ACE OF HEARTS

"Good night, Miss Jones," he said dismissively as he turned away and started back inside the saloon.

Libby reached out and grabbed his arm to stop him. The touch was electric and left her momentarily speechless. Reed looked back at her, frowning.

"But I'm good—real good," she finally blurted out. "Let me show you how good I am!"

"There's no need, but I'm sure the boys inside would love a demonstration." He walked on.

Fury replaced Libby's desperation. "Mr. Weston!" she called as he sat at the table with his friends, already engrossed in a new hand of poker.

Reed looked up to find himself staring down the barrel of her gun. "Miss Jones?"

"I didn't want to let you get away without seeing just how good I am with my sidearm," she said coolly. "Why don't you hold one of your cards out a little away from you?"

Reed was angry at her persistence, but he slowly obliged, silently hoping that she was as good a shot as she claimed to be.

All eyes were on him as he held out the card, and the men who were standing near backed safely away.

With a dead eye and a steady hand, Libby took careful aim and fired. Her shot pierced the center of Reed's ace of hearts.

Despite her ability, Reed was furious at her reckless display.

"Do you still think I should go home to my papa, Mr. Weston?" she taunted, smiling a bit smugly at him. "Or do you think I'm good enough to work for your show?"

WESTON'S

Lady

BOBBI SMITH

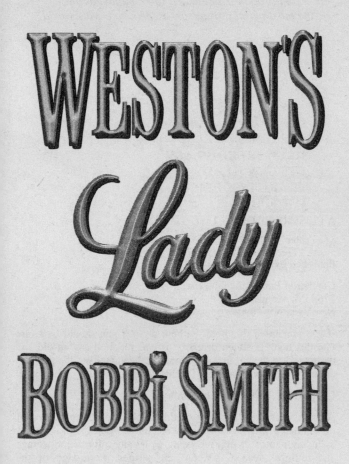

LEISURE BOOKS NEW YORK CITY

This book is dedicated to Dominic Joseph,
the most perfect grandson in the whole wide world!

A LEISURE BOOK®

May 1999

Published by

Dorchester Publishing Co., Inc.
276 Fifth Avenue
New York, NY 10001

ISBN 0-8439-4512-5

ACKNOWLEDGMENTS

I'd like to thank the wonderful people at United Magazine Company who have been so supportive of my career. They're fantastic! Mike Gilbert, to the first power, Gene Moutsatson, Karen Rembold, Dan Kuntz, Jeff Wardford, Dave Whitehead, Scott MacGregor, Jim Stoll, Mike Mary, Gary Parker, Gene Alfonsi, Bob Monnaville, Ron Scherer, Terry Massaro, Sue Good, John Jolly, Mike Gilbert, to the second power, Connie Hamm and Dave Shepard. I'd also like to thank three magnificent supporters of romance—Helen Everts, Sandy Leeds and Denese Pierson. And Georgann Vohsen, a wonderful fan and friend.

Prologue

Reed Weston was tired but smiling as he made his way to his hotel room. The trip into town had been a successful one for him and his brother Steve. They'd taken care of their family's ranch business and had even had some time left to make a few social calls and have a few drinks in the saloon. First thing in the morning, they would head back to the Circle W, but tonight, at least, they'd managed to have some fun.

Reed's smile widened as he thought of what Steve had just confided in him while they were drinking at the bar. It seemed his little brother believed he had found the woman of his dreams. Steve had confessed that he'd fallen in love with beautiful Kathleen Martin and was just about ready to propose. They'd concluded some business dealings with her father while they were in

1

town and had spent some time at the Martin home. Kathleen was a lovely young woman and would do his brother proud.

Reaching his hotel room, Reed unlocked the door and let himself into the darkened chamber. He was more than ready to get some much-needed sleep.

There seemed to be a hint of perfume in the air as Reed stepped inside and shut the door behind himself, and for a moment he wondered at it. Then he dismissed the puzzling scent as just his imagination. He turned to the bureau and struck a match to light the lamp there. He was shocked when he glanced up into the mirror and saw her.

" 'Evenin', Reed," Kathleen purred in a seductive voice from where she lay in Reed's bed.

"Kathleen—" He turned quickly and stared at the dark-haired beauty, shocked. This was the woman his brother wanted to marry!

"I've been waiting for you."

"But—how did you get in here? What are you doing here?" He did not move.

She slowly sat up, her movements deliberate and enticing. She let the cover she was holding slip so he could see the swell of her breasts. She wanted him to know that she was naked. "I wanted to see you, Reed. I wanted to be alone with you."

Reed knew a willing woman when he saw one, and the look in her eyes told him she was his for the taking. He swallowed tightly, ignoring the carnal desire that rose within him. His brother's words played in his mind—*"I love Kathleen, and I'm going to ask her to marry me."*

2

"Reed?" she said in a low, sultry tone. "Aren't you glad to see me?" She deliberately let the cover drop, revealing to him the full beauty of her bared breasts.

His body stirred at her ploy, but still he held himself under tight control. "You shouldn't be here, Kathleen."

"It's wicked of me to be so brazen, but I want you so much—love you so much. I just had to let you know."

Kathleen rose to her knees, offering herself to him fully. Reed almost took a step toward her. She was flawlessly beautiful. A man would be a fool to walk away from what she was offering, but his honor held him back. No matter how much he wanted to take her, he knew how his brother felt about her.

"You have to go. You can't stay." He made his words as cold as he could, wanting to discourage her.

But Kathleen was feeling so bold tonight, she wasn't about to stop now. She had daringly crept into his room and planned to seduce him. She'd wanted Reed Weston for as long as she could remember, and she intended to have him. Kathleen Martin always got what she wanted, when she wanted it. It had never occurred to her that Reed might not fall in with her plans.

"Can you stand there and tell me you don't want me?" she asked, leaving the bed and moving toward him. She stopped just a step away from him, noting with satisfaction that his jaw was locked and there was sweat beading his brow. "We both know that's a lie."

"You're a good woman. You have to leave—now!"

She lifted one delicate hand and rested it on his chest. "Do you really think I'm a 'good woman,' Reed? Do you really want me to go, darling?"

He was tempted to take her. She certainly was a man's fantasy come true. He had a beautiful, naked woman standing before him, and he couldn't believe he was denying himself. With all the strength he could muster, he almost snarled at her.

"Yes, I want you to go, Kathleen." He picked up her clothes and thrust them at her. "Get out of here, now, before I forget myself."

"But I want you to forget yourself," she countered, thinking he was just playing the gentleman and could still be hers.

Kathleen knew how easy men were to control. She'd controlled her father her whole life just by using her cajoling ways and a smile. Now, as she was offering herself, body and soul, to the man she'd dreamed about for so many nights, she was certain that she would get what she wanted—and she wanted Reed Weston.

Reed had always seemed distant, unattainable, even when he'd been at her home earlier that day, and she'd been emboldened by the challenge he represented to her. That was why she'd decided to come to him now, tonight. She wanted to show him just how much she loved him.

"This isn't a good idea."

"I want you to make love to me, Reed. We can be married and—"

"I am not going to marry you," he ground out quickly, fiercely. He was fighting not to give in to the burning desire he felt for her. He'd always found her attractive, but knowing how Steve felt, there was no way he was going to take advantage of this situation. He wouldn't be able to live with himself if he did.

For the first time, an element of understanding began to dawn in Kathleen's mind. "But Reed—" She tried the little girl pout that always worked with her father.

"Get out!"

She was incredulous as she asked, "You really want me to go?"

"Now!" he said as he fought against his body's baser urgings.

Kathleen had wanted Reed with a wild passion. She'd believed herself in love with him, but now, faced with his rejection, she was furious. The love that had filled her changed and became a burning hatred. How dare he send her away!

"You—You—!" she sputtered.

"Good-bye, Kathleen." Reed cut her off.

Kathleen took her things from him. Reed turned his back on her and went to stare out the window. She quickly pulled her clothing on, her emotions in turmoil. She'd never faced such complete and utter humiliation before.

She finished dressing and looked up at the powerful width of Reed's back. She wanted him to look at her. She wanted him to realize that he was making a big mistake. She wanted him to come to her and sweep her into his arms. She wanted him to tell her that he'd just been trying to protect her, but that he couldn't deny himself what they both wanted so desperately.

"Reed—"

"Kathleen." He said her name tautly, without turning around. "I haven't laid a hand on you, and that's the way it's going to stay. Now, go."

"You're going to be sorry for this, Reed Weston!" she seethed, angry at being so summarily dismissed.

He didn't respond. He didn't look around.

"I'll always remember that you sent me away, and someday you're going to regret it!"

With that, she was gone.

Reed remained standing at the window, staring out into the darkness. The temptation she'd presented to him had been real—Kathleen *was* beautiful—but he'd done the right thing in denying her. It wouldn't have been right to take advantage of her. Though, even as he thought about it, he realized she was far more worldly than he'd suspected. He'd believed her to be an innocent, but would an innocent have offered herself so blatantly to any man?

Putting the thought from him, Reed got ready for bed. Even as he settled in, though, he thought of Steve and wondered if he should say anything to him about his encounter with Kathleen. He finally decided against it. Nothing had happened; there was no need to bring it up.

Sleep was long in coming that night.

Reed was up and about with the sun, as was his habit. He finished his packing and was ready to head back to the Circle W. It was just a matter of meeting up with Steve and riding out after breakfast.

Reed waited quite a while for his brother, going over their business dealings and reviewing what they had to tell their father when they returned. Then he glanced at his pocket watch again. He was concerned that Steve had stayed too long in the bar the night before and had overslept this morning. They needed to be on the road, for there was much to be done today.

Determined to haul his lazy brother out of bed, Reed finally quit his own room and headed down the hall to rouse Steve. He knocked on the door and waited. When no answer came, he frowned, wondering what could be wrong.

"Steve?"

Still there was no answer.

Reed tried the doorknob and was surprised to find the door unlocked. He let himself in and stared about the empty room in confusion. Steve was gone. All of his belongings were missing. Worried, he hurried down to the front desk to see if anyone had spoken with Steve or had seen him that morning.

"Mr. Weston!" the desk clerk called, holding up a sealed envelope for him. "Your brother left this message for you when he checked out."

"He's gone?"

"Yes, sir. He left during the night."

"What did he say?" Steve was confused.

"I don't know, sir, I wasn't working then. But perhaps his letter will explain his departure." He handed Reed the missive.

"Thanks," he said absently as he took the letter and moved away from the desk.

It didn't make any sense that Steve had packed up and left in the middle of the night. When they'd been drinking at the saloon, they'd agreed to meet first thing this morning so they could get an early start for home. Reed couldn't imagine what could have happened to make his brother leave so unexpectedly—and without him.

Reed tore open the envelope as soon as he was in a more private place and quickly scanned the letter.

Reed—
  Something important of a personal nature has come up, and I have to head out tonight. I'll see you back at the ranch in a couple of days. Don't worry about me. Everything's fine.
                                    Steve

Reed was glad to know that there was nothing wrong, but he was irritated by his little brother's irresponsibility. This was a business trip, and their father was expecting them back that afternoon. The only reassuring thing was that Steve had left the note so his family would know that nothing was wrong. Returning to his room to get his belongings, Reed got ready for the long ride ahead of him. His father was waiting.

*   *   *

"I wonder what that boy is up to," George Weston said gruffly as he ate dinner with Reed two days later. "Steve didn't say in that letter just when he planned on showing up back here, did he?"

Reed could hear the growing annoyance in his father's tone. "He said he'd be gone a couple of days, so I think we'll be seeing him any time now."

"His work is waiting for him."

"I'm sure he realizes that."

Reed knew his father was a fierce taskmaster, but a man couldn't afford to be less than vigilant when it came to running a ranch. The work didn't get done by itself.

"George! Reed! It looks like Steve's riding in right now," called Andy, the ranch cook, who was standing in the kitchen where he had a clear view of the road up to the house. "And it appears he ain't riding in alone!"

" 'Bout damned time," George growled as he pushed away from the table to go meet his wayward son. For all that he sounded impatient, he was pleased that Steve had returned. He'd been worrying about him and wondering where he'd gone.

Reed followed his father out onto the porch. He was surprised to see that his brother was driving a carriage, and as the vehicle drew close enough for him to make out who was riding with him, Reed went cold inside. Kathleen was sitting next to Steve.

Steve reined in before the house, descended the carriage and then turned back to help Kathleen down. With his arm possessively around her waist, he faced his waiting family.

"Pa, Reed—I'd like you to meet my wife. Kathleen and I eloped the other night. We couldn't wait another day to be together."

Kathleen lifted her gaze to Reed and smiled. Only he understood the predatory look of challenge—and triumph—that shone in her pale blue eyes.

Reed stood alone in the privacy of his father's office, pouring himself a straight shot of whiskey. He'd managed to make it through dinner with Steve and Kathleen, but it had been difficult. Steve seemed so happy that Reed knew he could not tell him the truth of what had happened between him and Kathleen. Not that it mattered. Nothing had really occurred that night, and he was glad. Now that he knew what Kathleen was capable of, he didn't trust her at all. He would take great care to keep his distance from her.

Everyone had long since retired, and Reed was glad for the time alone. Tumbler in hand, he wandered out onto the porch. The night was dark, much like his mood, and he knew he had to come to grips with the situation. He would not do anything to ruin his brother's happiness. Steve loved Kathleen. Reed braced his shoulder against a post and took a deep drink as he stared out across the Circle W. The liquor burned all the way down, and he was glad for its searing intensity.

"Reed?"

At the sound of Kathleen's voice close behind

him, Reed tensed. He turned to find her standing before him, smiling as she gazed up at him.

"I wanted some time alone with you," she said, taking a step nearer.

"I don't think that's a good idea, Kathleen. I'm sure your husband's waiting for you. You'd better get on back upstairs."

"Steve's already asleep," she told him with a look that spoke volumes. "And what I want to say to you won't wait."

"If you're worried I'll tell him about the other night in the hotel—don't. You're his wife now, and he's happy. That's all that matters."

"Steve may be happy, but Reed, don't you wonder about me?" she asked, moving closer to rest her hand on his chest. "Don't you wonder if I'm happy?"

Reed set his glass aside and snared her wrist. "Don't," he ordered, anger flashing in his eyes.

"Don't what?" she asked, enjoying the fact that she was getting a reaction out of him. His control amazed her, and she wanted to find out what it would take to break his iron will.

"You're my brother's wife."

"But I could have been your wife," she said, shifting even nearer in spite of his grip on her arm. "I could have been in *your* bed." She rose and kissed him.

Reed reacted almost violently, grabbing her other arm and shoving her away from him.

"What the . . . ?" Steve's exclamation shocked them both. He'd awakened to find Kathleen gone from their bed and had come downstairs looking for her. The sight that greeted him—his wife in his brother's arms—left him stunned and outraged.

"Oh, Steve! Thank heaven you woke up and came after me! I didn't know what I was going to do! Reed grabbed me and—" She broke away from Reed and rushed to her husband.

"I can see what was going on." Steve's tone was barely controlled as he put his arms protectively around her.

Kathleen had always considered herself to be quite an accomplished actress, and this was going to be a true test of her abilities. Tears filled her eyes. She affected a look of terror and helplessness as she clung to her husband.

"This isn't what it seems," Reed told his brother as he met his condemning gaze straight on. He was angry at himself for not being prepared for Kathleen's cunning manipulations and angry at his brother for being so gullible as to believe her.

"I've got eyes, brother. I saw what happened!" Steve said coldly. "Go back upstairs, Kathleen." He put her from him without looking away from Reed.

"But Steve—" she protested, wanting to see the two of them fight over her. It thrilled her to think she could control these two strong men so easily.

"Reed and I have a few things to say to each other—in private. Go on."

Kathleen made a show of leaving them. She told Reed that he would regret that night he'd denied her in the hotel, and now she was proving it.

Steve waited until his wife had disappeared up

the steps inside before he turned on his brother.

"You bastard!"

He swung at Reed without warning, and his fist connected in a powerful blow that sent his brother reeling.

"Kathleen is my wife! You keep your hands off her!" Steve snarled as he advanced on his brother.

Reed and Steve had often fought as youngsters, and Reed had always won. Reed had no doubt that he could take Steve now, but he didn't even try. He could have told him the truth about Kathleen and what had happened, too, but he held back. His brother was so crazy about her, he would never have believed anything Reed might have told him.

"Do you understand me?" Steve demanded.

"I understand you," Reed answered quietly.

"If this is the way things are going to be between us now that Kathleen and I are married, we'll be leaving the Circle W. I can't stay here, not knowing what might happen to her when I'm not around to protect her."

"Steve, there's no reason for you to go—" Reed was shocked that his brother would even think of leaving.

"There's every reason!" he insisted, believing he would be keeping his wife safe from harm. "Kathleen and I will be moving out in the morning. Stay away from her 'til we're gone, Reed."

"What are you going to do? Pa needs you here, working the ranch with us."

"I don't care about the ranch. I care about Kathleen. She's the most important thing in my life. I'll do whatever I have to to make her happy."

13

"But Steve—" Reed took an impulsive step toward him, wanting, somehow, to make him understand.

"Get the hell away from me! I don't ever want to see you again! The next time I do, I just might not be able to control myself—and right now, it wouldn't take much for me to shoot you!"

Steve turned his back on his brother and on his life. He went upstairs to see to his bride.

The following morning, Reed watched from a distance as Steve and Kathleen rode away from the ranch. He wondered how long it would take his brother to discover the truth about the woman he'd married. He wondered, too, if he would ever see Steve again. He loved his younger brother. He had spent most of his life protecting him and keeping him out of trouble, but this time, there was nothing he could do to save him from himself.

Steve's abrupt, unexplained departure was devastating to their father. Steve offered no explanation for his actions, except to say that now he was married, he wanted to start a new life. Reed remained silent, revealing nothing of Kathleen's manipulations.

A great sadness filled Reed as he accepted his part in his brother's estrangement. He hoped that when Steve finally understood the truth, he would come home. They would be waiting for him.

Chapter One

"I am writing to let you know that your brother is dead."

Reed stared down at the note he held tightly in his hand, wondering how many times he'd read it during the past few days. Fifty? A hundred? It didn't really matter. The pain of the message had not lessened with time and neither had the horror contained in the rest of the letter. *"I don't think it was an accident. You are the only one I'm telling about my suspicions."*

"Are you all right, young man?" Mildred Kelly, an elderly, white-haired lady, was sitting across the stagecoach from Reed. She'd noticed the sudden haunted look on his face and was concerned that something was terribly wrong.

"I'm fine, ma'am, but thanks for asking," Reed

15

lied, glancing up to see the questioning kindness in her gaze.

Mildred didn't believe him, but she fell silent, sensing it was best not to ask the young man anything more. For all that he was very handsome and well-dressed and seemed polite enough, there was an edge of tension about him and a remoteness that discouraged any further attempts at familiarity or small talk.

Reed turned to stare out the window, his hand tightening into a fist, crumpling the letter he held. He wished he'd never received the letter from Joe Shadowens, Steve's right-hand man at the Stampede. He wished the last five years had never happened. He wished he could turn back the clock. But it was too late. He would never get the chance to change things. Steve was dead.

Thoughts of Steve haunted Reed. He hadn't seen him since that fateful day when he'd ridden away from the Circle W with Kathleen. Estranged though Steve had been from the family, their father had kept track of him. When he'd heard that Steve was trying to start up a Wild West show and needed money to finance it, he had made arrangements to secretly back him and had gotten the banker's solemn word that Steve would never learn the identity of his investors.

As it turned out, Weston's Wild Texas Stampede had become a great success, drawing big crowds wherever it played. George had been pleased to learn of Steve's accomplishment.

When their father had taken a fever and passed away the year before, Reed had sent word to Steve.

There had been no response. Steve had not attended the funeral or made any effort to contact Reed afterward.

His brother's indifference to their father's death had angered Reed, but he'd always hoped that one day they would have the chance to straighten things out between them. Now, sadly, Reed knew that day would never come. During one of the trick-riding performances the week before, Steve had been thrown from his horse and killed.

"I don't think it was an accident."

Joe's suspicions could not be ignored, and a grim determination had filled Reed. He'd sworn to himself that he would find out the truth of what had happened. If Steve's death hadn't been an accident, he would bring the murderer to justice.

It didn't surprise Reed that he hadn't heard the news of his brother's death from Kathleen. He was certain that she still hated him.

An official letter from Steve's attorney had arrived shortly after Joe's. The lawyer had requested Reed's presence at the reading of Steve's will. Reed had put the Circle W in the hands of his very capable foreman and had set out immediately for San Carlos, the town where Steve and Kathleen had settled after leaving the Circle W. Knowing how his brother had felt about him, Reed didn't know why it was important that he be at the reading, but as a last gesture of respect, he would attend as requested.

Now, as the stage rolled into town on schedule and drew to a stop before the stage office, Reed mentally prepared himself for what was to come.

It would be difficult—as difficult as burying his father had been—but somehow he would get through it. He shoved the letter into his pocket and climbed down from the stagecoach. He turned back and helped his traveling companion descend.

"Thank you, young man." Mildred smiled up at him. When he would have turned away, she touched his arm to stop him. "I hope everything goes all right for you."

"I do, too," he answered tightly.

Before she could say more, her family appeared, and she was whisked away, surrounded by love.

In contrast, Reed stood alone in the street, a solitary man. He took a deep breath as he looked around. For some reason, a part of him had half-expected Steve to meet the stage. Pain branded him with the undeniable knowledge that he would never see his brother again.

Reed's mood was somber as he picked up his suitcase. He headed for the town's only hotel, dreading the meeting with his brother's lawyer that same afternoon.

It was quiet in Charles Barton's law office as he prepared for the reading of the will.

Reed had arrived a few minutes early and had had time to introduce himself to the lawyer. He was standing at the window, looking out at the dusty streets of San Carlos, when he heard the door open behind him. Then he heard her voice.

"I'm Kathleen Weston. I'm here for the reading of my husband's will."

"Mrs. Weston." Charles nodded in cool welcome. "I'm Charles Barton, your husband's attorney, and of course you know Reed."

Kathleen had been prepared for a quick meeting with the lawyer. She had not expected anyone else to be there—especially not Reed. She stared at him in complete and utter disbelief.

"You're here? Why?" she asked in a breathless voice, her confusion very real.

Kathleen had always prided herself on her self-control, and she was struggling to keep her composure at the sight of Reed—so tall and darkly handsome.

Reed hadn't changed at all. He was still the best-looking man Kathleen had ever seen, and oh, how she still wanted him! The painful quickening of her heartbeat reminded her of just how much—even after all this time.

Again Kathleen realized that she'd made the biggest mistake of her life the night she'd eloped with Steve. The pleasure she'd gotten from her revenge had been short-lived, after which her life with Steve had been one of unending misery. She drew on her anger over Reed's long-ago rejection and her subsequent wretched marriage to school her expression to one of indifference to his presence.

"Mr. Barton requested my presence," Reed answered simply, thinking she looked as lovely as ever, but remembering that, in her case, beauty was only skin deep.

"Please, both of you have a seat. We can commence now that Mrs. Weston is here."

Kathleen sat down and closed her eyes at hearing herself called Mrs. Weston. *If only she'd been Mrs. Reed Weston!*

Reed took the seat next to her and waited for the reading of the will to begin.

"Are you all right?" Charles asked, thinking she was saddened by her husband's untimely death.

Kathleen looked at him and smiled tightly. "I'm fine. Please proceed."

The attorney nodded, then took out the document and began to read. " 'I, Steven Weston, being of sound mind and body as of this date of September 19, 1882, do hereby leave all of my worldly possessions and my controlling interest in the Weston's Wild Texas Stampede to my father, George Weston, and to my brother, Reed.' "

"What!" Any melancholy Kathleen might have been feeling was dashed at this pronouncement. She shot to her feet in outraged indignation, staring at the attorney in complete disbelief.

Charles calmly reread the text out loud.

"Surely, there must be some mistake," she said tightly.

"There's no mistake," he told her.

Kathleen glared at him, knowing Steve had done this to spite her.

"Please sit back down, Mrs. Weston. Mr. Weston assumed the will would cause some discontent, so he added this codicil. 'Any challenges to this will, including any made by my wife, Kathleen, shall be dismissed without question.' "

Kathleen paled at this news as she sank back into her chair. "How dare he leave me penniless?"

Barton gave her a smug, tight smile. "It's his

money, madam. He could do with it as he pleased."

"But he was *my* husband!" she countered.

The attorney leveled a cool, knowing regard on her. "Indeed. And you were *his* wife. Besides, from what Steve told me, you are hardly without funds. You are still a part-owner of the Stampede."

"I'll get an attorney of my own. We'll just see about these terms!"

Barton gave her a dismissive glance. Steve had warned him that there would be trouble. He was prepared for anything she might try. "The will is ironclad. Mr. Weston made sure of that."

"Mr. Barton?" Reed spoke up, stunned by what he'd just heard. "You say the will is dated last September?"

"Yes, sir."

"How could it be that Steve didn't know about our father's death? He passed away unexpectedly the previous spring, and I sent word as soon as it happened."

"In all of our discussions, Mr. Weston made no mention of the fact that he knew about your father's passing."

They both turned to Kathleen at the same time, realizing what must have happened to Reed's urgent message.

"Perhaps you can enlighten us on this matter, Mrs. Weston?" the attorney asked, his tone incisive. Steve had told him of his wife's betrayals and deceptions. He knew the truth of her character and what she was capable of.

"I don't know what you're talking about," she

21

answered quickly. "If you gentlemen will excuse me?"

She rose and swept from the office, her body rigid with anger.

Reed and Charles exchanged looks.

"Steve expressed his concerns about her to me when we drew up this document. I can see now that his thoughts on the matter were valid."

"I can't believe she would keep something that important from him."

"Be that as it may, you have your work cut out for you, Mr. Weston," Charles went on. "You're now Mrs. Weston's partner in the Wild Texas Stampede."

Reed nodded, his expression grim at the realization. "How big is her share?"

"She owns thirty-five percent of the show."

Reed didn't say anything. His thoughts were too troubled.

"What are you going to do with the Stampede?" the lawyer asked.

"For now, it looks like I'll have to take over the day-to-day running of it."

"The next scheduled performance date is the weekend after this one, in Los Santos. It is my understanding that the crew has assembled there to await word from Kathleen about their future."

He nodded. "I'll speak with Kathleen and head for Los Santos right away."

"If you should decide to buy her out and need any help with the negotiations, I'll be glad to handle it for you."

"I appreciate your offer." Reed stood, wanting

22

to get away from the office so he could have time to think.

"Mr. Weston?" Charles spoke up.

At Reed's questioning look, he went on.

"I want you to know that I respected your brother a great deal. He was a fine and honorable man."

"Thank you."

"Did you and your father provide for some of the financing for the Stampede?"

Reed was surprised. "Yes, we did, but it wasn't public knowledge."

Charles smiled sadly. "Steve was never sure, but he suspected you were the one who'd helped him in the beginning."

"We loved him."

"Your brother and I spoke at length about his decision not to leave the Stampede to his wife. His personal life, as you can imagine, was not what he'd hoped it would be. I even suggested at one point that he begin divorce proceedings, but he refused. He was a man of honor, and he would not forsake his wedding vows."

Reed nodded, knowing Steve had always been a man of his word.

"The show had become his whole life, and he knew that Kathleen didn't love it as much as he did. He was very sad about his estrangement from your family. He hoped remembering you in the will would make amends for the years you were apart."

"I understand." And he did, more than he

wanted to. Obviously, his brother had discovered the truth about Kathleen.

"If you need me at all, just let me know."

"I'll be in touch."

They shook hands. Charles handed him the papers he needed, and Reed quit the office.

As Reed stepped outside, his thoughts were troubled. The last thing he wanted to do was spend any time with Kathleen. He would love to buy her out and be done with it, but until he knew exactly what had happened to Steve on that last, fateful day, he was going to keep the show intact, exactly as it had been. He needed to find his brother's murderer—or proof that his death was an accident. That was all that mattered to him.

Kathleen was furious as she stalked about the parlor of her small home. She was Steve's wife! She should have inherited everything! How dare Steve leave it all to his brother! Oh, how she despised Reed Weston! And now she was going to be forced to deal with him as the co-owner of the show! It was infuriating!

Her mood was vicious as she tried to figure out what to do next. Her original plan to sell the whole show and start enjoying life had been destroyed by the reading of Steve's will. She was trapped, for all her personal funds were tied up in the Stampede. She longed to be free of it—as she was finally free of Steve—but unless she could convince Reed to buy her out, her life would be even more desperate than it had been before. Unless—

A knock at the door startled Kathleen. She

hadn't been expecting anyone, and she was cautious as she opened the portal.

"Reed—" She stared up at him, wondering why he'd come to her and what he wanted. She took care to keep her expression cool, revealing none of her thoughts. She had to admit, though, that the sight of him did still have the power to stir feelings deep within her—feelings she'd thought long dead.

"Kathleen, I'd like to talk to you for a moment, if you have the time?"

"Come in." She held the door wide, playing the lady, when in truth, there was nothing ladylike about what she was feeling.

"Thanks." Reed entered the house and followed her into the parlor. "I'm sorry about Steve."

"So am I," she answered, but for altogether different reasons than Reed. She glanced down at the skirt of the black gown she had donned that morning and realized just how much she hated wearing black. She was going to be forced to wear the awful color for the full length of her mourning, and she told herself that she was in mourning over the fact that she had to wear black—not because her husband was dead. The traitorous, decadent thought almost made her smile, but she thought better of it.

They sat down in the parlor facing each other.

"I understand we're now the owners of the Stampede," Reed began.

"Yes, we are. I was hoping you'd consider selling the show. There's so much about it that reminds me of Steve, I just don't think I can bear to continue as we were."

"I don't think Steve would want me to do that. The Stampede was his pride and joy. He built it up from nothing to be the success that it is, and I feel I owe it to him to keep it going."

Kathleen hid her disgust with his sentiments. She affected a look of sadness, hoping to touch Reed. "Then perhaps you'd consider buying my share? It pains me to be constantly reminded of him—and of how he died."

"I should think you would want to build up the show in his memory."

"The only memory I have is of watching them carry Steve's lifeless body off the parade grounds."

"You were there and saw the whole thing?"

"Actually, I was in our wagon when I heard the screams from the crowd. I came running out. It was so terrible! It was during an act that Steve and I usually performed together. I should have been riding with him, but I was feeling ill that night. By the time I reached his side, he was already dead."

Kathleen wasn't lying in her recounting of that dreadful night. The moment had been painful for her. She'd been in the midst of making love to her lover, when they'd been interrupted. She was just thankful that no one had burst in on them to tell her of the tragedy. She lifted a tear-filled gaze to look up at Reed, hoping he would not doubt her tale of torment.

"It must have been awful for you."

For a moment, Reed almost believed the pain he saw in her expression. Kathleen was a very beautiful woman, and he remembered how lovely she'd been all those years ago standing before him, offering herself to him. But then he reminded himself of her actions at the ranch after her elopement and of how Steve had been murdered—not accidentally killed—in the show.

For all that Kathleen might truly be sorry Steve was dead, there was the possibility that she had been behind the whole thing. She had not known about the changes in his will before his death, so she would have benefitted the most from his "accident." He wouldn't trust her, no matter how helpless and innocent she might look.

"It was terrible, and that's why I'd like to get away from the show."

"My funds are all tied up right now. I don't have the cash to buy you out." Reed went on, "I was hoping you would help me run the Stampede."

Kathleen lifted her gaze to Reed's. He seemed earnest enough, and she began to wonder. All those years ago, she'd needed and wanted him, but he'd turned her away. He seemed different now somehow, and this would give her the perfect opportunity to get him right where she'd always wanted him—in her bed.

True, she did despise him, but it would be the ultimate victory for her to finally seduce him. She smiled to herself at the thought. And seducing him would be a pleasant distraction while she disentangled herself from the show. She just might end up winning everything she'd always wanted, too.

"I'll be glad to do whatever I can to help you," she offered.

"I appreciate it," Reed answered. "I know how hard this is going to be for you, but I'm hoping, if we work together, we can make the Stampede an even bigger success—for Steve."

"I hope so," she agreed, but not caring in the least about Steve or his memory. The bigger the success of the show, the more money she'd ultimately get when she sold her share.

"The attorney told me the crew is waiting for us in Los Santos. I can be ready to ride out first thing in the morning, if that's all right with you?"

"I can be ready to go then."

"Good. Also, I was thinking that perhaps our first performance should be a memorial for Steve."

"That would be wonderful."

Kathleen showed him out, thinking that for the first time in ages, she was actually looking forward to returning to the Stampede. Reed was going to be there with her!

Chapter Two

Libby Jones heard the carriage pull up in front of the house. She looked out the window of her second-floor bedroom to see her handsome fiancé, John Harris, climb down out of his conveyance and walk up the steps to the front door. Eager to see him, she quickly finished dressing, making sure she looked her best. John liked her to be perfect, and she wanted to please him. Once Libby was certain she was ready, she started downstairs, looking forward to being with him.

Libby pondered how it was she'd come to be staying with Madeline Kelvin. It had all happened so quickly. One day, she and her brother Michael had been struggling along, trying to make a living on their small ranch just west of town, and the next Michael had gotten word that he'd been hired on by the railroad. They'd been thrilled by his good fortune. The only trouble had been that he'd needed to leave right away if he wanted the job. There was no way Libby could go with him, and no way Michael would leave her all alone. But then John had come to her and proposed so unexpectedly—and so romantically—that he'd swept her off her feet.

Everything had seemed to fall into place then. The only sad part was that the wedding couldn't take place until the bans had been published, so Michael wouldn't be able to attend. That troubled Libby, but he had told her he would be with her in spirit, just before he'd headed off to start his new life.

Madeline Kelvin was a close friend of John's, and she had offered to chaperone Libby until the wedding. So here she was, living in the home of one of the wealthiest people in Salt Creek.

Though Madeline had been most gracious during the two weeks she'd been staying with her, Libby still felt a bit uncomfortable. She would have preferred staying alone out at her own ranch, but John had said that was unacceptable for his fianceé. Libby was going to be glad when the wedding was over, so she and John could begin their life together.

John . . . At the thought of her tall, blond, sophisticated intended, she smiled. John was a bit older than she was and quite well off. His job as the banker in town made him a mainstay in the community. They had come to know each other through town dances and church picnics. When he'd proposed and told her she was the woman he wanted, she'd been amazed. She'd never suspected that he cared for her.

Libby grew excited now as she reached the bottom of the staircase and heard John speaking through the closed study door. She hadn't given love much thought, but she supposed she must love him to feel this way every time she saw him. She hurried forward, ready to knock on the door and announce herself.

"The arrangements have all been made?" Madeline was asking John.

Libby smiled. She assumed they were speaking of the wedding arrangements.

"Yes. I promised them I would deliver her into their hands tomorrow evening."

"And the payoff will be good?"

"The payoff will be excellent. You know how much he likes virgins."

There was a telling silence.

"Libby has no idea that any of this is happening, does she? She honestly believes you're planning to marry her." Madeline laughed derisively.

Outside the door, Libby actually took a step backward at the other woman's statement. *She honestly believes you're planning to marry her.* Her hand dropped to her side as she stared uncomprehendingly at the closed portal.

"That's what's so refreshing about Libby. She's such an innocent. He's going to enjoy having her, and she's spirited enough that he's going to enjoy taming her, too. Do you suppose she knows I'm here?"

"No. I haven't sent the maid up to get her yet."

"Good, that gives us time to toast our little plan."

"It is a fine plan, but what if her brother shows up looking for her?"

"He won't be back for months. His job will keep him away at least that long. When he does come back, I'll just tell him that Libby backed out of the wedding at the last minute and left town looking for him."

"Do you think he'll believe you?"

"Why wouldn't he? If she had left me at the altar, it wouldn't be my job to let him know. As the aggrieved party, I would hardly be expected to spread the word that I'd been jilted."

"What about their ranch?"

"What about it? It's not worth much, and if there's no one here to pay the taxes and take care of it, the bank can take possession."

"So you're going to make money twice off her."

"Exactly."

Libby was shocked senseless by what she was hearing. Tears threatened as she backed farther away from the door. She was increasingly horrified as the meaning of what she'd heard sank in. John's proposal of marriage had been a lie! He didn't love her. He never had! She'd been a fool to think he cared about her! It had all been a sham!

"Miss Liberty? What are you doing standing out here so quiet-like?" asked BethAnne, the maid, as she came up on her in the hallway.

At her question, the study door flew open and John came out, followed immediately by Madeline.

"Why, Libby—My darling fiancée, I didn't know

32

you'd come down to join us already," he said smoothly, reaching out to take her arm in a steely grip. He could tell by her stricken expression that she'd been listening to their conversation.

She tried to pull away from him, but he held her fast.

"Why do you look so surprised to see me? I told you I'd be calling on you tonight. Let's go into the study so we can speak privately. Madeline, BethAnne—if you ladies will excuse us?" His voice was smooth and controlled.

"Of course," Madeline responded. "Come, BethAnne, there's something I wanted you to tend to in the kitchen."

"BethAnne! Wait!" Libby called out to her, believing that the maid was the only one who could help her.

BethAnne glanced back questioningly, sensing that something wasn't right, but Madeline stepped between them.

"Now, BethAnne. I'm sure John and Libby need some time alone. Let's go and give them their privacy." Madeline herded the servant away down the hall.

John drew Libby into the study. He shut and locked the door behind them with a frightening finality. Only after he'd pocketed the key did he release her. Libby unconsciously rubbed at her arm where he'd been holding her, wanting to erase the vileness of his touch.

"Well, darling, just how much of our little conversation did you overhear?" He closed in on her threateningly.

"I don't know what you're talking about," she answered quickly, nervously.

"Of course you do." He smiled thinly at her, not at all amused by her attempt to lie. He stopped before her.

Libby backed up, wanting to keep some distance between them.

"You can't escape me, Libby dear, so you may as well just relax. I have plans for you—big plans. You're going to make me a wealthy man."

"I can't make you rich. All I have in the world is the ranch."

"Oh, no, darling, you have much more than that to offer." He reached out to touch her cheek, then took her by the arms and drew her toward him.

"Don't!" Libby tried to resist him.

But John wasn't about to be denied. He wanted a little taste of her before he had to let her go. It was not a romantic kiss or a loving kiss. It was one of domination and power. She was his to do with as he pleased. There was nothing she could do to stop him. The thought urged him on. His hand sought her breasts, and he fondled her roughly.

"Do you know how much some men will pay to bed a virgin?" he chuckled as he drew back for a moment.

Libby felt violated by his touch, and she blanched at his crudeness. She went still as she stared up into his eyes. What she saw there horrified her. There was no tenderness, no affection. There was only lust and greed.

"You are so naive. It's part of your charm. You're bringing me quite a high price. It was such

34

Her brother had insisted she learn to defend herself, and she prayed now that his lessons on how to use a knife paid off.

a stroke of good fortune when your brother was offered that job."

"Get away from me!"

Somehow, Libby managed to jerk free of him, backing away. Out of the corner of her eye she caught sight of a letter opener on the desk. She snatched it up and held it before her. It wasn't much, but it was the only weapon she could find at the moment. Her brother had insisted she learn how to defend herself, and she prayed now that his lessons on how to use a knife paid off. She really wished she had her father's six-gun, but it was safely stowed in her trunk upstairs.

"If you think that little thing is going to stop me, you're sadly mistaken."

"We'll see."

He made a grab for her arm, but she stabbed at him and made contact. He swore and jerked back.

"You little bitch!"

John lunged at her. As he did, Libby slashed out at him and cut his cheek. He roared his fury and kept coming. Her effort had not been enough to stop him. He knocked her backward, and the letter opener flew from her hand. Standing over her, he glared down. His expression was murderous as blood oozed from the deep cut on his cheek.

"If I hadn't already promised to deliver you tomorrow, I'd teach you a lesson right now that you'd never forget!"

Libby was quaking with terror inside, but she refused to let him know it. She returned his hate-filled look measure for measure, enjoying the sight of his bloodied face, glad that she'd managed to injure him at least that much. "And if I had a gun, I'd teach you a lesson *you'd* never forget! I'm pretty good with a knife, but I'm even better with a gun."

John saw the loathing in her green-eyed glare and smiled tightly as he wiped at the blood on his cheek. He was tempted to beat her within an inch of her life, but held himself back. She was worth too much money unscathed. He gripped her arm and forced her to her feet.

"Since you don't have either a knife or a gun right now, I suppose I'm safe," he remarked sarcastically.

Her continued mutinous expression infuriated John, but he could do nothing more than lock her up for the night. He hoped she would be taught a lesson in obedience after he handed her over tomorrow. She needed one. He realized then that it was a good thing they weren't really betrothed. He doubted she would have survived one year of being married to him, let alone a lifetime. He expected complete and unquestioning obedience from his women, not defiance.

Without another word, John unlocked the door and dragged her from the study, up the stairs to her bedroom. He opened the door and shoved her inside.

"Have a pleasant night, my dear." He stood over her for a moment, enjoying the flicker of uncertainty that he saw in her expression, then took the key out of her door. "Sweet dreams. This time tomorrow night, I venture to say, you'll be wishing you were back here with me."

"Never!"

"We'll see."

Striding from the room, he closed and locked the door from the outside. She was trapped—a prisoner.

When Libby heard the key turn in the lock, a wave of sickness washed over her. How could she have been such a fool? As soon as she was certain John had gone, she rushed to her trunk and dug through her personal things to find her father's gun. Only when her hand closed around the ivory handle of the weapon did she breathe a sigh of relief. Somehow, some way, she was going to save herself. She was getting out of this place tonight!

What an innocent she'd been to think that John loved her! She knew men for what they really were now, and she would never make that mistake again.

Libby heard the key in the door again and almost panicked. She sat down on the bed and slid the gun beneath the covers beside her just as Madeline came through the door.

"Well, my dear, I just came up to check on you."

"Why bother?"

"I had to make sure our merchandise wasn't damaged," she said smugly, looking her over. She stayed in the doorway, not trusting Libby. "It's good to know that John controlled himself. He does have a temper sometimes."

Libby was tempted to draw her gun now, but knew John was still downstairs and she probably wouldn't get out of the house. She would have to wait, but it wasn't easy.

"Get a good night's sleep. Tomorrow is your big

day," Madeline cooed as she backed out of the room and relocked the door.

Libby waited only until her footsteps faded away; then she jumped up and began sorting through her clothing. There was no time to waste! She found her riding clothes—a split leather skirt, blouse, vest, her hat, her boots and what little money she had. She took off the lovely gown she'd been wearing and donned the riding gear.

It was then that Libby noticed she was still wearing the engagement ring John had given her. Her flesh crawled at the thought. The ring had meant something to her once, but no more. She tore it from her finger and left it on the dresser where he would see it as soon as he walked into the room the next day. It wasn't much of a victory for her, but it was the only one she had for now.

After strapping on her gunbelt, she retrieved her revolver and double-checked to make sure it was loaded. If anyone tried to stop her, she was going to do whatever was necessary to save herself— even if it meant shooting first. Going to jail was infinitely preferable to the future John and Madeline had planned for her.

Libby needed help, but she feared the sheriff might be involved in this evil plot, too. As influential as John and Madeline were, she wondered if anyone in town would believe her or even listen to her story. And, as bad as her judgment had proven to be, did she dare trust anyone here? She knew she had to leave and never look back. She would head west and try to find her brother. Michael was the only person she could trust, the only person who truly cared about her. Michael was her only hope.

When night finally came, Libby was ready. She waited until she saw John ride off in his carriage before making her escape attempt. A tree grew close to her window, so with all the agility she'd learned as a young tomboy on the ranch, she climbed from the window and jumped out to grab the branch. It swayed dangerously under her weight, but it held. With utmost caution, she inched her way to the trunk and then climbed down. When she reached the ground, relief swept over her, but she could not let down her guard yet. As long as she was in town, she was in danger.

Moving silently through town to the stable, Libby was relieved to find that the stablehands had already bedded down for the night. She made her way to the stall where Raven, her horse, was kept and slipped a bridle on her pet before quietly leading him from the building. She finished saddling up outside and then mounted and walked the horse away.

Every fiber of Libby's being screamed for her to ride off at a gallop, but she didn't want to risk awakening anyone or alerting anyone. She needed a good head start if she was to make a safe getaway. Moving almost silently through the streets, she finally reached the edge of town and put her heels to the horse's sides. Only then, as she raced away into the night, did she allow herself to feel a moment of pure ecstasy. She had made it! It didn't

40

matter that she had little money to her name and only the clothes on her back. She was free of John and Madeline, and she was going to make sure she stayed that way!

Chapter Three

Reed and Kathleen made the two-day trip to Los Santos by stage, and Reed was relieved when they finally arrived. He'd managed to maintain a cordial relationship with Kathleen during their long hours together, but it hadn't been easy for him. He'd been glad for the company of other travelers on the way. The Stampede had camped a short distance out of town, and they reached the camping area late in the afternoon, having hired a carriage from the stable to take them there.

"Kathleen, it's good you're back." Joe Shadowens saw them arrive and came out to meet them. He eyed Reed, then put out his hand. "I'm Joe Shadowens."

"I'm Reed Weston, Steve's brother."

The two men shook hands.

"Glad to meet you," Joe said.

"It's good to meet you, too," Reed answered, neither man letting on that they had already been in contact. "I'll be running the Stampede with Kathleen now."

Joe looked surprised, but said nothing. "We've all been waiting to hear what was going to happen. No one knew for sure."

"Well, it's official. I'm the majority owner. We're staying in business."

"I can't wait to tell everybody. Come on, and I'll see about getting you your own wagon. Kathleen, do you need any help?" he asked.

"I'll be fine, thank you," she said with little enthusiasm. This was the last place on Earth she wanted to be, but there was no way out of it for the time being. "I'll see you both later."

Joe took Reed to a vacant wagon and showed him inside.

"I'm glad you're here. As soon as you're settled, come over to my wagon. I've got something I want you to see."

"I'll be there."

A short time later, when it was almost dark, Reed stood with Joe in the tented stable area. It was deserted, and they were glad. What Joe wanted to show Reed, he wanted to do in private.

Joe showed Reed the cinch of the saddle Steve had used on the night of his death. Reed's gaze narrowed as he studied the telltale marks on the leather. He looked up at the other man, his expression fierce.

"Who did this? And why?"

"I wish to hell I knew, Reed. I'd like to get my hands on him," Joe snarled.

"You're not the only one," he agreed, looking around to make sure they were still alone. He didn't want their conversation to be overheard. "Who had access to the saddle before it was time for Steve's performance?"

"It could have been anybody," he explained. "Things get pretty crazy around here when the show's going on."

"Damn."

"What are you planning to do?"

"I'm going to find the one who did this. I'm going to find the one responsible for my brother's death."

"But how?"

"I'm going to act as if this really was the tragic accident everyone wants me to believe it was. I'm going to keep the show going and pretend that I don't know a thing about your suspicions. Have you spoken to anyone else about them?"

"Only my daughter, Ann," he replied.

"All right. Let's keep it that way. Until I can prove who did it, we're going to operate as usual." He paused to draw a deep breath, knowing he had set quite a task for himself. He knew nothing about running a Wild West show. "I don't know what 'usual' is around here, though, so I'm going to be counting on you for help."

Joe nodded, ready and willing to do whatever he could to help his new boss. "Just let me know what you need."

"Fill me in on everything—and everybody. We'd

better go over the schedule, too, and then I'll meet with Kathleen. After all, she is part-owner."

Joe snorted in disgust at the mention of Steve's wife. "I don't like that woman. Never have. She's a hard one."

He was glad that Reed was taking charge of the Stampede. Things had been chaotic since Steve's death. They'd canceled several scheduled dates, and no one knew if the show was going to continue or disband. He'd feared that Kathleen would attempt to take over and run things, and he wanted nothing to do with her.

"I know, but I'm in charge of things now. I'm going to make Weston's Wild Texas Stampede the best show around. I'm going to make my brother proud."

Joe met his gaze and saw that Reed Weston was a man to reckon with.

It seemed to Libby that she'd been riding forever. She was exhausted, but terror and determination had driven her on. Over the last several days and nights, she'd stopped only long enough to rest and water Raven. Nothing else had mattered except putting as many miles as possible between her and John. She figured he'd be searching the main routes for her, so she'd kept to the back roads heading ever west.

Libby had seen a sign some miles back telling her that the town of Los Santos was just ahead. She had already made up her mind to stop there for the night. What little money she had wouldn't go far, so she hoped to find some kind of employment in town. She wasn't afraid of hard work. She would do whatever was necessary to take care of herself until she could locate her brother.

It was dusk as Libby reached the outskirts of Los Santos. She reined in before the hotel. As she dismounted, she saw a handbill posted nearby, and she stopped to read it.

COME ONE! COME ALL!
TO
WESTON'S WILD TEXAS STAMPEDE
SHOOTOUTS!
INDIAN ATTACKS!
TRICK RIDING!
FRIDAY NIGHT—7 P.M.
SATURDAY AND SUNDAY MATINEES

Libby remembered reading about Wild West shows, but she'd never thought she'd see one. Grabbing her saddlebags, she hurried inside and approached the counter.

"I need a room, please," she told the clerk.

"Yes, ma'am." The clerk pushed the ledger to her to sign. "Will you be wanting a bath, too?"

"Yes." His pointed question only made her all the more miserably aware of how dirty and unkempt she was from her days of desperate travel.

"That'll be 50 cents."

Libby carefully counted out the money. Her funds were running dangerously low—she had only enough left for food and lodging for one more day before she was completely broke. She had to find some kind of job—and fast—if she was going to survive.

"What do you know about that Wild West show?"

"The town's all excited about the performance coming up Friday night. It's the biggest thing to come through here in as long as I can remember."

"Do you think they're hiring any help?"

"You never know," he answered noncommitally, glancing at her askance and wondering what kind of job she could possibly think of doing at the Stampede. "The man in charge is Reed Weston. He's here in town tonight, too. Last I heard, he was drinking over at the Diamondback Saloon."

"What's Reed Weston look like?" Libby didn't care if he was in a saloon or not. She was going to find him and ask him for a job. She'd heard that the shows had demonstrations of good riding and shooting, and she could do both.

"Weston's a tall man, dark-haired. More cleaned up than most of the other cowboys in town."

"Thanks."

Libby hurried upstairs and bathed as quickly as she could. She had to catch Weston while he was still in town. She sorely regretted that she'd had no chance to bring any other clothing with her. She knocked what dirt and dust she could off her skirt, blouse, and vest, and then put them back on. A quick glance in the mirror told her she was in a sorry state, but she didn't care. The most important thing was that she'd escaped John and Madeline.

Libby hurried back outside. She was going to

the Diamondback Saloon to find Reed Weston and get herself a job.

Reed sat at a table in the Diamondback playing poker with Joe, and Pete and Frank, two of the trick riders from the Stampede. They'd spent the last few days practicing for the show coming up this Friday night, and they were ready to let loose for a while and have some fun. Joe got up from the table as the hand ended and headed for the bar to buy another round just as a woman entered the bar.

"Who's that?" Pete asked Frank with a grin as he caught sight of the female. He thought he'd already made the acquaintance of all the girls who worked at the bar.

Reed glanced up and went still, his gaze riveted on the slender, beautiful blonde who stood just inside the door, looking around. At first glance, it was plain she was no ordinary saloon girl. Though she wore riding clothes that had seen better days, she held herself with a dignified calm that was surprising in the face of the lewd propositions being thrown at her by some of the drunken cowboys seated nearby. She ignored them with a look of disdain, making it all the more evident that she was a lady—and the Diamondback was no place for a lady. Reed wondered what she was doing in the saloon so late at night.

"Well, *oooeee*, honey, what's a woman like you doin' in a place like this?" a drunk named Al Lansing called out as he ogled her from the table where he sat with friends. "Come on over here to me. I'd sure like gettin' to know you better!"

"I'm lookin' for—"

"A good time!" Harley Oats finished for her as he reached out and snared her around the waist. He hauled her bodily onto his lap. "You sure are a sweet little thing!" he declared, groping her in full view of the others and earning their hoots of approval.

None of the men seated at the table with Al and Harley noticed her struggling against him. They were too busy enjoying the entertainment, but across the room Reed noticed. His gaze narrowed as he tried to determine if she wanted the man's attentions or not. A female just didn't walk into a place like this and not expect some kind of trouble.

"Let me go!" Libby defended herself against Harley's mauling as best she could, but his grip on her was firm.

"Why else would you have come in here, except to have a good time?" he insisted, enjoying her struggles. It was almost as if she was dancing on his lap, and he was feeling real good about holding her so close. It gave him ideas of how they could spend the rest of the night.

After her ordeal with John, Libby had had all the manhandling she was going to stand for one lifetime. She tore herself free of Harley's hold. "I didn't come in here to be attacked!"

"Honey, we ain't attackin' you. We're plannin' on pleasurin' you real good!" Al told her.

"Come on, little lady," a man called out from another table. "There ain't no reason for you to play hard to get. Them boys'll pay you for showin' them some fun!"

Al stood up and made a move in her direction. He wanted to put an end to the standoff. He'd gotten hot just watching her with Harley, and he wanted his share of the good times.

Reed had been looking on in silence and thought the blonde was holding her own quite well until Al started toward her. He realized then that she might be in trouble. He pushed his chair back, ready to go to her aid, when she took care of matters herself.

Libby had never been so glad that her brother had taught her how to defend herself. She saw the man coming toward her, and in one smooth move, she drew her gun and faced him down.

"Stay back!" she ordered, then swung around to point the gun at the others as a warning. "All of you!"

Al and Harley both went pale.

Reed hid a smile at her display of daring. She was one hell of a woman, whoever she was.

Joe looked on in silent approval from the bar.

"See here, now!" Ed, the barkeep, bellowed when he saw the firearm. "Put that gun away! There ain't gonna be no shootin' in this saloon!"

"I'd be more than happy to put my gun away— if your customers will sit back down and mind their own business," she shouted back, not taking her eyes off the two who were threatening her.

"All right, boys. Enough funnin' for tonight," Ed ordered. "She ain't one of my regulars, so leave her alone. Get on back to your drinkin'."

50

There was grumbling all around as Al sat back down. Most of the patrons had been enjoying the little show, and once she'd showed them what she was made of, they'd started hooting with delight. There weren't many women around like this one.

"All right, missy, now you just head on out of here," Ed demanded, wanting her gone. He made money off drinking, and she was disrupting business.

"I'm not going anywhere until I find the man I came in here looking for!"

At her announcement, everyone stared around the saloon, wondering what lucky fellow she was after.

"You sure Harley isn't the man you're wanting, honey?" Al joshed, laughing loudly at his own humor. Harley just scowled at him from across the table.

Libby ignored him as she called out, "I'm looking for one Reed Weston. I was told he was in here tonight."

Reed was surprised by her announcement. He wondered how she knew his name and what she could want with him.

"I'm Reed Weston," he said easily.

Libby turned in his direction, and her eyes widened slightly at the sight of him. Reed Weston was probably the best-looking man she'd ever seen. His hair was dark and so were his eyes. There was an air of power about him, and although he appeared at ease, relaxed almost, she sensed there was nothing relaxed about him. He was watching her carefully, his gaze assessing.

51

For a moment, Libby considered leaving without speaking to him, but she realized she had no choice. She was desperate. She needed to find work right away, and Reed Weston was her only hope.

Slowly, Libby slid her gun back into her holster and started toward Reed's table. There were two other men sitting with him, but she didn't pay any attention to them. Reed Weston was her sole focus.

"I'm Liberty Jones," she said as she came to stand before him. "I need to talk to you."

Reed stood and pulled up a chair for her. "Have a seat."

"If you wouldn't mind, I'd prefer to speak with you outside." She was well aware that everybody was still watching her, and what she had to say, she wanted to say in private.

Reed couldn't imagine what she wanted with him. He knew it had to be important, though, for her to have braved entering the Diamondback alone to find him.

"Of course," he agreed, curious.

"We'll hold the game for you," Pete told him.

Reed nodded, and Libby started from the room, leaving him to follow. They both tried to ignore the comments of the others as they passed by. For all that Reed was annoyed by the ribald remarks being thrown their way, he did find himself watching the gentle sway of her hips as she led the way out the swinging doors. He brought himself up short, irritated. This was no time for him to be thinking about women that way. It was difficult enough dealing with Kathleen. He had one goal and one goal only, and that was to find his brother's murderer. He would let nothing deter him.

Libby didn't stop walking until she was safely outside on the sidewalk. When she spun around to face Reed, her expression was as determined as her mood.

"Mr. Weston, I understand that you run the Wild Texas Stampede, and I need a job."

"A job? Doing what?" Reed was surprised by her statement and momentarily distracted as he found himself gazing down into the greenest eyes he'd ever seen.

"I can shoot as good as any man, and I can ride just about anything with four legs," she told him.

He couldn't believe she was serious. "But you're a woman. I don't hire women to perform in the show."

"Why not? I'm good, and I can prove it to you." She had to convince him of her ability. If it meant actually showing him what a good shot she was, she would do it—right then and there.

"No. I'm not interested. Look what just happened with Harley," Reed answered curtly. The last thing he needed in the Stampede was a woman who looked like her. He had enough trouble. He didn't want any more, and that was exactly what she looked like to him—trouble. "Women shouldn't be shooting guns. They should be home, taking care of their families. I suggest you go back home to your daddy, like a good little girl, and let him take care of you proper-like."

53

Anger flashed in Libby's eyes at his tone. She was nearly frantic, but fought down her desperation. She couldn't display any weakness. "I can shoot a playing card out of a man's hand at a hundred paces."

"Good night, Miss Jones," he said dismissively as he turned away and started back inside the saloon.

Libby reached out and grabbed his arm to stop him. The touch was electric and left her momentarily speechless. Reed looked back at her, frowning.

"But I'm good—real good," she finally blurted out. "Let me show you how good I am!"

"There's no need, but I'm sure the boys inside would love a demonstration." He walked on.

Fury replaced Libby's desperation. She had gone through hell twice! First with John, and just now in the saloon. She was not about to take no for an answer! She needed a job and she was going to get one. She'd show him how good she was, and then he'd be certain to hire her.

Following Reed back inside, Libby drew her gun and stood waiting just inside the door. The noise level was loud, but it quieted as the men noticed her standing there with her gun in hand.

"Mr. Weston!" she called as he sat at the table with his friends already engrossed in a new hand of poker.

Reed looked up to find himself staring down the barrel of her gun. "Miss Jones?"

"I didn't want to let you get away without seeing just how good I am with my sidearm," she said coolly. "Why don't you hold one of your cards out a little away from you?"

Reed was angry at her persistence, but he slowly obliged, silently hoping that she was as good a shot as she claimed to be.

All eyes were on him as he held out the card, and the men who were standing near backed off.

With a dead eye and a steady hand, Libby took careful aim and fired. Her shot pierced the center of Reed's ace of hearts.

Despite her ability, Reed was furious at her reckless display.

"Do you still think I should go home to my papa, Mr. Weston?" she taunted, smiling a bit smugly at him. "Or do you think I'm good enough to work for your show?"

Libby hoped she'd impressed him with her daring and accuracy. She hoped he'd be interested in finding a place for her with his traveling show, but the cold, furious look he turned on her dashed all her hopes.

"I told you I don't hire women for the Stampede, Miss Jones," he ground out, more determined than ever to get away from this troublemaker. "If you're looking for employment, I suggest you get a job working here. Maybe the barkeep could use a little extra help—you could wait tables and help keep the boys in line."

Reed tossed some money on the table and left the room. His gaze was hard and his body rigid with anger as he walked past her. He did not speak to her again.

"Hey, Harley, it's a damned good thing you

55

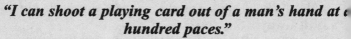

> *"I can shoot a playing card out of a man's hand at a hundred paces."*

didn't mess with her! Think what she mighta shot off of you!"

Laughter followed Reed as he disappeared through the swinging doors.

Libby was tempted to use her gun again—this time on Reed. How dare he dismiss her so rudely! There wasn't a man within a hundred miles who was as good with a gun as she was, and she'd just proven it to him and to everybody else in the bar!

Libby stood there a moment longer, gun in hand, then turned away from the leering, knowing looks and fled into the night. Tears burned her eyes, but she dashed them away. This was no time for hysterics. She had to find a job! John was sure to be looking for her, and she had to stay ahead of him. Joining up with the Stampede would have been perfect. They would have been constantly on the move, and she would have been surrounded by people. She would have been safe. But now her situation was dire. In one more day, she would be destitute, completely without funds and with no way to earn any. She had to do something—but what? Libby headed back toward the hotel, her mind racing to form a plan—any plan—that would save her from the fate she knew awaited her.

"Miss Jones?"

The man's voice came out of the darkness behind her. Alone and suddenly frightened, Libby stopped. She rested her hand on her gun as she turned back to see who'd followed her down the street.

"What do you want?" she asked, suspiciously

eyeing the man she'd seen standing at the bar in the Diamondback.

"I want to talk to you."

"Why?"

"I think I can help you." Joe smiled at her, wanting to put her fears to rest.

"I don't understand. Why would you want to help me? You don't even know me."

"Miss Jones, I know a lady when I see one," he answered. "My name's Joe Shadowens. I work for the Stampede."

"You do?"

"Yes, ma'am. I tend to the stock and gear. I've been with the show since we started up."

"But how can you help me?"

"That was some fancy shooting you did in there. You handled yourself real well, but the boss wasn't too happy with you."

"I wasn't trying to make him happy. I just wanted him to hire me," she told him, almost sorry she hadn't missed the card and hit Reed Weston. At least if she was in jail, she would have three meals a day and a roof over her head.

"And that's why I came after you. If you're serious about wanting a job with the Stampede, I'm offering you one."

"What would I have to do?" She was suddenly cautious.

"I heard you say you could shoot and ride. I need someone to help me with the horses."

"But Weston said he didn't want any women working in the Stampede."

"What Reed doesn't know can't hurt him."

"I don't understand."

"You need a job, right?" Joe thought he'd read her correctly when he'd seen a flash of desperation in her eyes while she was talking to Reed. This pretty girl was in some kind of trouble. "You can't go home to your daddy, can you?"

"My father's dead."

"Do you have any kin?"

"A brother, but he's working for the railroad, and I don't know how to get in touch with him. That's why I need the money. Once I've saved enough, I can go find my brother."

"How'd you come to be here all alone?" Joe asked, wondering how someone as beautiful and intelligent as Miss Liberty Jones had ended up in this town, alone and unchaperoned, talking to him in the middle of the night.

"It's a long story, and one I'd prefer not to go into. If you're serious about offering me a job, I'll take it."

"Good. There is one thing, though."

"What?"

"Knowing how Reed feels about having you with the Stampede, you're going to have to stay away from him—maybe even disguise yourself."

"How?"

"If you dressed like a boy, no one would think twice about you being with the show. We take on youngsters all the time, so you'd fit right in."

"And your Mr. Weston would never find out I'm there?"

"Not unless you tell him. Your secret would be safe with me."

"Why are you being so kind?" She was leery of his seemingly genuine concern for her.

"I have a daughter just about your age, and if she were in trouble, I'd move heaven and hell to help her."

Libby swallowed against the sudden tightness in her throat. It had been so long since anyone had shown her any real kindness. "Thank you, Mr. Shadowens."

"Just call me Joe. Everybody else does."

"Thank you, Joe. I promise you won't be sorry."

"I know that." He grinned at her.

"My friends call me Libby."

"Well, Libby, I'd be honored to be your friend. Do you have clothes you can use for your disguise or do we need to find you some?"

"I've only got what I'm wearing."

The news surprised him, but only confirmed what he'd suspected about her. "I'll bring you some boy's things tonight and then you can join up with me tomorrow. Where are you staying?"

"I've got a room at the hotel."

"All right, I'll be over right away. In the morning, just come on out to the campgrounds and ask for me. Anybody with the Stampede can tell you where to find me. It's going to be hard work, you know. It won't be easy."

"I can handle it," she said fiercely, prepared to do whatever she had to to save herself from being found by John. "But what about your boss?"

"We'll make certain that you don't see much of him. I'll keep you down with the horses. If your disguise is good enough, he won't recognize you even if he does run into you. He'll never know you're there."

"Good. I'd like to keep it that way. The last thing I want to do is meet up with him again."

Having seen the way Reed had stalked out of the saloon, Joe was certain the feeling was mutual, but he said no more. "What room are you in?"

She told him, and he promised to get the clothes to her as quickly as possible. They started off in different directions, but Libby stopped and turned back.

"Joe?"

He looked at her.

"Thank you."

He nodded and smiled. "You just wait for me in your room. I'll be there shortly with everything you'll need."

She returned his smile and hurried away. She'd never believed in guardian angels before, but Joe was changing her mind.

Chapter Four

Reed was weary as he let himself into his private wagon at the campgrounds. He was glad he kept a bottle of whiskey on hand. He needed another drink, for the thoughts that had haunted him—and taunted him—on the ride back would not be dismissed.

Opening the liquor, Reed took a drink straight from the bottle as he settled in at the small table. The whiskey burned, and he was glad for the reminder of its power. He wanted it to ease the tension within himself. He drew a deep breath and closed his eyes.

Reed sat in solitary silence, but the peace he sought still eluded him. Instead of forgetfulness, an image of Miss Liberty Jones, gun in hand, dominated his thoughts. Reed opened his eyes and took another drink, wanting to erase the vision of her from his mind. This was no time to be thinking about women—sharpshooters or otherwise.

Reed's grip tightened on the bottle, and he lifted it to his lips again. In the time that he'd been with the Stampede, he hadn't learned anything that would help him find whoever had cut Steve's cinch, and he'd found no indication that his brother had had any enemies. Everyone seemed truly saddened by his death—even Kathleen.

At the thought of Kathleen, Reed took another swig. He'd never trusted her after that scene at the ranch. He knew what an accomplished actress she was, and as far as he was concerned, she wasn't above suspicion in Steve's murder. Things could not have been good between the two of them if Steve had cut her out of his will. But for all his suspicions, Reed was going to have to pretend he trusted her while they worked together to run the show.

Reed took one more drink, then set the bottle aside and started to undress. He stretched out on the bed and folded his arms beneath his head. As he lay there, a vision of Liberty Jones as she'd looked in the saloon that night returned—her golden hair tumbling loose about her shoulders, her green eyes flashing fire as she gave him a haughty look of disdain for refusing to hire her for the show, the gun held expertly in her hand as she took careful aim to prove his judgment wrong.

Reed smiled in the darkness. There was something about her that had touched him—something that, for all her ability to defend herself, made her seem vulnerable. It certainly had taken a lot of nerve on her part to walk right into the Diamond-back that way and seek him out. And even his re-fusal to hire her hadn't discouraged her. She'd been determined enough to try to convince him otherwise by demonstrating just how good she re-ally was in front of all those men. He was damn glad she was a good marksman. He could have been maimed for life if she hadn't been. His smile broadened for a moment, then faded.

Reed wondered why Liberty needed a job so desperately. She was an attractive woman. She should have been married, living on a ranch some-where, raising a passel of children.

It occurred to him, then, that she might be in some kind of trouble. The thought gave him pause. He'd been so caught up in his own grief and anger over Steve's death that he hadn't even con-sidered her situation. But now, alone in the dark-ness, he did, and he found himself scowling. He thought of the condition of her clothing, and his scowl deepened. His active imagination conjured up an image of Liberty going hungry because he hadn't hired her. He swore out loud at the thought and tossed uncomfortably on the bed, his con-science tormenting him more than the lumps in the mattress.

Reed realized then that he probably could have found something for her to do around the Stam-pede. Disgusted with himself for being so callous, he vowed silently that in the morning he would send someone into town to check on her. If she needed any help, he would see that she got it.

Satisfied, Reed rolled over and sought the forgetfulness of sleep. But it still proved elusive, and he knew it would until he'd found Steve's killer.

Libby finished pinning her hair up and then donned her hat, making sure no errant strands escaped her taming. She took a deep breath and turned toward the mirror to stare at her reflection. She studied herself in the mirror, and finally, after a long, critical moment, she smiled. She really did look like a boy!

Libby had taken care to bind her breasts so no tell-tale curves would be revealed beneath the shirt she wore. Of the three pairs of pants Joe had brought her, she'd chosen the baggiest to disguise her hips. With her hair up and out of the way, she definitely could pass for a youth of about fourteen. And certainly after working outside with the animals all day, she would be as dirty as any of the other hands. Dirt was an excellent camouflage. She was bound and determined to fit in. She did not want to draw any undue attention to herself.

Libby would never have guessed that dressing up like a boy would be liberating, but wearing the pants allowed her a freedom she'd never had before—and she liked it. This disguise would certainly keep her safely hidden from John. She doubted he'd ever recognize her dressed this way.

The fear that John might catch up with her was always with Libby. Only when she'd lost herself in the crowd of workers at the Stampede would she feel halfway safe again. Anonymity was what she wanted. The fewer people who knew who she really was and where she was, the better.

65

Libby had told Joe when he'd brought the clothing to her that she wanted to go by the name of Bert Jones while she was working at the show. If she was going to be a boy, she'd better have a masculine name. He'd agreed.

Joe had reminded Libby before he left that she was to meet him at the campgrounds at dawn, so now that the sky was finally lightening in the east, she knew it was time to go. Before she'd changed into her boy's clothes, she'd settled up with the desk clerk and claimed her horse from the stable. Raven was now tied up behind the hotel in a quiet area where she would be able to ride out unnoticed.

Libby gave herself one last confident, reassuring smile in the mirror, then turned away. She was ready to leave behind the life she'd always known. She gathered up what few things she owned and headed for a future filled with adventure, uncertainty and possible danger.

Libby was about to walk out the door when she stopped and rummaged through her bundle of personal belongings. Taking out her holster and gun, she strapped it on. She would take no chances. Her very life was at stake.

"What do you mean she's gone?" Reed demanded late that morning when Mark Devlin, one of the hands from the show, reported back to him after making the trip into town.

"I asked around town about her like you told me to do, and the hotel clerk said that Liberty Jones

66

had checked out early this morning and no one had seen her since."

"Damn," Reed swore under his breath, though he didn't know why the news irritated him.

"I heard all the talk about what she did last night in the Diamondback. She must be good with a gun." Mark grinned. "Did you change your mind about hiring her?"

"No. The Stampede's fine just the way it is." Reed's answer was curt, discouraging any further questions about his interest in the lady trick-shot.

"If you want me to keep looking for her, I can ride out again and take a look around," he offered.

"Never mind. Go on back to work. We've got a lot to do before the show Friday night."

The news that Liberty Jones had disappeared troubled Reed, but he told himself that by sending Mark to check on her, he'd done everything he could, so it wasn't his problem. There was nothing more he could do for her.

Putting thoughts of Liberty from him, Reed concentrated on what was most important to him—vengeance. He'd been talking to everyone, introducing himself, asking questions, casually trying to pick up any hints that someone might have held a grudge against Steve. He'd come up empty-handed. If he hadn't seen the cinch on the saddle, he wouldn't have believed someone had killed his brother.

For a moment, Reed considered contacting the sheriff in the town where the accident had happened, but he realized it was too late now. There was nothing the law could do. It was all up to him. The realization weighed heavily on him.

Kathleen was angry as she walked around the campground early that afternoon. She'd been unhappy before Steve died, but now she was even more miserable. At least, when he'd been alive, she'd had enough money to do as she'd pleased. Now she was being forced to exist on her meager personal savings and her investment in the Stampede.

God . . . how she hated the Stampede!

Kathleen looked around, trying not to let the disgust she was feeling show. The Stampede had been all Steve's idea. He'd wanted to prove to his father and brother that he could be a success on his own, and he'd managed, somehow. But now here she was, left alone to live out her existence as Steve's widow, and that didn't sit well with her at all. She was a young woman. She wanted to enjoy life—heaven knew she'd had little enough pleasure since that fateful night when, in a fit of rage, she'd decided to teach Reed a lesson and elope with his brother.

Many were the nights that Kathleen had silently cried herself to sleep, realizing what a foolish mistake she'd made. Reed had been the man she'd desired—he'd had the power and the money. Like a fool, she'd married Steve just to spite Reed, and she'd been facing the consequences of her rash and foolish actions ever since.

Somehow, some way, she was determined to get what she wanted this time. Reed was here, close by. As partners, they would be working together. One way or another, he was going to be hers. Then her dreams would really come true—she would have the fortune she'd always coveted and the man she'd always longed for.

A smile curved her lips at the thought as she returned to her wagon and closed the door behind her. Caught up in her scheming, she was taken completely unawares when two strong arms reached out from the darkly shadowed interior and grabbed her. She gasped as she was pulled against the solid wall of a man's chest.

"I've been missing you, woman. It's about time you came back here," Lyle McKenna said as he nuzzled her neck. He'd been waiting to get a minute alone with her, and his passions had grown hot. He boldly cupped one of her breasts and squeezed.

"Don't!" Kathleen protested, twisting away from him. There had been a time when she'd welcomed Lyle's attentions, had encouraged him, even. He was tall, fair-haired and good-looking in a rugged sort of way. He'd been with her in her wagon when Steve had been killed. But she didn't want him anymore—not with Reed so close by. Reed's was the only touch and kiss she wanted.

"Don't?" Lyle stared at her, stunned by her icy refusal. His body was ready for her, and he fully intended to get what he'd come for. He gave a low chuckle. "So, you playin' hard-to-get? I got something that's hard, all right. I've been thinking about this all day. It's been almost a week since we've had any time alone."

"Things have changed," Kathleen insisted, walking away from him.

"You ain't telling me you're playing the mourning widow, are you? We're alone here."

"My life has changed. It will never be the same." She was thinking quickly, trying to come up with a way to discourage him without angering him.

"It will always be the same between us, sweetheart. I know exactly what you want and need, and I plan on giving it to you."

He followed her and grabbed her wrist, hauling her back into his embrace. He didn't bother with subtleties, knowing just how fast and hard she liked their lovemaking to be. He loved her. She had become his whole world, and he was not about to let her end their relationship. Ignoring her protests, he lifted her skirts and caressed her knowingly. When she swayed against him, he smiled.

"You know you love it."

"I don't," Kathleen retorted. She was angry that her body was betraying her by responding to Lyle when Reed was the man she hungered for in her heart and in her mind. She closed her eyes, letting thoughts of Reed fill her. She imagined it was Reed stripping away her clothing, baring her breasts to his kisses. That it was Reed laying her on the bed and moving between her thighs in a passionate, near-violent possession.

"Move, woman!" Lyle demanded.

"Don't talk!" she cried, not wanting the sound of his voice to intrude and ruin her fantasy.

Lyle felt her shudder as her desire peaked, and

he joined her in that release. He was smiling and sated as he collapsed on top of her. His pleasure was short-lived.

"Get off of me!" Kathleen pushed at his shoulders to dislodge him. She quickly shifted away and got up. "How dare you!"

Lyle was surprised by her reaction, and he rolled over to look at her as she stood beside the bed. "What's wrong with you?"

"I told you, my life has changed. Nothing can be the same anymore. We can't go on this way."

"So, marry me," he offered.

Kathleen was absolutely shocked at his proposal. She had been using him for sex, and only for sex. He meant nothing to her. "Marry you? I can't marry you. I'm in mourning."

"I could tell," he said sarcastically, getting up. "I like the way you mourn, Kathleen."

Lyle reached for her again, but she eluded him. "As long as Steve's brother is here, I can't carry on like this."

"What's he got to do with anything? Steve's dead, and you're very much alive." He leered at her, wanting her again.

Kathleen recognized the look in his eyes and moved farther away from him to don her wrapper. "You'd better go."

Annoyed, Lyle began to dress. When he was finished, he reached for the doorknob, then looked back at her. "It's not over, Kathleen. I'll be back."

With that, he was gone.

Kathleen breathed a sigh of relief and made a mental note to see that the lock was changed on the door as soon as possible. She wouldn't let this happen again. Reed was here. After all this time, he was still the one man she wanted above all others. It seemed love and hate were very close, after all.

Thinking about Reed, she realized that using the direct approach when she'd dared to go to him that night hadn't worked. This time, she would be smarter. She would use her wiles and play the mournful widow. She would draw on his sympathies and play up to him. As co-owners, they would have to work together running the Stampede. This new relationship would afford her endless opportunities to have Reed all to herself.

Heat flushed through Kathleen at the thought. She was eager for those moments to come. Reed had never married in all these years, and she could only hope that his staying single meant he'd realized his mistake in sending her away. She hoped so. If it did, she would spend the rest of her life helping him correct that mistake.

Kathleen was sorry now that she'd reacted so angrily at the reading of the will. She had to think of a good reason for her emotional outburst besides greed—something that would convince Reed that she truly had been a good wife to Steve. She would do it. Lying came easy to her, and besides, her future depended on it.

Libby's confidence was growing as she made her way through the campgrounds, heading for the grandstand to watch the rehearsal that was about to begin. She'd put in a full day working the stock and had kept pace with the other hands—all men. Not one of them had paid any particular attention to her. They'd accepted her as who she said she was—one Bert Jones, orphan and drifter—and she was relieved. The work was hard but honest. The horses were some of the finest animals she'd ever seen.

Reed Weston had only come around once that day, and the minute she'd seen him, she'd made sure to go in the opposite direction. She had no intention of tempting fate or pushing her luck. Her luck had held so far, and she was thankful.

Things had gone smoothly that morning when she'd met up with Joe. She'd been relieved to find out that he had arranged for her to have her own tent. It wasn't much, but it offered her some element of privacy. Joe had told her it was hers for as long as she wanted it. He'd set it up close to his wagon, so if she ran into any trouble, he'd be within shouting distance. After telling her how he'd wanted her to work with the horses, she'd been on her own. The day had passed quickly, and when she'd heard about the practice for the show the following night, she'd been eager to attend.

"Hey, Bert! Come on and sit with us!"

Libby looked up to see Mark Devlin motioning for her to join him. She'd met him earlier that afternoon, and he'd seemed nice enough. She was tempted to flee, though, for one of the men with him had been in the Diamondback, sitting at the table with Reed Weston the other night. Instead, she headed his way. It was important that she fit in and that she make friends.

"Didja meet Pete, yet?" Mark asked as she sat down nearby. "Pete, this is Bert. He just joined up with us today."

Pete didn't even give her an interested glance as he said hello, and Libby was thrilled. She sat down in front of him so he couldn't get a good look at her again, and settled in to watch the show that was about to begin.

Libby was fascinated by the action being played out on the parade grounds below. She'd had no idea the Wild Texas Stampede was so exciting. She'd known there were more than 50 horses used in the show, for she'd worked with some of them that day. Now, as the main procession began, she watched in awe. Music was playing from the Stampede's own cowboy band when the first rider entered the arena.

Libby recognized Reed Weston immediately as he led the way. He was dressed all in black and was riding one of the most magnificent horses she'd ever seen. It was a black stallion, and Reed looked arrogant and powerful riding him. She hated the man. She wanted to look away, to ignore Reed completely, but somehow her gaze was drawn back to him, to the easy way he sat in the saddle and controlled his mount.

Libby found herself wondering if he controlled everyone in his life as easily as he did the horse. The thought angered her, for she remembered far too clearly how he'd dismissed her without even giving her a chance to prove her worth.

"Who's that?" she asked Mark, pretending not to know his identity.

"That's Reed Weston. He just took over running the show when his brother, Steve, the original owner, was killed."

"What happened?"

"It was an accident. Steve was thrown during a show a few weeks ago."

"That must have been terrible."

"It was. Steve was a good man, and a damned good rider. We all respected him."

"What about this Reed? Do you think he's as good as his brother was?"

"I hear tell he's every bit as good a shot, though I haven't seen him practice yet."

"So he's in one of the acts, too?" She was surprised and curious.

"That's why it's 'Weston's Wild Texas Stampede.' Steve could ride and shoot with the best of them. Stands to reason his older brother should be just as good."

Libby was fascinated as she turned her attention back to the scene before her. There were at least forty riders circling the parade ground and some were Indians. She'd noticed them earlier in the day in the camp area. "What do they all do?"

"Well, the first group of riders are our Indians," Mark informed her. As the warriors rode past, he explained how Steve had made arrangements for them to leave the reservation to tour with the show. "During the actual parade on Friday night, they'll all be in war paint. In the show, we have a re-enactment of an attack on a settler's cabin, one of a cavalry fight and then, as part of the finale, they raid a stagecoach. That's our 'cavalry' follow-

Libby's gaze was drawn back again and again to Reed Weston as he led the parade.

ing up behind them. The trick riders are next, then the ropers."

Libby watched the procession. She was in awe of the talent of the participants in the show, but in spite of all the different riders, her gaze was drawn back again and again to Reed Weston as he led the parade.

"Looks like Miss Kathleen ain't going to be riding again any time soon," Pete remarked.

"Who's Miss Kathleen?" Libby asked, glancing back at them.

"Steve Weston's widow," Mark explained. "She used to do some trick riding in the show with Steve. We were wondering if she was going to make an appearance tomorrow. Since she's in mourning, I guess she's not."

Libby was surprised that a woman was a performer in the show. From the way Reed had sounded last night at the Diamondback, he didn't want any females in the Stampede.

As the rehearsal started up in earnest, Libby looked on spellbound. She was enjoying every minute of the performance until it was time for Reed Weston's act. She was tempted to leave. The last thing she wanted to do was watch him do anything, but she knew if she got up to go right then, everyone would wonder why. Feeling trapped, she stayed where she was as he rode out to the center of the grounds.

No one had seen Reed shoot before. Everyone grew quiet as they waited for the first target to be thrown. Gunfire erupted as the targets were thrown into the air, and by the time Reed was finished, he had managed to hit ninety-five of the one hundred targets. He was every bit as good as his brother had been.

Libby was irritated to discover that Reed was so good. She'd wanted him to fail. She'd hoped he'd make a fool out of himself in front of all those people, but he'd been fast and accurate. Reed Weston obviously knew how to handle a gun. Of course, she did, too, and she would have welcomed the chance to go head-to-head with him in the show. She would have enjoyed besting him in public.

The rest of the show was as amazing as the beginning had been. Libby knew if they were this good in rehearsal, they would be even more exciting in full costume. She understood why the Stampede was such a success.

Libby ate a solitary dinner in the company's food tent and then retired to her quarters, glad that the day had passed without incident. As she bedded down that night, she calculated that with any luck, she would only have to work at the show for two months. By then she would have enough money saved to be able to go find Michael. It was a reassuring thought.

Reed was not looking forward to speaking with Kathleen again, but he could delay no longer. She was part-owner. He had to find out what her plans were, what she wanted to do.

Kathleen was in her wagon, pondering her future. Her life seemed particularly boring right then. She'd managed to avoid Lyle since that first encounter, and she was glad about that. The farther away from him she stayed, the better. But Reed was another story. She wanted to be with Reed, but he had been so busy taking charge of things that she'd had no chance even to see him. She was growing frustrated and wondered how she could manage to get him alone.

It was then, as Kathleen was plotting what to do next, that she saw Reed coming across the grounds toward her wagon. There wasn't much time to plan, but she had always been quick-witted and today proved no exception. When the knock came at the door, she was ready.

"Kathleen? It's Reed. I need to talk with you."

She waited. Drawing a deep breath, she forced herself to tears. She picked up one of Steve's shirts that she hadn't discarded yet and made her way to the door. Slowly, hesitantly, hoping this worked, she opened it.

Reed was stunned by the sight of her tears. "Kathleen—Are you all right?"

"I—I don't know," she said in a ragged, throaty voice. She actually saw concern in his expression and that emboldened her.

"Did something happen?"

She stepped farther back, wanting to lure him inside where no one could see them.

"It's just—I was thinking about Steve." She sighed raggedly, hiding a smile of triumph as Reed followed her inside. "I was going through his things and, well, I found this shirt."

She held it out so he could see it.

"It still has his scent on it." Her voice broke as

79

she said the last, and she began to sob in earnest. Strategically, she turned and took a small step in his direction.

Reed was helpless to do anything but open his arms to her in her distress.

Kathleen went quickly into them. She pressed herself against him, ever so lightly, as she continued to cry. He felt so strong and warm, she wanted to stay there forever, but she knew this wasn't the time. She had to play the game out. If she made her move too soon, she would ruin her chance. She had found heaven in his arms. If it had taken Steve's death to bring him back to her, so be it.

"It's just so hard," she managed. "I try to be strong, but there are times when—"

Reed was amazed at how fragile Kathleen felt to him. He could feel the shudders wracking her as she cried. He found this tormented woman to be a very different person from the Kathleen who'd been so furious at the reading of the will. He wondered if she was finally realizing just how much she'd lost when Steve died.

Reed didn't say any more, but held her until she quieted. There was nothing he could do that would make things any better for her.

"I'm sorry to be so emotional," Kathleen said, finally forcing herself to move away from him. She didn't want to. She would have preferred to stay in his arms forever, but she had to take things one day at a time. She had already attained one goal—she'd gotten him inside the wagon and had gotten him to hold her. She looked up at Reed and managed a sorrowful smile. "Thank you."

Reed nodded. "You know tomorrow night's Stampede is in Steve's memory."

"I know, and I was wondering if you thought I should participate. Steve and I did have a riding act together. I could do that, if you think I should." She made the offer, sounding reluctant, although she would have been more than thrilled to get out of her mourning dress for a while, even if it was only for a performance.

"There's no need. Everyone will understand and respect your state of mourning."

She took out a lace handkerchief and dabbed at her eyes. "All right. Is there anything you want me to do?"

"No. It's entirely up to you. Whatever you feel you're capable of tomorrow."

"I'll see how I feel in the morning. We can talk then."

Kathleen watched from the window as Reed left the wagon and moved off across the grounds. Her gaze lingered on him until he was out of sight. He would be back to speak with her in the morning. At the thought, she turned away and let the curtain fall back. It wouldn't do for anyone to catch sight of her smiling so brightly when she was supposed to be tormented by her husband's death.

Chapter Five

Libby was busy grooming a horse late the next afternoon when she happened to glance up and see Reed across the campgrounds. She stopped what she was doing to keep an eye on him, ready to make herself scarce if he headed in her direction. While she was watching, a beautiful, dark-haired young woman, clad in black, approached him and, after taking his arm, continued on with him.

"Is that Steve Weston's widow?" she asked the man working nearby.

Lyle looked in the direction she'd indicated to see Kathleen with Reed. He scowled and tensed when he saw the rapt look on her face as she gazed up at the other man. He wanted to go over there and tear her away from Reed, but he controlled the urge. It wasn't easy. "That's her."

82

"Pete and Mark said last night that she has a riding act in the show."

"She did, but I doubt she'll be doing it anymore."

"Why?"

"She and Steve always rode together. It was during their act that he had the accident."

"It was? What happened? Was she hurt, too?" She was shocked, for she had not heard that before.

"I heard talk that she was feeling sick that day, so Steve did the performance alone. Somehow, he fell and was trampled by some horses." Lyle managed to sound regretful as he related the details of what had happened.

"She must be devastated over her loss," Libby said as she watched the way the other woman was clinging to Reed, looking very delicate and helpless. Reed seemed to be completely absorbed in what she was saying to him, and for some unknown reason, that irritated Libby.

"I'm sure she is." Lyle's gaze was on them, too. The way Kathleen was acting angered him. Before Steve's death, all she'd wanted was to be free of him, and now that she was, she was playing this widow-thing up as though Steve had really meant something to her—and Lyle knew better. He knew what she really wanted, what she really liked. He smiled to himself at the memories, making up his mind to find a way to get her alone.

As Lyle fell silent, Libby turned her attention back to the horse she was grooming. She did manage one last glance at the widow. Kathleen certainly was an attractive woman—even dressed in mourning as she was. She was so petite and fragile looking. Libby knew that women who looked the most helpless were usually the ones most capable of taking care of themselves.

Currying the horse with harder strokes, Libby looked down at her own attire and grimaced. She had nothing in common with Kathleen Weston. Kathleen was beautiful and rich. Kathleen was a co-owner of the Stampede. While here she was broke, doing a man's job, disguised as a boy. No, they were nothing alike—except for being alone.

Libby knew she should be proud of being able to take care of herself, but it didn't lessen the sting of knowing that Reed had refused to hire her to work in the show, when Kathleen had been a regular performer all along.

Lyle couldn't stand it anymore. He'd been watching Kathleen with Reed Weston for too long, and he was determined to get her away from the other man.

"I'll be back," he told Bert.

He left the boy working with the horses to go speak with Reed. It took him a minute to catch up with the two of them.

"Mr. Weston—" Lyle started off politely since they hadn't talked before except in passing. All he really wanted to do, though, was hit the man.

Reed stopped and both he and Kathleen looked back in his direction. "You're Lyle, aren't you?"

"That's right."

"Just call me Reed."

"All right, Reed. I wanted to talk with you about your shooting act in the show," he began.

"What about it?"

"Well, don't you think it's boring? Anybody who's halfway decent with a gun can hit those targets. The audience is paying to be entertained. We owe them a good show."

"Reed's a wonderful shot!" Kathleen bragged. "You certainly aren't as good as he is." She looked up at Reed almost worshipfully.

"I may not be, but there are others in the Stampede who are. Maybe you ought to let them take that part of the act, while you just stick to leading the opening parade."

Something about this over-confident cowboy irritated Reed. Not that the man wasn't right about there being other, better shots in the show. He was certain there were any number of performers who could match or pass his expertise. "I appreciate your sentiments, but since this is Weston's Wild Texas Stampede and I'm the boss, I'm going to be performing in the show."

Lyle shrugged as if it didn't matter to him, but he was furious over Kathleen's defense of the other man. He walked away, not trusting himself to say anything more.

The stands were crowded as it drew near seven o'clock. The people in town had turned out in full measure, and they were eager to see Weston's Wild Texas Stampede.

Libby had handled every job Joe had given her, and as the time came for the entry parade, she found herself an out-of-the-way spot from which to watch the procession. She was as excited as a young child as she waited for the action to start.

When the music began, Libby was caught up in the moment. She watched in breathless delight as Reed led the way. She'd thought he looked impressive the other night, but tonight, dressed as he was in buckskins and wearing polished boots and a new Stetson, she thought he looked even more handsome.

The realization that she was thinking of him as a good-looking man brought Libby up short, and she forced the thought away. She didn't even like Reed Weston!

Libby turned her attention to the Indians who were coming next. As Mark and Pete had told her during rehearsal, they were wearing war paint and looked as threatening as any war party that had ever ridden the range. The cavalry followed, looking equally impressive. The trick riders who came next entered at a gallop, giving a preview of their acts to come, and the crowd roared its approval at their daring stunts.

The Stampede progressed on schedule. Each act drew thunderous applause from the audience. When Reed made his appearance, silence reigned. His accurate shooting earned a rousing reaction from the awe-struck crowd.

Again, Libby found herself hoping he would fail—that he wouldn't prove to be as good as he'd been in rehearsal the night before, but Reed surpassed his previous record. He hit ninety-seven of

Reed's accurate shooting earned a rousing reaction from the awe-struck crowd.

the one hundred targets. Reluctantly, she was forced to admit that he was good.

It was as the finale featuring the Indian raid on the stagecoach drew near that Libby went to help with the team. She noticed Joe rushing around with a worried look on his face and sought him out to see what was wrong.

"Joe? What's the matter?"

He stopped long enough to answer her. "I can't find Shorty. He rides shotgun on the stage, and nobody's seen him for hours."

"Can I help you look for him?"

"Yeah, check out the stable area and see what you can turn up. We've only got a few minutes before it's time to go on."

Libby raced off to do what he'd asked. To her horror, she found the man in one of the more secluded spots in the stable, curled up with a bottle of whiskey. He was drunker than a skunk.

"Shorty! Get up! It's time for the stagecoach raid!" Libby shouted.

He looked up at her, bleary-eyed, and gave her a drunken smile. "Sure, Bert, I'll get up. I'm ready to ride. I just gotta take this here bottle with me."

"Let's go!" she told him angrily. She doubted he could still do his routine, but she had to get him to Joe so he could see what shape Shorty was in. Joe would have to decide if he wanted him in the performance or not.

Shorty got to his feet and staggered out of the stable. "How much time we got?"

"Not much. Joe's been looking for you. We've got to hurry!"

Shorty was unsteady on his feet, but somehow managed to stay upright. Libby thought about putting an arm around him to help, but decided against it. She didn't want to risk his discovering that she wasn't the boy she appeared to be.

"Joe!" she called out as she saw her friend in the distance.

Joe saw them coming and ran to meet them. His expression was at first relieved, but then turned furious as he noted the other man's condition. "Shorty, you're fired! I warned you about drinking on the job! Get outta here now! I don't ever want to see your face around the Stampede again."

"Ah, but Joe—" Shorty began, realizing despite his liquor-induced haze that his boss was serious.

"Get out of here now. I don't want drunks working for the Stampede."

"But—"

"Go!"

Shorty was angry, but too drunk to do anything about it. He staggered away, taking another deep swig from the bottle.

As he moved off, weaving as he went, Joe swore under his breath. There wasn't much time left, and he desperately needed someone to ride shotgun with him.

"Think you can play his part, Bert?" Joe asked, turning to Libby. "I need you."

"What's he do?"

"He rides shotgun on the stage with me. All you have to do is hang on tight and shoot at the attacking Indians. Can you handle it or should I get somebody else?"

"I can do it," Libby answered, thrilled that Joe thought enough of her to ask.

"Come with me. There's not much time."

Libby trailed after him to the place where the stagecoach stood ready and waiting for them. He handed her a holster and six-gun to wear and then helped her climb up on top before giving her the shotgun.

"They're loaded with blanks, so there's no danger. Did you watch the rehearsal last night? Do you remember what's supposed to happen?"

"They chase the stage around the parade ground a few times and then you outrun them."

"That's the script," he said, nodding his approval. "Are you ready to ride?"

"If you are." She was confident as she settled in the driver's box with Joe.

"Looks like you're getting your chance to work in the Stampede after all," he told her with a chuckle as he slapped the reins on the team's backs.

She grinned at him and held on as they made their way to the entrance. She'd show Reed Weston!

Joe took the stagecoach into the arena at a good clip. As they made the first turn, the warriors came charging out from a different entrance, whooping and hollering. The roar from the crowd was deafening as Libby climbed up on top of the stage and began firing. As scripted, several of the Indians took deliberate falls, and the crowd cheered even louder.

The team was running at top speed when it happened. Joe had been controlling them with a steady hand, but suddenly he lost the reins and fell from the driver's box.

"Joe!" Libby cried as she saw him tumble to the ground. This definitely wasn't part of the act.

She had to think fast, for she knew the runaway stage was headed straight for the stands, where it might crash and injure innocent people—not to mention herself. She tossed her shotgun aside, then scrambled forward, trying to get a firm hand-hold on whatever she could so she, too, wouldn't be thrown from the vehicle.

All around her she could hear the approving roar of the crowd. They thought Joe's fall was a regular part of the act. When some of the warriors reined in to see to the fallen driver, the fans in the stands thought they were taking him captive. The rest of the warriors kept riding in hot pursuit of the stage. They were no longer acting, they were trying to help.

Libby reached the driver's box and was horrified to see that there was no way she could get to the reins. They were dragging in the dirt behind the team as the horses raced blindly on. She had to act, and act quickly. Her decision was made in a split second, for she knew if the horses continued to run wild, they could charge into the stands and possibly kill someone. Giving no thought to her own safety, Libby climbed down in front of the driver's box to make a grab for the horses' harness.

It was one of the most difficult things Libby had ever done, but somehow she managed. Hanging on for dear life, she worked her way forward inch-by-inch between the racing horses.

The crowd in the stands jumped up at Libby's display of daring horsemanship and bravery. Everyone was amazed at the stunt. The audience applauded raucously as she finally reached the lead horses.

Libby managed to climb on one's back. She yanked with all her might on its bridle to halt the team's breakneck pace. The horses slowed awkwardly. They bucked wildly at being so restrained, but Libby kept her seat.

Fighting to keep hold of the stubborn horse, Libby felt her hat loosen and then fly off. Her hair, freed from its restraining pins, tumbled about her shoulders in a glorious mass of golden curls. As she brought the horses to a full stop, it was revealed to all that the "man" riding shotgun was not only a crack shot and an unusually courageous rider, but a woman as well! Her secret had been disclosed in front of everyone.

The performance continued as the Indians closed in on the stage. The audience had no idea that this wasn't the way things were supposed to go. They were cheering and screaming in excitement over her handling of the runaway team. Her horsemanship had been superb. They'd never seen anything like it by a female before.

Libby thought fast. She was worried about Joe, but wanted things to work out right for the Stampede. She couldn't let on that this had been a real accident. In a brazen move, she drew the six-gun Joe had given her at the start of the performance and began blasting away at the now "attacking" raiders. The warriors were glad to see that she'd stopped the team. They played along with her and scattered as if in terror. They allowed themselves to be driven off by the lady gunslinger.

The crowd was going crazy. A woman had saved the day! She'd stopped a runaway team of horses, driven off the raiding party and saved the stage-coach!

Libby was trembling as she climbed down from the lead horse's back. She wanted to run back to Joe, to find out how he was, but she was forced to continue the act. She could see that Joe was being helped from the parade ground by some of the other performers, so she turned to the audience and waved, playing up to the crowd.

No one in the stands understood that Joe's fall had not been part of the act. They were roaring their approval, cheering and shouting for more excitement. Everyone was wondering who the mysterious heroine was. They were amazed by her talent.

"Who is she?" one man shouted to another.

"I don't know. Does anyone know who Weston's lady is?"

The question was repeated again and again. They all wondered why Weston's lady hadn't been billed as the star of the show. She certainly had been the highlight of the night.

As the remnants of the stage chase were cleared away and Libby made her exit, the closing parade began. Reed led the way, but for all that he was smiling and waving to the audience, he was furious. He had watched what had happened with Joe and the stagecoach raid in stunned disbelief. What could have been a tragedy had been transformed into a major success, and by none other than Miss Liberty Jones! He had no time to deal with the situation right now. The parade came first, but as soon as things quieted down, he was going to find out exactly what was going on.

The crowd's cheers were deafening as he rode out at the forefront of the parade. Everyone there was attributing the exciting new act to him and lauding his showmanship.

Libby wanted nothing more than to find out about Joe's condition, and then disappear for the night, but there would be no getting away. She would now have to appear driving the stagecoach at the end of the parade.

"Damn, Bert! You had us all fooled!" one of the other hands told her, laughing at his own inability to recognize that Bert had been a woman—and a darned pretty one, at that. "That was one smart trick! Reed's good! Real good to put one over on us like this!"

"I'll tell him you said so," she replied sarcastically, though no one else suspected her true feelings on the matter.

She made her way to where the stagecoach was ready and waiting for her to take the reins.

"Well, Bert, what's your real name?" Mark asked as he stood by the stagecoach.

"Liberty Jones," she replied. "But my friends call me Libby."

His eyes widened slightly at her announcement.

So this was the woman Reed Weston had been looking for the other day—the woman who'd caused such a stir at the saloon the other night! And all this time she'd been right there under all their noses, and no one had known it. She was some kind of female. That was for sure.

"Nice to meet you, Libby," he replied with a grin as he helped her climb up onto the driver's box to take the stagecoach out for the parade. "Be careful while you're out there. One of the reins snapped while Joe was driving. That's why he lost control and fell. I've fixed it temporarily to get you through the parade, but it won't hold forever. So watch out."

"I'll be careful. Just find out how Joe is for me, will you?" she asked worriedly.

She was shocked by the news that the reins had been damaged. She had seen how careful Joe was with the equipment and the livestock, and she was horrified that such a freak accident could have occurred.

On cue, Libby urged the team forward. The horses trotted out onto the parade grounds to a standing ovation from the crowd.

"There's Weston's lady!" the shout came.

The noise level grew as the audience expressed its pleasure with her daring riding and shooting. The stage attack had been magnificent. She was going to be the talk of the town for weeks to come. Weston's lady was a star!

Libby deliberately didn't look Reed's way as they lined up for the final bow before the stands. She brought the stagecoach into line expertly and waved again to the audience, who responded with great fervor to her friendly gesture.

Reed waited until the cheering had died down, then urged his horse forward for the closing ceremony.

"And now, ladies and gentlemen," he announced, "I'd like to introduce to you Mrs. Kathleen Weston."

Kathleen walked out from the secluded spot on the sidelines where she'd been watching the show. She didn't know who the little bitch was who'd just earned such thunderous applause from the audience, but she intended to find out. She wondered why Reed had kept the other woman's performance a secret from her. As co-owner, she was entitled to know exactly what was going on, and she resented being left out of any decision concerning the acts.

"As you all have heard by now," she began when she reached the center of the parade ground, "my dear husband, Steve, the founder of the Wild Texas Stampede, was killed in a tragic accident just a short time ago. We have dedicated this performance tonight to his memory. With the help of Reed, my husband's brother"—Kathleen looked toward Reed and waited quietly while he acknowledged the crowd—"we are going to continue the Stampede and try to make it bigger and better than ever—just the way Steve wanted it to be. We want to make Steve's dreams come true. Thank you so much for your support and kindness. Good night."

The Stampede was over with her announcement. Kathleen led the way, walking gracefully back to her seat to watch the procession file out. She kept her expression carefully schooled into one of earnest pain.

As the stagecoach moved past her, Kathleen looked up at the young woman driving it. Her expression hardened. A flare of anger seared her again as she got a close-up look at the female who'd caused such a stir with the audience. The woman was beautiful—blonde, young, shapely in the outrageous pants she wore and absolutely gorgeous. Kathleen had heard the people in attendance calling her "Weston's lady" and that had infuriated her, too. There was only going to be one Weston's lady in this Stampede, and that was her— not some little troublemaker who'd made her "debut" dressed like a boy. Kathleen would see to it.

Libby could well imagine what Reed was thinking, and she wasn't interested in hearing any of it. As soon as she'd parked the stagecoach where it belonged, she jumped down and hurried to where Mark was standing. She would deal with Reed Weston later. Right now, she needed to know how her friend was. She hoped his injuries hadn't been serious.

"How's Joe?"

"Nobody knows for sure. His daughter, Ann, sent for the doctor from town, and he's checking him in his wagon right now."

"Thanks."

Libby didn't waste any time talking with the other members of the Stampede. There would be time enough for explanations about her hidden identity later. She rushed off toward Joe's wagon and knocked softly when she reached it.

"Yes?" Ann Shadowens answered, opening the door only slightly. "Oh, it's you—come on in." She gave Libby a welcoming smile as she held the door wide for her.

"I'm Libby." Libby entered. She had never met Ann before, but she knew the girl would be nice if she was Joe's daughter. Ann was a petite, pretty blonde, whose warm manner put her instantly at ease.

"Papa's in there. He told me he wants to talk to you." She eyed Libby with interest, having had no idea that "Bert" was a girl.

"He's all right, then?" Libby pressed, her concern very real.

"The doc says he will be. He broke his leg and will have to be off of it for a while, but he'll heal. Come with me."

Ann led the way to the small room at the back of the wagon that served as Joe's sleeping area.

"Doc, I want you to meet Miss Liberty Jones," Joe said with pride as he saw her coming. His face was battered and swollen, but he had a smile for her as she went to stand by his bedside. "She's a fancy shot and one helluva horsewoman."

"Joe." Libby was thrilled to see that he could still smile. "You're really all right—I was so worried."

"Yes, ma'am. The good doc here says I'm going to be fit as a fiddle," he told her.

"I'll be leaving now," the doctor said as he

picked up his medical bag and started from the wagon.

Ann went along with him to see him out, leaving Libby and her father alone.

"From what I hear, you did one fine job controlling that team," Joe complimented Libby.

"Thanks."

"No, thank *you*. It could have been deadly out there. You saved the day."

"And I also lost my hat." Libby managed to smile, but she knew it wasn't funny. She was well aware of what Reed Weston thought of her and believed her hours with the Stampede were numbered.

"So I heard. Well, we had them all fooled for a little while, didn't we?" He chuckled at the thought of how shocked Reed probably had been.

"I guess I'd better start packing up my things. I appreciate all you did for me, Joe." She had faced the fact that she would have to leave. Reed Weston would never let her stay on.

"What do you mean, you're going to start packing up?" He glared at her.

"We both know how Reed feels about my being with the Stampede. It's better if I just go ahead and leave now, before he shows up to throw me out."

"You aren't going anywhere. I heard that crowd cheering for you, and I ain't never heard anything like it before in all the time I've been with this show. They all believed you were supposed to save the day that way. They had no idea it was real."

"So?"

"So, let's make it a regular part of the show. How could Reed refuse, knowing how excited the audience was about you and your stunt? He'd be a fool to let you get away!"

Libby said nothing, her thoughts on her encounter with the Stampede's boss at the Diamondback. "I don't think this is such a good idea."

"Leave everything to me. I'll handle it," Joe assured her.

Ann returned then. "I understand my father had a hand in bringing you to the show."

"Yes, he did."

"I'm glad," Ann said, smiling at her. "Things could have been much more serious out there today if you hadn't been along to control the team. Thank you."

"I'm just sorry it happened at all. Mark told me one of the reins broke, and that's why you lost your seat."

"It's unusual for reins to break. I checked them myself before the performance." Joe frowned. "Accidents happen, though, and even though I'm a little the worse for wear, things have turned out all right."

"Thank God."

"Things will turn out for you, too. You'll see. You stay close. I imagine Reed's going to be looking for you real soon."

"I think you're right."

Libby said her good-byes. She was greatly relieved that Joe was going to be all right. Drawing a deep breath, she left the wagon and started for her own tent.

* * *

"Reed?" Kathleen had been searching for him since the end of the show and finally found him near the stagecoach. "I need to talk to you."

"What is it?"

"Don't you think you should tell me when we're adding a new act to the show? I had no idea that we'd changed the attack on the stagecoach. As co-owner, I should always be consulted about such things. We'd just spoken, but you never mentioned anything about a new script."

"As a co-owner who was so eager to be bought out, I thought you wouldn't be too concerned about day-to-day operations."

"Well, I am." She drew herself up, her head held high. "From now on, I'd like to be informed as to what's going on."

"By all means," he responded, just wanting to appease her. Until he got the chance to be alone with Miss Liberty Jones and find out just what she was up to, he didn't want to talk about tonight with anyone else.

Kathleen had expected an argument from him. She was surprised by his easy acquiescence. "Who is this woman everyone's calling Weston's lady?"

Inwardly, Reed grimaced. "I met her the other night in town. She worked out quite well, don't you think?"

"The audience certainly was impressed."

"Yes, it seems they were most impressed. Now, if you'll excuse me, I've got some business to attend to." Without another word, Reed strode away. There was only one woman he wanted to talk to right now—and it wasn't Kathleen.

Kathleen was shocked as she watched him walk away. How dare he dismiss her without even a backward glance?

She had the sudden urge to slap him, but controlled herself. She wanted to build on their relationship as co-owners, not destroy the tenuous understanding they'd established so far. Trying not to appear too irritated, she managed a benign expression as she started back to her own wagon.

"Mr. Weston!" a man called out to Reed.

Reed stopped at his call and waited as he hurried over to speak with him. "Can I help you?"

"I just wanted to compliment you on the wonderful show," the man told him. "I'm Randolph Page, the editor of our local paper. That was quite an original idea, having a woman disguised as a man in the stagecoach attack. She was wonderful. I know everyone's been calling her Weston's lady, but I wondered if you could tell me her real name? I'd like to mention her in the article I'm going to write about the Stampede's performance tonight."

Reed grew even more frustrated. The crowd's reaction to Liberty Jones had told him that she had won their hearts. If she got even more publicity, he would be forced to keep her on with the show. There was no way to avoid telling the newspaperman, though.

"Her name is Liberty Jones," he finally answered. "Isn't she wonderful?"

"She was fantastic! Look for the article in tomorrow's paper!" The editor hurried off toward his office.

Reed headed toward Joe's wagon again in hopes of finding Liberty. His path took him through the dispersing crowd, and he was stopped numerous times by the townspeople. They all complimented him on the show and told him how exciting Liberty's performance had been. He hid his displeasure and thanked them all for attending.

As Reed continued on, he thought about what had happened during the stagecoach attack. He was forced to admit to himself that he doubted any man could have done a better job handling that runaway team. Not that he wanted to change his position about adding a woman to the show. He didn't want to do it, but it almost seemed he had no choice. In just one performance, Liberty Jones had made a name for herself. She'd become *Weston's Lady*. His expression was thunderous at the realization.

"Mr. Weston!" An elderly woman hurried up to speak with him. "I'm so sorry to hear about your brother's death. It's always a tragedy when someone young dies, but you did him proud tonight. I'm sure he would have been pleased."

"Thank you, ma'am." Her kind words touched him. He hoped she was right.

"And your lady was just marvelous! What a clever idea to have her disguised as a boy! You certainly had all of us fooled."

"I'm glad you enjoyed the show."

"That we did. The Stampede was a great success. I'm sure you're going to sell out wherever you go. Word of how great Weston's Lady is will travel fast. Good luck to you and God bless you," she told him as she patted his arm before moving off to join her waiting family.

Reed stalked off. He greatly resented having been put in this position, and there was going to be some hell to pay.

It was then that Reed saw her. Liberty had just come out of Joe's wagon and was heading for a nearby tent. He watched her move, studying her, wondering how he could have been so blind as to have missed her before. Though her figure was hidden by the boyish clothing she wore, there was no mistaking her now that the golden mass of her hair had tumbled free. Liberty Jones hadn't disappeared from town. She'd been right here the whole time.

Some foreign emotion taunted Reed, but he ignored it. He didn't like being put on the spot this way, but there was no escaping the fact that he was trapped. Weston's Wild Texas Stampede had just created a new star, and now he had to deal with her.

Reed swore under his breath and quickened his pace. She wouldn't get away from him this time.

"Liberty Jones!" He called her name in a gruff voice that reflected his black mood.

Libby stopped. She recognized his voice, and her heartbeat quickened. She had known this moment was going to come sooner or later. She had just hoped it would be later. Slowly, she turned to face Reed. She lifted her chin defiantly as she met his harsh gaze straight on.

"You wanted something?"

"Yes," he said coldly. "I want to see you in my wagon—now. I think we have a few things to discuss."

Chapter Six

Reed opened the door to his private wagon and stood back to let Libby enter ahead of him. She swept past him, her manner dignified and lady-like, in spite of her masculine attire. Something about her controlled, almost icy manner annoyed Reed. He didn't like being made a fool of, and she'd just accomplished that very nicely. He followed her inside and shut the door firmly behind them.

"Have a seat," he said, motioning her to one of the chairs at the small table.

"No, thank you. I prefer to stand." Libby felt more in control if she remained standing. If she sat down, she would be forced to look up at him, and she didn't want to give him that advantage.

"Have it your way," Reed said sharply. "It appears, Miss Jones, that you don't listen very well.

It seems you didn't hear a thing I said to you the other night at the Diamondback."

"Really?"

"Yes, really." What little patience he had with her was fading fast. "As I recall, I told you I wasn't hiring for the show. And I especially wasn't hiring any women."

"I hired on as a boy," she retorted.

Reed's gaze raked over her, and he gave her a sardonic look. "So I see. How ingenious of you."

At his expression, she countered, "You wouldn't give me a chance! Joe did! I'm good—damned good! And I just proved it tonight. The performance could have been a disaster, but I managed to stop the runaway team in time! Think what would have happened if the horses had run into the stands."

"But they didn't."

"Because I managed to rein them in!" she insisted. "People could have been injured or killed, but they weren't—thank God—because I acted fast enough to keep it from happening. In fact, everything turned out so well that the crowd was fooled completely. The audience thought it was a regular part of the act!"

"So I could tell," he said flatly. His tone reflected his irritation with the entire situation.

"I can help you with the show," Libby went on, trying not to sound desperate. If he fired her, she had no money and nowhere else to go.

"I don't need your help, Miss Jones."

His arrogance stung her, but she couldn't give up. "But you wouldn't want to disappoint your public, would you? You're a businessman, Mr. Weston."

Reed's gaze raked over her assessingly. He could not explain to himself why he was glad she was going to be there where he could keep an eye on her. She meant nothing to him. This was a business deal only, and yet—

"You know, you're absolutely right, Miss Jones," he began thoughtfully. "You *are* worth a lot of money to me. And it's for just that reason that I'm going to keep you on in the Stampede. You wanted a job with Weston's Wild Texas Stampede—well, now you've got one. You're officially Weston's Lady."

Reed's statement was so reminiscent of John's words that it sent a shiver of terror down Libby's spine, and his hot gaze upon her unnerved her. Her temper flared. She was never going to be helpless before a man again!

"Know this, Reed Weston," she began, the fire of her anger glowing in her eyes, "I *am* worth a lot of money to you, and I'll earn every cent you pay me for my work in the Stampede, but that's the only place I'm going to be Weston's Lady."

"We both know you're not a lady, and I'm not even sure you're much of a woman." Even as he said it, Reed knew it was a lie. She looked beautiful as she challenged him. Her hair was a glorious golden mane of unruly curls about her shoulders, and high color stained her cheeks.

His cruel comment stung, and Libby reacted without thought. She swung out at him.

Reed read the flash of fury in her eyes, and he

anticipated her attack. He snared her wrist to stop her when she would have slapped him, and he jerked her to him.

In that instant as he stared down at her, his awareness of everything except Liberty faded. Even dressed as she was, he thought she was gorgeous. She had proven that she was spirited and brave, and despite his harsh words, he was very aware that she was all woman. Reed could no more have stopped himself from kissing her right then than he could stop breathing.

Reed drew her near, slowly, deliberately. He wanted this—no, he needed this. He needed to taste of the fire of her passion. He bent to her.

Libby's eyes widened at the sudden change in him. She found herself frozen, held captive by the unfathomable look in his eyes.

Their lips met, and time seemed suspended. His mouth settled over hers like a possessive brand, claiming her sweetness for his own.

Libby had meant to fight him, yet something about his nearness and touch mesmerized her. Her heartbeat quickened, and her pulse raced. She was lost.

The logical part of Libby didn't want this. She knew Reed was cold-blooded and mean. She knew he really didn't care about her. He was just like John—concerned only with money—and she didn't want anything to do with him. Yet his kiss was a tempting challenge, and she instinctively responded to that challenge. The few gentle embraces she'd shared with John before that horrible last night had been pleasant enough, but nothing like this. Reed's kiss was exciting and arousing and—

Just as she was about to be swept away, Libby regained her senses. This was Reed Weston. She couldn't stand the man. What was she thinking of, kissing him this way? In an act of pure self-defense, she drew her gun and pressed it hard against Reed's side as she tore herself from his hold.

"I'll earn my salary working in the show—not in your wagon," she said coldly. She was angry with herself for having enjoyed his kiss, and she was angry with him.

Reed went still at the feel of the cold metal pressed against his side. He drew back and looked down at her, giving her a slight, mocking smile. "I wouldn't have it any other way."

"Any relationship we have will be strictly business," Libby continued. His smug, almost amused expression annoyed her so much that she still held her gun on him. "Remember, I'm Weston's Lady only when I'm acting in the Stampede."

His gaze narrowed dangerously as he regarded her. "We're performing a matinee tomorrow. There's an early practice. Be there. We need a new driver for the stagecoach, and we have to figure out what else you're qualified to do in the show. We have to give the public what it wants—and they want Weston's Lady."

"Don't worry." She continued to glare at him, but sensing no further threat, she slowly holstered the gun. "I'll be ready. Good night, Mr. Weston."

"Good night, Miss Jones. And—Liberty?"

She had started for the door, but paused to glance back at him questioningly.

"Your gun wasn't loaded."

Heat stained her cheeks as she realized the weapon she'd pulled on him was the one from the show—it held only blanks. He could have disarmed her and overpowered her at any time, but he hadn't. She hurried from the wagon, his knowing laughter following her as she went. The farther she got from him, the better.

Libby sought the safe haven of her tent. As she reached it, she found that Ann had been watching and waiting for her.

"Are you all right?" Ann asked, her expression worried.

"Yes, why?"

"I was just coming outside when I heard Reed call out to you that he wanted to see you in his wagon. I was worried that he might have been a bit harsh with you."

Libby gave Ann a friendly smile. She was tempted to confide in her, but she was still not quite ready yet to trust anyone fully. She'd been taught too painful a lesson with Madeline and John, and it would take a while to recover.

"Reed and I managed to work things out. Your father was right. Reed realized that I could make money for the Stampede, so he agreed that I should stay on with the show."

"He didn't fire you? That's wonderful!"

"No. He realized the audience loved the 'act,' just like your father said. So I'm officially Weston's Lady and a member of the Stampede now."

111

"I'm so happy for you," Ann said with sincerity. "And thank you again for helping to save my father."

"I just wish the whole thing had never happened. Mark told me that one of the reins had been damaged. I guess that's why Joe lost his grip and fell."

"Damaged? How?"

"He didn't say much, just that he'd temporarily repaired it. He warned me to be careful when I drove the stage at the end."

"Well, I'm sure it was an accident. I'm just thankful my papa's alive."

"Me, too. Your father's a very kind man. Tell him what happened with Reed for me, will you?"

"Of course. He's resting right now, or I'd have you come in and tell him yourself."

"I'll visit him in the morning. You take good care of him, and if you need any help, let me know."

"I will. Thanks, Libby."

It was some time later when Reed finally had time to check on Joe. He wanted to make sure the older man was doing all right. If he was still awake, he was going to talk to him about the changes he'd made in the show. Since Joe had always been the regular stagecoach driver, they would have to choose someone new to replace him in the act until he was healed.

"Reed!" Ann seemed a bit startled at seeing him when she answered his knock at the door. Then she managed a sad smile as he moved more clearly into the light.

"Is everything all right?" Reed asked, puzzled by the look on her face.

"Yes, it's just that you looked so much like your brother standing there in the dark that for a moment I thought you were Steve."

"I wish Steve was here."

"Me, too," she answered, her tone distant.

"I know it's late, but I wanted to look in on your father."

"He's doing as well as can be expected. He managed to sleep for a while earlier, but he's awake now. You can come in and talk with him if you'd like."

"Are you sure he's up to it?"

"I'm sure. I know he wants to see you. Come on in."

Reed entered their wagon and followed her to where Joe lay in bed, his eyes closed. Reed could tell that the older man had taken quite a beating.

"Papa? Reed's here, and he wants to talk to you."

"Reed?" Joe opened his eyes and smiled as best he could when he saw his new boss.

"Hi, Joe," Reed said as he sat down in the chair next to the bed. "How do you feel?"

"Like hell, if you must know the truth," he said with a grimace as he tried to shift positions and found every movement was excruciating.

"I don't doubt it. That was quite a spectacular fall you took. You're lucky to be alive," Reed told him.

"I know. I wanted to stir up the crowd, but that was one heckuva way to do it. You weren't plan-

113

ning on this kind of excitement at tonight's show, were you?"

"No, I wasn't," he answered tersely.

"Are you angry?" Joe ventured, hearing the tension in Reed's voice.

"You know I told Liberty in town that night that I wasn't hiring anyone for the Stampede."

"She seemed like she needed a job, so I thought hiring her on wouldn't do any harm. If Shorty hadn't gone and gotten himself all drunked up, she would still be just one of the boys."

"Well, she's not 'one of the boys' anymore. If it's any consolation to you, the crowd loved her 'act.' They all thought Liberty's part in stopping the stage was planned. They even named her Weston's Lady. I had several people from the audience stop me and ask me about her. The editor of the town paper is going to mention her in his article about the Stampede. So, as of tonight, we have a new star in the Stampede. Weston's Lady is going to be performing regularly."

"You hired her on?" Joe was shocked and relieved at the news. He'd thought he was going to have to convince his boss to keep her on with the show.

"I did, and I'm thinking of arranging more acts for her. I know she can shoot, and judging from the way she handled that team today, I'd say she's a damned good rider, too."

"It looks that way."

"We've scheduled a practice for tomorrow morning, since we're doing the matinee tomorrow. I wanted to know who you thought should take your place as the stage driver?"

Joe thought for a moment, then answered, "Mark's about the best man at handling a team we've got. I'd have him do it."

"All right. I'll speak with him in the morning. Did the doctor say how long you'll have to stay off that leg?"

"About a month or so."

"Will you be able to travel with us?" Reed was worried about the discomfort Joe would suffer as they moved from town to town. He also valued his help running the show and knew he would miss him if he chose to stay behind.

"I don't care how much it hurts, I wouldn't miss being with you for anything. Especially now that Weston's Lady is going to be a regular. I still haven't forgotten how she shot that card you were holding at the saloon. She should be something to watch."

"She's something all right, and I haven't forgotten our little run-in at the saloon, either." Reed scowled as he stood up to go. "You take it easy. I'll look in on you tomorrow."

"Reed? Before you leave—I take it you didn't talk to Mark yet?"

"No. Why?"

"It was just something that Libby said earlier." At Reed's questioning look, he hurried on, "Mark told her one of the reins broke. That's why I had the accident."

"One of the reins broke?" He repeated, his gaze narrowing as he considered the implications of what Joe was saying. *First, Steve's cinch and now Joe's reins?* "How?"

"That's what I don't know. I thought maybe you could check on it for me."

Reed looked grim as he nodded. "I'll go have a look right now."

Their eyes met, and each understood what the other was thinking.

"I'll let you know what I find out in the morning."

"Thanks."

"Is something wrong?" Ann asked him, noticing his dark expression as she saw him out.

"No. I just want to check on some details about the accident. That's all. Good night, Ann."

She bade Reed good night, too, and remained standing in the doorway, her gaze lingering on him as he moved away. She saw him pause and glance at Libby's tent, then walk on. Only when he'd disappeared into the darkness did she turn back inside. All the while she'd been watching him, in her heart she'd been wishing he was Steve.

Libby was lying awake in her tent when she heard someone leaving Joe's wagon. She recognized Reed's and Ann's voices immediately. As she heard Reed bid Ann good night, she found herself holding her breath and wondering where he was going next. She heard his footsteps as he neared her tent and feared that he was coming to see her. The last thing she wanted to do was see Reed Weston again this night.

Nervous and a bit frightened, Libby reached out

in the darkness and grabbed her father's gun. This was one gun she knew was loaded with real bullets. She'd checked it right before she'd gone to bed to make sure. She didn't trust anyone right now. Never knowing when or if John might show up kept her constantly on guard, and after her last encounter with Reed . . .

Logically, Libby told herself, she had nothing to fear from Reed. If he'd wanted to force her to his will, he could have done it earlier in his wagon. It still embarrassed her to think of how he'd taunted her with the knowledge that he'd known all along her gun was useless.

Thinking about the moments before that embarrassed Libby even more. Why, she'd actually responded to his kiss! She shivered as she remembered the intensity of Reed's lips upon hers. His kiss had been a hot, demanding caress, unlike anything she'd ever experienced before.

Thinking back to the kisses she'd shared with John, Libby knew Reed's had been totally different. John's early kisses had been sweet enough, she supposed. She'd been an innocent to the ways of men then, and had accepted his embrace as what a kiss was supposed to be. But that night at Madeline's had taught her differently. Just the memory of John's vile, forceful touch and punishing kiss left her filled with revulsion. She couldn't believe she'd been so completely taken in by him. It would never happen again.

But then there was the memory of Reed's kiss— so sensual, so demanding. She had reacted differently to him. She'd almost enjoyed his embrace, but she had to fight the attraction. Reed was a man—and he was just like John. He'd proven it by telling her he was keeping her with the show because she was worth money to him.

A tear streaked down Libby's cheek as she lay alone in the darkness. She heard Reed pause nearby and she tensed, but then he continued on. As the sound of his footsteps faded away in the distance, Libby wept for the loss of her innocence. Pure though her body might still be, she understood too well now the ugly workings of the world. The knowledge left her feeling she was jaded. When she finally slept, the gun was next to her.

Mark was still working with the horses when Reed found him. He told him what he wanted to see, and Mark got the reins out for him to inspect.

"Here's what I had to repair," Mark said as he handed him the reins.

Reed studied the leather for a minute. "Was there anything wrong before the performance? Did you notice that it looked worn or possibly cut?"

Mark frowned. "I wasn't looking for anything like that when I fixed it, but now that you mention it, the break could have been caused by a cut. Why would someone intentionally cut the stage's reins?"

"I don't know. As careful as Joe is with the gear, he would never use anything that was damaged or worn in any way. He wouldn't take the chance that it might break during a show." Reed fell grimly silent. There was no point in asking Mark who had access to the team—Joe had already told him that everyone did at show time.

"I'll keep a look out and see if I notice anything else damaged in the equipment."

"Thanks. In fact, why don't you take over for Joe until he's back on his feet?" Reed instinctively trusted Mark and knew he would do a good job. He believed he was honest and hard-working.

"All right, and if you need anything else, just let me know." Mark was pleased to be asked. Everyone knew Joe was the unofficial second-in-command with the Stampede. It was an honor that the new boss thought so highly of him. He would do his best.

Reed took one last look around the grounds, then retired to his wagon for the night. It was late, well past midnight, as he lay awake trying to figure out who would have wanted to hurt Joe. Did someone know of Joe's suspicions about Steve's death and want to silence him? He'd thought Joe had kept his opinion about the cinch quiet. If Joe had mentioned it to others and had also revealed that he was trying to find Steve's killer, would the killer be coming after him next? Reed knew that from now on he'd have to take extra care. There would be no more "accidents" in the Stampede.

As he finally started to fall asleep, Reed's thoughts drifted to Liberty. He remembered the sweet fire of her kiss and the look on her face when he'd told her the gun was useless. A slight smile curved his lips as sleep claimed him.

* * *

Libby was up at dawn and ready to face whatever the new day held for her. Reed had said there would be an early practice, so she girded herself for the prospect of spending a good part of the morning in his company—something she would rather avoid.

Libby supposed the old adage, *Be careful what you wish for, you might get it*—held true. She'd wanted a job with the Wild Texas Stampede when she'd approached Reed that night in the saloon, and now she had one. She wasn't quite sure what Reed had planned for Weston's Lady to do in the show, but she would be prepared for anything. She donned her own clothing, and after checking her gun one last time, she headed for the parade ground. Libby was as ready as she would ever be.

Reed, Mark and several of the other hands were already there, ready to go to work, when she joined them. Kathleen was also in attendance, and that surprised Libby. She noted that the other woman's expression was distant and a bit disdainful as she watched her approach, and she wondered at her reaction.

"We're going to be making some major changes to the show," Reed was saying. He paused to introduce Libby to the others. "Everyone—in case you didn't know, this is Liberty Jones. Up until late yesterday, most of us thought of her as Bert, one of the hired hands, but now we know the truth. Liberty, do you know everyone?"

"I haven't met Mrs. Weston yet," she told him. Up close, Kathleen Weston was even more lovely than Libby had previously thought.

120

"Kathleen, this is Liberty, the new star of the Stampede," Reed said, introducing her.

Inwardly, Kathleen was seething. *This woman who'd been passing herself off as a boy was now going to be the new star of the Stampede?* She eyed Libby critically, noting her worn clothing, but also noting how pretty she was. She decided she didn't like her at all, and she greeted her coolly. "Liberty."

"It's nice to meet you, Mrs. Weston. My friends call me Libby," Libby returned, her instincts screaming a warning that she would have to be careful around this woman. Maybe it was the memory of the way she'd seen Kathleen gazing up at Reed so rapturously the other day, or maybe it was the iciness she saw reflected in her eyes that warned Libby all was not what it seemed. "I hope the show goes well with the changes we're going to make."

"I do, too," Kathleen said with emphasis.

"It will," Mark put in, still enthusiastic about the audience's response to Libby the night before. "Libby was the talk of the town last night. I went with some of the boys to pay a late visit to the saloon, and that's all they were talking about. This afternoon's show should be sold out again."

"How wonderful." Kathleen's tone was ambiguous. Before Steve's death, her riding act with her husband had been one of the highlights of the Stampede. Now, she was relegated to the invisible status of being Steve's widow, and it was infuriating.

"It will be wonderful, financially," Reed put in,

wanting her to understand that she would be profiting by Liberty's new role. "Liberty Jones is going to be a great attraction."

"You're billing her as Weston's Lady?" Mark asked.

"Yes."

"Where did that name come from?" Kathleen demanded.

"That's what the crowd was calling Libby yesterday when they didn't know who she was," Mark explained.

Kathleen nodded, then turned to Libby. "So what is it exactly that our new 'star' is going to do? What are you good at?"

Liberty recognized her underlying hostility and bristled. She didn't know why this woman should take an automatic dislike to her. "I was raised on a ranch, and my father treated me as an equal to my brother. I know how to shoot. Reed can testify to that."

The men laughed, and even Reed managed a smile. "She's definitely got a good eye."

"Oh?" Kathleen asked, wondering what had gone on that she didn't know about.

"At the Diamondback the other night, Libby decided to give Reed a firsthand demonstration of just how good she was with a gun," Mark offered.

"You actually went into one of the saloons in town? Why?" She turned to the other woman, her expression horrified. No good woman would ever do such a thing.

"I needed a job, and I wanted to work for the Stampede. I'd heard that Reed was the man to see, and he was in the saloon. I wanted to impress him and I thought actions would speak louder than words, so I had him hold up a card and I shot it."

"Is this true?" Kathleen looked at Reed, unable to believe what she was hearing. "You didn't tell me any of this."

"There was no need to tell you," he answered simply, liking the way that Liberty had related their first encounter. If everyone thought they'd had a secret plan from the beginning, so much the better for advertising for the show. "I was impressed by Libby and, it seems, so is everyone else." He deliberately used the name she preferred.

"And we all saw that she knows her way around a horse, too," Mark said, having witnessed her bravery firsthand the day before.

Libby smiled at Mark. "I can throw a knife, too, if you're interested. What did you have in mind for the act today? Are we going to recreate the same scene that we did yesterday?"

"I'd like to—without the driver breaking a leg," Reed answered. "Mark's taking over for Joe as the driver, so we'll have to plan exactly how we're going to do this."

"Are you two going to have a shoot-out of some kind?" Mark asked, looking from Reed to Libby. "It would be quite a draw if you went head-to-head in a competition—especially after the scene at the bar the other night."

"I'll do whatever you want me to do," she offered.

Kathleen bristled at her willingness. "Do you think it's really necessary?"

Reed glanced at Kathleen. "If Libby's the one the audience wants to see, Libby's the one we're going to give them." He turned to Mark. "I want you to bring the stagecoach around so we can see what we can put together, but first there's one other thing I have to say."

They all fell silent as they waited for Reed to speak.

"We've had two serious accidents here in a short period of time, and I'm telling you right now, there aren't going to be any more. I want everyone to double check everything. We are not going to put anyone else's life at risk. Two accidents were two too many. Is that understood?"

They all murmured their agreement.

"Good. I expect you all to take care—of yourselves and each other. I'm going to be watching to make sure you do."

When Reed had finished speaking, Mark hurried off to get the stagecoach.

Kathleen excused herself, having seen and heard more than she wanted already. She didn't like this Liberty Jones being around Reed so much. She didn't care how good she was with a knife, gun and horse. Libby was just a stupid cowgirl. Kathleen was not going to let her come between them. Reed was going to be hers.

Chapter Seven

"She hit all of them!" Mark exclaimed, impressed by Libby's first shooting demonstration. The boys who'd been at the saloon hadn't been lying. Not only was she pretty, but she could ride and shoot with the best of them.

After finishing the rehearsal for the stagecoach performance, they had come to an open area to let her show them how good she really was. She hadn't missed one of the fifty targets Mark had thrown for her.

"Libby, you're as good as any man I've ever seen," Mark said.

"Thanks." She flashed him a warm smile, appreciating his kind words, as she holstered her gun.

Reed had been standing a short distance away, watching, and Libby sought him out.

"So it wasn't an accident when you shot the card

I was holding the other night. You really are that good." He was amazed by what he'd just seen.

"No, it wasn't an accident," Libby responded, glad that her aim had been perfect this morning. "But I was wondering, do you think the audience will find it boring just watching me shoot targets? Shouldn't we plan something a little more exciting?"

"Like what?" Reed was pleased that she was thinking about the audience's reaction to the show.

"Mark suggested earlier that we should have some kind of a competition—the two of us. What do you say?" Libby gave him a challenging look.

Reed saw the daring glint in her eyes and decided to return her challenge. "I know how good you are with a gun, but how much do you trust me?"

Theirs gazes met and locked. They stared at each other for a long moment. A thrill shivered through Libby at the reckless look in his eyes.

"I guess I have no choice," she finally answered, knowing she was trapped. Without this job, she was destitute. Staying on with the Stampede was her only hope of survival, and Reed Weston owned the Stampede.

Her answer bothered Reed. He didn't know why she should mistrust him. He wasn't the one who'd been deceiving everyone. She was. "You're right, you don't have a choice about trusting me if you want to stay with the show. Go stand in front of those hay bales. I've got an idea."

"What are you going to do?" Mark asked as Reed drew his gun and took aim at Libby.

"We're adding another act to the show. Liberty was worrying about boring the crowd, so we're going to make sure we keep them awake. Liberty— don't move."

Reed didn't say another word, but began to fire. Those who were working nearby preparing the grounds for the matinee all came running to see what he was doing.

Libby stood stock-still as he'd ordered, holding her breath as Reed's bullets flew around her. Only when he'd fired his last shot did she let out a sigh of relief and step away. She turned to find that he'd outlined her shape in the hay bales with his shots. Impressed, but not about to give him too much credit, she faced him and nodded in acknowledgement of his perfect aim.

Reed was looking quite confident as he watched her coming toward him. Her gaze was serious, and she was focused only on Reed as she took out her gun. His expression didn't change as he waited for her to join him.

"It's your turn," she said quietly.

Reed accepted her challenge. He moved to stand in front of the stack of bales and waited.

With a steady hand and eye, Libby duplicated his trick. In spite of his confidence in her, Reed found himself holding his breath until she'd fired the last bullet. He was glad that his judgment of her abilities had been correct.

"That's some fine shooting," Mark said, complimenting them both.

They just smiled at him, but reserved cautious looks for each other. They discussed where to set up the shooting display so as not to endanger the crowd. It was decided that they would put a sheet behind each of them with their outline painted on it, so it could be shown to the audience when their shooting was done.

"Would you like me to do a knife-throwing act?" Libby offered.

"Pick your target. What would you like to do?" Reed asked, not doubting her ability with a knife one bit.

For an instant, an image of using John as her target hovered in her thoughts, but she turned serious. "I don't have a knife with me, but I could hit a target someone's holding up, if you'd like. Mark could do it, if you don't want to."

"No, you're Weston's Lady. If you work with anyone in the show, it will be me," Reed declared, surprising himself.

"Here," Mark spoke up, handing her the knife he carried. "Will this do?"

Libby took it and weighed it in her hand, studying the blade. "This is a nice one. Thanks."

Mark nodded and stepped back, interested in seeing how good she was at this.

"All right," Libby said, turning to Reed. "Who's got a cigar?"

"A cigar?" Reed frowned as one of the hands hurried to bring one to him.

"Yes, if you stand sideways in front of the hay bales and put a cigar in your mouth. I'll try to cut it off."

"Try?" he repeated, glancing at her.

Mark chuckled, but said nothing as Reed took up his position.

"I'm as ready as I'll ever be."

"So am I," Libby told him.

She took careful aim and did exactly what she'd told him she would do. Everyone was thrilled with her accuracy—Reed the most of all.

"Shall we put that in the show?" Libby asked, smiling at Reed as he stared at the ruined cigar.

"As long as your hand stays steady, it's fine with me."

That settled, they set out to decide what they were going to do as the final act for Weston's Lady.

"Just how good are you on a horse?" Reed asked point-blank.

"I can hold my own," she answered. She had matched him in everything he'd wanted her to do so far, and she wasn't about to show any weakness now. "What did you have in mind?"

"I was thinking we could do some trick riding together."

He quickly explained his idea. He was pleased when both she and Mark agreed that it might work and they should give it a try.

"That should really excite the audience," Mark remarked.

"Have you ever ridden standing up before?" Reed asked Libby.

"When I was little, my brother and I used to try stunts like that all the time. I should be fine."

"Let's give it a run-through then."

Mark brought the horses for them. Libby had

specifically requested her own mount for the action to come. She was used to her horse and they understood each other.

When they finally decided exactly what they were going to do, Reed and Libby mounted up, ready to see if it could actually be done.

Libby put her heels to Raven's sides and raced down the center of the parade ground with Reed in hot pursuit. He gained on her and swooped down to snare her around the waist. He hauled her from her horse's back and held her to him as he rode.

As Reed kept tight control over his mount, Libby carefully shifted her position until she was sitting in front of him. As she settled back against the hard width of his chest, Reed's arms came around her, and her hips were settled tightly against his. The shock of that intimate contact surprised them both. They had known they would be touching each other during the ride, but neither had expected to feel this sudden jolt of awareness between them.

Libby realized that she'd made a mistake agreeing to do this act with him, but it was too late to back down. She would brazen it out, but she wanted to get away from him as quickly as she could afterward.

Their plan had been that she would maneuver around him until she was standing up behind him on the horse; then they would race the length of the parade ground with her waving to the crowd. Eager to escape his hold, she started to move away. It was as she began to try to shift to the back of the saddle that she started to slip from Reed's grip.

Reed feared Libby was about to fall and made a desperate grab for her, crushing her to him. He reined in hard, afraid of losing his grip on her entirely. As he brought the horse to an immediate stop, he found himself staring straight down into her wide, frightened eyes. Her breasts were pressed tightly against his chest, and the way she was breathing heavily from fear and exertion only left him that much more aware of their position. He scowled, struggling for control over the unbidden desire she roused in him.

"Why did you stop?" Libby asked, trying to sound annoyed as she quickly masked her fear and pushed herself away from him.

"I thought you were falling," he growled.

"There's no way I could have fallen with the grip you had on me," she retorted, very much aware of the hard heat of his body where they were still in contact. He was all male, but she didn't even want to think about that. They had a show to put on. That was all she cared about.

Reed hadn't completely released his grip on her until she spoke; then he realized just how tightly he had been holding her. He eased his grasp, and she shifted farther away from him. He couldn't decide if he was glad or not. Her hips were still tight against him, and there could be no escaping that contact in the way the act had been set up.

"What if I kick out of a stirrup and you use that to help you change positions?" Reed asked, trying to think of a safer way for her to get behind him.

Libby nodded. "Let's practice it once now while we're sitting still to make sure it works."

Libby moved so she was fully facing him. She braced herself by gripping his shoulders and waited for him to kick free of one of the stirrups. When he did, she slipped her booted foot into the stirrup and stepped around him, still clinging to his broad shoulders to help pull herself up behind him. Bringing her knees up beneath her, she manipulated herself to a crouch on the horse's back, and in one smooth, easy motion, she stood up. She fought for her balance, but managed to remain standing.

"You did it!" Mark shouted.

With a laugh of triumph, she slid back down to dismount. "Do you want to try it again from the start?" She asked Reed.

"We'd better. We're not going to be able to rein in during the performance."

Mark raced to bring her her horse. Then she and Reed rode to the far end of the ground to start over.

This time, their execution was perfect. Libby was so intent on making sure she didn't get too close to Reed that she was able to move around him with more ease. The steady gait of the horse was smooth, and her only truly frightening moment was when she was actually standing behind Reed. When she finally achieved the right position, she was exhilarated. Reed carefully slowed the horse to a stop before the center of the stands.

"What do you think?" Reed asked Mark, after he'd helped Libby down to the ground.

Mark had always thought that Kathleen was a decent horsewoman. She had done a few trick rides before Steve's death, but compared to Libby, she'd been an amateur. "The performance was fantastic. I've never seen another woman who could ride this well."

"And neither have I," Reed admitted, finding himself amazed by her abilities.

The memory of holding her crushed against him as they rode brought other thoughts to his mind, but he shoved them away. Libby had made it perfectly clear that she wanted nothing to do with him, and he felt the same way about her. They were doing this performance for the show and for no other reason.

"You didn't have any problems? Using the stirrup works best for you?" Reed asked Libby as he, too, dismounted to stand with her and Mark.

"This last time was fine. I think we've got it worked out just right. What do you want me to wear during the performance? I figured you probably wanted me to be Bert for the stagecoach act."

"Your boy's clothes will be fine for that," Reed told her as he eyed her garb critically. "What else do you own?"

Libby swallowed tightly as she admitted, "Only what I have on and the boy's things Joe gave me."

Reed found himself frowning as he wondered again about her background. Every woman he'd ever known had had more clothes than she knew what to do with, and here Libby had only the clothes on her back. He knew nothing about her personally, except the little she'd mentioned about

133

her adventures with her brother. Other than that, she was a mystery to him.

"How much time do we have, Mark?" he asked brusquely.

"A little over four hours until show time."

"Come with me," he ordered Libby.

"Where are we going?" She balked. She had seen his scowl and thought he was angry about something.

"I'm taking you into town. We're going to do some shopping."

Libby was humiliated and quickly protested, "There's no need to. I—"

He silenced her with a look. "If you're going to be Weston's Lady in the Stampede, you have to dress the part."

His statement did not ease Libby's humiliation; it only intensified it. Still, she hid her distress. She would not let him know how dire her situation really was.

Reed turned away to speak with Mark, giving him instructions about what to prepare for the performance that afternoon. When he'd finished, Reed was ready to head into town.

"There's one thing I want straight between us before we go anywhere," Libby said firmly as she stood her ground before him. "I want you to take the cost of any clothes we get out of my pay."

"We'll work the payment schedule out."

"We're not 'working out' anything. I'm paying for any clothing we buy. We have to agree on this, or I won't go with you."

He saw the glint of determination in her eyes.

"Agreed. Now, let's go. We don't have a lot of time."

They mounted up and rode out. Libby knew Reed was right. If she was going to be a star in the show, she had to look like one. She thought back to the last time she'd been concerned about looking good, and she remembered that terrible day at Madeline's house and how excited she'd been waiting for John to arrive. She'd primped endlessly, wanting to look her best for him.

Libby glanced down at the clothes she wore now and grimaced. Her innocent dreams were as tattered and worn as her clothing.

Pain filled her as she thought of how, up until her experience with John, she'd only believed in the good in people. When John had come along and swept her off her feet, she had trusted him. Libby realized that she should have known he hadn't really cared for her, but she'd been too filled with girlish notions of love and marriage to understand that much of what he'd said had been lies. How could she have known that people as respected as John and Madeline could be so vile?

She'd learned her lesson the hard way. The Liberty Jones who'd thought she loved John didn't exist any longer, and the new Liberty Jones wasn't about to trust anyone with her heart and soul ever again. Her brother Michael was the only person in the world she could believe in, but he was gone, and she was alone. It was up to her to take care of herself. And she would. After all, she'd gotten this far on her own—she was now a star for the Stampede. That thought soothed her damaged spirits, and Libby smiled slightly.

Reed noticed the change in her expression and thought she looked even more lovely smiling. The thought annoyed him, but he couldn't stop himself from remarking on it.

"You're smiling," he said.

Libby quickly glanced over at him, a little startled that he'd noticed. "I was just thinking about the show."

"And?"

"I think the performance is going to be great."

"I hope you're right. If the audience response is the same as yesterday, you'll be well on your way to making quite a name for yourself."

For just an instant, she looked haunted. The possibility that John might learn of her whereabouts through the Stampede's publicity suddenly scared her. "But only in the towns we play in, right?"

"We send out handbills and put up posters in advance of our performances, so we get the word out far and wide." He noticed that she had an almost frightened look about her. He couldn't imagine what she could be afraid of. "Are you worried about something?"

"No, not at all. I wanted to be in the Stampede, and now I am." She gave him a smile that she hoped would make him stop asking questions.

"So tell me, Liberty, is Los Santos your home? Is this where your family is?" He suddenly wanted to know more about her.

"My parents are dead, and my brother is off

working for the railroad." She kept her answer short and avoided telling him where her hometown was. She did not want to reveal too much about herself. The less anyone knew about her, the better.

"Why did you decide you wanted to work for the Stampede?" He sensed there was a lot more to her story than she was telling him, considering her lack of clothing and the way she'd looked a moment ago when he'd mentioned all the publicity she'd be getting. Reed wondered if she was running from something—or someone. A husband, maybe? The thought brought him up short.

"I needed a job, and when I saw your handbills posted around town, I thought you might be able to use me. What about you? Why are you running the Stampede? It was your brother's show, wasn't it? How did you end up with it?" She artfully deflected the conversation away from herself.

"Yes, Steve started it up on his own when he married Kathleen. I've been running the family ranch near Crawford's Gulch. After Steve died, Kathleen talked about selling the Stampede, but it was doing so well, I wanted to keep it going. I thought I owed my brother that much."

"Well, if our first show was anything to judge by, he'd be proud of you. The audience certainly enjoyed it."

"I've booked several more towns for us. We'll be moving out on Monday."

"Good," she said, and she meant it.

"Steve had also booked some dates that we

Bobbi Smith

didn't cancel, so we'll be on the road for quite a while."

This news pleased her even more. She didn't want to stay in one place too long. She wanted to keep moving. "What about your ranch? Who's taking care of it?"

"My foreman is, and he's been with the family for years. The Circle W will be fine."

Libby asked him more about the ranch, and the rest of the ride passed quickly. Before they knew it, they were on the outskirts of Los Santos.

"There's a small clothing store on the main street. I guess we can start there and see what we can find," Reed told her.

Milly Adams looked up as the door to her shop opened.

"Why, aren't you the lady from the Wild West show?" she exclaimed. "I saw your performance last night, and you were wonderful!"

Libby smiled warmly at her. "Thank you."

"No, thank *you*. The show was so exciting. If I hadn't had to work today, I would have gone back a second time to see you again. You were that good!"

"We're glad you enjoyed the Stampede, ma'am."

"Why, you're Reed Weston, the owner, aren't you?" she asked.

"Yes, ma'am."

"It is a pleasure to make your acquaintance. You're a very shrewd man to include a woman as brave and exciting as Miss Jones here in your production. She steals the whole show."

"That she does," he agreed, glancing at Libby to

see that she was actually blushing a bit at the woman's gushing praise. "And that's why we're here. We decided she needed some new clothing for her performances. We were wondering if you had anything that might suit her."

"Why, it just so happens that I do!" Milly was eager to please them, and even more eager to gain the attention that would result if Weston's Lady from the Wild Texas Stampede shopped at her store. "Come look at these things!"

A short time later, Libby was in the dressing room trying on a leather split skirt that was decorated with fringe, with a leather vest and a blouse to match. As she was slipping them on, Milly returned to the dressing room to give her a pair of hand-tooled leather boots that happened to be just her size. They were decorated with lone stars on them.

"You're going to look marvelous in this outfit. I can't wait until your husband sees you in them," she was saying.

"Husband? Oh, he's not my husband—" Libby quickly corrected her.

"But I thought if you were Weston's Lady—" Milly was confused.

"Only in the performance not in real life. I work for Mr. Weston."

"Well, he certainly is a handsome man." Milly looked back over her shoulder to where Reed was patiently waiting for Libby. He was out of earshot, so she knew they could speak openly.

"I suppose he is," Libby hedged.

"There's no 'suppose' about it," Milly told her. "He's one good-looking man."

"He's my boss, so I don't think of him that way."

Libby glanced out to see Reed standing at the window, staring outside. She paused to study him for an instant, seeing him through the shopkeeper's eyes. Reed *was* devilishly handsome, tall and dark. There was a pride and sense of power and authority in his bearing, too, that impressed people. She stood transfixed as she gazed at him, remembering his kiss from the night before and the practice of their riding act earlier that morning. He was attractive, she finally admitted to herself, but she didn't care. She knew what men were really like now. Reed was only interested in her because of the Stampede—nothing else.

"Well, let's see what he thinks of this outfit," Libby said, changing the subject.

She moved past Milly into the shop to model for Reed.

"What do you think?" Libby asked.

Reed had been lost in thought and hadn't heard her come out of the dressing room. At the sound of her voice, he turned quickly. A slow smile spread across his face at the sight of her. The skirt fit her perfectly and the fringe swayed as she walked toward him. The vest matched the skirt, and the boots were just what the outfit needed to make it special.

"You look wonderful," he complimented her.

Libby could almost feel his warm, approving gaze upon her. In spite of herself, she found she was blushing a little at his open appraisal. "I thought I could wear this for the shooting act."

"It would be perfect," he agreed.

She nodded and hurried back into the dressing room, where Milly waited to help her change.

"I have a lovely dress that you could wear for evening—" She started to hold up an emerald satin gown for her to look at, but Libby quickly stopped her.

"No, I won't be needing that. Thank you." She knew she couldn't afford it.

"Pity. Let me go see what else I have."

Carrying the gown, she left Libby alone while she went to check.

"Is there something wrong with that gown?" Reed asked as she brought the gown back out.

"I thought Miss Jones would like it, but she said she doesn't need it. She says she only needs things for the show."

"Will it fit her?" he asked.

"It should."

"Tell her I said to try it on. There might be an occasion when she might need it in the future."

"Yes, sir. I'll tell her you said so." Milly picked up a few more items and carried them back to where Libby was waiting.

A few minutes later, Libby emerged from the room once again, this time to find Reed sitting in a chair by the mirror. When he heard her coming, he looked up.

Libby looked positively beautiful as she made her way to him. The emerald gown fit her as if it had been made just for her. The color emphasized her pale complexion and highlighted the beauty of her golden tresses. The neckline was modestly cut, yet hinted at the fullness of her bosom, and his gaze lingered there for a moment before he lifted it to hers.

"We'll take the dress," he told Milly.

"Do you really think it's necessary?" Libby countered, wondering how long it would take her to pay off all her purchases.

He ignored her question as he spoke to Milly. "She'll need shoes to go with it, too."

"Yes, sir." The shopkeeper was thrilled with his taste—and his budget.

When Milly moved off to give them a moment to speak alone, Libby glared at Reed.

"I thought we were only getting clothes for the show!"

"There will be times when you're going to need to look like a lady," he told her.

His comment stung her, reminding her of his harsh words of the day before. "Then I guess it's more of a costume than any of the other clothes, isn't it?" She turned away and hurried back into the dressing room.

"Do you know what else you're interested in?" Milly asked Libby as she went to the backroom to help her out of the gown.

"Do you have any pants?"

"Pants?"

"Yes. I want a pair of men's pants to fit me."

"But you're a lady!" she protested.

Libby gave her a benign smile that hid the truth of what she was feeling. "There's a very tricky riding act I have to put on, and I really think I should be wearing pants of some kind."

"Oh. Well, let me take a look and see what I can find—"

She bustled outside again and was gone for a few minutes. When she finally returned, she had several pairs of men's pants with her. She waited as Libby tried them on. The first pair was too big and nearly fell off her, but the second pair fit her like a second skin. Libby was amazed at how comfortable the pants were to wear, and with the boots and blouse she thought the outfit looked feminine, even though it was traditionally male attire.

"What do you think?" she asked Milly.

"Well, I—" She wasn't sure what to think. She'd never seen a lady dressed this way before. Of course, yesterday in the Stampede Miss Jones had been wearing boy's clothing, but this outfit was different from the nondescript things she'd had on then. This outfit drew attention to her—to the curve of her hips and her long legs.

"I understand," Libby told her with a grin. "Let's see what Mr. Weston thinks."

Libby walked outside to find Reed, leaving the shopkeeper behind. She was watching him closely as she called out to him.

Reed turned from where he'd been looking at some other merchandise to see Libby coming toward him. He stood still, taking in the sight of her. He'd thought she couldn't appear any more beautiful than she had in the gown, but he'd been wrong. Dressed as she was in the men's pants that hugged her long, slender legs, a blouse and her new boots, she looked ravishing. His throat went dry, and for a moment he was speechless.

"I thought pants would be appropriate for the riding act."

"Pants?"

"I know a real lady wouldn't be seen wearing these, but we've already established that I'm no lady, so it won't matter. It will make my maneuvering around you easier."

A rush of unwanted desire slammed into him as he remembered the positions they'd found themselves in during practice. At the idea of having her, so clad, sitting before him on his horse's back, he swallowed tightly. "Whatever you think will work."

She was surprised that he didn't put up more of a fight about it. She felt victorious as she returned to the dressing room where Milly was waiting. "I'll take this outfit, too."

"You were the talk of the town today with your stagecoach act. I can just imagine how excited everybody will be once they see you in your other performances."

"I hope you're right."

"You just wait and see. Everyone's going to be so impressed with you. You're a star."

Milly gathered up the clothing and went out front to package it up. Reed walked up to the counter as she was wrapping the clothes.

"Pick out another dress for her, something for day wear, and whatever underthings she might need," he told her.

The shopkeeper hurried to do as he'd asked. As

she selected the necessary garments and began to wrap them, too, she wondered if there wasn't more to their relationship than Miss Jones had let on. The young woman had declared that she wasn't Weston's Lady, but he certainly was acting as if she was. *And,* Milly thought, *what woman in her right mind wouldn't want to be Reed Weston's woman?* She certainly would have jumped at the chance if he'd been interested in her and she'd been single. Still, she did not question her good fortune at the business they'd given her today. They had been the best customers she'd had in ages, and she was thrilled that she'd had the items they'd wanted in stock.

By the time Libby had dressed and come back out to join Reed, Milly had her clothing all bundled up and ready to go.

"Thank you, and good luck to you!" Milly called to them as they left her shop. She couldn't wait to let all her friends know that they had paid a visit to her store.

"I'm paying for the gown," Reed told Libby in a tone that brooked no argument as they rode out of town.

"I don't want to owe you for anything," Libby insisted, not wanting his charity.

"Think of it as part of our business arrangement. If the clothes you're wearing are all that you own, it's only logical that you'll need a few other things now that you're not disguising yourself as Bert."

He was right, and she knew it. She didn't say any more.

It wasn't until she was back in her own tent getting ready for the show that she found the other, more feminine articles he'd purchased for her without her knowledge. His boldness in daring to take charge this way angered her, yet his thoughtfulness touched her. Troubled by her mixed emotions, she began to get ready for the performance. Show time was drawing near.

Chapter Eight

Reed had finished dressing for the show and was about to start for the parade grounds when a knock sounded at his door.

"Kathleen—" He'd been caught up in thoughts of Liberty and was surprised to see the other woman. He deliberately stepped outside to talk with her.

"I've been trying to find you for hours. Where have you been?" Kathleen asked, looking worried. In reality, she was hurt that he hadn't invited her inside so they could talk privately. She doubted anyone would question her need to meet uninterrupted with her brother-in-law and business partner.

"I had to take Liberty into town. She needed clothes for her performances."

"You bought her clothes?" *Libby got new clothes,*

147

while she was forced to wear black! "I could have gone with her. You shouldn't have bothered. You're more needed here," she continued, furious, but taking care not to let her anger show in her voice.

"I didn't think about it. There was little time, so we left as soon as we'd finished our early practice."

"How did the practice go?"

"Liberty will be performing in four acts in the Stampede, including the stagecoach raid."

"Are you pleased?"

"Very. I think you'll be impressed, too. I still have to speak with Joe before the show starts. Do you want to go with me, or shall I see you later?"

"We can speak later."

With that, he locked his wagon door and headed off to meet with Joe. He found Ann outside their wagon, and she told him to go on inside. Joe was resting in bed, looking as comfortable as possible considering his battered condition.

"We're just about ready to start," Reed told him as he sat down in a chair beside the bed.

"Libby worked out all right?"

"Yes. She's going to do a shooting act, a knife-throwing demonstration and a riding act along with the stagecoach performance. I took her into town and bought her some clothes, so I guess we're as ready as we'll ever be. The people in town were still talking about her, so I think the Wild Texas Stampede has found itself a star."

"Is she excited?"

"It's hard to say," Reed remarked thoughtfully. "It occurred to me as I was getting ready for the show that in all the time we spent together today, she told me very little about herself. The only clothes she had, other than the boy's outfits you gave her, were the ones on her back. So while we were in town, I had the shopkeeper put some extra things in for her."

"She isn't going to like that. Our Libby's a proud one."

"'Our' Libby? I hardly think she's 'my' anything." He grimaced, thinking of their conversations.

Joe laughed. "She's a spirited one, all right, but she'll do you proud."

"I'm counting on it. The way we've got the shooting challenge and the knife throwing set up, if Libby accidentally misses, Kathleen may end up the sole owner of the Stampede."

"Then you tell Libby I said to make sure she doesn't miss! The last thing I want is Kathleen to be my boss." He was not joking.

This time it was Reed's turn to chuckle. "If Liberty ever does shoot me, it won't be by mistake. How soon are you going to be able to get out and watch a performance?"

"The way I'm feeling, a few more days."

"Well, take it easy and rest up. I'd better get over there. I'll let you know how it goes."

"I'll be waiting to hear," he said as Reed stood to go.

"From now on, we're doing a double check on all equipment, too," Reed told him.

"Good. We can't be too careful," Joe agreed. "I just keep praying the bad times are over."

"So do I."

Reed left the wagon and stopped to speak with Ann. "Are you going to watch the show this afternoon?"

"I wouldn't miss Libby's official debut for anything. She's going to be wonderful."

Reed hoped Ann was right. He had a feeling she was.

Back inside, Joe was feeling a bit relieved. It appeared that Reed was quite taken with Libby, though he probably hadn't realized it yet. He was distracted by her, and Joe was glad. She was giving Reed something else to think about besides his brother's death, and that was good.

The stands were packed with people as the Wild Texas Stampede got underway. From the opening parade to the closing finale, the crowd was spellbound and enthralled. They cheered wildly during the stagecoach raid, roared over the shooting demonstration and held their breaths when Libby was handling her knife. When Reed and Libby began their trick ride, they fell silent as they watched in awe.

On the sidelines, Kathleen watched in silence, too, but her silence wasn't caused by any sense of awe. Her silence came from pure, unmitigated outrage. How dare that other female climb all over Reed that way! In public, no less! And she was wearing pants, too! It was positively scandalous!

Kathleen was determined not to stand by and let Libby turn the show into a mockery of what it once was. As part-owner of the Stampede, she was going to find Libby when the performance was over, and she was going to tell her she was fired! In a huff, she marched away, determined to confront the other woman—and get rid of her!

Libby was thrilled as she and Reed rode from the parade ground. Everything had gone perfectly! She was amazed that absolutely nothing had gone wrong. The way her luck had been going, she'd expected trouble and lots of it.

"Good job," Reed told her, over his shoulder, as he reined in.

"You were fantastic!" Mark exclaimed as he came running to help Libby down from behind Reed. "It couldn't have gone any better."

"I didn't miss during the shooting," Libby said with a grin, glancing up at Reed.

He smiled down at her. "I appreciate that."

"I thought you might."

"That ride wasn't too bad either!" Mark said. "Did you hear the crowd? They never stopped cheering. You're on to something, boss. Looks like Weston's Lady is quite a hit."

"Yes, she is," Reed agreed, his gaze meeting and holding Libby's for a long moment. He was thinking of their ride, and the softness of her curves pressed so tightly against him. It was a memory not easily forgotten.

"I'm just glad things went well," she told them, looking away from him. The moment had seemed intimate even though they were in the midst of a crowd of people.

"We all are." Reed started to ride off so he could

When Reed and Libby began their trick ride, the crowd fell silent as they watched in awe.

"*Mr. Weston, please! I want to get your picture with Weston's Lady!*"

tend to his horse, when a photographer from town came hurrying up.

"Wait! Mr. Weston, please! I want to get your picture with Weston's Lady!" the man exclaimed. "It will only take a few minutes, and I'd really appreciate it!"

Reed dismounted and went to stand beside Libby as the man readied his equipment. When he finally had everything set up, he told everyone else to move away.

"Now, both of you, hold still. Put your arm around her, Mr. Weston. She is, after all, *your lady*!"

Reed did as he was told, holding Libby's slight curves to his side. She felt soft and warm against him. He forced himself to remember that he had to keep smiling for the picture. Which was hard to do, since he really wanted to turn to her and—

"All right. I'm ready. Don't move!" the photographer ordered. When he was done, he looked up and smiled at them. "That was wonderful. I'll bring you copies."

"Thank you. We'd like that," Reed told him before going off to tend to his horse.

Libby moved away from Reed then and started back to her tent. She hadn't gone far when Kathleen's voice rang out commandingly from behind her.

"Wait just a minute! I want to talk with you!"

Libby stopped and turned to face her. "Did you see the show?" she asked, thinking the other woman was going to praise her for the flawless performance.

"Yes, and that's exactly what I want to talk to you about."

Libby was surprised by the vehemence in her voice. "Is something wrong?"

Kathleen looked her up and down, making a point to stare at her tight-fitting pants. "I am tempted to fire you this instant! Weston's Wild Texas Stampede has a reputation to uphold. This— this—" She sputtered as she searched for the right words to describe the outfit. "This outrageous attire you've chosen to wear is completely inappropriate for a family event. I am certain that your talents would be better displayed somewhere else—perhaps working at the Diamondback? I can make arrangements for you to pick up your pay and—"

"And nothing!" Reed snarled, appearing out of nowhere to confront Kathleen. He'd heard what she was saying and was angry. "If you have a problem or a complaint about anything in the Stampede, Kathleen, you come to me. I'm the one in charge here. I'm the majority owner. I run this show."

"But this—this—" Kathleen was horrified that Reed had caught her in the middle of her confrontation with Libby. She'd thought she could get rid of the girl and then tell him later that Libby had quit for no reason. Now she was trapped, actually caught in the act. Drawing upon her superior acting abilities, Kathleen forced herself to tears. She stared pointedly and disapprovingly at Libby. "This isn't Steve's dream! This isn't what Steve wanted the Stampede to be."

"Steve wanted the Stampede to be successful, Kathleen, and that's exactly what Libby does for the show—she makes it a success. She's our star, our draw. She's popular with the audience. Everyone loves her!"

"But—"

"I won't hear any more of this. The Stampede's making money. That's what matters to me, and that's what would have mattered to Steve."

She gave him a tortured, teary-eyed look. "What do you know about your brother or what he would have liked? How often had you seen him in the years before he died? Oh, how I wish Steve were still alive!"

With that pained cry, she made a dramatic exit, leaving Reed and Libby staring after her.

Libby was shocked. It was obvious the other woman hated her. Then to hear Reed defend her strictly because she made money for them hurt her more than she could say. It reaffirmed what she'd thought earlier. She was a commodity to Reed, just as she'd been to John. That was why he'd bought her the clothes for the show. Not because he wanted her to look good, but because she would make more money for them if she was in costume, looking her best.

"Are you all right?" Reed asked, seeing Libby's suddenly strained expression.

"I'm fine," she managed and gave him a tight, cold smile.

He wanted to say more, to reassure her in some way, but something about her expression stopped him. He nodded and walked away.

Libby was a little startled when Ann approached her after Reed had gone from sight.

"I heard what Kathleen said to you!" she told her angrily.

"You were listening?" Libby was surprised that Ann was so furious.

"I hadn't meant to. I was coming over to tell you what a good job you did, when I accidentally heard what she was saying."

Libby was embarrassed that Ann had overheard everything. "I didn't know what to say to her."

"I hate that woman," Ann said. "You watch out for her. Don't ever turn your back on her. She is one of the most vicious people I've ever known. All her talk about wishing Steve had never died—" Ann's gaze burned with the intensity of what she was feeling.

"I don't understand," Libby said, caught off-guard by the rawness of the other woman's emotions. Ann had seemed so gentle-spirited to her. A chill went down her spine as she saw the fierceness of her anger.

"Kathleen's a liar and a cheat. She's the reason Steve's dead. Everything that's happened here is because of her! Kathleen didn't care about Steve."

"Are you sure?" This news amazed Libby.

Ann cast her a knowing look. "I'm sure. How could she love him and then sleep with other men? Her latest was Lyle, right before Steve died."

Libby was shocked. "But she loved her husband, didn't she? She was just crying and saying—"

"Kathleen never loved Steve. So be careful

around her, Libby. I like you, and I don't want to see you get hurt."

Libby gave her a gentle, calming smile. "I like you, too, Ann. Thanks."

Ann lifted her gaze to stare off in the direction Kathleen had gone. "She is an impressive actress, isn't she? No one would ever guess how evil she really is."

With that, Ann walked away, leaving Libby alone with her thoughts.

Libby was troubled as she made her way to her tent. Ann's hatred for Kathleen was a little frightening. She wondered why she felt that way. Then her thoughts turned to Reed. For a moment, when he had come to her defense, she'd almost believed he was protecting her honor, but she'd been wrong. He'd only been protecting his profits.

At the realization, her determination strengthened. She would start thinking the same way he did. She would concentrate on saving the money she needed to go find Michael. Only when she was with her brother again would she feel safe and protected.

Lyle had been watching Kathleen for days now, ever since their last encounter, hoping for a sign that she was missing him and wanting him, but he'd been disappointed. She'd ignored him completely. Tonight, he'd had enough. He was going to find out exactly what she was up to. He was not a man she could use whenever she felt like it and then just throw away. He wasn't about to let her go—not without a fight.

159

Lyle waited until long after dark before making his way to Kathleen's wagon. There was no light coming from inside, so he figured she'd already bedded down for the night, and that was fine with him. That was right where he wanted her—in bed, waiting for him. He smiled at the thought as he reached for her doorknob in anticipation of the long, hot night to come.

Lyle's smile faded quickly when he found the door locked. He glanced around to make sure no one was nearby watching, then took out the key she'd had made for him and put it in the lock. Lyle's growing excitement was jarred when he found the key wouldn't turn, and when he tried to force it, his frustration grew even more. And then he realized what she'd done—Kathleen had changed the lock!

Lyle wanted to roar his anger. He wanted to pound on the door until she opened it and let him in. He wanted to smash the door in and take what he wanted—her! Instead, he left, managing to contain his anger for now. He would deal with Kathleen later—on his own terms.

Inside the wagon, Kathleen waited in silence until she heard him walk away. Relief flooded through her once she knew he was gone. Lyle definitely had a mean streak in him, and she'd been hoping she wouldn't have to deal with it.

Letting out a sigh, Kathleen sought sleep. She'd had a long, frustrating day dealing with Reed and Libby, and she was glad that it was over. The confrontation with Libby hadn't gone at all the way she'd planned. She hated the other woman, and

160

she'd wanted to get rid of her. But then Reed had shown up and ruined everything.

It infuriated Kathleen that Reed had taken Libby's side against her. She was going to have to think of a different way to handle him. What she was doing now obviously wasn't working as well as she'd hoped.

As she fell asleep, Kathleen willed herself to dream of Reed. He was her fantasy, and soon, if she had her way, he would be her reality.

Reed stood alone in the darkness, staring out across the parade ground. The show had again gone off without any trouble. There had been no accidents. It had been a good day.

He sighed heavily, pleased with the way things were going—particularly with Liberty's performances. She'd been magnificent, and the audience had responded to her as warmly today as they had the night before.

Reed frowned slightly, finally admitting to himself that he was responding to her, too. He didn't want to. He had no time for any involvements. He wanted to find the man responsible for what had happened to Steve and Joe. He had to find out why someone wanted them both dead.

"You look troubled, Reed," Ann said as she appeared by his side.

"What are you doing out here so late?"

"I wanted to talk to you when I knew we could be alone. I've been doing some serious thinking about who might have been responsible for Steve's accident and for my father's."

He turned to look at her, and seeing her troubled expression, he waited for her to go on.

"Kathleen is not the pure, devoted wife she would have you believe," Ann said venomously. "I happened to overhear her argument with you earlier, and I couldn't believe it when she said she wished Steve was still alive. She is such a liar and a cheat! She made Steve's life a living hell before he died! She had lovers, and she flaunted them before him."

"How do you know?"

"Because I saw her. Lyle was her latest. I'd see him sneaking out of the wagon whenever Steve was away taking care of business. If I were looking for someone who had a motive to want Steve dead, I'd start with Kathleen."

"But why would she try to hurt your father?" He could see no connection.

"Maybe she thought Papa knows more than he does. I'm not sure. All I do know is that Steve was a good man, and he didn't deserve what happened to him." Her eyes filled with tears at the memory of that tragic night.

"You cared for my brother," Reed said quietly, seeing her distress.

"Yes. Steve meant a lot to me. I miss him." She moved away then, leaving him alone.

Reed remained standing in the darkness. His thoughts were deep and troubled. Kathleen had been the first one he'd suspected. Certainly, she would have had the most to gain by Steve's death. She hadn't learned of the changes in his will until the actual reading, and he remembered all too clearly her reaction to the shocking discovery. Now, though, he had to consider Lyle as a possible suspect, too. Did the other man want Kathleen so badly that he'd commit murder to have her? Or was it someone else entirely?

The thought was sobering. The members of the Stampede were certainly glad that he had taken over the show for his brother. They seemed pleased that they were back performing again. If there was another reason for the accidents, it eluded him.

"Look at this!" Ann called out excitedly to Libby the next morning as she held up a copy of the Los Santos newspaper.

Libby hurried over to see what Ann was so excited about, only to find the picture the photographer had taken of her and Reed the previous day prominently displayed on the front page.

"Oh, my—" She stared down at the likeness, her initial delight at seeing herself so glorified giving way to a sense of terror. *What if John saw this picture?* It was a chilling thought. There was no denying the picture was of her, even though the caption read, "Weston's Lady rode into town with Weston's Wild Texas Stampede and delighted all who saw her performance." Anyone who knew her would recognize her immediately.

"You look beautiful," Ann told her proudly. "And the article is wonderful, too."

Libby quickly scanned it, dreading what she would find. She was right to worry. Her name was proclaimed in the article. If John saw it, he would know exactly where to find her. She could only hope and pray that a copy of the paper never fell into his hands. Fine publicity though it was for the show, it would mean nothing but danger for her if he found out about it.

"I'm sure Reed will be pleased," she finally said, wishing they were leaving town that very day instead of having one more performance later that afternoon.

Ann cast her a quizzical look. "You don't sound very excited about it. I'd be thrilled to be featured in an article this way. They make you sound so wonderful. Did you read the whole thing? *Stampede owner Reed Weston and his lady are a heavenly match. From their straight-shooting performance to their trick-riding display, the two are pure magic. Weston's Lady, Liberty Jones, is a rare talent, indeed. There is one more show, so don't miss it!*" "

Libby hid her fears behind a smile. "You're right. This is a great article."

"You're going to be so famous, you probably won't even talk to me anymore," Ann said with a laugh.

"That would never happen," she assured Ann.

"I've got to go show this to my father. He'll be excited about it, too."

Worry consumed Libby, yet she knew there was absolutely nothing she could do, except keep a careful look out for trouble. She told herself that by the time John got a copy of the Los Santos paper—if he ever did—she'd be gone with the show.

*   *   *

Kathleen had thought she was angry the day before, but the article in the paper today left her seething. *Stampede owner Reed Weston and his lady are a heavenly match!* She was beside herself with fury. *Weston's Lady, Liberty Jones, is a rare talent, indeed.* She had never hated anyone as much as she hated Libby right then.

The urge to scream, rant and rave was nearly overwhelming. *Weston's Lady!* She snarled as she threw the paper across the room, sick of staring at the picture. The other woman looked positively gorgeous in her tight pants as she stood next to Reed. A sneer curved Kathleen's lip as she glared down at her own black dress. She was trapped in the role of grieving widow, and there was nothing she could do to change things.

Her frustration mounted. Kathleen told herself that she had not died when Steve did. She was very much alive and very much a woman. That much was obvious every time she saw Reed. She wanted him—oh, how she wanted him. Nothing had changed since that night so long ago when she'd gone to his hotel room in the hope that he loved her as much as she loved him. If only she could turn back the hands of time and relive that fateful night. Everything would have been different between them. She was sure of it.

Drawing a ragged sigh, Kathleen tried to decide what to do next. Her plan to play the grieving widow had worked to a degree. They were maintaining a friendly relationship, although after the confrontation with Libby, she wondered if she'd damaged her relationship with Reed. She hoped not, but there was only one way to find out. She would go to Reed and apologize. She would play up to him and lead him to believe that she thought he was absolutely brilliant in choosing Libby to be the star of the show. This particular lie wouldn't be easy, but lately it was beginning to seem that everything was a test of her acting prowess. She was glad that, so far, she had managed to be convincing.

Determined, Kathleen primped one last time before the mirror and left her wagon. She'd just closed the door on her way out when Lyle appeared at her side.

"I came to see you last night, but it seems you changed the lock," he said in a quiet voice as he fell into step beside her.

"I told you things couldn't be the same anymore."

"That's why I came over so late. I didn't want to make things awkward for you. I just needed to see you." His meaning was unmistakable.

Kathleen paused and turned to look up at him, touching him on the arm. "It was a difficult day yesterday. Tonight—I'll come to you tonight."

He managed to control his eagerness. *Tonight!* He wanted her so badly, he ached. He was tempted to just carry her off right then and there and be done with it, but he controlled his baser urges. "All right. I'll see you tonight—late."

She gave him a slight smile and hurried on, hoping she'd gotten rid of him for the time being. She'd worry about meeting him tonight—tonight.

"Reed!" Kathleen called out when she finally located him on the grounds some time later.

At the sound of her call, Kathleen saw Reed look up and frown. His reaction hurt her, but she refused to let him know it. She was going to impress him with her changed attitude.

"Do you have a moment or two? I'd like to talk with you about something," she said as she went to him.

"What's wrong now?"

"Absolutely nothing," she told him. "I just wanted to apologize for the way I acted last night."

"There's no need—" he began.

She cut him off. "There is every need. I overreacted. What you've accomplished with the Stampede since Steve's death is wonderful. I don't know what I would have done without you being here to help run things. I suppose I was just missing Steve a lot last night. I'm used to seeing him riding in the show and, well, I spoke out foolishly. I hope you'll forgive me."

"There's nothing to forgive, Kathleen." Reed was watching her intently. After hearing what Ann had had to say about her the night before, Reed was feeling more cautious than ever around her. For all that she was pretending to have changed today, the truth was, she was the same woman who'd come to him in his hotel room and the same woman who'd lied to Steve about what had really happened when he'd walked in on them at the ranch all those years ago. He could never forget that.

"I'm slowly coming to realize that Steve's not coming back—ever," she said softly. "I'm alone now, and that's very frightening to me."

"There's nothing to be afraid of. The show's profitable, so your income is secure." The idea that Kathleen might be afraid of being alone in the world almost made him laugh, but he controlled it. He doubted she'd ever been afraid of anything.

"The show is profitable thanks to your Liberty Jones. But since Steve's accident, I've learned there's more to life than money." Her expression was carefully schooled to one of wistful sadness that she hoped would touch Reed's heart. She was disappointed when he didn't respond to her as she'd hoped.

"I'm sorry he's gone, too. The only thing we can do is take each day as it comes and honor his memory as best we can. That's why I want to make the Stampede a success."

"And you're doing that—thank you." She met his gaze, hoping he saw the earnestness of her emotions in her eyes. "I'm sure you must have a lot to do to prepare for the show tonight."

"It's going to be a busy day."

"If you find you need me for anything, just let me know."

Reed gave her an agreeable response, but knew she was the last person he would rely on. Trusting Kathleen might prove to be a deadly mistake.

Chapter Nine

Libby found herself getting excited as show time neared later that afternoon. She was standing in a quiet spot near the sidelines, watching the audience file into the stands across the way. She'd passed a peaceful day, resting up for the performance and trying to avoid Reed.

Libby told herself she didn't care about the man. She didn't even like him! But there was something about Reed that made her uneasy and kept her off balance—and that troubled her. She liked to be in control of herself and her emotions. She couldn't take any risks. Her life was already too dangerous and complicated right now.

As hard as Libby had tried, though, there was no forgetting the kiss that Reed had given her in his wagon. She hadn't been able to put the memory from her. When Reed had slipped his arm around her waist to have their picture taken, his simple touch had sent a shiver of awareness up her spine. Libby told herself that none of what she was feeling mattered. She would be leaving the Stampede as soon as possible. She had to find Michael and make sure she stayed ahead of John.

John. Memories of the man and his terrible threats haunted her. She rarely made it through the night without waking up in a cold sweat, shaking from the power of a nightmare in which he burst through the door of the tent to get her. It sometimes took her hours to fall asleep again, and she was beginning to wonder if she would ever feel secure again.

"Are you ready to ride?" Reed asked as he rode up and reined in beside her.

"I'm ready."

Libby looked up at him and flashed a confident smile, hoping he would go away. Suddenly, out of the corner of her eye, she saw a man who looked like John in the crowd. Her smile froze and all color drained from her face as she quickly turned to look his way, trying to see where he'd gone.

John! Had it been John?

Panic set in, but she knew she couldn't run. A shiver of dread trembled through her as she struggled to locate the man in the milling crowd, but he had disappeared from sight. Terror clawed at her. Could it have been him? She clasped her hands together to still their shaking as she tried to calm herself.

"Liberty? What is it? Are you all right?"

The sudden change in her shocked Reed. She

looked positively ashen, and she was visibly trembling. He noticed the direction of her gaze and tried to see what had caused such a reaction, but he could discern nothing unusual. He saw only the townspeople making their way into the stands, seeking the best seats they could find so they could enjoy the show.

"Just a moment of stage fright," she lied, trying desperately to sound casual as she kept Reed's horse between her and the stands. "I guess I'd better get ready for the entrance parade."

Reed watched Libby rush off, and he wondered what she'd seen that had frightened her so much. She'd looked almost terrified for a moment. Again he realized how very little he knew about her. She'd been very close-mouthed about her past, revealing little to him. She was a mystery to him—and that was beginning to bother him.

Reed scowled. Where had Liberty come from? She had appeared in the saloon that night out of nowhere. How was it that she had only owned the clothes on her back? Was she was running from something? Was she in trouble with the law? Or was she fleeing from a relative? An abusive father? Possibly a husband?

The thought that she might be running from a husband troubled Reed more than he cared to admit, but he had to face the possibility. He grew determined to discover the truth. His scowl darkened. He glanced in Libby's direction, wanting to reassure himself that she was safe, but she was already gone from sight. He told himself he was being ridiculous to worry about her so much.

She'd made it perfectly clear to him that she didn't want anything from him but a job. He smiled as he remembered her pulling her gun on him.

Yes, Libby was fine, and Reed made up his mind that she was going to stay that way. No harm was going to come to her while she was with his show. He would see to it personally. He put his heels to his horse's sides and rode off to organize the entry parade.

The parade went perfectly. The audience cheered wildly as the procession circled the parade ground. Libby rode with her head held high, maintaining her poise, but inwardly she was quaking. She kept her gaze riveted on the stands, trying to spot the man she'd seen earlier.

Libby's mind had been racing since she'd left Reed. She'd been trying to figure out what to do if the man in the crowd was John. She'd left her sidearm within close reach just inside her tent door, in case he found her there and tried to grab her and take her away. The others in the show might not come to her defense quickly enough, so she had to be ready.

John no longer had any claim on her. They were not betrothed any longer. He had no right to come anywhere near her. She wanted to make sure it stayed that way.

For just an instant, Libby considered confiding in someone—maybe Reed or Joe or even Ann— but she stopped herself. John and Madeline's betrayal ran deep. Madeline, a pillar of the community, had taken Libby into her home with the promise of chaperoning her, only to prove as evil as John. Haunted by the horrible memories, Libby knew she couldn't trust or rely on anyone. She would take care of herself, and she would make sure John never got the chance to hurt her again.

The stagecoach act went off perfectly. Mark was proving an able replacement for Joe. He handled the team with perfect ease until the time came for him to fall from the stage. He performed his stunt, and, as planned, Libby saved the day and ran off the attackers, all to the audience's delight.

"Let's have a hand for our very own Liberty Jones—Weston's Lady!" the announcer called out.

Hearing her name broadcast so loudly had never before troubled Libby, but today it did. Just knowing John might be there made her want to ride from the parade ground as quickly as possible so she could lose herself behind the scenes. Her smile never wavered, but she urged the team to gallop from the ground. Her unexpectedly hurried exit forced the next act out earlier than usual, but they managed to handle the transition smoothly.

Libby was nervous as she prepared for the shooting act with Reed, which was coming up soon. She couldn't wait to be done with the show today, but she knew there was no rushing things. The only reassuring thought she had was that at least this time her gun was loaded with real bullets.

"I hope you can steady yourself long enough to shoot straight when we go on," Reed said as he sought her out. He smiled to lighten his words. "You're edgy today. Is something wrong?"

"I'm fine," she lied.

"So you're up to the challenge of shooting real bullets at me in a few minutes?"

She turned on him, her gaze narrowing. "I'm always up to the challenge of shooting at you."

"I didn't doubt that for a minute, but are you up to missing?"

Libby managed a slight smile and nodded. "I'm just a little tired today. I didn't get a lot of sleep last night. But I promise you, I'll miss."

He accepted her explanation for the time being without further argument, but he didn't believe a word of it. "I'm counting on that."

When it was time for their performance, Libby was back in control. Everything went smoothly. Her aim was perfect, and her shots were true. She pretended to herself that John was standing behind Reed, and she was shooting him every time she got off a shot. It was amazing how accurate she could be.

She held on to the same thought when it came time for her knife-throwing demonstration, and her aim proved true.

The end of the Stampede couldn't come soon enough for Libby. She was relieved when they completed their daring ride, and she and Reed were taking a bow before the grandstand. Staring up at the cheering crowd, she tried to find John. She wanted to know where he was, to locate him before he could find a way to trap her.

Before today, Libby had resented the title "Weston's Lady," but suddenly it took on a different meaning for her. If John was there, he might interpret it as meaning she was Reed's now. Maybe that would discourage him from coming after her.

Reed always kept a protective arm around Libby's waist to make sure she didn't fall when they were riding together. He felt her suddenly begin to tremble as they were waving to the crowd, and a fierce surge of anger filled him. He wheeled the horse around and rode from the arena, keeping a tight hold on her.

"You're riding with me in the finale," he ordered when they were out of sight of the audience.

Libby stiffened at his command. "Why?"

"Because there's something wrong, and I intend to find out what it is. If I have to keep you with me constantly until I have some answers, then that's just what I'll have to do."

"There's nothing wrong," she insisted, trying to slip free of his unyielding grip.

"Don't even think about getting down," he told her.

Reed turned to issue orders to the rest of the Stampede's performers, and then they were riding out again in the closing parade. Libby controlled her urge to fight him. She didn't want to make a scene, especially not during the parade. They made the last ride together and were done for the night.

"Libby, I want to talk with you," Reed told her as they dismounted and he turned his horse over to one of the hands.

"About what?" Libby looked up at him, keeping her expression neutral. All she wanted to do was go to her tent and hide.

175

He gave her an exasperated look. "You know what. I want to know what's frightened you so badly that you're shaking."

"Reed!" Mark called out to him, distracting him from his purpose. "Can I talk to you for a moment?"

Reed was torn. He wanted some straight answers from Liberty, but Mark never bothered him unless it was something important. He knew he had to go see what he wanted. "I'll be right there," he answered Mark, then looked back down at Libby. "Don't go anywhere. Wait for me here."

Libby wasn't about to stay right there in plain sight. The last thing she wanted to do was talk to Reed about any of this. It was none of his business. The moment he turned his back, she slipped away. She knew better than to go back to her tent. That would be the first place he'd look for her. She went to the stable area to see to her own horse, certain she could lose herself there for a while.

Mark was glad that he'd been able to get Reed away from Libby. For some reason, it had looked as if the boss was mad at her, and he couldn't imagine why. She'd performed expertly again tonight and deserved only praise. Mark didn't want anything to happen to her. He liked Libby. She was different from any woman he'd ever known. She was braver, smarter and far more talented with a gun, that was for sure, and the sight of her in those tight pants wasn't anything to ignore either. He didn't want anybody giving her trouble, and that included Reed.

"What is it, Mark?" Reed asked as he went to speak with the other man. He was irritated at being interrupted with Libby, but business was business.

"I wanted you to take a look at something." Mark led him off, quickly making up an excuse as to why he'd interrupted him.

When Reed returned to where he'd told Libby to wait for him, he found that she had gone. He swore under his breath and went looking for her. She couldn't have gone too far, and he had no intention of letting her get away from him. He intended to find out exactly what was going on tonight.

Libby stayed back in her horse's stall, watching and waiting for the opportunity to slip away unnoticed. The stable was deserted, and now she was only waiting to make sure the grounds were, too. It had been a good half an hour since she'd left Reed, and she hoped that he'd gotten distracted by his business with Mark and had gone off to do something else. She didn't want to see him again until tomorrow. By then, she hoped he would have forgotten what he'd wanted to talk to her about.

It was almost dark now, and the longer she lingered there, the safer Libby felt she was from John. Certainly, if he'd been at the Stampede's performance, he would have come looking for her by now. She'd seen no sign of him. Libby decided that it must have been her overactive imagination that had made her think she'd spotted him in the stands in the first place. She was safe—for the time being. She started to sigh in relief and let her guard down.

"Liberty." Reed's tone was sharp as he spoke from behind her. He'd been looking for her for the better part of half an hour. With each passing minute, he'd grown more fearful that something terrible had happened to her. He was glad that he'd finally found her—even if it was in the dark, deserted stable.

"Yes?" Libby tensed as she faced him, her moment of relief short-lived. She might be hidden from John, but Reed had managed to find her.

"Why are you hiding here?" He wasn't in any mood to play games. Standing where he was, he had successfully blocked her only escape route, so he had her undivided attention.

"I'm not hiding. I came here to take care of my horse."

"And that's why you're standing here, working on him in the dark?" He'd seen the wariness in her expression when she'd turned to him and knew she wasn't going to make this easy.

"I was just about ready to quit," she said a little too quickly.

"Good, then we can talk."

"About what? It's getting late now, and I need to get some rest. Like I told you before, I didn't sleep very well last night."

"That's part of what I want to know. Why aren't you sleeping well? What's bothering you? What are you afraid of?"

"I'm not afraid of anything."

"If you're not afraid of *anything*, what about

anyone? Are you in trouble? Is someone looking for you?"

"I'm not in trouble," she told him. "Leave me alone."

"Let me help you, Liberty," Reed offered.

"I don't need your help."

Reed noticed that she had avoided answering his most important question about not being afraid of anyone, and his suspicion about the real cause of her fear grew. He persisted. "Who is it you're running from? A husband?"

She glared at him as she answered him vehemently, "I am certainly not running away from a *husband!* How could I when I've never been married?"

Her answer was so heated that Reed believed her without question. He was surprised at how relieved he was at the news. "I can't help you, if you don't tell me what's wrong."

"I didn't ask for your help. Just leave me alone. I work for you in the Stampede. Period. The only help I want from you is to hand me my pay every week."

"Libby—" He sensed the growing tension in her as she verbally sparred with him, so he deliberately changed tactics. Altering his tone so he no longer sounded commanding or condemning, he took another step toward her. "I'm concerned about the way you were acting tonight because I care about you. I want you to be happy. If you're not happy, it's going to show up in your performances."

Libby gave a scornful laugh. "So you're still worrying that I'm going to shoot you? Well, you can relax and go on about your business. If my aim gets that bad, I'll quit."

"That's not what I was talking about. If you're unhappy, how will you convince the audience that you're enjoying what you're doing?"

Her gaze turned cold as she regarded him in the darkly shadowed stall. "So that's it. I'm the Stampede's star, and I'm worth money to you. It seems that's the only thing you're concerned about—making a profit."

"Damn it, Libby! My wanting to help you has nothing to do with money. Tell me what's wrong, and let me see if there's anything I can do to change things for you."

She stared up at Reed and quieted, mesmerized by the emotion she saw in his expression. Was the tenderness and concern she saw there real? Could it be that he really wasn't like John?

The possibility frightened her. To find out if that was true, she would have to take a chance—she would have to trust him. That realization stopped her cold. She couldn't afford the luxury of being wrong again, not after both John *and* Madeline had betrayed her.

For a moment, her conflicting emotions held her unmoving.

"You're afraid of me for some reason, but there's no need to be."

Reed took a step closer to her. She looked so beautiful and so very alone right then. Her hair was loose about her shoulders in a cascade of golden curls, and she was still wearing the pants that fit her so perfectly. She was a woman like no other he'd ever met.

True, Libby had deceived him by hiring on as a boy, but he understood why now. Desperation had been driving her. There was something in her past she was fleeing, something terrible enough to frighten her into running away with only the clothing on her back, and he wanted to save her from it.

Reed felt an overwhelming need to take Libby in his arms. Staring at her as she faced him so bravely, refusing to give in to the fears that threatened her, he knew he would protect her with his very life. He would slay her dragons for her—if she would only tell him which dragons they were.

"Libby—" He reached out to her and drew her to him.

Libby was tormented. She wanted to believe that Reed was as good and honorable a man as she thought he was, but doubts about her own ability to judge people assailed her. As Reed enfolded her in his strong, warm embrace, she found herself wanting to lean against him and be safe.

His lips sought hers then, and she gasped at the contact, so sweet, so powerful. His kiss was heavenly, and this time, she gave herself over to the full pleasure of his embrace. For just this moment, she could forget the fear that haunted her days and terrorized her nights. For just this moment, she could lose herself in the wonder of Reed's touch.

When he parted her lips and tasted her more deeply, she gave a whimper of excitement. She had never known such a sweetly intimate kiss before. Delight coursed through her, and she clung to him, thrilling at his nearness.

At the sound of her pleasure, Reed crushed her even more tightly against him. He wanted to erase the fear and uncertainty that seemed to rule her very existence. He wanted to keep her this way, close to his heart.

He marveled at how perfectly she fit against him. Her breasts were pressed fully to his chest, and her hips nestled against his. It seemed as if they were made just for each other. He lifted her in his arms and carried her a short distance from the stall to a quiet, dark corner where he laid her upon a clean bed of straw. He followed her down, his lips seeking hers again and again in passionate exchanges.

Libby gasped at the heat of his body covering hers, yet she reveled in the closeness. She gave no thought to the fact that they were in the stable. She didn't care. Right then, there was just Reed and the glory of his kisses.

When Reed's hand sought her breast, she went still. John's touch had been harsh and almost cruel. He'd seemed to enjoy inflicting pain on her. She experienced none of those feelings with Reed, though. His caress left her breathless—and wanting more. An ache grew within her, and Libby moved against him, instinctively knowing that he alone could satisfy the mysterious need that was growing inside the womanly heart of her.

When Libby moved so enticingly against him, Reed went still. As caught up as he was in the heat of the moment, he still had enough sense about him to wonder if she knew what she was asking of him. He would have liked nothing more than to bury himself deep within her, but he was certain she was an innocent. He wouldn't act on her sensual invitation until he was sure that it was what she wanted, too.

"Libby—" Her name was almost a groan as he broke off the kiss for a moment. He lifted one hand to frame her face as he gazed down at her, his eyes burning into hers. She was tempting. Lord knew he wanted her. But he had to be sure that he wasn't taking advantage of her. Their joining would be nothing more than a mindless coupling, if she didn't believe in him. "Do you trust me? You have to trust me."

Libby had been gazing up at Reed, enraptured. He was so handsome and so strong. It would have been so easy to give herself over to him, to forget all her fear and loneliness. His touch and his kiss had swept her away from the ugliness of her reality. She had been spellbound—until he'd spoken of trust.

Trust. Did she dare let down her defenses and trust Reed?

The memories of John's betrayal returned, and their effect on her was like a knife to her heart. She stiffened, frowning, pushing herself away from Reed. She was embarrassed that she'd forgotten herself so completely.

"Libby?" He let her go, sensing her troubled mood.

"No—No, I can't do this—" She got up, needing

183

to get away from him as quickly as she could. She didn't care how she looked as she hurried from the stable; she just knew she had to go.

Seeing the almost distraught look on her face, Reed made no effort to stop her. Every fiber of his being wanted to go after her, to take her back in his arms, to convince her that she could be safe with him, but he didn't. If he went after her, he might frighten her even more. The decision to believe in him and to trust him had to be hers.

Logical though Reed was being, reason did nothing to ease the sweet ache of desire that lingered within him. He got up slowly. He did not hurry from the stable.

Kathleen smiled brightly at Horace Kelly, the mayor of Los Santos, and Lee Daly, the local physician.

"I'd be delighted to join you for dinner," she told them eagerly. "And I'm sure Reed would, too."

"What about Miss Jones? Will she be able to come?" Horace asked quickly. He was quite taken with the beautiful young star of the show and wanted to meet her.

Kathleen hid her irritation, but it wasn't easy. "I'll check with her, too. Shall we meet you in town? I'm not sure where Reed and Liberty are right now, so it may take me a moment or two to locate them."

"That would be wonderful. We'll be waiting for you at the restaurant."

"We'll be there. Thank you so much for the invitation, gentlemen."

Kathleen waited until they had ridden away before she began her search for Reed. She had no intention whatsoever of looking for Liberty. She would convince Reed to go with her, and she would have him all to herself on the ride into town and back. Who knew? There was a hotel right there in Los Santos, and maybe she and Reed could spend the night.

The thought sent a surge of desire through her. Reed—there with her in a soft bed with no danger of being interrupted. She smiled at the fantasy and planned to do everything in her power to see that it came true.

Kathleen checked Reed's wagon but found no sign of him. She asked several of the hands, but none had seen him for some time. One man mentioned that the last time he'd seen the boss, Reed had been heading for the stables, so she started off in that direction to see if he was still there.

Kathleen was nearing the stables when she saw Libby come rushing out. Her clothing and hair were disheveled. She wondered what had been going on. She stopped a short distance away, watching and waiting to see if anyone else would follow her out of the stable. It was quiet for a moment and then Reed emerged from the stable.

Anger seared her soul. She had seen Libby's condition, and she knew what had been going on in there between the two of them. She wanted to rail at the injustice of all that was happening, but managed to adopt a sweet manner instead. Somehow, she was going to get him away from that little slut. Reed was hers!

"Reed?" Kathleen called out as she hurried to speak with him.

He looked up at the sound of her voice. The last person in the world he wanted to see right now was Kathleen. His thoughts were on Libby. She was the only woman he wanted to be with. "What is it? Is there some kind of trouble?"

"No. Everything's fine. In fact, everything is better than fine. We have been invited to dinner with the mayor and the local physician. They're waiting for us at the restaurant in town. I told them we'd be there shortly."

"I really shouldn't leave tonight—" He did not want to make small talk with the dignitaries of Los Santos.

"But I told them we'd be there. They're expecting us," she said, managing to look suitably sorry that she'd put him in such an awkward position.

He girded himself for the night to come, knowing it was going to be a long one. "All right. Give me a few minutes, and I'll be ready to go."

"I'll be waiting for you." And she knew she would wait for him for as long as it took.

A short time later, they were on their way into town. They took the small carriage, and Reed drove. The moon was bright, giving them enough light to make the trip easily.

Kathleen enjoyed having the opportunity to sit so close to Reed. She made sure that she leaned against him at every opportunity. Her thigh was carefully pressed against his in an innocent, yet exciting way. She actually found herself anticipating bumps in the road. Their conversation was less than witty, but she hoped after a glass of wine or two, he might become more open with her. Reed seemed tense and uncommunicative for some reason.

The trip was over too quickly as far as Kathleen was concerned, but she still had the rest of the night to look forward to. If she had her way, they would be spending the night together there in town.

"Horace Kelly and Lee Daly, this is Reed Weston," Kathleen said as they met.

Both men had stood up when they'd approached the table, and they quickly shook hands with Reed.

"It's a pleasure to meet you, sir," Horace told him, impressed by all he'd seen at the Stampede.

"Same here," Lee said.

"Where's your Lady?" Horace asked Reed with a sly smile. He had been anxiously anticipating meeting the beautiful, daring young sure-shot.

Reed was momentarily perplexed, but before he could say anything, Kathleen answered.

"She was too tired to join us this evening, but she sends her warmest regards." She gave Reed a benign smile, leaving him to wonder if she had really spoken to Libby or not.

"Too bad," Lee replied. "We were looking forward to finding out how she got to be so good at riding and shooting. I've never seen another woman with talent like that."

"She is special," Reed agreed.

Kathleen bit back a nasty retort. "Our audiences seem to respond to her. She's made quite a name

187

for herself in the last few days. We're very proud of her."

"I'll say. All I heard about all day Saturday was what a surprise her performance had been on Friday night. Of course, there was other talk, too—that you'd arranged that whole scene at the Diamondback just to make sure everyone showed up for the Stampede."

Reed simply smiled, allowing them to think whatever they wanted.

"It was a brilliant idea. You caught the men's attention with the scene in the saloon, and then surprised us all with her unexpected appearance in the show. Well done, Weston. You're quite a showman."

"I appreciate your compliments, but Liberty is the one you should be telling all this. She's very talented, and I'm really glad she's accurate with a gun."

"So you're using real bullets in the shooting part of your act, are you?"

"That's right. The element of danger has to be there, or it wouldn't hold the same fascination for the crowds."

"You're a braver man than I am," Horace told him.

"I trust Libby with my life," Reed said. The statement gave him pause and made him realize that he truly did trust her with his life every time they performed—and she was forced to trust him, too.

"We're so sorry about your husband and your brother," Lee said.

"He must have been a wonderful man to have

created such a fantastic show," Horace agreed.

"Steve always knew what he wanted in life and how to get it," Reed said, remembering how his brother had declared himself in love with Kathleen all those years ago. He wondered sadly if Steve had ever regretted eloping with her. Reed believed that he had, judging from the changes in the will, and the thought saddened him.

"My husband was a fine man," Kathleen said, looking a bit tearful at the mention of Steve. "He was well loved by everyone, and he is missed."

The waiter approached them then, and they ordered their meal. When it came, they enjoyed a companionable time together. As they finished the dessert, Kathleen began her ploy. She hoped and prayed that it would work.

"Well, gentlemen, I don't know about you, but I am just exhausted tonight."

"It has been a long day for you," they agreed, realizing how late it was becoming. "Thanks so much for joining us this evening."

"It's been our pleasure, believe me," Kathleen said. She'd been pleased to have the undivided attention of all three men—even if they did spend most of the night talking about Libby. Right now, though, she wanted to get away from the mayor and the doctor and enjoy the attentions of only one man.

They said their good nights and parted company. Horace and Lee wished them much success on the rest of their tour.

As Reed escorted Kathleen outside to where they'd left the carriage, she knew this was her only chance. She'd thought it through. Her premise was believable. She only hoped it would work on him. For all that he'd made clever conversation with the mayor and doctor, he had said very little directly to her.

"Reed, I was thinking—"

He cast a guarded glance her way.

She wanted to make her idea seem perfectly innocent. She wanted him to believe that she'd just thought of it—not that she'd been planning this moment for long hours.

"Since it's so late, I thought maybe we should spend the night here in town and not head back to the Stampede's campground until tomorrow morning. What do you think?"

Chapter Ten

Reed had always known Kathleen was devious, but her acting ability was proving far superior to any he'd ever encountered before. He was certain now that she'd manipulated the whole evening to her advantage. She had been calculating and careful, qualities that would have served her well in planning her husband's untimely "accident." But Reed was prepared for her.

"You can stay here in town if you want to, but I'm going back to the Stampede tonight."

"But we've only got one carriage," she protested. "Surely, you wouldn't leave me here alone without transportation?"

"You're the one who wants to stay," he pointed out, refusing to be drawn into her intrigue. "I'll walk you over to the hotel and help you get registered, but I'm not spending the night. I've got too much work waiting for me."

"It will wait for you," she said softly, hoping her tone was suggestive without being aggressive. "You don't have to go."

His gaze hardened as he looked at her. "I'm going. Now, it's up to you. What do you want to do? If you choose to stay, I'll send one of the hands into town in the morning to pick you up."

Kathleen was not about to back down. She didn't want it to look as though she'd only planned to stay to lure him to her bed. "I'll stay, if you're sure it's not too much trouble for you?"

"That'll be fine. Let's see about getting you checked in."

She took his arm as they made their way to the hotel. It was a quiet evening, and she was soon registered.

"Will you walk me upstairs?" she asked when he would have gone.

Reed didn't like the idea, but didn't want to seem callous. "All right." He would see her to the door of her room and then leave.

"Would you like to come in for a while?" she invited him when they'd reached her room, lifting her gaze to his. For so long now, she had wanted this man. She longed to entice him to her. She wanted him with a hunger that would not be denied.

"No. Good night, Kathleen."

Reed would have loved to have been in that hotel room with a beautiful woman right then, but the beautiful woman he wanted to be with wasn't

Kathleen. It was Libby. She was the only woman he was interested in.

Frustrated as Kathleen was by his refusal, she still made sure she sounded pleasant when she told him, "Well, be careful on your ride back. I'll see you some time tomorrow."

"We'll be packing up to leave, so the sooner you return the better. What time do you want me to send someone for you?"

"Eight o'clock will be fine. Good night, Reed."

He nodded, they watched her disappear into the room and close and lock the door. Only then did he leave. Once he was away from Kathleen, Reed couldn't get out of town fast enough. Libby was back at the Stampede, and that was where he wanted to be.

After she'd left Reed at the stable, Libby had found another secluded spot beyond the grandstand. She'd needed the time alone there to pull herself back together. Why was it that the moment Reed touched her and kissed her, she forgot all her best intentions? The power he wielded over her angered and troubled her.

Libby had remained there, hiding from reality— and hiding from Reed. She'd feared that if he found her, she wouldn't have the will to stop him if he tried to kiss her again. Not that she would have wanted him to stop— The confusion of her thoughts had only darkened her mood more. And then she'd seen them—Reed and Kathleen—riding away from the campgrounds together in the small carriage.

Libby had been stunned that Reed had gone off with Kathleen. True, she was his sister-in-law, but Ann had told her what kind of woman Kathleen truly was. Knowing he wouldn't be coming for her now, she left her retreat and walked back toward her own tent.

"Hey, Bert!" Mark called out laughingly as he saw her crossing the grounds alone, still wearing the pants she'd performed in. "You don't look very happy tonight."

She smiled at Mark. She was coming to like him more and more. He seemed open and honest and nice. He'd been nothing but kind to her. Even when she'd been in disguise, pretending to be Bert, he'd been a friend to her. "What are you doing roaming around after dark?" she asked.

"I was just checking on the stock one last time before bedding down," he told her. She had such a lonely look about her that he asked, "You want to go with me?"

"Sure."

Libby fell into step beside him. Something about Mark made her feel comfortable and unthreatened, and that was just what she needed right then. She looked up at him, seeing the proud way he carried himself. He was not as strikingly handsome as Reed was, but there was something about Mark that she liked. He always had a quick, easy smile for her and a kind word. Mark had a rare confidence about himself that set him apart from the other men in the show. She was sure that was why Reed had picked him to take Joe's place in the stagecoach raid. He had been sure that

Mark could handle the additional responsibility.

"Where's home, Mark?" She truly was curious. He had no accent or drawl to hint at his place of birth.

"St. Louis. I was born and raised there."

"How did you end up here in Texas?"

He grinned at her. "I wanted to experience the Wild West firsthand. My family owns a successful shipping line. I could have stayed in St. Louis and worked in the business, but there was this restlessness in me. I needed to see more of the world."

Libby nodded, understanding his wanderlust. "My brother Michael is the same way. He had to see more of the country than just the few acres we owned. That's why he took the job with the railroad."

"And he left you behind, alone?" he asked, frowning at the thought of leaving a lovely young woman defenseless.

"I wasn't alone at the time."

"But you are now."

She paused, realizing how close she was to revealing too much about her past. "No, I'm not. I've got the Wild Texas Stampede. It's my home now."

Mark noticed how she'd deflected his question, and again he wondered about her background. "I'm glad you feel that way. I love it, too. There are a lot of good people here."

"How did you come to be in the Stampede?" Libby asked.

"I left St. Louis about three years ago and started traveling west. I didn't have any particular place in mind when I headed out. I was looking for adventure. I met Steve in Kansas City. He had just started up the show then. It was very small, but he was determined to make it work. I asked him for a job, and after I proved to him that I could handle a horse, he hired me."

"What was Steve like? Was he anything like Reed?"

Mark looked thoughtful for a moment. "In some ways, they're very much alike. Once you were Steve's friend, you were his friend for life. He was a very loyal, very honest man. Reed seems to have those same qualities, but I think he's more cautious about trusting people than Steve was."

"So you liked Steve?"

"Very much. He gave me the chance to see a part of the West I would never have gotten to experience any other way, and I'll always be grateful to him for that. I like Reed, too. I haven't known him all that long, but he strikes me as a smart man, and it seems like he's going to do a good job with the show."

They finished taking care of the stock a short time later, and Mark walked Libby back to her tent.

"Thanks for keeping me company," Mark told her.

"It was my pleasure, believe me," she answered, and she meant it. Talking with him had helped to distract her from thoughts of Reed and Kathleen. "I'll see you in the morning."

"Good night."

Safely in the haven of her own tent, Libby sought sleep. She wanted to relax, but the image of Kathleen sitting so close beside Reed in the carriage stayed with her. Reed had asked her to trust him, yet for all that they'd shared passionate kisses earlier that evening, he'd gone off to spend the night with Kathleen.

An unexpected surge of some emotion—jealousy?—shot through her, troubling her even more deeply. Libby told herself she was being ridiculous. She didn't care about Reed, so it didn't matter what he did with Kathleen.

With that final thought, Libby rolled over and closed her eyes. Try as she might, though, she could not forget the memory of Reed's lips on hers and his passionate caresses when they'd been together early that evening.

Kathleen ordered a hot bath once Reed was gone. She regretted that she hadn't been able to convince him to stay with her. They could have had a fine time, but she made up her mind to enjoy every minute of her stay in the hotel just the same. The maid brought the tub in to her room and filled it with hot water, and Kathleen couldn't wait to luxuriate in it. It seemed an eternity since she'd last had the chance to pamper herself. She stripped off her dreaded widow's weeds and climbed into the tub to soak in its welcoming warmth.

Kathleen remained lazing in the tub until the water cooled, then washed and toweled herself off. That done, she stood before the full-length mirror to look at her body. She turned sideways, then studied herself from the front and back. Her breasts were high and firm, her hips nicely rounded. She thought she looked quite attractive, and her resentment over the society-dictated year of mourning deepened. Wearing the heavy black widow's weeds was like being buried alive. She was young and pretty, and she wanted to enjoy her life.

Muttering to herself, Kathleen climbed into the solitary bed. The sheets felt cool against her bare flesh. She regretted again that Reed was not there to help warm the sheets up. She certainly would have enjoyed making love to him. A smile curved her lips as she imagined him lying next to her. It would have been wonderful.

She sighed wistfully, still clinging to the hope that one day soon he would really be hers and come to her of his own free will. She wondered how much longer it would take. She wasn't a patient woman.

As she was considering how long she would wait for Reed, she remembered her promise to Lyle that she would meet him tonight. A throaty, wicked chuckle escaped her at the thought of him waiting endlessly for her to come to him. She wondered how long he would wait for her. She wondered, too, how angry he would be when he discovered she wasn't coming. The thought that she could control Lyle this way pleased her. It made her feel powerful. It would be amusing when she finally saw him again tomorrow.

But until then, she was just going to enjoy the softness of her lonely bed and dream of what the future might hold for her with the man she'd been dreaming of for so long—Reed.

Thrill to the most sensual, adventure-filled Historical Romances on the market today...
FROM  LEISURE BOOKS

As a home subscriber to the Leisure Historical Romance Book Club, you'll enjoy the best in today's BRAND-NEW Historical Romance fiction. For over twenty-five years, Leisure Books has brought you the award-winning, high-quality authors you know and love to read. Each Leisure Historical Romance will sweep you away to a world of high adventure...and intimate romance. Discover for yourself all the passion and excitement millions of readers thrill to each and every month.

SAVE AT LEAST $5.00 EACH TIME YOU BUY!

Each month, the Leisure Historical Romance Book Club brings you four brand-new titles from Leisure Books, America's foremost publisher of Historical Romances. EACH PACKAGE WILL SAVE YOU AT LEAST $5.00 FROM THE BOOKSTORE PRICE! And you'll never miss a new title with our convenient home delivery service.

Here's how we do it. Each package will carry a 10-DAY EXAMINATION privilege. At the end of that time, if you decide to keep your books, simply pay the low invoice price of $16.96 ($19.98 CANADA), no shipping or handling charges added.* HOME DELIVERY IS ALWAYS FREE.* With today's top Historical Romance novels selling for $5.99 and higher, our price SAVES YOU AT LEAST $5.00 with each shipment.

AND YOUR FIRST FOUR-BOOK SHIPMENT IS TOTALLY FREE!

IT'S A BARGAIN YOU CAN'T BEAT! A Super $21.96 Value!

LEISURE BOOKS A Division of Dorchester Publishing Co., Inc.

GET YOUR 4 FREE* BOOKS NOW— A $21.96 VALUE!

Mail the Free* Books Certificate Today!

Get Four Books Totally
F R E E* —
A $21.96 Value!

(Tear Here and Mail Your FREE* Book Card Today!)

PLEASE RUSH
MY FOUR FREE*
BOOKS TO ME
RIGHT AWAY!

Leisure Historical Romance Book Club
P.O. Box 6613
Edison, NJ 08818-6613

AFFIX
STAMP
HERE

* * *

Lyle was restless, and he was growing more and more tense with each passing minute. It was nearly midnight, and still he'd seen no sign of Kathleen since the end of the show. She'd said she would come to him late that night, but how late was she going to be?

For several hours, he'd been doing nothing but lying in his bed thinking of her. He was on fire with the need to have her, and he would not be denied again. Tonight, Kathleen would be his, as she had been for months now. Steve's death should have made things better between them. It should have brought them closer together, not separated them as it had.

Lyle had been serious when he'd proposed to Kathleen the last time he'd been with her. He wanted her for his own. If it meant he'd have to marry her to keep her in his bed, he would do it. If that was what she wanted from him, he would oblige. They just needed some time alone together so they could talk things out, and he wanted that time to be tonight.

Another hour passed before his patience was finally at an end. What had been desire was now rage. Unable to remain waiting where he was any longer, Lyle went after Kathleen. When he found her, he was going to teach her a lesson she wouldn't soon forget. He was not a man who could so easily be ignored and dismissed.

Lyle was glad to see that the grounds were deserted. The night was quiet, so he would have to take care not to draw undue attention to himself as he tried to rouse Kathleen. Her wagon was dark, and the thought that she'd gone to bed, completely forgetting that they were to meet tonight, enraged him. He walked around the wagon looking for a way inside and was pleased when he found one window partially open. After making sure no one was watching, he pried it more fully open and climbed inside.

"Kathleen?" he called softly, in a voice just above a whisper.

Heat was pounding in his body, and he decided that if she was there, he wouldn't be angry. He would just make love to her all night to make her realize what she'd been missing. They were good in bed together—very good.

Lyle made his way to her small bedroom, expecting to find her asleep there since she hadn't responded to his call.

"Kathleen?"

He stepped inside the cramped room, and his anger returned full force. Her bed was empty. It had not been slept in.

Where was she? And more important—who was she with?

Lyle was tempted to stay, to wait in her bed for her. He wanted to be there when she finally did return, but common sense warned him off. He would confront her, but on his terms—not hers.

Rage simmered within him as he climbed from the wagon, and he began to plan what he was going to do when he saw her again. No one saw him, and he was glad. He made his way back to his own bed and passed a sleepless night, waiting for the dawn.

It was late when Reed finally reached the Stampede. The ride had seemed shorter coming back. He wasn't sure if it was because he didn't have Kathleen beside him or because he was eager to return, but whichever it was, he was glad.

All seemed peaceful as he stabled the carriage and tended to the horse. He took one last walk through the grounds to make sure everything was quiet. Standing across the way from Libby's tent, he found himself watching over her, wanting to make sure that no one was around bothering her.

"Reed? What are you doing out here?" Mark said, coming upon him in the dark.

"I was just enjoying the peace and quiet. I only got back a few minutes ago from having dinner with the mayor and one of the other townspeople in Los Santos. I wanted to make sure everything was settled before I went on to bed."

"It's been quiet all night," Mark assured him.

"Good. I'll talk to you first thing in the morning."

Satisfied that things were as Mark had told him, Reed went on to his wagon. He was glad to be there. He was glad he'd gotten away from Kathleen.

Libby was on his mind when he stretched out on his bed a short time later. He remembered the excitement of her kiss and how wonderful she'd felt in his arms earlier that evening. For an instant, he thought of how good it would feel to have her there with him and to be making love to her.

With a growl of irritation at the direction of his wayward thoughts, Reed pounded on his pillow several times under the pretense of plumping it, but in reality he was easing his frustration. He finally fell asleep, but his dreams were filled with visions of Libby, and he got little real rest.

"Where was Kathleen? Did she spend the night in town?" Joe asked Reed the following morning when Reed found him sitting outside his wagon for the first time since the accident. Joe had just seen one of the hands ride back into camp in the carriage with her.

"We were invited to dinner with the mayor last night, so Kathleen and I rode in to dine with him and the town doctor. She decided she wanted to stay there since it was so late, but I came on back. I had too much work to do here."

"We've got to pack up and move out today, so it's going to be a long day and a busy one."

"You're feeling better I take it?"

"Much. I wish I could get up and get going. This sitting around doing nothing is driving me crazy."

"Take it easy. Mark's doing a fine job in your place. There's no need for you to worry."

Joe's mood turned more serious. "Have you learned anything new about my accident—or Steve's?"

"Nothing," Reed told him in disgust. "It's frustrating, knowing there's a murderer in the show and not being able to find a clue to prove who it is."

Joe nodded, his expression grim. "Maybe we'll never know."

Reed looked over at him, his gaze reflecting the fierceness of his resolve. "One way or another, I'm going to find out who's responsible for Steve's death. No matter how hopeless it may seem, I am not going to give up—ever. I owe my brother that much."

They were silent for a moment; then Joe spoke up. He had an idea he'd been considering, and he thought this might be the time to suggest it.

"I've been doing some thinking, since I don't have much else to do right now, and I was wondering whether you'd consider taking Libby and riding on ahead into King's Crossing to do some advance publicity for the show. You know how excited everybody was about her here in Los Santos. Your run-in with her at the Diamondback was great for business. Maybe you could do something like that again. I don't know that word about her has reached King's Crossing yet, and it certainly couldn't hurt to try something a little different."

Reed felt he belonged with the Stampede, but the prospect of spending some time alone with Libby was appealing. "I really should stay with the Stampede. You need me here."

"I'm moving a little bit now, and you just said Mark was doing a good job. It would be good for business if you and Weston's Lady stirred up the crowds in the next town before we go there."

Reed saw the logic to his reasoning. His own personal feelings on the matter only made Joe's suggestion that much more attractive to him. "If she's interested, we could do it. I'll check with her and see what she thinks."

"You'd have a good two days in town before we roll in."

"I'll let you know what we decide."

Reed left Joe to seek out Libby.

Ann had been watching them talk from where she was sitting inside their wagon, and when Reed moved away, she came outside to speak with her father.

"Is Reed going to do it?"

"I think so."

"Good." She said no more, but went on about her work.

Joe sat in silence, relieved for the moment.

Reed heard the sound of gunfire and knew he'd found Libby. One of the hands had told him that Libby had decided to do some practicing, so he'd gone in the direction the man had pointed to ask her if she was interested in Joe's idea.

Reed came over the top of the low rise to find Libby taking careful aim as Mark tossed clay targets in the air for her. He remained where he was, admiring her expertise from afar.

"Good job!" Mark told her as she blasted the last target from the sky with expert ease. "Maybe we should start calling you 'Dead Eye' instead of Weston's Lady."

"Thank you—I think," she said with a laugh, thinking "Dead Eye" sounded a little gruesome.

Reed was looking on and listening, and it occurred to him then that he had never heard Libby laugh before. The revelation touched him. He felt a pang of jealousy as he watched her with Mark. Having seen her fear the day before, he wondered why she'd been so guarded with him and yet seemed at ease with Mark. He frowned.

"There's Reed," Mark said as they started back toward the campgrounds.

"I wonder what he wants?" she said. Standing on the top of the rise as he was, Reed was silhouetted against the sky. She couldn't read his expression, and he looked so mysterious that a shiver ran down her spine.

"I think we're about to find out," Mark responded as they walked to where Reed was waiting for them.

"That was some nice shooting," Reed complimented her when they drew within earshot. "I like it when you practice. You know how I feel about you getting rusty."

"Don't worry, I'll keep on her." Mark assured him with a grin. "We won't let her miss. It wouldn't look good for the show if the boss got shot. Did you need some help?"

"I need to talk with Libby. Joe came up with a great idea for publicity, and I want to see if she's interested."

"What is it?" Libby asked, curious.

"Joe suggested that we ride into King's Crossing ahead of the show and do some early promotion. Since our little encounter at the Diamondback created so much excitement in Los Santos, Joe was thinking we could do some shooting demonstrations ahead of time to stir up interest in

205

your act in the next town. What do you think?"

"That sounds like a good idea," she agreed. Riding out ahead of the show suited her just fine. Even if John had heard about her and managed to track down the Stampede, she wouldn't be there.

"So only the two of you will be going?" Mark asked, glancing between them as they made their way back toward the wagons.

"It'll be fine," Libby reassured Mark.

"You're sure?"

"She'll be fine," Reed said. Then he glanced at the other man, for he sensed Mark was concerned about Libby. "She's got a gun, and she knows how to use it."

"I'll be glad to ride along, if you want someone with you to help set things up."

"If Joe was healthy, I'd take you up on the offer, but I need you here. If there's any trouble, I don't know that Kathleen can handle it on her own. And even though Joe is moving a little better, he won't be anywhere near normal for at least a month."

Mark fell silent, not pleased that Libby would be traveling alone with Reed, but having no power to change things. He supposed Reed was right— she could handle herself quite nicely should a difficult situation arise. She'd certainly proven that to them often enough.

"How soon do you want to leave?" Libby asked Reed.

"Will an hour give you enough time?"

She nodded. "I don't have that much to pack."

"I'll meet you at the stables. I have to speak with Kathleen before we go."

Libby shouldn't have been caught unaware by his need to talk with Kathleen. When she'd fallen asleep the night before, she'd thought that the two of them were spending the night together somewhere. It hadn't been until this morning that she'd learned through general talk around the camp that Kathleen had stayed overnight in town, but Reed had returned by himself around midnight. For some reason, she'd found the knowledge comforting, although she wasn't sure why.

"Got any ideas what you're going to do in town?" Mark asked.

"I'll probably take a shot at him again," she said, casting him a sidelong glance. She hoped he didn't realize she was being half-serious right then.

"I wish I'd seen you that night at the Diamondback," he said smiling. "Pete and the other guys are still talking about it."

"I had to do something to get his attention," she said simply.

"I'm just glad Joe was impressed with you." Mark looked down at her, thinking she was one of the prettiest women he'd ever seen—and a good shot on top of it.

Libby sensed a deeper meaning to his words, but chose to ignore the implication. She didn't need any more complications in her life, no matter how nice Mark was. "Well, I'd better go get ready. I'll see you when you get to town."

"We'll be following right behind you," he told her. "Be careful."

"We will."

* * *

"I can be ready to ride out with you and Libby in half an hour," Kathleen announced as soon as Reed had told her his plan to do advance publicity for the Stampede.

"No, you misunderstood me," Reed insisted. "Libby and I are going into King's Crossing by ourselves. I need you to stay here and run things with Joe and Mark."

"That's ridiculous. Joe and Mark can handle everything here. They're only packing up and moving on. How difficult can it be for them when they've done it hundreds of times before? I won't be needed here. I'll come with you."

"It wouldn't be proper for you to ride with us. You're in mourning."

"If we're talking about being proper, what's proper about Libby traveling unchaperoned with you?" she challenged hotly. She did not like the idea that they were going to be alone together for several days—Reed and his "Weston's Lady."

"That's really none of your business, Kathleen."

He sounded so cold that she stopped arguing. "You're absolutely right. I was just concerned with the image the Stampede would be projecting."

"The image we'll be projecting is that the Stampede is a thoroughly entertaining show and that it shouldn't be missed by anyone in town. That's all that's important."

Realizing she was treading on dangerous ground with him, she lightened her tone and smiled. "You'll be careful on the trip?"

"You don't have to worry."

"But I do," she said, and then, impulsively, she

stood up on tiptoe and kissed his cheek. "I'll be thinking of you while you're gone."

Everyone around the area saw her kiss him—everyone, including Libby and Lyle.

Reed was disgusted by her move. He was tempted to wipe his cheek off right then and there, but he managed to control the impulse. "I'll see you when you get to King's Crossing."

"Yes, you will."

"Kathleen?" Lyle had been watching from nearby and the sight of her kissing Reed had been all he could stand. He'd heard the talk of how she'd gone into town with him the night before, and he was wondering just what was going on between them. He wasn't about to stand by and let her get away from him. She was his!

"Yes, Lyle?" Kathleen was instantly grateful that Reed was with her as she confronted Lyle for the first time since she'd gotten back. She knew he must be furious with her, and she supposed she was going to have to make it up to him in some way, but now certainly wasn't the time.

"If you'll excuse me, I have to get ready. I'll see you later, Kathleen." Reed was glad to get away. Seeing Lyle and Kathleen together reinforced his suspicions about their possible guilt, and he wasn't ready to confront them yet.

Lyle hated Reed. Since he'd shown up, Kathleen had changed. She was a different woman now, and he didn't like it. He waited until the other man had moved out of earshot before he spoke again. "I don't like being lied to, Kathleen."

"Is there something you want, Lyle? If not, I

have a business to tend to." She tried to be aloof.

"You know damned good and well what I want," he snarled in a low voice. He was tempted to grab her right there and show her.

"I can meet with you later, if you'd like," she said softly, her gaze narrowing as she followed Reed's progress through the camp. If Reed was going away with that little bitch, Libby, there was absolutely no reason why she couldn't have a little fun while he was gone. She was getting tired of hoping and praying he'd come to her. Last night had been particularly frustrating. She wanted a man, and if it had to be Lyle—well, she'd just have to make do. For the time being, anyway.

"That's what you told me yesterday."

"Something came up."

"I know something came up," he countered tightly. He was tempted to grab himself for emphasis, but knew this wasn't the time or place. "It was 'up' all night."

"Be quiet." She tried to hush him, knowing how crude he could sometimes be.

"Why?"

"Because you want me, and you're not going to get me unless you control yourself." She saw the dangerous glint in his eye. "Come to my wagon at midnight. I'll be waiting."

"You'd better be, woman. I waited long enough for you last night."

She gave him a wicked look as she recognized the heat in his tone. "No, you didn't. You can never get enough of me, and you know it. Besides, we both know I'm well worth the wait, don't we?"

He was almost panting after her.

"I'll see you tonight, Lyle." She walked away and did not look back.

Lyle remained standing there a moment longer, watching her go and waiting for the pounding heat in his groin to ease. He wondered how long it was until midnight. It couldn't be soon enough.

Chapter Eleven

*The Office of Carroll and Condon, Publishers,
New York City*

"This sounds so exciting. It would be perfect for
Sheri, don't you think?" Dawn Scarola asked
Brooke Borneman as they sat at their desks.

As readers for the publisher, it was their job to
go through periodicals from across the country
and find interesting articles that might translate
into good story ideas for Carroll and Condon's
Dime Novel series. The ultimate decision about
which articles were selected would be Mr. De-
Young's, of course, but Dawn and Brooke were the
ones who got to pick out the most exciting stories—and this story about the lady sure-shot from
Texas sounded wonderful.

"Listen to this, Brooke," Dawn said as she began

to read aloud from the account. "*Stampede owner Reed Weston and his lady are a heavenly match. From their straight-shooting performance to their trick-riding display, the pair is pure magic. Weston's Lady, Liberty Jones, is a rare talent, indeed.* And did you see their picture?" She held up the paper. "Look—isn't he handsome?"

"He's the best-looking cowboy I've seen since Sheridan St. John's husband Brand came here with her for a visit a few years ago."

"I remember everybody talking about him. Was he as handsome as this Reed Weston?"

Brooke studied the picture in the newspaper thoughtfully for a moment, then smiled. "It's a tie. They are both splendid examples of mankind's finest efforts."

"You are so sophisticated," Dawn remarked, laughing. "Why don't you just say they're really cute?"

"They're that, too!" Brooke laughed with her friend as they turned their attention back to the article again.

"What are you two so interested in?" Thea Lynch asked them as she came back into the room followed by Kelly Bloom and Jennifer Bonnell.

"Not what," Dawn corrected. "Who. His name is Reed Weston, and he owns a Wild West show in Texas."

The three women hurried over to look at the picture.

"He is definitely one handsome man," Jennifer agreed.

"What do you think about this Liberty Jones

wearing pants?" Thea asked the others. "Isn't that a bit outrageous?"

"Frankly, I think she's a lucky girl," Dawn said.

"You know, you're right. She is a lucky girl. Think about the exciting life she must lead. She gets to travel, and she's surrounded by handsome cowboys. Maybe we should move out West." Brooke was thoughtful.

"And join a Wild West show?" Dawn's imagination started to run away with her. She tried to picture Brooke performing in the Stampede. "What could you do? Some trick riding? Or are you good with a gun?"

"Neither, I was thinking we should convince Carroll and Condon to relocate and open an office there. Someplace like St. Louis, say. It's a big city, and then we'd be a lot closer to all those good-looking cowboys."

"That would be fine with me, especially if they all look like this Reed Weston."

Tim DeYoung walked into the room just then, interrupting their reverie. Dawn called him over.

"We've got Sheridan St. John's next book right here for you!" Dawn announced excitedly, holding up the article on Weston's Lady. "You know how popular Wild West shows are right now, don't you? They've been playing in big cities all across the country and drawing thousands of people to the performances. Buffalo Bill's even got his own show. If Sheri chose to do a series on this Weston's Lady, it would be wonderful."

"It most certainly would," Brooke put in. "Sheri knows the West, and in this story, she would have a strong heroine in a Texas setting. I can see it now—" She paused, then said dramatically, " 'Liberty Jones, Lady Sharpshooter, or The Adventures of Weston's Lady.' Isn't that a great title? What do you think?"

Tim was listening with interest. Westerns were their best sellers, and he trusted Dawn's and Brooke's judgment implicitly. They hadn't been wrong yet in the stories they'd picked. "Send a wire to Sheri and see if she's interested."

"I'll do it right away," Dawn promised, giving Brooke, Thea, Kelly and Jennifer a triumphant smile. She couldn't wait to see what their bestselling author did with the idea. If anyone could write a page-turner about Liberty Jones and Weston's Wild Texas Stampede, it was Sheri.

The wire went out that afternoon.

John Harris was in his office when a knock came at the door. He looked up, irritated at being interrupted. He didn't want to talk with anyone. He just wanted to be left alone.

"What is it?" he called out in a sharp voice.

The door opened, and Nell, one of his tellers, came in. Her approach was timid, for the boss had become decidedly mean-tempered ever since the accident that had scarred his cheek and forever marred his good looks. She tried not to stare at him as she spoke, but the sight of the hideous, jagged mark down his cheek could not be ignored. She tried her best to be calm, but he did look frightening, and the way he was scowling at her only made him that much more intimidating.

"Miss Kelvin is here to see you, sir. I told her I'd check and see if you were busy. If you don't want to be disturbed, I'll tell her to come back another time," Nell offered quickly, wanting to get away from him as fast as she could.

John was surprised that Madeline would be so brazen as to come to see him here at the bank. Whatever it was she wanted, he knew it had to be important. "No, send her in. I can spare a few minutes."

"Yes, sir." Nell hurried to do as he'd requested.

John rose to greet Madeline at the office door. His curiosity was piqued by her unexpected appearance. "My dear—this is a surprise."

Madeline graciously thanked Nell for showing her in, then waited until the other woman had closed the door behind her on the way out.

"A pleasant one, I hope?" she said, giving John a smug smile.

"You tell me." He remained cautious as he gestured for her to sit down in one of the chairs in front of his desk while he returned to his own seat.

"I have something I think might interest you—in fact, I know you're going to be very interested indeed."

"I don't like teases, Madeline," he said tersely. "What are you up to?"

John's attempt to intimidate her didn't bother Madeline at all. She merely smiled coldly at him, for she was his equal in every way. Opening her purse, she drew out a folded newspaper.

"Henderson, the man you hired to find Libby, paid me a visit just a little while ago. He brought me a copy of the paper from Los Santos."

"So?" John didn't like being led on. If Madeline had something to say, she should just say it. "Henderson told me over a week ago that he was giving up searching for Libby. He said he had no idea where she'd gone and doubted he'd ever be able to find her."

"Well, I guess when you upped the reward you were offering for information on Libby's whereabouts, you made it so irresistible he decided to keep on looking a little while longer."

"And?"

"And I think you're going to be very glad you offered the extra cash."

"Why? What did he find?" he demanded tersely, wanting to believe that they'd located her, but refusing to let himself get excited—yet.

"Oh, just a picture of your beloved fiancée on the front page of the Los Santos newspaper, that's all."

John's eyes widened at Madeline's words. He reached up and touched his cheek. The pain from the wound Libby had inflicted on him had lessened over the weeks since she'd fled, but it had not eased entirely. Many nights he'd lain awake, wracked with pain and longing for vengeance. His voice was tight when he spoke. "So you're telling me that the little bitch has been in Los Santos the whole time?"

"Not necessarily the whole time, but that's where she was just a few days ago. Henderson was passing through and happened to see a copy of the paper lying around in a bar called the Diamondback. Here, take a look." She handed the newspaper to John and waited to see his reaction. She felt quite satisfied with herself when he finished reading and lifted his gaze to hers. The look in his eyes was cold and deadly. "I knew you were going to enjoy that article."

"Very much. I'll be riding for King's Crossing this afternoon. With any luck, I can get there before the show has moved on. Libby's not going to get away from me this time."

"It was rather humiliating for you when you didn't have her for your 'friend' that day," she said pointedly.

"Humiliating wasn't the word for it." John shot her a nasty look, irritated with her for reminding him of what had happened after Libby had escaped them. The man he had promised her to had not been pleased, and he had let John know it in no uncertain terms. His anger had only inspired John to make sure that some day he got even with Libby. That day was about to come.

Madeline openly studied the hideous scar on his cheek, knowing that even after it was fully healed, he would still bear Libby's mark. "Are you planning to have a heartwarming reunion with your fiancée?"

"Most certainly."

"I wish I could be there to watch when you two lovebirds are reunited," she said, giving an exaggerated sigh of disappointment at being excluded.

"Don't even hint at it. You're not coming with me," he said flatly. "Libby and I have a few things to settle, and they're going to be settled in private."

218

"Pity. Oh, well," she said. After all the trouble Libby had caused, she would have enjoyed watching the girl suffer at John's hands. "By the way, I paid Henderson the reward you'd promised, so you owe me quite a handsome sum of money."

"It's worth every penny," he told her. "I'll have one of the tellers write you a draft."

"That will be fine," she said easily, standing to go. "Have a safe and happy trip to King's Crossing. I'll be looking forward to hearing how finding your long-lost betrothed turns out."

"I'm looking forward to telling you about it." His smile was thin as their gazes met.

Madeline smiled at John in return and then left him. She was pleased that Libby was going to get just what was coming to her.

Reed and Libby had left the Stampede that morning and had been riding for long hours. It was late in the afternoon when stormclouds began to gather in the distance and roil their way.

"The sky isn't looking too friendly," Reed remarked, studying the countryside to see if there was someplace nearby where they could seek shelter. "We'd better put on our slickers."

They quickly donned their rain gear, knowing it would be little enough defense if the storm turned out to be as bad as it threatened.

"Let's pick up our pace," Libby suggested.

They put their heels to their mounts' sides, but even their swift horses couldn't outrun Mother Nature's savage intent. The storm swirled around them, breaking overhead with a fierceness that startled them. Just as the downpour drenched them, they found a rocky outcropping where they were partially protected from the full wrath of the storm. They dismounted and, keeping a tight grip on their horses' reins, they huddled there, hoping to escape the worst of the blinding rain.

Lightning split the sky, and the accompanying thunder was so loud and powerful that the earth seemed to move with the force of it. The horses reared and tried to bolt, but somehow Reed and Libby managed to control them.

"Are you all right?" Reed asked, moving nearer to Libby to try to shield her body with his.

"I think so," she said, as Reed stepped in front of her and blocked the fierceness of the wind-blown rain. His protective gesture gave her a moment to draw a ragged breath. "Thanks." She'd always appreciated the broad width of his chest and shoulders, but never more than she did right then.

He grinned down at her. "You're Weston's Lady. It's my job to make sure nothing happens to you."

Libby smiled weakly back up at him. She was sure he'd meant to reassure her with his statement, but it had reinforced her belief that he only cared about her because she was worth money to him. Why else would he have gone off with Kathleen last night? And she'd seen him kiss Kathleen that morning.

They fell silent, waiting for the rest of the storm to pass. It was harsh. The wind and rain battered the land, but finally, after almost half an hour, the downpour began to weaken.

Even though cold rain was dripping down his neck, Reed enjoyed having an excuse to stay close to Libby this way, protecting her. He wished he could protect her from all the troubles that threatened her, but until she relented and confided in him, this would be the best he could do. When at last the rain stopped, he knew it was time to move away.

"I think it's about through," he told her, regretfully stepping back to take a look at the sky.

Though it was still dark, the threat of the hard-driving rains and damaging winds was over.

"Are you all right?" Reed asked.

"I'm wet, but I'll live," she told him. The shield of her slicker had offered little real protection. She was soaked to the skin.

"Me, too," he agreed.

They both shed their slickers and got ready to ride.

"Do you plan to make camp any time soon?" Libby asked, realizing she'd be miserable if she tried to keep riding in her wet clothing. She desperately needed to change. She only hoped that the things in her bag were still dry.

Reed glanced Libby's way, having been preoccupied up until now with taking care of his mount. The sight that greeted him left him momentarily speechless. Libby's blouse and riding skirt were soaked and clinging to her like a second skin. The blouse, in particular, was practically transparent and molded suggestively to her every curve. He could make out the details of the feminine undergarment he'd purchased for her at the shop, and he swallowed tightly, forcing his gaze up to her face and away from the swell of her breasts pressed so revealingly against the damp fabric.

"I thought we could keep going for a while until we find a dry place."

Libby took a look around and knew he was right. Sleeping in mud had little appeal to her. "You're right, but give me a minute. I have to change these clothes."

"Go ahead. I'll take the horses and wait for you over here."

"Thanks." She handed him the reins and got her bag down to find some dry things.

"And I promise I won't look," Reed told her.

"You're a smart man, Reed Weston. I'd hate to have to put on a shooting demonstration out here where there would be nobody to see it but us."

"As I told Mark, you've got a gun and you know how to use it. You're safe with me."

He was smiling as he walked their horses a short distance away to give her the privacy she needed. He played the gentleman as Libby shed her soaked garments and donned some of the boy's clothing Joe had given her.

"It's safe for you to turn around now," she called out to Reed.

Reed came back to her to find that she'd almost transformed herself back into Bert. This time, though, instead of stuffing her hair up under her hat, she had simply plaited the heavy, wet length into a single braid that hung down her back. It still amazed him that he had seen her working as a stable hand at the Stampede and hadn't immediately recognized her. There was no mistaking her beauty now, no matter how baggy and ill-fitting the boy's things were.

"It's not exactly fashionable, but it'll do for the rest of today. I'll change into my fringed costume tomorrow before we get into town. I'll need to look my best then."

Reed thought that Libby had looked pretty good a minute or two before in the wet blouse. As he realized the direction of his thoughts, he brought himself up short. He had to admit that he was glad she'd changed. At least now he could keep his mind on the reason they were making this trip— the Stampede. If Libby had stayed in her wet clothing, he doubted he could have thought about anything with any degree of logic. Libby had been too tempting, too beautiful to ignore.

They mounted up and headed out. They kept going until they finally passed beyond the storm's path. They were relieved to be on dry ground. After finding a relatively secluded spot near a small pond, they made camp just as the sun was setting.

Reed tended to their horses, while Libby built a small campfire and prepared the food that he'd brought along for them. It was filling fare, and they ate hungrily. By the time they'd finished, night had fallen.

Reed got up to check on their horses one last time. On his way back to sit with Libby, he realized his shirt was still damp, so he took it off and spread it out, as best he could, near the fire.

Libby had begun to unbraid her hair while Reed was gone. Because her hair was so thick, it was still wet, and she wanted to brush it out so it could dry better overnight. When Reed reappeared, he was naked to the waist, and her eyes widened at the sight of him. She'd seen her brother shirtless, but he had never looked the way Reed looked. Reed was a magnificent specimen of manhood. His shoulders were broad, his arms and chest powerfully muscled. There wasn't a spare ounce of flesh on him, and she felt her throat go dry as she stared up at him. She had never thought of a man as beautiful before, but she did now.

"Something wrong?" he asked, seeing her strange expression and wondering at it.

"No. Nothing," she said quickly.

"My shirt's wet. It needs to dry out a little. It shouldn't take too long."

Libby shrugged as if it meant nothing to her that he was sitting half-naked across the campfire from her, his skin bronzed by the golden flames. She told herself that the kisses they'd shared the day before at the stable hadn't meant anything either. She told herself that Reed would stay on his side of the campfire, and everything would be just fine. She didn't care if he looked great with his shirt off. It didn't matter. She worked for him in the Stampede. He was her boss, and that was all there was to their relationship.

Almost nervously, Libby finished freeing her hair from the constraints of the braid and began raking her fingers through the damp mass of pale curls. She realized then that she needed to brush it out, so she retrieved her hair brush from her saddlebags and set to work on it. It was awkward for her to brush out the back, and she struggled along on her own for some time before Reed spoke up.

"Libby?" Reed said her name quietly. "Would you like me to help you?"

He had been mesmerized by the rhythmic motion she'd been using in her struggle to tame the unruly curls. In the firelight, her hair was the color of sunshine—several glorious, almost shimmering shades of blond. It was stunning, and he ached to run his hands through the golden mass.

Libby knew she shouldn't accept his offer. She knew it was far better if he just stayed right where he was across the fire from her, but she found herself accepting. "Thanks."

Reed went to sit down behind her. He reached around and gently took the brush from her hand. With slow, deliberate motions, he began to work his magic upon her.

Libby found herself entranced by his touch. He was firm without being harsh. His touch was gentle and sensuous and left her wanting more than just to enjoy his ministrations to her hair. Suddenly in her thoughts, she was in the stables, back in his arms, kissing him. His embrace had been her heaven and her hell. His kiss was seductive, his touch arousing. Yet she couldn't allow herself the luxury of believing it had meant anything. It had been a momentary lapse in her own rigid self-control, and she wouldn't allow it to happen again.

Yet, Libby wondered, if Reed did try to kiss her right now, would she stop him? Would she be able to refuse him? Could she send him from her? She knew the answer. The answer was no. She wanted Reed to kiss her again—she wanted it desperately.

Her heartbeat quickened at the thought. A shiver ran through her, and she surrendered to his gentle assault on her senses. She waited—wondering, hoping, aching for him to cast the brush aside and take her in his arms. She wanted him to kiss her as he had the night before. It had been so wonderful. She closed her eyes, hoping—

But Reed made no move to kiss her.

"Here's your brush," he said, stopping suddenly and handing her the brush. He knew he had to get away from her, or Libby might have a very serious reason to use her gun on him. Damn, but she was irresistible. She was so beautiful, he ached to hold her and kiss her again!

As soon as she'd taken the brush from him, Reed made a quick retreat to the other side of the campfire. The farther he stayed away from her, the better. She was too tempting. It would have been so easy to make love to her, but he knew he couldn't. He would not take advantage of her that way. He would not destroy what little trust she had in him right now.

Stretching out on his hard bedroll, Reed thought about staying up longer until he was sure his shirt was dry, but he decided against it. He didn't want to sit and watch her any longer. He wondered as he lay back and closed his eyes whether he'd get any rest tonight at all.

"Good night, Libby."

"Good night." Her answer was quiet, almost emotionless.

Reed did not open his eyes to look at her, though he was sorely tempted. He made up his mind to pretend to be asleep in the hope that he soon would be.

Libby sat glaring at Reed. She was furious—and hurt. It had felt so wonderful to have his hands upon her, but then he had just gotten up and moved away without a second thought. An ache grew in her heart, for she remembered all too clearly how he'd spent part of the previous night with Kathleen and how the other woman had kissed him that morning.

Irritated, Libby lay down and pulled her blanket up over herself. The last thing she wanted was for Reed to catch her watching him. She told herself she didn't care about him. It was good that they stayed away from each other. Her life was complicated enough right now. She didn't need anything—or anyone—else to worry about.

Midnight.

At long last, it was midnight. Lyle had thought the day would never end. He'd deliberately worked harder than ever, just to make the time go by more quickly. He was burning with the need to make love to Kathleen, and he wouldn't be able to rest easy until he did.

Lyle left his own bed and made his way through the grounds to Kathleen's wagon. He took one quick look around, saw that there was no one watching and tried her door. He didn't realize until it opened that he'd been half-expecting to find it locked. A self-satisfied smile curved his mouth.

For all her standoffish ways lately, Kathleen still wanted him as much as he wanted her. He let himself in and locked the door.

"Don't light any lamps." Kathleen's voice came from her bedroom in the back.

"But I love looking at you, woman," Lyle told her as he made his way to her bedside. He knew she probably wanted to keep it dark for fear that someone might see them together, and that irritated him. They had been lovers for months now, and he'd thought with Steve dead, she would come to him openly. Somehow, he was going to have to convince her that he could make her happy. He would start right now, tonight.

"Shhh," she whispered.

Lyle could hear her shifting in the bed to accommodate him. Never one to waste time, he stripped off his clothes and went to her. Aching with the need to have her, he plunged deep within her.

Kathleen was everything he'd ever wanted in a woman. She was beautiful. They were perfect together. Lyle wanted only to please her. He kissed her hungrily as he ground fiercely against her. He knew she liked it hot and hard, so he gave her what she always wanted. His hands were restless as he caressed her. He wanted her to respond as wildly to him as he did to her.

And Kathleen did. She had needed this. True, Lyle wasn't the man of her choice, but she would bide her time and make do with what she could get. The shield of darkness helped her be mindless in her response to him. She became only a creature of the flesh and gave herself over to his possession.

Lyle increased his rhythm, grasping her hips and bringing her more tightly against him. She gasped at the sensation and clung to him as waves of ecstasy swept over her. He felt Kathleen's excitement and met her in that release. Groaning his pleasure, he collapsed heavily on top of her.

"Oh, baby, you are one hot piece," he said in a husky voice as he lay unmoving upon her.

Kathleen's desire was sated momentarily, but she was not happy. No matter how hard she tried, there was no way to convince herself that the man who had just made love to her was anyone but Lyle. She sighed. Someday . . .

"I've been missing you, woman," he said, bracing himself over her on his elbows.

"I could tell," she said, giving him a smile. She was glad for the covering of darkness so he couldn't see the look in her eyes.

He leaned down to kiss her again, and she felt him grow hard within her.

"You are something. You got me wanting you again already."

She made a throaty sound that she hoped sounded like a purr to him. She didn't want to talk to him anymore. She didn't want any declarations of undying love. She just wanted to forget Reed's indifference to her. She wanted to pretend for just a little while that life was wonderful. Taking the aggressor's role, Kathleen pushed on his shoulders and rolled him onto his back.

"I like the way you think, Kathleen," he told her as she began to move against him.

Kathleen knew he wouldn't be happy if he knew what she was really thinking, so she said nothing, but smiled at him in the night. "I thought you might," she said throatily.

And then the talking ended, and there were only the sounds of their heated coupling.

When Lyle crept from her bed hours later, Kathleen was glad to see him go. No matter how hard she'd tried to pretend in all these years, no man satisfied her as she was sure Reed could—not Steve and certainly not Lyle.

Kathleen lay awake, staring into the pre-dawn darkness, wishing it had been Reed who'd made love to her for hours on end. She wondered where he was with Libby. She wondered, too, if he was coming to care for the other woman. The thought infuriated her. She wouldn't stand by and let that little slut have the one man she wanted above all others.

Sleep did not come the rest of the night for Kathleen as she lay awake imagining Reed and Libby alone together on the trail. She couldn't wait to get to King's Crossing. She wanted to do everything in her power to keep the two of them apart.

Chapter Twelve

Neither Reed nor Libby slept well overnight. They were up with the dawn and on the road soon after. They stopped only once so Libby could change into her fringed outfit and then headed straight into King's Crossing. It was mid-morning when they rode down the main street.

"I've got to meet with the sheriff to make sure everything's set for the Stampede when it arrives. I also need to check with him and see if it's all right for us to put on our demonstrations. You can come with me, or we can check into the hotel first and you can rest up while I take care of business," Reed told her.

"Let's get our rooms first. Then I can take a look around while you're talking to the sheriff."

They reined in before the Castle Hotel.

"I can't think of a better place for the Castle Hotel to be than in King's Crossing," Libby remarked as she dismounted and tied up her horse.

"I was thinking the same thing when I saw the Royal Flush Saloon back there." Reed chuckled as he came to her side and they entered the hotel.

It didn't take them long to check in. As soon as they'd taken their belongings up to their rooms, Reed went to take care of Stampede business. Libby stood in the window of her room staring down at the street below. She saw Reed emerge from the hotel and make his way to the sheriff's office down the block. She didn't want to stand there watching him, but somehow, she couldn't look away from the sight of his tall, broad-shouldered form moving so easily down the street. There was an aura of confidence and power about him. She'd only known Reed for a short time, yet she was finding herself drawn to him in ways she hadn't thought possible after John's betrayal. Not that it mattered. He'd made it quite clear that she meant nothing to him. Her gaze remained on him until he'd disappeared into the sheriff's office. Only then did she turn away from the window.

The bed with its clean white sheets was tempting, and Libby sat down on the side to test its comfort. Its softness was inviting after the night she'd just passed on the hard ground, but she was feeling a little too restless to try to nap just yet. She decided to help Reed with publicity by posting the handbills they'd brought with them to advertise the show. Gathering up the notices, Libby started from the room. She paused at the door for a moment, considering leaving her gun behind, but then thought better of it. There was no guarantee that John wasn't lurking around somewhere, and she couldn't afford to take any chances. It would take only one mistake where he was concerned, and she would be in real danger.

Libby started at the far end of the main street and began nailing up the handbills in prominent places. Several people stopped to talk to her, and she could tell that there was a lot of excitement about the Stampede's imminent arrival. She worked her way down the street and found herself in front of the Royal Flush Saloon. She had just put up a handbill when two men came staggering out of the saloon.

"What have we got here, Vance?" one man asked his buddy as he leered first at Libby, then at the notice she'd just put up. He recognized her immediately as Weston's Lady from her picture on the poster.

The man named Vance stared at her, too, then grinned stupidly. "Damnation, Tom, it looks like we got us a real live Wild West star right here in King's Crossing!"

"Good morning, gentlemen." Libby smiled politely as she stepped back away from them a bit. The smell of hard liquor was heavy upon them.

"Good mornin' to you, too, darlin'," Tom responded. "That's you on that poster, ain't it? You're Liberty Jones, Weston's Lady."

"Yes, I am."

"And you do some performin' in this Wild Texas Stampede? Says here on the poster that you do some fancy shootin' and trick riding." He leered at her. Everyone knew that actresses were whores, and this one was one pretty piece. He was all set to try some of what she was selling.

"Yes, I do." Libby tensed, seeing a change in his expression and sensing things might get ugly with these two. She forced herself to smile sweetly at them. "The Stampede's coming to town tomorrow, and we're going to be putting on three performances this weekend."

Vance and Tom were staring at her. Their faces were slack from the liquor they'd imbibed, but in their eyes, Libby could read the ugliness of their thoughts. She knew she should get away from them as quickly as she could.

"And what are you doing until the show gets here?" Vance asked, his voice loud, his words slurred.

"I'm helping do advance publicity for the Stampede."

"I'll just bet you are!" Tom hee-hawed. "Well, I can help get word out about you real fast, honey. Since you're such a good trick rider, why don't you give me and Vance a sample of your talent? What do you say?"

Both men were ogling her with obvious intent. They were in the mood for some fun and thought this Weston's Lady was the one they wanted to show them a good time.

Vance was practically drooling with excitement as he advanced on her and grabbed her left arm. "I can take you for a bucking bronco ride right now, sweet meat. Let's go."

Tom closed in on the other side at the same time and tried to catch her other arm.

"Don't!" She evaded him, but the handbills went flying as she went for her gun.

Libby knew a moment of panic when Tom knocked the gun from her hand before she could even aim at them.

"We ain't lookin' for no trouble. All we're wantin' is what you're sellin'!" Tom snarled, grabbing up her gun and taking her by the other arm to help Vance control her.

Vance's grip was bruising as he dragged her toward the alley that led around to the back of the saloon. "What are you fighting us for? We'll pay you, if it's money you're wanting."

"Let me go!" She continued to struggle against them as she looked around for some help, but there was no one around she could appeal to. She fought them as hard as she could, but they still managed to force her down the narrow walkway between the buildings and out of sight of anyone who might have come to her aid.

"Say, baby, we know what you showgirls are like." Vance chuckled.

"Damn, maybe she's one of them gals who likes it rough?" Tom was having a difficult time keeping his hold on her.

"I guess we're going to find out."

"I am not a whore!" Libby cried.

Both men laughed at her. "If you don't want to charge us, that's fine with us."

Vance shoved her back against the wall as they reached the rear of the building. He was rough as

235

he tore at her blouse and chemise, baring her breasts to their hungry gazes.

Libby never stopped fighting. She hadn't escaped John to end up in a back alley with these two creatures! "Get away from me! What do you think you're doing?"

"We're just having some fun. Don't fight us so much, girlie. Relax and enjoy yourself. We can make this real good for you," Tom told her, looking on as Vance pawed at her.

Libby was horrified. She struggled, trying to free herself, but Vance's hold was brutal. He groped at her breasts, his touch painful. "Get away from me!"

"You know you don't mean it," Vance said as he clamped a hand over her mouth to silence her.

"Oh, yes, she does!" Reed snarled as he came upon the scene. "Both of you get the hell away from her before I shoot you where you stand."

Fury pounded through Reed at the sight of Libby being so mauled. He wanted to shoot both men without hesitation for daring to touch her, and it took all of his will power not to do it right then and there.

Vance and Tom were shocked by this stranger's interference.

"We ain't doin' nothing wrong. She's looking for some fun, so we're obliging!" Tom said quickly, puzzled by the man's deadly expression.

"That's right!" Vance added. "C'mon. We'll share. You can have some, too! She's just some actress known as Weston's Lady from that show that's coming to town."

"You're right about one thing," he said coldly. "She is *Weston's Lady*."

"Yeah, so?" Vance frowned.

"I'm *Weston*."

Both men went still at his statement. Vance's hands dropped away from Libby.

Reed saw Libby's torn blouse and bared breasts before she struggled to cover herself, and fury unlike anything he'd ever felt before filled him.

The minute Vance let her go, Libby ran to Reed's side.

Reed immediately put a protective arm around her shoulders and drew her close. His gun never wavered as he asked her, "Are you all right?"

"Yes."

"We didn't mean nothing! We thought she was a—" Tom began.

"Don't say it!" Reed snarled, his gaze narrowing dangerously as he seriously considered putting these two six feet under. "This woman is a lady, and she deserves to be treated like one."

"What's happening here, Weston? What's going on?" Sheriff Bruner asked as he came running up to them. He'd been summoned by some of the townsfolk who had heard the commotion in the alley and had gone for help.

"They were assaulting Miss Jones, and I was just lucky enough to get here in time to stop them," Reed explained.

Bruner took one look at the pretty young woman clinging to Reed. He saw the tattered condition of her clothing and drew his own sidearm. "I'll take it from here, Weston."

Reed nodded tightly and slowly holstered his gun.

"Let's go!" Bruner ordered. "You got a lot of explaining to do!"

"But we didn't do nothing—" Vance was protesting.

Reed glanced at the man sharply, ready to defend Libby's honor if necessary.

"I know what you were trying to do. You're damned lucky Mr. Weston got here in time to stop you or I'd be tempted to shoot you myself right now," Bruner told them. He stepped forward to take their guns.

"That one's mine," Libby managed in a shaky voice when she saw him take her weapon from Tom.

The sheriff handed Libby her sidearm, then turned his attention back to the drunks. He motioned for them to move up the alley toward the street. He glanced at Reed and Libby.

"I'm sorry this happened, ma'am. If you want to come by the jail and press charges—"

"Later," Reed said harshly, answering for Libby. He wanted to get her away from there as quickly as he could.

The sheriff nodded and herded the two away to the jail, leaving Reed and Libby alone.

Reed was rigid with fury as he realized the danger Libby had faced all alone. He thanked God that he'd left the sheriff's office when he had. If he'd stayed there any longer, he would have been too late to save her. His expression turned even more threatening at the thought. As good as she was with a gun, there were going to be times when she wouldn't be able to protect herself. Powerful emotion swelled within him, and he knew then and there that he would never let anything hurt Libby again.

The fear that had filled Libby turned to anger with herself as the sheriff took the two drunks away. She couldn't believe she'd been so vulnerable. She'd vowed that she'd never allow herself to be caught in that kind of situation again, and if it hadn't been for Reed showing up when he had— In spite of her determination to be brave, she shuddered as she realized what might have happened to her.

"Are you all right?" He felt her tremble and was worried about her.

"Yes," she lied, refusing to let him know how scared she really had been. She stepped away from him, knowing it would be all too easy to get used to relying on his strength. She felt a little lost without his arm around her, but refused to give in to the desire to return to the safe haven of his arms.

"They didn't hurt you?" He was amazed at what a strong woman she was. Most of the females he'd known would have been crying hysterically after such an assault.

"No, thanks to you."

"Can you cover yourself?" He would give her his shirt if she needed it.

"I think so." She quickly drew the fabric of her blouse together, covering her breasts as best as she could.

"Let's get you back to the hotel."

She nodded and stayed by his side as they left the alley.

A few people had gathered around, having heard that there was some excitement going on. Reed stayed close to Libby. He wanted to protect her from stares as they made their way to the Castle Hotel and hurried upstairs to her room. He opened her door for her and followed her inside. She quickly distanced herself from him. Something about being alone with him in such a small room seemed too intimate.

"Are you going to be all right by yourself or would you like me to stay with you for a while?" he asked.

"I'm fine. I'm just angry that I let them get the upper hand. I should have realized—"

"You should have realized what? That a decent woman can't walk down the streets of this town in broad daylight without being attacked? This was not your fault."

After all the insults and humiliation she'd endured during the assault, Reed's words were most welcome. Libby looked up at him, remembering how fiercely he'd protected her when he'd come to her rescue. She had never been so glad to see anyone as she had been to see Reed in that alleyway. She could only imagine what would have happened to her if he hadn't shown up when he did. "Thanks."

Reed saw the depth of her emotions mirrored in Libby's eyes. As much as he wanted to take her in his arms, he held himself back. He was certain that she was still skittish after her run-in with the other men and he didn't want to do anything to hurt her or scare her. He simply reached out and touched her cheek in a gentle, unthreatening caress. "I'm glad I got there in time. I'm glad you weren't hurt."

"I'm unhurt because of you." She lifted her gaze to his, and they stood staring at each other for a long, quiet moment.

"I'd better go." Reed forced himself to move away from her mesmerizing influence.

"I'll get cleaned up, and then I'll be ready for our demonstration this afternoon."

"Are you sure you still want to do it?"

"I'm Weston's Lady, remember?" She managed a smile. "If we've got a performance to put on, I'll be ready." .

Reed had never known another woman as brave or as emotionally strong as Libby. His gaze dropped to where she was holding her damaged blouse together. "What about clothes? Do you need something else to wear?"

Libby's expression faltered as she, too, looked down at her ruined blouse. "I could wear one of the boy's shirts, I guess—"

"I'll take a look around town and see if I can find something to replace the blouse. And what about the two drunks? I'll need to talk with the sheriff again. Do you want to press charges against them?"

"Just tell him to keep them locked up until they're sober and warn them if they ever come near me again, I'm going to shoot first and ask questions later." She meant it.

241

"I'll tell him."

Reed started from the room. As he opened the door to leave, she called out to him.

"Reed—"

He looked back at her questioningly.

"Thank you."

Reed simply nodded, gave her a reassuring smile and left. He waited in the hall outside her door until he heard her lock it securely behind him.

Once Reed had gone, Libby stripped off her ruined blouse and went to the washstand. The water was cold, but she didn't care. She was going to feel dirty until she scrubbed every place where those terrible men had touched her. She began to wash, using lots of soap. Glancing up at her reflection, she noticed a bruise forming on the side of her breast, and she trembled as she realized how close she'd come to being seriously hurt. The thought made her scrub twice as hard. She wanted to banish the memory of that horrible attack.

Reed left the hotel and paid a visit to the small clothing store he'd noticed earlier that day. When he emerged a short time later, he was carrying a package of new clothes for Libby. She'd been constantly in his thoughts, and he was coming to understand that she must have had a hard life before she'd joined up with the show. She'd been alone in Los Santos with only the clothes on her back, desperate for a job, and he'd refused to hire her. Reed had to smile at her resilience and determination. There weren't many women who could do what she'd done and still maintain the air of innocence she had about her. Libby was a very special woman.

Reed stopped in at the sheriff's office to relay Libby's decision on handling the two men and to reaffirm the time and place for their demonstration that afternoon.

"Are you sure this is how she wants to handle it?" Sheriff Bruner asked, surprised.

"Yes, but I'd make sure they understand that she's dead serious about shooting first."

"I'll tell them," he said. "After what they tried to do today, I wouldn't blame her."

"Me, either. In fact, I might even help her," Reed told him. "I'll see you about three o'clock at the empty lot by the mercantile."

"I wouldn't miss it. Are you two as good as your handbill says you are?"

"Better," Reed boasted, and with a laugh, he left the sheriff to go back to the hotel and get ready for the performance.

It was a little after two when he went to Libby's room to give her the new clothing. She answered his knock quickly. She was wearing some of the boy's clothing, and he was glad he'd made his purchases.

"Here," Reed said, handing her the package.

"What's this?" She gave him a questioning look.

"I found a few things I thought might fit you. If you don't want them, just let me know, and I'll take them back."

"That was very thoughtful of you." Libby smiled at him.

243

He was pleased that she was happy. "I'll be back to pick you up in about half an hour. That should give us enough time to get set up for our 'show.'"

"I'll be ready and waiting," she promised.

When he'd gone, Libby quickly opened the package. She gasped in surprise and delight at the sight of the garment on top. It was a beautiful fringed white leather split skirt and matching blouse. The workmanship on it was wonderful. She had never seen anything like it before. Reed had also bought her a simple blouse to replace the one that had been ruined. For a moment, Libby allowed herself the pleasure of enjoying the clothing, but then reality returned and she immediately worried about the cost. She was certain the leather outfit was very expensive, and she was bound and determined to reimburse him fully for the expenditure.

Still, for all that she feared she'd never be able to pay Reed back, Libby was unable to resist the chance to wear the white garments. She quickly undressed, then slipped them on and turned to stare at her reflection in the mirror. She smiled. If it were possible, the outfit looked even more lovely on. Libby made up her mind to wear it that very afternoon. She strapped on her gunbelt, checked her revolver to make sure it was loaded, and was ready and waiting for Reed when he knocked on the door a short time later.

"Libby—" Reed said, staring at her in open admiration. The supple leather garments fit her perfectly. "You look beautiful."

"Thank you. I've never owned anything like this before. It's lovely."

"When I saw it, I thought it might look good on you, but I had no idea just how good."

She blushed a little, but was secretly pleased at his compliment. "I'm ready to go, if you are."

"How steady is your gun hand?"

"Like a rock," she reassured him, laughing.

"Good. After the rough morning you had, we don't need any mishaps this afternoon."

A good-sized crowd had gathered at the lot, eagerly waiting for the demonstration to begin. Reed and Libby could hear the buzz of excited conversation as they approached.

"Good afternoon, ladies and gentlemen," Reed began. "I'm Reed Weston, the owner of Weston's Wild Texas Stampede, and this is Miss Liberty Jones, who is also known as Weston's Lady. We've come into town early to give you a taste of the entertainment you can expect from the Stampede when it arrives here in King's Crossing tomorrow night. Our first show will be on Friday afternoon, and we're hoping you'll all come out over the weekend to see us."

"What are you going to do today?" someone called out.

"Liberty and I are going to demonstrate a few of the trick shots we do in the show. Liberty—" He nodded toward her, wanting her to go first.

She smiled at him and waved to those gathered there. "If Mr. Weston will hold up that ace of hearts, I'll show you a little trick I think you might enjoy."

Reed held the card out to the side, away from his body. Libby distanced herself from him. When

245

she was far enough away, she took out a small hand mirror she'd brought with her and turned her back on Reed. She lifted the mirror and took out her handgun.

The crowd fell silent in anticipation of what was to come. The thought that she was going to try to hit something as small as a playing card amazed them. The fact that she was going to do it while taking aim by looking in a mirror thrilled them even more. They waited, collectively holding their breaths, to see how she would do.

"Is the doc around, just in case?" someone called out, and the crowd gave a nervous laugh, then fell silent again.

Libby smiled. With expert precision, she took careful aim in the mirror and squeezed the trigger.

Reed held up the card for all to see, and the crowd erupted into wild, approving cheers as they saw the bullet hole in the middle of the heart.

"As you can see, our Miss Jones is an excellent shot," he told them.

They roared in agreement.

Reed and Libby went on to demonstrate several other shooting techniques. When they had finished, the townspeople came forward to compliment Libby on her ability and to tell them both that they were looking forward to seeing the whole show on Friday.

Gossip about her run-in with the drunks that morning had already spread, and several people came up to make sure she was all right. Libby was touched by their thoughtfulness and thanked them for their concern.

"What do you think? Shall we do the same thing tomorrow or come up with something different?" Reed asked Libby as they made their way back to the hotel.

"Let's think up something new. We want them to know that there's more to the Stampede than just shooting tricks."

"The responsibility is all yours," Reed told her. "I'm open to suggestions. In fact, we can discuss it over dinner tonight, if you want?"

"I'd like that."

"The hotel dining room looks like it serves decent fare. I'll come for you about six o'clock."

"That'll be fine," Libby said, pleased that they would be spending the evening together.

When they reached the hotel lobby, Reed went on up to his room while Libby stopped at the front desk to order a bath to be brought to hers. If she was going out to dinner with Reed, she wanted to look her best. She didn't know why it was suddenly important to her, but it was.

Libby paused. The last time she'd cared about pleasing a man had been that horrible night with John. She firmly pushed the memory away. This was Reed.

She returned to her room and went through her things. She found the gown he'd bought for her in Los Santos. At the time he'd insisted they buy it, she'd questioned the need for it. But now, for tonight, its simple yet elegant style was perfect, and she was actually looking forward to wearing it for him. She found herself hoping he thought she looked pretty.

The bath was hot and luxurious, and Libby enjoyed every minute of soaking in the warm, scented water. She washed her hair and had an hour left before Reed had said he would come for her. Lying down on her bed to relax for a while, Libby felt positively decadent. It had been so long since she'd had the chance to do absolutely nothing this way, she wasn't even sure she knew how anymore.

Libby was determined to give it her best effort, though, and as she lay on the bed, she let her thoughts drift, enjoying the peace and quiet. She thought of how thrilled she'd been when Reed had come to save her that morning. It was a reassuring thing to know that men did exist who were honorable—men like Reed. He was her hero.

Libby smiled to herself as she remembered how angry she'd been with Reed when they'd first met. She'd resented him for not hiring her for the show that night at the Diamondback, and she'd been furious with him for his cold indifference to her. That had changed now, though. Today, he had saved her from certain harm.

Libby remembered how Reed had asked her to trust him that night in the stable and how she'd panicked at the thought. Reed had proven by his actions today that he was nothing like John. He had put himself in harm's way to save her, and she could not imagine John ever doing that. The revelation was liberating. Reed was different—and maybe, just maybe she could trust him.

Excitement filled her, and she got up from the

bed to start to get ready for Reed's arrival. Tonight, she was going to dine with Reed, and she was going to enjoy every minute of their time together.

Chapter Thirteen

"You look beautiful," Reed said, his gaze warm upon Libby as he stood in the doorway.

"Thank you," she told him with a smile as she accompanied him downstairs. She had taken great care with her appearance, and she was most pleased that he'd noticed. "This is a far cry from what Bert would have worn, that's for sure."

"I like Libby's taste better." Reed gave her an easy grin as he escorted her into the dining room.

Libby had been in his thoughts all day, and he was beginning to realize that even though they'd only known each other a short time, there was something very special about her. He knew now that he should have recognized that he'd met his match after their first encounter that night at the Diamondback, but he'd been too caught up in his worries about Steve to think about anything else—

until today. When he'd found her being attacked by the two drunks, he'd realized how much he cared about what happened to her. It had been a revelation—one he was still coming to grips with.

They entered the restaurant and sat at a table near the back. The fare was simple yet delicious, and they both relaxed, enjoying the quiet pace of the evening.

The restaurant was a little crowded when they first arrived. Several of the other people dining there had attended the shooting demonstration that afternoon, and they stopped by their table to compliment them.

"We can't wait for the actual Stampede to show up!" one elderly lady told them excitedly as she clung to her husband's arm. "It's going to be so much fun!"

"Thank you," Reed said, pleased with the response they were getting. "We hope you enjoy it."

"I know we will, if today was any kind of preview of what's actually in the show!"

Libby was watching Reed from across the table. After the couple had gone, she said to him, "You're very good with people."

"My brother, Steve, was better," he told her. "The more I work with the Stampede, the more I realize what a brilliant idea Steve had when he started it up. He built the show into what we have today, and it's turned into a real crowd-pleaser. People from places like King's Crossing and Los Santos don't get the chance to see the bigger shows in the cities, so they're really enthusiastic when we come to town. Steve understood that."

"You sound quite proud of him. Were you close?"

At her question, Reed's easygoing expression darkened. "At one time we were." He paused, remembering. "Then something came between us and—"

"Something—or someone?" she asked astutely.

He glanced up at her. His expression was guarded now. "Someone," he finally answered.

Libby had suspected that would be his answer, and she also suspected who that someone was. "Was it Kathleen? Did she cause your estrangement?" Libby had sensed Kathleen had feelings for Reed.

"Yes. It was Kathleen." He sounded disgusted.

"What happened?"

Reed was quiet for a moment, then looked at Libby. He attempted to smile, but it was more of a grimace. "I've never told anyone the whole story before."

"Why not?" She was truly surprised. Surely his relationship with his brother had been worth fighting for.

"There was no point then. Steve would never have believed me. It would only have made him angry. He honestly loved Kathleen—in the beginning."

"It was that terrible?"

Reed looked at Libby. "I hope I never have to deal with another situation like that again." He shook his head at the memory of that night in the hotel room.

"I understand," Libby said, seeing the pain in his eyes.

"Steve and I had been in town taking care of ranch business for our father. Steve had just told me how much he loved Kathleen and how he planned to propose to her. We had a couple of drinks at the bar and then went back to our hotel rooms." He paused, frowning. "When I entered my room, I found Kathleen waiting for me. I sent her away because I knew how Steve felt about her. I didn't love her, but he did."

"That was a wonderful thing to do." Libby was impressed that Reed had done the honorable thing. She thought of John and knew what he would have done with a willing woman. The thought made her shudder.

"Kathleen didn't think so. She was furious, and she vowed she'd make me regret sending her away. The next morning when I got ready to head back to the ranch, I went looking for Steve and found out that he'd left already. That was strange, but I didn't think too much of it, until he showed up at home a few days later—with Kathleen. They had eloped the same night that she'd come to me."

Libby was amazed at the other woman's conniving ways. "It must have been difficult for you to stay quiet about what happened."

"It wasn't easy, but I knew he loved her. I was hoping it would work out. I was hoping she would be happy with Steve. They stayed on at the ranch for a while. One night, though, Kathleen cornered me and tried to kiss me. Steve walked in on us, and when he demanded an explanation, she lied and told him that I was the one who had gone after her."

"And he believed her?" Libby could see the pain in Reed's expression as he relived the memory.

"He loved her," Reed said simply. "They left the ranch the next day and never came back. It broke my father's heart."

"If your brother hated you so much, how did you end up owning the Stampede?"

"Evidently, Steve eventually realized the truth about Kathleen, but I had no idea until I attended the reading of his will a short while ago. That was when I discovered that he'd left everything to our father and me. The hell of it was, Pa had been dead for some time. I'd sent word to Steve about his funeral, but I never heard from him. At the time, I thought he didn't care, but at the reading of the will, I realized that Kathleen must have intercepted the message and never told Steve the truth."

"I heard she was a cold woman, but I never thought she was vicious, too."

"Vicious—" Reed looked up at Libby, wondering whether he could trust her, wondering if he could tell her the whole truth. Libby hadn't been with the Stampede at the time of Steve's accident, so there was no way she could have been involved in what had happened.

"Now that you're co-owners with Kathleen, you have to deal with her almost every day, don't you? It must be difficult for you."

"It isn't easy, especially since—"

Libby was puzzled when he stopped in mid-sentence. "Since what?"

Reed looked at Libby, and in that moment, he decided to trust her with what he knew. "Since I don't believe Steve's death was an accident."

"What?" Libby's eyes widened in shock at his statement. "I don't understand."

"Besides myself, no one knows what I'm about to tell you except Joe and Ann." He paused.

She waited for him to go on.

"Steve was murdered."

"I don't understand. I thought he fell from his horse during a performance—"

"He did fall, but only because someone had cut his cinch. Someone wanted him dead, but they wanted it to look like an accident," he told her fervently, his eyes aglow with the fierceness of his need to find his brother's killer.

"Oh, God—" She was shocked. "Who would have done such a thing? And why?"

"That's what I've been trying to find out. That's why I've kept the Stampede together just as it was when Steve was alive. Everyone who worked for the show on the night of the accident is still with the show, and I'm going to find the one responsible. Joe's accident was no accident either. The reins were cut. Someone must have realized that he'd found out the truth and was trying to shut him up."

"Do you think it was Kathleen?" Libby was horrified that she could even think such a thing.

"Logically, since she didn't know about the changes in Steve's will, she would have had the most to gain by Steve's death. Or it might have been Lyle. It's my understanding that they were lovers. Either one of them might have wanted him dead. But I have no proof and no witnesses."

"You didn't go to the sheriff in the town where it happened?"

"No. I didn't get Joe's letter until after the Stampede had left that town. He wrote to me and told me of his suspicions. By then, it was too late. There would have been nothing the sheriff could have done, since we couldn't prove anything. So, I'm determined to solve this on my own. I checked with Joe when I arrived to see who would have had access to Steve's horse right before his performance, and Joe said it could have been anyone."

Libby frowned at his statement. "That's strange—unless Joe's changed things since Steve died."

"What's strange?" He looked up at her questioningly.

"As Bert, I worked with the horses. There was only one person in charge of readying the main performers' mounts, and that was me. I made sure everything was ready just before they went out for their part of the show."

Reed was thoughtful. "He must have changed things."

"Joe's very serious about his job. But how could his reins have been cut, too? I was right there with the stage coach until he sent me off to find Shorty. Once we'd located him, Joe fired him on the spot, but there was no time for Shorty to cut the reins in revenge. Who could have done it?"

"I don't know, but I plan to find out."

"I wish I could be more help."

"I just wish I could find the one who did it. Steve was a good man. He didn't deserve what happened to him."

Libby saw the sadness in him as he thought of his brother. "If I see or hear anything that will help you, I'll let you know right away."

"Thanks." Reed nodded. "The longer it goes on, the harder it's going to be to prove anything. I keep expecting the one responsible to make a mistake, to say something incriminating, but so far, I've been coming up empty-handed." He shook his head as he lifted his gaze to Libby's. He suddenly realized how dark their conversation had been, and he feared he'd ruined their evening. "I'm sorry."

"For what?"

"I shouldn't have burdened you with this. We were supposed to be having a pleasant dinner. You've had a difficult enough day."

"I just wish there was something I could do to help."

"I know. I wish I could have done something to save my brother. But it's too late."

"You are helping him," Libby said gently. "You're keeping his dream alive. Without you, the show would have closed. You said yourself, Steve's plan for the Stampede was a wonderful idea. You're making it bigger and better than ever. He'd be proud of you and of the show."

"I'd like to think so. I know he'd like Weston's Lady," he told her, his gaze meeting hers across the table.

She smiled at him and reached out and put her hand on his. "You'll find the one who did it. I know you will."

"I hope you're right." He looked down at her hand on his, wondering how such a simple touch could cause such an immediate reaction in him. He deliberately directed their conversation away from the show. He wanted to know more about her and her family. "What about your brother? What's he like?"

"My Michael's wonderful," Libby told him, slipping her hand away from his. "He's a few years older than I am, and he works for the railroad."

"Do you get to see him very often?"

"As often as he can get away, but he's been real busy lately," she answered, not really lying.

"I'm looking forward to meeting him," he said. "You never did tell me where you grew up."

"Michael and I had a small ranch near Westland."

Reed hadn't been to that part of the state, but he'd heard the grazing lands were good there. "Are your folks still there on the ranch?"

"They died some years ago."

"Are you planning to go back one day?"

At his question, her expression suddenly looked a bit cautious.

Reed was pleased that Libby had told him more about herself tonight than she had in all their previous conversations. He had wanted to win her confidence, and he was making progress, but he could tell it was going to take more time.

"No. There's no reason to. There's nothing for me there anymore."

Reed wanted to know how she'd come to be alone in Los Santos that night, but something in her manner told him not to press her any further right now.

"So you're starting a whole new life for yourself with the Stampede."

"You could say that," she said with a smile, glad that he hadn't asked her any more direct personal questions. "Actually, since I joined the Stampede I've already led two different lives. I was Bert, and now I'm Weston's Lady."

As she said it, Reed smiled at her.

"I'm glad you're Weston's Lady," he said softly.

"So am I," she answered, her gaze lingering on him—on the broad width of his shoulders, on the strong, lean line of his jaw. He was not only a handsome man, he was a hero. He'd proven that today when he'd rescued her in the alley. He had championed her at a time when she thought she'd lost all faith in men.

Libby had thought Reed arrogant before, but now, knowing about his brother's death, she understood his reaction to her at their first meeting. He had cared only about finding the one responsible for Steve's death. He hadn't had time to concern himself with anything else. As she studied him now, she remembered all too clearly the power of his kisses that night in the stable, and she wondered . . .

The waiter's approach ended her fantasy and the intimacy of the moment. They finished eating without saying any more, both sorry that the evening had to come to an end.

Reed had been watching Libby in the flickering lamplight, unable to look away. She was a vision. With her hair styled up and away from her face, she looked like the most elegant of ladies. He remembered all too clearly, though, how much he'd enjoyed brushing out her thick mane of hair just the night before, sitting by the campfire. He almost wished she'd worn it down tonight. His gaze drifted lower to the emerald gown, which fit her perfectly. The bodice was modestly low and hinted temptingly at the fullness of her womanly curves. He would never have dreamed that the wild, gun-toting woman who'd tried to convince him to hire her for the Stampede in Los Santos would turn out to be his "lady," but she had—and he was glad.

"We'd better call it a night," Libby finally suggested, knowing they had another busy day planned tomorrow.

"I know," he agreed reluctantly.

He stood and held her chair for her as she rose. Together, they left the dining room, unaware that others were watching them and thinking them a most handsome couple.

"Thank you for saving me today, Reed. If it hadn't been for your help this morning—" Libby turned to him when they reached the door to her room.

"Shhh," he said quietly. "Let's don't even think about this morning."

"All right," she agreed. She looked up at him then, and her breath caught in her throat at the depth of emotion she saw shining in his eyes.

"Well, good night." Reed stared down at her, unable to look away. Libby was so beautiful, he could no more have left her at that moment than he could have stopped breathing.

"Good night."

There was no one else in the hall, so he bent to her, capturing her lips in a soft exchange. When she returned his kiss without reserve, Reed took her in his arms and clasped her to his heart. Libby gave a soft moan as his mouth moved possessively over hers. She thrilled to his nearness, and a sweet ache grew within her.

Reed's breathing grew ragged at her passionate response. Logically, he told himself there was still much he didn't know about Libby and her past, but none of it mattered right then. All that mattered was that she was in his arms willingly. He wanted her. There was no doubt about it. It was with his last bit of rapidly failing self-control that he broke off the embrace and put her from him.

"You might want to start wearing your gun when you're with me," he said, giving her a lopsided grin.

"Why?" she asked breathlessly, wondering why he'd stopped kissing her and why he'd let her go so abruptly. She had loved being in his arms.

Reed's grin widened as he realized her question was serious. She truly was an innocent. He lifted one hand to touch her cheek. "Good night, Libby. Sweet dreams."

He opened the door to her room for her and waited until she'd gone inside. Once he was certain she was safe, he returned to his own room and got ready for bed.

Reed intended to go straight to sleep. He needed to get some rest, but there was no rest to be found in his solitary bed. His body was on fire with his need for Libby, and no matter how he sought comfort, he found none. With a groan of irritation, Reed got up and dressed again. There was only one cure for what ailed him, and he couldn't have that. He was going to have to satisfy himself with a shot of whiskey at the Royal Flush and maybe a mind-numbing poker game to take his thoughts off the ache in his body.

There were only a few men in the saloon as Reed entered and went to stand at the bar.

"Whiskey—straight," he ordered. He was determined to do some serious drinking, if necessary, to help him get some sleep this night.

"Gee, cowboy, it sounds like you've had a rough day," the bargirl said as she sidled up next to him. She leaned back against the bar, thrusting her bosom out to give him a better view of her cleavage, and smiled.

"You can't imagine," he growled. For a saloon girl, she wasn't unattractive. Had he met her a few months before, he might have been tempted, but he felt no stirring of desire for her.

"Maybe I can help?"

"I don't think so," he told her shortly.

"You never know. You're Reed Weston, aren't you? The owner of the Wild Texas Stampede."

"That's right."

"What do you say I show you how to have a good time tonight?" The girl deliberately ran the tip of her tongue over her lips in a suggestive manner.

Reed picked up the tumbler the barkeep had set before him and downed the liquor in one swig. It was fiery, but it gave him just the jolt he needed to deal with his emotions. "I appreciate your offer, but I'm not interested."

"I can make it real good for you," she pressed, moving a little closer to lean lightly against him. He was a real good-looking man, and she was going to enjoy treating him right.

"I'm sure you could, but I need to get back to the hotel. Here," he said as he handed her enough money to buy herself a drink. "Enjoy."

"Thanks, Weston, but I would have enjoyed having you more than just having a drink."

He gave her an easy smile, but left her. For all that he was sure she could deliver on her promises, he had no interest in bedding her. There was only one woman who interested him, and that was Libby. There was no point in even looking at anyone else.

Libby had gone to bed, but sleep proved elusive. She thought only of Reed and the magic of his kiss. She thought about his advice to start wearing her gun whenever she was with him, and now she understood what he'd meant. He had wanted her.

The knowledge thrilled her, and she freely admitted to herself now that she had wanted him, too. She had never responded to John the way she did to Reed. His kiss had been heavenly. She had loved being in his arms, and she had not wanted him to leave her.

As she lay in the darkness, Libby suddenly knew a driving desire to go to Reed and tell him the truth of her feelings. She got up and began to dress. She paused to look at herself in the mirror and saw how the excitement of thinking about Reed had brought heightened color to her cheeks. After running the brush through her hair, she went to the door and started to open it.

It was at that moment that Libby remembered Reed's tale of how Kathleen had gone to his hotel room, and she stopped, going cold inside. She stood there staring down at her hand on the doorknob, desperately wanting to go to him, but fearing that he would find her actions too brazen, that she would remind him too much of Kathleen.

Want him though she did, Libby knew she couldn't take that risk. She drew a ragged breath and let her hand drop away. She would not go to Reed's hotel room. If he had wanted her with him, he would have told her. He obviously didn't want her, just as he hadn't wanted Kathleen that night so long ago.

A single tear traced a path down her cheek as Libby slowly undressed and went back to bed. Loneliness filled her as she lay down. She longed to sleep, so she could forget, but it was not until the early morning hours that she finally found solace. When she did drift off, her dreams were of Reed and the wonder of his embrace.

*   *   *

Kathleen couldn't wait for the Stampede to get in to King's Crossing. She had been separated from Reed for only a day, but it seemed an eternity to her. For so long she had prayed for a time when they could be together, and finally they were—running the Stampede. Now, if she could only convince him of how much she loved him, her life would be perfect.

The Stampede had been traveling all day and had made camp several hours before. They were not due to arrive in King's Crossing until late the following day. Frustrated and missing Reed, Kathleen knew what she had to do. When darkness fell over the campsite and everyone had bedded down, she crept from her own wagon and went to Reed's. She'd kept a duplicate key to his wagon so she could let herself in.

Kathleen went straight to Reed's bedroom. It was a small area at the back of the wagon, and she sat down on the bed, caressing his still-rumpled sheets. She closed her eyes. In her mind, Reed was there with her, wanting her. She lay back and gave a soft moan as she imagined the ecstasy she would find loving him. She didn't know how long she'd been lying there, when a voice cut through her dreams.

"That's how I love seeing you—ready and waiting for your man," Lyle said in a low voice. He had been on his way to her when he'd seen her leave her wagon. He'd followed her from a distance, for he'd wanted to make sure that no one was watching them. Once he'd been certain that it was safe, he'd quickly slipped inside the wagon after her.

"Lyle!" she gasped, horrified. She'd wanted to be alone with her fantasies of Reed. She hadn't wanted to be with Lyle tonight.

"I always knew you had a wild side to you, but I never knew you liked making love in other men's beds," he said, stripping off his shirt. "I like the way you think. I'm going to enjoy every minute of having you right here on the boss man's sheets."

Kathleen didn't want Lyle. She wanted Reed. She didn't want this to happen, but she was trapped. If she protested, Lyle might get angry. "I didn't know you were watching me."

"I'm always watching you, honey. You're my woman." He dropped his pants and came toward her. "Since Steve's dead I can have you whenever I want you, and I want you now."

She wanted to scream at him that she was not his anything, but she held her tongue. She saw no way out of the situation, so she forced herself to play the role Lyle wanted—difficult though it was going to be, lying in Reed's bed. Lifting her arms, she clasped him to her.

Lyle was ready. Just thinking about Kathleen was enough to get him hot for her. He spread her thighs and buried himself in her. It didn't matter to him that she wasn't ready. He'd worry about taking care of her later. Right now, he needed release, and fast. With a driving pace, he thrust against her, and when he reached the pleasure that he'd sought, he groaned loudly.

"Damn, you're good, woman. I'd do anything for you. You know that, don't you?" He rose to look down at her. The look in his eyes was feverish. "I am so damned glad Steve's out of the way. There's nothing to keep us apart now. Nothing!"

"I know," Kathleen said as she lay unmoving beneath him. She wondered how her secret trip to Reed's bed could have turned into such misery. Determination filled her. She refused to feel used. Keeping her eyes closed, she reached for the man above her, arousing him again. This time it would be her turn to enjoy their coupling. This time, at least in her mind's eye, she would be with Reed.

It didn't take much encouragement to excite Lyle again. He'd always known how much she wanted him. He began to move, ready now to see that she was pleasured, too. He took his time, caressing and kissing her. She grew wanton under him, and he knew he was a good lover. As Kathleen grew more and more bold and demanding, Lyle sought to satisfy her. He had never known her to be so wild before, and he was enjoying every minute of it. He was pounding against her, giving her everything he had as hard as he could, when she cried out.

"Reed!"

Lyle stopped moving, and he wrapped his hands around her throat, threatening to strangle her. "What the hell did you say?"

Kathleen had been so caught up in her dreams of Reed that she'd forgotten herself. Lyle's hands at her throat cut off her breath and shocked her into awareness of what she'd just called out in the heat of their mating.

"Oh, God—"

"Not God, Kathleen!" he snarled, his hands bruising her throat. "You said Reed!"

Her eyes widened in terror as she saw the fury in his expression. "I—I didn't—"

"You sure as hell did, you little bitch! I'm making you, and you're thinking about that bastard?" he said in a cold, deadly voice.

"I love him! I've loved him all my life!" she protested as tears stung her eyes. She knew there was no point in lying any more. "I only married Steve to spite him!"

"You're a fool!" Lyle snarled. "Reed doesn't want you. He doesn't want anything to do with you. If he had, he would have married you years ago."

"I can make him want me!"

He was tempted to beat her within an inch of her life, but instead he tore himself away from her, leaving her lying on the bed, gasping for breath. "You're my woman, Kathleen. No one wants you more than I do. I hope your lover boy appreciates that I just took you in his bed. Maybe I'll tell him when I see him again."

Kathleen was frightened by the fury she could see in Lyle. She remained unmoving as he dressed and left the wagon without speaking to her again. Trembling, she rose and put on her own clothing. She was just starting from the wagon when she saw a letter on the table. The handwriting she recognized as Joe's, and she picked it up, trying to read it in the darkness. There was enough moonlight for her to be able to read most of what was in the letter.

*I am writing to let you know that your brother
is dead, and I don't think it was an accident.
You are the only one I'm telling . . .*

Horror filled her. Joe thought someone had
killed Steve! In a moment of terror, she realized
that she must be one of the suspects, for neither
Joe nor Reed had told her any of this.

Pain stabbed at her heart. She wondered if Joe
really hated her that much—or even Reed. He had
never said a word to her about the possibility that
Steve had deliberately been killed.

Suddenly, her blood ran cold.

Lyle.

The memory of his words returned to torment
her. *I'd do anything for you. You know that, don't
you? I am so damned glad Steve's out of the way.
There's nothing to keep us apart now. Nothing!*

Could Lyle have done it? Would Lyle have done
it?

The questions tormented her. She dropped the
letter back on the table and silently fled Reed's
wagon for what little safety and privacy she had
in her own.

Kathleen was desperate to talk to Reed, but she
couldn't go to him. There was no way to explain
how she had gained the knowledge that Steve had
been killed without admitting that she'd gone
through his personal things. She had thought she
was trapped when Lyle had cornered her in Reed's
bed, but now she was truly caught up in a deadly
web of deceit and lies.

Chapter Fourteen

Sheri smiled up at Brand as they sat next to each other in the stagecoach. They were the only passengers on this leg of their trek from Phoenix to the town of Coyote Run, Texas, where they planned to meet up with the Stampede. The trip was long and arduous, but Sheri knew it would ultimately be worth every inconvenience. Liberty Jones sounded like the perfect heroine, and she couldn't wait to meet her and interview her. Sheri was certain this was going to be a great book.

"I hope we get there in time." Sheri had originally wanted to meet the Stampede in King's Crossing, but it wouldn't be possible to get there before the show left.

"With any luck, we will," Brand told her. He knew how excited she was about starting the research for her next novel.

"I am missing Becky already, though," she remarked, her thoughts drifting to their young daughter. They'd left her behind in Phoenix with Sheri's cousin Maureen, her husband Charles and their young son, Bud, so Sheri could concentrate on her writing while they were away.

"I'm sure she's having quite a time. You know how Maureen and Charles love to spoil her. She's not suffering, that's for sure," he reassured her.

"I know you're right. It's just hard being away from her. I have to admit, though, I am enjoying having you all to myself." Her smile turned sensual as she thought about the long, passionate nights they'd been spending during their travels. Having a young child often prevented intimacy between them, and they were taking full advantage of their time alone.

Brand recognized the welcoming glow in his wife's eyes and didn't hesitate to act on it. He took her in his arms and kissed her.

"I knew I was going to like having this stage coach all to ourselves," he said huskily.

"I do like the way you think," she murmured, reveling in her husband's undivided attention.

Brand drew her across his lap and held her close. He was tempted to do more. They were, after all, alone, but he controlled himself. They were old married folks now. They had to behave themselves.

"New York really thinks a series about a Wild West show will be popular?" He turned his thoughts back to her writing career.

"Oh, yes, especially this particular one—Wes-

271

ton's Wild Texas Stampede with its female star.
Liberty Jones sounds fascinating. She's a sharpshooter and a trick rider. I need to learn as much
as I can about the life she leads with the show."

"You do like doing your research."

"This will be fun, but not as much fun as doing
the research on my first *Brand, The Half-Breed
Scout* novel, all those years ago."

"It's hard to believe it's been almost six years
since you left New York and came out to Fort Mc-
Dowell to do research on me," he said, giving her
a knowing look.

"That was definitely hands-on." She lifted one
hand to his caress his cheek.

"And I loved every minute of it." He looked
down at her, his blue-eyed gaze warm upon her.
He sought her lips in a sweet reward.

"That's what you say now, but you didn't feel
that way back then. As I recall, you were pretty
anxious to send me back to New York," she teased
when they broke apart, breathless.

"You distracted me from my work."

"Good." She kissed him again.

"Yes, it was good," he said gruffly, fighting temptation. He set her away from him.

"You always did have great self-control," she
complained good-naturedly.

"I'm just protecting my wife's reputation."

"And you're doing a fine job, in spite of my ob-
jections."

"I'll make it up to you tonight."

"Promise?"

He turned a steady, hungry gaze upon her. "Promise," he repeated.

"I love having something to look forward to."

"I'm glad I inspire you."

"You definitely are my inspiration," she told him. "Just look at what *Brand, The Half-Breed Scout or Trail of the Renegade* did for my career."

"I am always happy to oblige."

They eagerly awaited the stage's arrival at their overnight stop. It couldn't come too soon.

The crowd broke into enthusiastic applause as the entire cast of the Stampede came out for their final bows. This was the first show in King's Crossing, and the audience had loved every minute of it.

Kathleen stood on the sidelines watching the crowd's reaction to Libby, listening to the thunderous applause for her. It rankled her that Libby was so popular. She longed to be rid of her, but could think of no way to get her out of the show.

Annoyed as Kathleen was by the crowd's love for the other woman, she was even more troubled by the memory of the letter she'd found in Reed's wagon. When they'd reached King's Crossing and had met Reed and Libby again, she had not said a word about her discovery. There was no logical way she could have justified being inside his wagon when he was not there with the show. So she'd kept quiet about what she knew, but the revelation had been haunting her. *Had someone killed Steve? If so, who?*

Memories of Lyle's words during their lovemaking that night would not be ignored—*I'm so damned glad that Steve's out of the way.* Had Lyle been the one? Could he have been the one? Certainly, he had a temper, but was he capable of murder? She could think of no reason for him to want Steve dead. He had had nothing to gain by Steve's death. They were already lovers. But if it hadn't been Lyle, then who had done it?

The questions tormented her. Kathleen had thought Steve's death a tragic accident. She had never hated the man she'd married, she just hadn't loved him, and her lack of feeling for him had taken a toll on the marriage. She would never have wished ill on Steve, but she was not overly sorrowful about being a widow. Her newfound freedom had given her the opportunity to try to win Reed's love again, but things were not turning out as she'd hoped they would—especially not with Libby around.

Disgusted with everything in her life, Kathleen turned away from the sight of Reed and Libby accepting the crowd's adulation. She stalked off across the campgrounds.

"Excuse me, ma'am."

The man's call jarred Kathleen from her thoughts, and she looked up to see a nicely dressed man hailing her.

"What?"

"I was hoping to meet Miss Jones, and I didn't know where would be the best place to speak with her."

"Her tent's over there," she told him, pointing toward Libby's abode.

"Thanks."

Kathleen didn't pay too much attention to the man, except to notice that he had an ugly scar on his cheek. As popular as Libby was, there was no telling who would come to see her. Kathleen went back to her own wagon.

John was elated. In a matter of minutes, he was going to have Libby in his power once again. This coming reunion made every dollar of the substantial reward worth it. He made his way to the tent the woman had pointed out and, after taking a quick look around to make sure no one was watching him, he slipped inside. He stood just inside the door and stared around at Libby's things.

"Well, my sweet fiancée, it looks like you're going to be mine at last," he muttered to himself.

A cruel smile curved his lips. His satisfaction with the situation was mingled with the fury he'd felt during her performance. When he'd seen her throwing the knives, it had been all he could do to control his driving need to attack her right then and there. She was going to pay for what she'd done to his face. He reached up and lightly touched his scar. Very soon, she would pay.

John wanted to laugh out loud, but he controlled the urge. Later, he would celebrate his good fortune in tracking her down. Right now, he had to figure out how to corner her and get her away from the Stampede. The tent was too flimsy for the reunion he had in mind. Every word they said could be overheard, and he didn't want that.

He had to find a more private area, where he could get her alone.

Sneaking from her tent, John made his way to where the performers exited from the parade ground. He found a secluded spot and waited there for Libby to pass by. He would follow her and find the opportunity he needed. He could afford to be patient. He knew exactly what he wanted, and he would do whatever was necessary, wait as long as it took, to achieve that goal—getting Libby back.

Libby had been feeling uneasy all evening. She told herself she was just imagining things, but every now and then she got the feeling that someone was watching her. Which, of course, was true. The entire audience was watching her. She kept smiling through the show, and she was pleased that the performance went smoothly. Now, as they rode from the arena area, however, she was glad the night's show was over.

"I'm going to visit Joe for a while. I'll speak with you later," Reed told Libby as they dismounted near the stables.

"Do you want me to take Raven for you?" Mark asked as he came up to take the reins of Reed's horse.

"No, I'll tend to him myself tonight. Thanks," she said, leading her own horse into its stall.

"Let me know if you need anything," Mark said as he moved off.

Libby unsaddled Raven and began to brush him

down. It was a calming, mindless job that she enjoyed.

John waited, staying out of sight, biding his time. He watched until most of the crowd had dispersed and the stable area appeared deserted. He had seen Libby go in, but he hadn't caught sight of her coming out. He knew this was his chance. He was going to claim her for his own now. He touched his gun reassuringly. He had worn it beneath the jacket he'd donned, and he knew he could get to it easily should the occasion arise.

Quietly, John passed through the maze of stalls, searching for some sign of Libby. He was confident he hadn't missed her, and the farther he had to go, the better he felt. He wanted to get her alone, and he wanted to catch her unawares. He wanted to see her expression when they came face-to-face again.

And then he found her.

John smiled in victory. He wanted to grab her and drag her bodily out of there, but he fought down the need to physically overpower her. Someone would see them and try to stop him. When they left together, it had to look as if she was going willingly.

"Hello, my love," he said in a low voice, meant for her ears only.

"John!"

Libby's blood ran cold at the sound of his voice, and she knew that her sense of foreboding had been right. She spun around to face him, the brush she'd been holding flying from her hand as she went for her gun.

277

"Don't even think about it," he snarled, his own sidearm already drawn and aimed straight at her. He reached over and grabbed her gun, tossing it aside, out of her reach.

"What do you want?" Libby demanded, her heart pounding wildly. She had been terrified that this moment would come, and now that it finally had, she was facing her worst nightmare. John had found her. She told herself she would not panic.

"I never thought you were stupid, my dear," he sneered. "You know what I want. I've come to claim what's mine."

"I don't know what you're talking about." She backed a little away from him. "I left the ring at Madeline's. You have no claim on me."

He closed in on her, madness shining in his eyes. "I'm not letting you get away from me again."

He reached up and touched her cheek, tracing an invisible line down her face that matched the gash on his. When she visibly shuddered at his touch, he smiled.

"Look at my face, Libby. See what you did to me? I'm going to make you pay for this. I'm going to cut you just as you cut me!"

"I'm glad I cut you! I should have aimed for your heart instead!"

John laughed softly, dangerously. "You are such an amusing little slut, but I'm growing weary of your bravado. Since I no longer have anyone interested in buying you, I'll just have to keep you for myself. I plan to enjoy every minute of our time together."

"I'm not going with you. I'm staying right here with the Stampede."

"They're not going to want you. Once I'm through with you tonight, you won't be anyone's star! I want you to suffer as I've suffered. I'm going to make you sorry you ever thought of using that letter opener on me." He took a menacing step toward her.

"I'll never be sorry I cut you, but I will always regret that I didn't have my gun that night. If I'd had it, you wouldn't be here right now! You'd be dead!"

He merely gave her a knowing look. "Well, you didn't have it, and I am here right now. Let's go. I am your betrothed, and you are coming with me."

"I'll scream!"

"Go ahead," he said indifferently. "There's no one around to hear you. I made sure of it before I came back here to get you. So let's be on our way, darling. There's so much I want to do to you once I've got you alone!"

"I don't know who you are, but Libby's not going anywhere with you," Reed ground out as he came upon the stranger holding a gun on Libby. He had drawn his own gun and was ready for trouble. He'd always known that one day the secrets from Libby's past would come back to haunt her. It looked as though he'd been right.

"That's where you're wrong, *friend*," John said coolly, not taking his gaze off Libby. "I'm Libby's fiancé. Isn't that right, darling? We had a slight disagreement some weeks ago, and I've been searching for her ever since. Now that I've found her, I've come to take her back home with me where she belongs."

Reed cast a quick glance over at Libby and saw the terror in her eyes. He instinctively knew that this man was the reason she'd been so desperate to find a job back in Los Santos. This man was the reason she'd come to him with only the clothes on her back. Reed had no idea what had happened between them, but he would not allow her to face her fears alone.

It came as a revelation to him that he loved Libby, and he would do whatever was necessary to keep her safe. She was obviously too proud to ask for his help, but she was going to get it anyway.

"Ah, but Libby *is* home. The Stampede is her home now," he said quietly.

"You're wrong. My name is John Harris. Libby and I are engaged, and we're going to be married. See, I have her ring right here." He dug in his pocket and pulled out a large diamond. "So it's time for her to come with me now."

"You're the one who's wrong." Reed didn't waiver in his defense of her. "There's no way Libby can be your fiancée."

"Why not?" he demanded.

"Because she's married to me."

"What!" John roared, his shock real.

"Why do you think she's called Weston's Lady? Libby's my wife, so I'd appreciate it if you'd put that gun away and back out of here. My wife isn't going anywhere with you."

"You're lying! She isn't wearing any ring!"

"Tell him, Libby."

"I'm married to Reed, John. We just haven't had time to get a ring yet."

John blanched at the news, his hatred eating him alive. He was tempted to shoot her right then and there, but he knew he'd be dead in the next instant, and he valued his own life much more than any desire for revenge.

"If I ever see your face around the Stampede again, Harris, I'll make sure you're locked up for quite some time."

John turned to Libby, his fury plain to see. "This isn't over, my dear!" he threatened. "One day when you least expect it, I'm going to come for you, and your husband here isn't going to be able to save you. Remember that!"

"Are you threatening my wife?" Reed thundered. "Mark!"

Mark heard his call and came running. "What is it?" He looked between Reed and the stranger, wondering what was going on.

"Mark, escort Mr. Harris out of here, before I decide to shoot him and he has to be carried to the undertaker's. And I'll take that gun," Reed commanded.

Mark quickly disarmed John and handed Reed the weapon.

"Now, get the hell out of my show, Harris, and don't ever come back—if you value your life."

John glared at Reed Weston, hating him. "I'll see you again, Weston! You, too, Libby! You can count on it!"

"Take him into town, Mark," Reed said, disgusted. "Make sure he's got a ticket on the next outbound stage."

Mark dragged the cursing John away. Only when they were out of sight did Reed turn back to Libby. He slowly holstered his gun and opened his arms to her.

Libby flew into his arms and clung to him. She was trembling and hid her face against his chest. She had been strong for so long, but suddenly she couldn't help it. She began to cry.

Reed felt her shudder and held her even closer. He reached down with a gentle hand and lifted her chin so he could see her face. "Libby? Are you all right?"

"I am now," she managed, trying to smile but failing miserably.

Emotion surged through Reed at the sight of her distress. He thanked God that he'd returned when he had, or Harris might have taken her away from him. He pressed a gentle kiss to her cheek.

"I think it's time you told me the truth," he said solemnly.

"I know." She nodded and moved away from the protective shelter of his arms. It had felt so good to have his strength to rely on that she felt a little lost. She drew a ragged breath and tried to calm her fears.

Reed picked up her gun and handed it back to her, then kept a supportive arm around her as they walked slowly back to his wagon. Neither spoke again until they were inside, sitting at the small table facing each other, a single low-burning lamp illuminating the room.

"You were engaged?" Reed asked quietly.

Libby looked up at him, knowing she had to tell him the truth, but dreading it. "Yes."

"What did he do to you?" He knew it was a sordid story, but he wanted to help her. He wanted to do whatever he could to make her life easier.

Her expression was haunted for a moment. "I was such an innocent. I thought he loved me, but now I realize how silly I was to believe his lies."

"Why? You're a beautiful woman. I can't imagine a man not falling in love with you," he said fiercely.

"No, you don't understand. John's the banker in Jung's Station, my home town. My brother and I owned only a small ranch. When Michael got the job with the railroad, he had to leave and I couldn't go with him. That was when John suddenly proposed to me." She paused, remembering how starry-eyed she'd been. "I was so enamored of him. I couldn't believe he loved me. I was so thrilled that I said yes right away."

Reed reached across the table and took her hand in his. "But did you love him?"

Libby lifted her gaze to his, and he could see her torment.

"At first I thought I did. John swept me off my feet. It all happened so fast, and it was so wonderful that the handsomest, richest man in town had proposed to me. John wanted me to come into town to live. He said it wasn't proper for me to stay alone at the ranch, so he arranged for me to move in with a friend of his. Madeline is one of the pillars of society in town. I was to live with her until we were married. The wedding was scheduled for the week after our bans were posted." She sighed wearily. "Everything went perfectly—for a while. John came to see me regularly, and then—"

In her mind, all the horrible memories of that night returned, and she went pale. Reed tightened his grip on her hand.

"It's all right, Libby. You're safe with me."

She looked up at him, tears filling her eyes. "I know." She paused to gather her thoughts, then went on. "I was so excited that John had arrived. I hurried downstairs to see him. That was when I heard his conversation with Madeline though the closed door. They didn't know I was there, and I found out the truth about what he really planned to do with me."

"What?" Reed couldn't imagine.

"I was right to have my doubts about him loving me. He didn't. He had just seen an opportunity and had taken advantage of it."

"I don't understand." He was frowning.

"John planned to sell me to another man."

"What!" He was shocked.

Libby blushed and felt awkward and embarrassed as she explained to him, "Evidently John knew a man who would pay to bed a—virgin."

Reed tensed visibly at her words, knowing that if Harris had been there at that moment, he would have shot him.

"John had made all the arrangements to sell me to this man. If I hadn't listened at the door that night, I would never have known." She looked up at him. "He and Madeline caught me listening. He dragged me into the study and—"

Reed quickly stood and went to her side of the small table. He pulled her to her feet so he could hold her, and Libby did not resist. She went to him willingly and was enfolded in his embrace. She'd known in the stable that this was where she longed to be. Being in Reed's arms was her haven—and her heaven.

"You don't have to tell me any more, if you don't want to," he told her gently.

"No, it's important that you understand everything that happened," she went on. "He started to attack me, and I managed to get away from him, and then I found a letter opener on the desk. I cut him with it when he came at me again."

"I'm proud of you." Reed wrapped his arms more tightly around her as he imagined her fighting off the other man. He had never known a woman as brave as Libby. "How did you manage to get away from him?"

"They locked me in my room that night. He told me he was going to take me to the other man the very next day. I knew I had to escape, so I took only my gun and the clothes I had on. I climbed down the tree outside my window and managed to get away. I'd been on the run for days when I finally met up with you in Los Santos."

Reed gave a low groan, remembering how he'd treated her. He cupped her face with his hands and looked down at her. "Oh, God, sweetheart, I'm sorry. If I had known—"

She shook her head. "It's all right now."

Reed found himself half smiling at her brave words. "It is, isn't it?"

Without saying anything more, he claimed her lips in a cherishing exchange. Libby lifted her arms and looped them around his neck. She returned his kiss in full measure. Reed had never known such ecstasy. He parted her lips and deepened the kiss. Crushing her to him, he savored her nearness. She was a spirited woman, a courageous woman. He had never known anyone like her. Having her in his arms was pure bliss for him. When she moved restlessly against him, he wanted more—needed more.

Reed bent and scooped Libby up in his arms. They stared at each other as he carried her to his bed and laid her upon its welcoming softness. He followed her down, covering her body with his own, reveling in the glory of her nearness. She fit against him perfectly, and he sought her lips once more, tasting her sweetness.

Libby was lost in a haze of sensual pleasure. She hadn't been certain of her feelings until now. This was Reed. He had confronted her demons for her and protected her from the ugliness of her past. She loved him. She held him close, feeling as though she could never get enough of him. His lips left hers to seek the softness of her throat, and she eagerly arched to him, thrilled by the sensations the touch of his mouth was arousing in her. She gave a soft, rapturous moan.

Reed heard her moan, and heat pounded through him. He sought the fullness of her breasts with a gentle caress. Unbuttoning her blouse, he slipped the garment from her shoulders and brushed the straps of her undergarment down, baring her breasts to his kisses.

"Oh, Reed—" she gasped, having never known such intimacy before. She clung to him, seeking the hardness of him, wanting to be closer to him, wanting more.

He rose to claim her lips again.

"I love you, Libby," he told her, the words a hoarse whisper against her mouth.

She opened her eyes to gaze up at him, all the love she felt for him shining in her eyes. "I love you, too."

They stared at each other for a long moment, treasuring the sweetness of their declaration.

Libby made the first move, reaching up for Reed and drawing him back down to her, offering herself to him. There had been a time when she thought she would never trust again. There had been a time when she thought she would never fall in love, but Reed had changed all that.

Reed went to her, caressing her, kissing her. The fire of his need was building, and he wanted nothing more than to bury himself deep within her welcoming heat. This was Libby. Only she could satisfy the burning ache within him.

Reed could have surrendered to his need. He could have taken her right then. He could have made love to her all night, but the memory of her story about John's betrayal helped him keep himself under control. She had been hurt once. He would not be the one to hurt her again.

Drawing a shuddering breath, he went still. It

took all his willpower not to continue. God knew he wanted her, but she had been through too much for him to take advantage of her innocence. He loved her and respected her, and he was going to treat her like the lady she was.

"Reed?" she said his name softly, wanting him to kiss her again, not understanding why he'd stopped. She'd been enjoying his kisses and his touch, and she wanted more. She caressed him, her hands sculpting the muscles of his back and moving lower to his hips, innocently urging him on.

"Libby, don't."

"Don't?" She stopped, shocked that he didn't want her to touch him. Suddenly, she feared that he didn't want her at all, and tears welled up in her eyes at the humiliating realization.

He saw the look on her face and gave a guttural groan. "Ah, love, don't cry. It's not that I don't want you. It's that I want you too much. There's nothing I want to do more than make love to you right now, but I'm not going to."

She could only stare up at him in confusion.

"Libby, I won't use you this way. Not after what happened to you with John. You deserve better."

"But I love you, Reed."

"I know, sweet, and I love you. Will you marry me? Tonight? There's a justice of the peace just a little ways out of town. We could leave right now."

"Oh, Reed," she gasped at his ardent proposal, but she didn't believe he meant it. "You don't have to marry me just because you told that lie to John."

He frowned. "That's not why I'm proposing to you."

"It's all right, really."

"It's not all right. John had nothing to do with my proposing. I love you, Libby, and I want you with me all the time. Marry me. Now. Tonight."

Libby gazed up at him, cherishing the fierce look of devotion on his face. "I love you, Reed Weston."

"Prove it," he demanded.

She slipped a hand behind his neck and gently urged him down to her. Her mouth met his in a delicious kiss that held the promise of heavenly delights to come.

"We'd better hurry," she whispered against his lips. "It's getting late."

They got up from the bed, and Reed began to help her with the buttons on her blouse. It was difficult for him to cover that sweet flesh, though, and his progress was slow. Each button that he fastened required a kiss, and he was becoming distracted from his original purpose.

"If you keep this up, we may never leave the wagon," Libby told him, as she arched against the heated brand of his mouth at her throat.

"Mmmm . . ." he responded, hating the thought that he had to let her go.

"We can stay here if you want," she offered.

Libby gave a throaty chuckle as Reed finished the last button and put her away from him.

"Let's ride, woman. We've wasted too much of the night already."

Chapter Fifteen

"I now pronounce you man and wife," said Art Lansing, the justice of the peace, as he stifled a yawn and smiled at the happy couple standing before him. "You may kiss your bride."

Reed needed no further encouragement. He gathered Libby to him and sought her lips in a tender exchange.

"Congratulations, Mr. and Mrs. Weston."

"Thank you."

They left his home and started back to the campgrounds. The ride to the justice's small cottage had seemed an eternity to Reed and Libby, but going back, the miles flew, and they were glad. They couldn't wait to get to the wagon and start their honeymoon.

Reed had considered taking her to the hotel in town for the night, but he feared they might run into John. He wasn't sure what he might do to the man if he saw him again—especially after hearing Libby's story.

Reed had never thought the sight of the Stampede's tents and wagons would thrill him, but tonight they did. They were back. They were home.

After quickly tending to their horses, Reed put his arm around Libby, and they walked quietly to his wagon. Before Libby could say a word, he lifted her in his arms and carried her up the few steps and over the threshold.

"Tomorrow, we'll go into town and I'll buy you a ring," he promised as he set her on her feet and closed the door.

"It doesn't matter."

"Yes, it does," he growled, holding her close. "I want everyone to know that you're mine."

Libby looked up at him and smiled tenderly. "I love you, Reed."

Determined to show her how much he loved her, too, he didn't say a word. He simply took her hand and led her back to the bedroom.

Libby suddenly felt a bit shy. They were married. The realization was exciting—and a little frightening. She wasn't sure what she was supposed to do, and her uncertainty showed in her expression.

"Don't worry, love," Reed said in a gentling tone. "You're mine now. I'll never let anything or anyone ever hurt you again."

"Oh, Reed—" It had been so long since she'd felt safe. His words were just what she needed to hear, and she went to him, offering herself to him, wanting only to love him and be loved.

They began to undress. The need they'd felt for each other had grown with time, and they were both eager to know the glory of their wedded union.

Libby slipped beneath the covers, a little embarrassed to be so unclad before him. But Reed would have none of it. He went to her and drew away the blanket.

"You're too beautiful to hide from me," he told her, his voice deep with emotion as he gazed down at her. Her breasts were high and firm, her waist was small enough to be spanned by his hands and her legs were long and shapely.

"Do you really think so?" She saw the flame in his eyes and smiled slightly. She had never been this way with a man before, and she wanted to please him.

"You're perfect, Libby."

Reed still was wearing his pants, and, sensing how nervous she seemed to be, he decided not to shed them just yet. He stretched out beside her and pulled her to him. The touch of her silken flesh against him fired the heat of his desire, and he knew he was going to be hard-pressed not to hurry their lovemaking.

"I love you," he told her as his lips found hers.

That first kiss was all it took to ignite the firestorm of their passion. There would be no stopping this time. There would be only shared love and pure ecstasy.

Reed's hands were restless as he traced arousing

paths over her satiny curves. Libby responded with an untutored ardency that thrilled him more than the techniques of any practiced seductress. His mouth left hers to seek the sweetness of her throat and then moved lower to press hot kisses to her breasts. She gave a throaty purr as he explored that sensitive flesh, and she arched sensuously to the plunder of his lips. Her unspoken invitation urged him on. He slipped his hands down to caress her hips and thighs. She began to move against him in an instinctive, age-old rhythm.

Leaving the bed for a moment, Reed stripped off his pants and went back to her. Libby's eyes rounded at the sight of him so unclothed, but then she smiled in womanly welcome.

"You're beautiful, too," she said, admiring the powerful width of his chest and shoulders, the leanness of his waist and the male strength of him. She reached for him, eager to know more.

Reed fit himself to her, molding their bodies together. The touch of him against her was so foreign to Libby that she was surprised for an instant, but then she relaxed and opened to him as a flower to the sun. He was strong and hot and all male, and she wanted him. She wanted this. He moved between her thighs, seeking out the womanly heart of her. As he positioned himself to make her his own, Libby gasped at the invasion.

"I'm sorry," Reed told her. He kissed her and went still, waiting for the pain to ease, waiting for her to accept him more fully.

"I'm not," she said, gazing up at him, thinking

she had never seen a more handsome man—and he was her husband. She didn't know how fate had brought her to this magnificent moment, but she was thrilled. As dangerous as her life had been since she'd fled John, this night in Reed's arms made it all worthwhile. Reed loved her. He had truly made her "his lady." "Love me," she whispered, encouraging him to move.

At her sensual command, Reed could no longer deny himself. He began his rhythm, catching her up in his passion, taking her to ecstasy and beyond. Libby had never known such intimacy and she reveled in it. She caressed him, seeking to please him as he was pleasing her. His response was exciting and urged her to even greater boldness. A thrilling tension grew within her as she gave herself over to Reed's mastery, and when passion's promise crested within her, she cried out his name. The knowledge that he'd pleasured her took him to the heights as well. He strained against her as he, too, reached love's pinnacle.

They lay together in ecstasy's aftermath, their bodies still one, their limbs entwined. Neither had ever known such joy before. Reed cradled her to him, his hands tracing worshipful paths over her body. Libby clung to him, treasuring their closeness. They rested, secure in the fullness and completion of their love.

"I knew loving you would be wonderful, but I didn't know it would be this wonderful," Libby finally told him.

"Neither did I. If I had, I would have done something about it sooner."

Her head was resting on his chest, and she loved the rumbling sound of his voice as he spoke. "I almost went to you at the hotel the other night."

He glanced down at her, surprised. "You did?"

"I was ready to go to your room, but then I remembered what you'd told me about that night in the hotel with Kathleen, and I didn't want you to think that I was anything like her."

He gave a soft laugh. "You're nothing like Kathleen, but it's good that you didn't go to my room. I wasn't there."

"You weren't?" She was surprised and lifted her head to look at him questioningly.

"No. I tried to sleep after I left you, but I was wanting you too much. I ended up in the bar, drinking for a while."

"I'm sorry."

"Don't be. It made me realize a few things, especially after one of the bargirls propositioned me."

"She did?" She was instantly jealous.

"Yes, but I turned her down. I realized as I was talking to her that there was only one woman I wanted, one woman I needed, and that was you, sweetheart. I love you."

"I love you."

Libby shifted her position so she could kiss him, and Reed crushed her to his chest. His desire was reignited, and they came together in a mating that was as fast as it was explosive. They reached passion's peak together and collapsed into each other's arms, sated and exhausted.

"I'm glad you turned down that bargirl," Libby said breathlessly.

He kissed her. "There was never any doubt."

They lay together, enjoying the newness of their love and the thought of what the future held for them. They loved long into the night, falling asleep only as dawn's first light brightened the eastern sky.

Kathleen was up with the dawn. All night, her dreams had been haunted by visions of Steve. She'd awakened more frustrated and angry than ever before. Nothing in her life was turning out as she'd hoped it would. Unless she could find a way to win Reed away from Libby, her future stretched bleak and empty before her.

After dressing, Kathleen wandered about her wagon. She had not spoken with Lyle since the other night and that was fine with her. The farther away from her he stayed, the better. She feared he might have been the one who had harmed Steve, and she wanted nothing more to do with him. All his protestations of love and devotion meant nothing to her. He meant nothing to her.

Her mood was black as she left her wagon and looked around. She hated the Stampede with an ever-growing passion and longed to be away from the show. Until Reed got the money to buy her out or until she could find another buyer for her part of the ownership, she was stuck with nowhere else to go.

That thought didn't sit well with Kathleen. She wondered how much longer she could stomach watching Reed with Libby. It was infuriating, watching them together. *Weston's Lady*. She sneered at the thought. *Weston's Whore* was more like it, she thought smugly. She admitted freely that she hated the other woman. Libby had the one thing in this world that she wanted—Reed.

Kathleen glared at Libby's tent as she walked past it. She honestly believed there had to be some way to rid the show of her unwelcome presence.

In her fantasy, Kathleen pictured herself alone with Reed, convincing him that she loved him. But she knew it was just that—a fantasy. And so her dark mood remained as she made the rounds of the camp ground to make sure everything had gone well overnight.

Libby awoke first, and she lay quietly beside Reed, studying him while he slept. In slumber, there was an almost youthful look to his features. He seemed younger, less guarded. The hard line of his jaw was eased, and he was smiling slightly as he slumbered on, unaware of her loving scrutiny. Libby hoped he was smiling because he was dreaming of the night just past. She let her gaze drift lower, across the broad, heavily muscled expanse of his chest and then even lower to the blanket's edge that shielded that most manly part of him from her view.

Heat burned her cheeks as she realized just how brazen she was being, but she told herself it was all right, for she was looking at her husband. Reed was hers. And she did love him so.

As she was gazing at him, his eyes opened, and

her blush deepened even more at having been caught.

"Good morning," he said in a sleep-husky voice. A thrill went up her spine.

"Good morning," she returned, suddenly realizing that she was lying next to him completely unclothed, with the blanket covering her only to her hips.

"This is the most beautiful morning view I've ever awakened to," he murmured, reaching out to pull her down to him. His lips sought her breasts as she shivered in sweet anticipation of what was to come.

The idea of making love in the daylight shocked Libby. She would have said something, but his lips were too persuasive, his touch too enthralling. Caught up in the excitement of loving him again, she cast all her cares to the wind and gave herself over to his expert guidance. She gloried in his coming to her, and she cried out her love for him as he took her to the peak of excitement and beyond.

"What a wonderful way to wake up," she sighed, holding his head to her breasts and savoring the joy of having him in her arms.

"We can arrange to make this a daily practice, if you'd like," he offered with a wicked grin.

"I'd like!" she agreed, giving him a quick kiss. "We'd better get up, don't you think?"

"No," Reed groaned. "I want to stay right here with you for the next six months. We can have one of the boys bring us food occasionally, and the rest of the time they can just leave us alone."

"I like the way you think, Mr. Weston, but I do believe you'd be missed in the Stampede."

"No, I wouldn't. No one would think twice if I didn't show up, but they certainly would miss you if you didn't. You're my star, you know, Mrs. Weston."

"I think I like being your star."

"I like you being my wife better."

"Really? Why is that?"

"Do I have to show you?" he complained with a smile, the fire of his desire shining in his eyes.

"I guess you do."

It was some time later when they finally left the bed. They did so regretfully, but knowing it was time to start tending to Stampede business. As much as they would have liked the real world to go away, there would be no hiding from it.

"Reed?" Libby said his name quietly as she finished dressing, donning her pants, blouse and vest. She had managed to forget about John during the long, hot, dark hours of the night, but now that she faced the light of day, the memory of last night's confrontation returned.

"What?" He glanced her way and saw her troubled expression. "What's wrong?"

"I just wanted to thank you for coming back for me when you did last night. I don't doubt a word of what John said, and you saved me from him." Libby went to Reed and pressed a gentle kiss to his cheek.

"I don't want you to worry about him anymore. He was very brave when he was cornering a defenseless female, but I doubt he'd be anywhere near that brazen if he had to deal with a man."

"But I'm not a—" She started to protest that she wasn't defenseless, but he stopped her.

"Men like Harris are cowards. A real man would never do the things he's done. From now on, he'll have to get through me to get to you, and that's not going to happen. I'm going to protect you, Libby—with my life. You're safe now."

She kissed him again and sighed. "I know. For so long, I couldn't trust anyone, but now—"

"Now you have me, and I don't think we're ever going to see Harris again."

"I hope you're right."

"Mark took care of things for us last night. With any luck, John caught the first stage out of King's Crossing this morning."

"If he did, life would be perfect."

"You mean it's not perfect now?" Reed gave her a mock-hurt look.

"You're right. It is perfect now. I just married my hero."

He kissed her one last time. "We'd better see about business, and I suppose it would be a good thing to make our big announcement at practice this morning."

"I'll go back to my tent and start moving my things in here with you. Then I'll meet you in front of the grandstand."

Reed was tempted to kiss her one last time, but he knew if he did, they probably wouldn't get around to taking care of business for another hour or so, and it was well into the morning already.

Libby started from the wagon, her heart light,

her mood happy. It had been so long since she'd allowed herself to relax and enjoy life, but today she was going to do just that. She felt almost giddy as she stepped out into the sunshine. It was a perfect day. Reed loved her. She smiled to herself and headed off toward her tent, unaware that Kathleen was coming her way.

Kathleen saw Libby coming out of Reed's wagon wearing the same clothes she'd had on the night before. She also saw the look on her face. If ever she'd seen a woman who'd just spent the night with a man and was quite pleased about it, it was Libby. Emotions Kathleen had long managed to suppress erupted. She charged forward to confront the woman who was ruining her life.

"How dare you flaunt yourself so blatantly coming out of Reed's wagon!" she shouted, no longer caring who heard.

Libby had been caught up in her dreams of the future and was not prepared for a confrontation with Kathleen. "Kathleen, I—"

"You slut!" With all the power she could muster, she slapped Libby.

The force of her blow sent Libby sprawling. She'd known Kathleen was a cold woman, and she was certain she didn't like her, but she'd never expected that Kathleen might physically attack her.

"How dare you spend the night with Reed? He's mine! You might be Weston's Lady in the Stampede, but I'm the woman he loves! I'm the one he's going to marry!" Kathleen stormed, completely losing control. "I lost him once years ago, but I will not let him get away from me again! I have

301

suffered enough for one lifetime being married to Steve. Reed is mine! You stay away from him!"

The sound of her shrieks disrupted the quiet of the morning, and some of the others came running to see what was wrong.

Reed had just finished dressing when he heard the commotion and opened the door to see Libby getting back to her feet, wiping blood from the corner of her mouth. He suddenly feared that John had returned, and he was reaching for his gun as he stepped out of the wagon. It was then that he saw Kathleen. She looked like a wild woman as she stood before Libby, hands on her hips.

"You are nothing but a low-class whore!" Kathleen screamed.

"You're wrong, Kathleen," Libby told her, trying to stay calm as she got back to her feet.

"I know a slut when I see one! I won't have this kind of behavior going on in the Stampede!" she shouted. "I'm firing you right now! Get your things and get the hell out of my show!"

Fury filled Reed. He had tolerated Kathleen for as long as he could, but this was the end. He stepped from the wagon. "I run this Stampede, Kathleen. You have no power to fire anyone without my approval, and you're not ordering Libby to do anything."

He went to Libby and slipped an arm about her. She glanced up at him.

"You all right?"

She nodded in response.

"There's something you need to know," he ground out as he faced Kathleen.

Kathleen glared at the sight of his arm so protectively around Libby. *She* was the one he should be holding and helping! *She* was the one who needed his support and love. Not Liberty. She was almost beyond reason as she lifted her gaze to his.

"Libby and I were married last night."

All color drained from Kathleen's face, and she began to shake as she stared at the two of them. It seemed she'd been waiting her whole life for Reed to realize how much he truly loved her, and now this little tramp had stolen him!

"That's ridiculous," Kathleen said, refusing to believe him. "Libby's a tramp! Why would you marry her when you know how much I love you? I never loved your brother. You know you were the one I was meant to marry. I only married Steve to spite you—"

From the back of the crowd that had gathered, Ann's screams of outraged fury interrupted Kathleen. She came running toward them. "Kathleen! You bitch! I hate you!"

Reed and Libby watched her approach. There was a madness in Ann's eyes, and a tenseness about her that was almost frightening. She seemed completely unaware of anyone but Kathleen.

Ann stopped before Kathleen, glowering at her with a hate-filled gaze. "How can you talk to Libby that way when you are worse than the lowest streetwalker!"

Kathleen sensed the insanity in Ann, and she

303

took a step back away from her. "This has nothing to do with you. Go away! You're acting crazy!"

"You're damned right I am!" Ann screamed. "I can't stand it any more, and I'm not going away. This has everything to do with me. You ruined Steve's life. You never loved him. But I did! I loved him. I loved him more than life itself." She was sobbing.

Kathleen shot her a disparaging look as she sneered, "If you loved him so much, then why didn't you just take him? I didn't want him. You could have had him—with my blessings!"

At her words, Ann grew even more deranged. *"Because he loved you,"* she cried. "I begged him to leave you, but he wouldn't. I told him how much I loved him, how much he meant to me, but he wouldn't divorce you. He knew what a tramp you were, and he forgave you!"

Kathleen shrugged. "What does it matter now anyway? Steve's dead."

Ann went completely still at her words, and then in a violent move threw herself bodily at Kathleen. Her hands closed around the other woman's throat. Kathleen tried to fight her off, but she had little luck against her mindless madness.

"I hate you! You're the reason Steve's dead," Ann was screaming. "You were the one who was supposed to die that night. Not Steve! You were supposed to be riding that horse. I wanted *you* dead! Not Steve. I loved him!"

"Oh, my God!" Reed and Libby looked at each other as the horrendous truth was revealed to them.

Lyle had been drawn to the scene by the sound of Kathleen's shouts, and he ran to rescue her from Ann's attack. Mark grabbed Ann around the waist and hauled her away from the other woman.

"I hate you, Kathleen! I hope you rot in hell for all the pain you've caused all these years," Ann continued to yell as she fought Mark's hold with all her might.

"What are you saying?" Reed demanded, confronting Ann as Mark restrained her.

"I wanted *her* to die that day!" She looked at Kathleen as she strained against Mark's iron grip. "Not Steve! I would never have hurt Steve. I loved him! I only wanted him to be happy! That's why I wanted her dead. If she were dead, then he would love me."

"Somebody go for the sheriff," Reed ordered tersely.

One of the hands hurried off to make the ride into town.

Reed stared at Ann, knowing she was out of her mind. She was the one who had cut Steve's cinch that day. She was responsible for his death. His jaw tightened as he fought for control. "What about your father's accident? Why did you cut his reins?"

"Papa's reins? No—I didn't cut his reins—" She looked totally confused at his question.

Mark made the mistake of easing his grip on her when she calmed a bit, and Ann took advantage of it. In a violent move powered by her insanity, she broke free from him and ran headlong toward the stables.

"I'll get her, Reed," Mark called out, following after her.

Reed looked to Libby, and she rushed to his side.

"I'm sorry," she told him in an emotion-choked voice. She looked up at him and saw his torment. Uncaring that others were watching, she drew him down for a gentle kiss.

Kathleen had been standing stock-still. As she watched Ann disappear into the stable, she began to shake with the force of all that she was feeling. *Ann had been the one who'd killed Steve.* The knowledge hammered through her, enlightening, yet horrifying her. Ann.

Fury held her in its unrelenting grip, and watching Libby kiss Reed proved the last straw. She had to get away! She started to move and only then became aware of a man holding her in a gentle, yet supportive way.

"Are you all right?" Lyle asked. He could feel her trembling beneath his hands, and he wanted to help her if he could.

"You!" Kathleen shrieked at the sound of his voice, suddenly focusing on who was holding her.

In a quick move, she tore herself free from Lyle as if she couldn't bear to be near him. She turned on him aggressively, and with all the power she possessed she slapped him.

"Get away from me, and stay away from me!" she shouted at him, not caring that she was humiliating him. She knew only that she couldn't bear the sight of him.

Lyle stared down at her. For the first time, he

saw revulsion in her eyes and realized that she had never cared for him in all the time they'd been together. She had only used him when it had suited her. He'd always hoped that she did care for him and would come to love him, but no more. He expected anger to rise within him. He felt nothing. He let his gaze go over her features one last time, committing to memory all that he saw there. His heart ached, then hardened.

"Good-bye, Kathleen," he said quietly.

Without another word to anyone, Lyle turned and walked away from her. He did not look back. He never would. It was done.

Kathleen was glad that he was going. She never wanted to see him again. Her life had just come crashing down around her, and she didn't need his sympathy. She spun away from Lyle to find Reed and Libby both watching her.

"So that note was right. Steve was murdered. He didn't die in an accident," she said coldly.

"You knew about Joe's letter? How?"

"I happened to be in your wagon the other night while you were in town, and I found it."

Reed was outraged that she'd dared to go through his things, but he knew he should have realized that she would try anything to achieve her ends.

Kathleen sneered at him, not caring that he was angry with her. All her dreams had been destroyed. Any hope she'd ever had that he would be hers was gone. "I'm sure you thought I had something to do with Steve's death. That's probably why you wouldn't buy me out when you first showed up. You were trying to trap me. Well, I'm sorry to disappoint you, Reed darling. I might not have loved Steve, but I never wished him any harm."

"I'll have a bank draft drawn up for your share of the Stampede tomorrow," Reed said curtly.

"Thank you. I can't wait to be done with this hell hole." She gave Libby one last, long, disparaging look. "There is no accounting for some men's taste in women. Who would ever have thought that Reed Weston would love a woman who dressed like a boy?" She turned then, her head held high, and started to walk away.

Kathleen had just moved away from the crowd as Mark's shout alerted them to danger.

"Look out!"

They looked up to see Ann galloping from the stable on one of the stallions. She was heading straight for Kathleen.

Chapter Sixteen

Kathleen heard Mark's warning shout. She turned to see Ann riding a massive stallion, charging toward her. Even from this distance, Kathleen could see the look of deadly intent in Ann's eyes. Terror seized her, and she screamed, running for her life.

Ann cared only about one thing—making Kathleen pay! Now that her own terrible secret had been found out, she had nothing left to lose. She'd eluded Mark and grabbed the first saddled horse she'd been able to find. Now she was riding straight for Kathleen. She wanted her dead! All the misery in her life was the other woman's fault. She was going to end it here and now. It wouldn't bring Steve back, but then, nothing would bring Steve back.

Reed reacted instinctively. He shoved Libby out of harm's way and threw himself between Kathleen and the horse. He waved his arms and shouted at the galloping steed to deflect it from its murderous path.

Ann was a decent rider, but she was concentrating so hard on riding down Kathleen that she was caught off guard by Reed's unexpected heroic act. Spooked by his intervention, the stallion reared in fright. Ann only had time to cry out once as she lost her seat and was thrown violently from the panicked horse's back.

Libby ran to where Ann lay unmoving on the ground as Reed grabbed the stallion's reins.

"Ann!" she cried.

Libby knelt beside her crumpled body and carefully turned her over. She was silently praying that Ann would be all right, but to no avail. The fall had killed her. Her neck had been broken. Tears streaked down Libby's face as she stared at her. Her death was a terrible waste—just as Steve's had been.

"How is she?" Reed came running to join Libby once he'd brought the horse under control, and so did Mark, Kathleen and the others.

Libby looked up at her husband. "She's dead."

"Ann! Where's Ann!" Joe's shout came from just beyond the accident scene. "What's happening here? Where's my daughter?"

The crowd parted, and Joe came hobbling painfully toward them on crutches. He hadn't moved around much since his fall, but when one of the hands had told him about Ann's confrontation with Kathleen, he'd been desperate to get to her.

He'd feared what might happen between the two women.

Reed stood up and went to the older man. He blocked his path, not wanting him to see Ann this way, but Joe would not be deterred.

"You don't want to see this, Joe."

"Why not? What's happened?"

"Ann was on horseback, trying to run Kathleen down, when she was thrown," he explained, knowing there was no easy way to tell Joe of her death.

Joe looked at him, his expression tormented and angry. "Where's my Ann? Where is she?"

Reed saw that Joe would not be turned away, so he stepped back to allow him to go to his daughter.

"Oh, dear God, no!" Joe's voice was full of anguish as he painfully made his way toward his daughter. Somehow, he managed to sit on the ground next to her limp form. He gathered Ann in his arms, all the while crying her name.

Joe sat there, rocking her, silently demanding of God why the last hour had happened, and knowing that there could be no turning back the clock, no denial of her death. It was real. He had lost his beloved daughter.

Reed encouraged the others to go about their business, then sent one of the hands into town for the undertaker, knowing there was nothing any of them could do for Ann now.

"Reed—" Kathleen said his name softly and reached out to touch his arm as he walked near her.

He stopped and looked her way. "Are you all right?"

She nodded tightly. "Yes, thanks to you. That

311

was a very brave thing you did. You could have been hurt or killed trying to save me."

He met her gaze, and for the first time he saw contrition in her eyes. "You don't have to thank me."

"Yes, I do. I know you'll find this hard to believe, but you just proved me right. I have loved you for what seems like forever, because I knew you were a wonderful man. You just showed me how wonderful you really are," she told him sorrowfully. "You put yourself at risk to save my life. You could have just stood by and watched me die, but you didn't. You were brave and courageous, and that only reinforced what I already knew about you. You are a hero, Reed Weston."

They stood looking at each other for a long moment. Then Kathleen rose up on tiptoes and pressed a soft kiss to his cheek. Tears burned in her eyes as she gently caressed his face.

"I won't bother you anymore, and I hope you and Libby are very happy together." Her voice was choked with emotion as she turned and hurried off.

Libby had been standing off to the side watching Reed take charge, and she was surprised when she saw Kathleen seek him out. She stayed where she was, though, allowing Reed to have a moment with her alone. When Kathleen finally walked away, Reed looked up in Libby's direction, and Libby smiled reassuringly at him. He joined her then, and they stood together a little distance away from the grieving Joe.

"This is all such a terrible waste," Libby said sadly.

"Of all the people I suspected might have been involved in Steve's accident, I never once thought of Ann."

"I know, but she loved him so much. I guess she couldn't bear living without him—" She fell silent for a moment as she imagined the guilt Ann had been living with in the weeks since Steve's death. "Think how horrible her life's been since that night he died. I don't know how she lived with herself."

"And Joe—" Reed looked at the older man and knew he was going to have to get the truth out of him about what had really happened.

"He told me that night we first met, when he offered me the job with the show, that he was helping me because he had a daughter about my age, and if she were ever in trouble he would move heaven and hell to save her."

"It looks like he just tried, but sometimes it's impossible to save people from themselves."

They shared a sorrowful, knowing look.

"Is there anything I can do to help?" Libby asked.

"Just keep a look out for the undertaker. I'm going to take care of Joe."

Mark came to them with a blanket, and Reed took it from him. "Give me a hand with him."

Mark nodded and followed him as he approached Joe.

"Joe, let us help you," Reed offered. "We need to get Ann inside."

"God help me, she's dead, she's dead," he moaned, so desperately tormented that he was barely coherent.

313

"I know, and I'm sorry."

Reed covered Ann with the blanket and then lifted her gently in his arms. Mark helped Joe up and steadied him as they made their way toward his wagon. Mark opened the door for Reed, and he entered and carefully laid Ann on her bed. As he came out of her bedroom, he closed the door behind him. Mark had just helped Joe inside and settled him at the table. Reed gave him a nod of thanks.

"I need to talk to Joe privately," Reed told Mark.

"If you need me, I'll be close by." With that, he left the two men alone.

"Joe," Reed said softly, understanding how distraught he was right then, but knowing they had to talk.

Joe looked up at him, his expression one of pure anguish. "She's dead, Reed. My Ann's dead!"

"I'm sorry," he said in a gentle tone, thinking Joe looked as if he'd suddenly aged thirty years. He looked like a haggard old man now. "But you need to tell me what happened, Joe. I think it's time I learned the truth."

Joe shook his head in defeat and exhaustion. It was over—Ann's life and his.

"When I wrote that letter to you, I didn't know who'd cut the cinch, but I knew it had been done deliberately," Joe said, his soul weary with the weight of the tragic burden he carried. "God, Reed, I loved Steve. Your brother was a good man. I would have done anything for him. That's why I wrote to you. I was angry that he'd been killed and I wanted to see justice done. And then, right after

I'd mailed the letter, I found out the truth."

"How did you find out?"

"I had confided my suspicions about Steve's accident to Ann and had told her that I'd written to you with the news that I believed the cinch had been cut. She gave me a terribly strange look and suddenly went to her room without another word. When I went to check on her later, I found her huddled in her bed, trembling and crying. I asked her what was wrong, and she told me that I had just condemned her to hang. I didn't understand at first, but then she explained how much she'd loved Steve and how he wouldn't leave Kathleen to be with her. She told me that she'd been determined to set him free so they could be together. She'd cut the cinch on the horse Kathleen was supposed to ride in that act, not knowing that Kathleen wouldn't ride that night. She didn't learn of the change in plans until too late—Steve had taken the fall and had been killed."

"And you'd already written to me," Reed said solemnly. He realized how very lucky he'd been that Joe had written the letter when he had.

"I couldn't let my daughter hang for murder!" Joe said frantically, passionately. "I loved Ann—I had to protect her. I thought I'd convinced her never to speak of that night again. That's why I cut the reins on the stagecoach myself. I wanted to convince you that there was a killer at work in the Stampede. I didn't want any suspicion cast on Ann at all."

"Your plan almost worked."

315

"Until this morning. Something must have set her off."

"She overheard Kathleen talking about Steve."

"That would have done it. I guess she couldn't control her fury and her guilt any longer." He stopped, knowing it was over. "I'm sorry about Steve, Reed. I'm sorry all of this happened."

"So am I."

"Will you be going to the sheriff in King's Crossing?" Joe girded himself for the answer to come.

Reed stared at him long and hard before he responded. "The one who committed the act has paid for the crime."

Joe nodded, feeling nothing. His life was over. Nothing else mattered now that his daughter was dead. "I'll be leaving the show today, after I've taken care of Ann."

"I'll have some of the boys help you with your things."

Reed turned and left him. There was nothing more to say. He would wait outside for the sheriff and the undertaker.

While Reed was inside talking with Joe, Mark walked Libby to her tent. They were both stunned by the drama that had been played out before them.

"I never thought Ann was capable of anything like this," Mark said.

"Neither did I. She was always kind to me."

"I guess love can make you do things you wouldn't ordinarily do. So is what I heard about you true? Did you and Reed really get married last night?" he asked.

Libby smiled up at him. "Yes, we eloped to the justice of the peace."

"Oh." Mark had not wanted it to be true. He had come to care about Libby and had wanted to court her himself. "Well, congratulations."

She was surprised, for she could have sworn she saw a flash of disappointment in his eyes. "Thank you. I think we're going to be very happy."

"I hope so. Who was that John Harris who caused all the trouble last night?"

"Someone from home. We had been engaged once, but I'd ended the engagement. He wasn't pleased, so I was fortunate that Reed showed up when he did at the stable."

"Well, I stayed in town with him and made sure he had a ticket for today's stage."

"It's good to know he's gone, so I won't have to worry about running into him again."

"I guess things will be pretty peaceful around here, now that we know how Steve's accident happened."

"We could all use a little peace and quiet."

Mark left Libby at her tent and went to take care of his own business. Though he was glad that she had found happiness with Reed, he regretted that he hadn't had more time with her. She was a delightful, beautiful woman, and he liked her a lot.

As he was making his way toward the stables, he met Reed coming out of Joe's wagon.

"How is he?" Mark asked.

"Not good. He'll be leaving the show today."

Bobbi Smith

Reed quickly filled Mark in on everything that had happened.

"Now that you mention it, I do remember on the night of Steve's fall that Ann was in the stable area. She could easily have gotten to his horse, and no one would have thought anything of it."

"And on the night of the stagecoach 'accident,' Joe sent Libby to find Shorty right before it was time to go on."

The two men shared a knowing look.

"I'm just glad it's over," Mark told him. "And, by the way, congratulations on your marriage."

Reed smiled for the first time. "Thank you."

"Libby's one helluva woman."

"I know." Reed paused, then changed the subject. "Did everything go all right in town with John Harris last night?"

"I told Libby I made sure he bought a ticket on the first stage out this morning."

"I think I'll ride into town once everything's settled with Ann and Joe, and make sure Harris got on that stage. We don't need any more surprise visits from him."

"You want me to keep an eye on Libby while you're gone?"

"Please. Harris is a mean bastard, and I wouldn't put anything past him."

Both men cared about Libby and were determined to keep her from harm.

They heard the sound of a rider and saw Lyle heading out of camp, his gear strapped to the back of his mount.

"I guess that scene with Kathleen convinced him

318

that it was time to move on," Reed said. He hadn't liked the man and was glad to see him leave.

"He was a good worker. We'll have to replace him."

"Speaking of replacing people, how would you like to take on Joe's responsibilities permanently? I can use a good right-hand man."

"I'd like that."

They shook hands.

"I'll talk with you more later. Right now, it's time I paid Kathleen a visit. If the sheriff shows up, come and get me."

Kathleen was packing. She knew there was nothing more for her here. It was time she went back to San Carlos and tried to pick up the pieces of her life. A knock at her door surprised her. After the scene with Ann, she was certain no one in the Stampede would want to speak with her again.

"Reed? What are you doing here?"

"We need to talk, Kathleen."

"Come in."

"You're leaving?" He looked around as he went to sit down at the table.

"There's no reason for me to stay. There's nothing to hold me here."

"Name a price for your share of the Stampede, and I'll have a bank draft drawn for you."

She told him a figure, and he agreed to it without argument.

"So, you were lying when you said you couldn't buy me out before," she stated flatly.

"I wasn't lying. I wasn't going to change a thing

about the show until I'd found out what had happened to Steve."

Kathleen looked over at him, her expression sad. "It's still so hard to believe—Steve and Ann, both dead." She shook her head. "And you suspected me for a while, I'm sure."

Reed shrugged. "I didn't know who had done it, but I wanted the culprit found. Now we know."

"Yes, we do." She was solemn.

"How soon do you plan to leave the show?"

"Today, as soon as I get everything together. You can mail the draft to me in San Carlos."

"All right." He stood to go. "Good-bye."

"Good-bye, Reed."

She watched him leave, her heart breaking. Ahead of her, the future looked bleak, but there was no turning back. She continued to pack.

Reed sought out Libby and found her moving her things into his wagon.

"Did you get everything settled?" she asked as he joined her there.

"As much as I can," he told her.

He looked so serious that Libby put down the clothes she was carrying and went to embrace him.

"I'm sorry things turned out the way they did, but I'm glad you finally found out who was responsible for Steve's death."

Reed stood still, just holding her. "So am I."

"How's Joe doing?"

"Not well."

"Are you going to tell the sheriff what he did?"

"No. There's nothing to be gained by it. He's leaving the show today, and so is Kathleen."

Libby wasn't surprised. "I'll miss Joe. He was kind to me."

Reed looked down at her, his expression tender. "I do owe him for that. If he hadn't hired you on as Bert that night, things would have been very different."

"I'm glad he hired me."

"So am I."

Reed kissed her, drawing her close to him, savoring the sweetness of her. Though his world had been dark today, Libby's love still shone brightly.

"I missed you while you were gone," she whispered against his lips.

The sadness in him touched her, and she wanted to erase all the pain in his heart. Without saying another word, she took his hand and led him back to their bed. Then she showed him just how much he meant to her.

"I love you, Libby," Reed said a short time later as he lay with her in his arms. The beauty of her love so freely given was his beacon in the storm of life. He had found safe harbor in the haven in her arms.

They got up and had just finished dressing when Mark came to report that the sheriff and undertaker had arrived.

"I'm going to ride into town with them to set everything straight," Reed told her.

"What about the show tonight? Do you want to cancel the performance?"

"No. You and Mark go ahead with practice. I'll be back in plenty of time."

He sought out Sheriff Bruner and told him what had happened, while the undertaker tended to Ann.

"Looks like you had a rough morning here," Bruner remarked, sympathizing.

"Did you want to talk to any more of the witnesses?"

"No, I've heard enough. Unless there's anything else you think I need to know, I'll be heading back to town now."

"Want some company?" Reed asked.

"Sure."

The two men rode out together.

"You've got some business to take care of in King's Crossing today?"

"One important thing for sure," Reed said, smiling. "Libby and I got married last night, and I want to get her a wedding ring."

"Well, congratulations. That's real good news. You two do make a handsome couple."

They reached town and parted company there. There was no jewelry store in town, so Reed checked at the mercantile and managed to find a simple gold band. He would have liked to get Libby something more impressive, but knew it would have to wait. As long as there was a ring on her finger proclaiming that she was his, that was all that mattered to him.

Reed went to the stage office next. John's threats could not be dismissed, and he wanted to make sure the man had left on the stage that morning.

"Can I help you?" the clerk asked as Reed entered the office.

"I just wanted to see if a man named John Harris made the stage on time."

The clerk got out the ledger and checked. "I do have his name down as having purchased a ticket, so he should have used it."

"Are you sure?"

The clerk thought it a strange question, but answered, "Things are always busy around here at departure times, but I'm sure if he bought a ticket, he used it. What did he look like?"

"He had a scar on his cheek."

"Oh, that man," the clerk said. "Yes, he was here at boarding time."

"Thanks."

Relieved to know that much, Reed started back to the Stampede campgrounds. For all that Harris might have gotten on the stage here in King's Crossing, he could very well have left it at its first stop and be on his way back to the Stampede to cause more trouble right now. Libby didn't trust Harris, so Reed knew he had to be on guard. He would be prepared for him if the time came, for there was no telling what the man might try next.

When Reed had ridden for town with Sheriff Bruner, Libby knew she could delay no longer. She wanted to say good-bye to Joe. She made her way to his wagon and knocked softly on the door.

"Come in," came his gruff response.

She let herself in and found him sitting at the table, his head resting in his hands.

"Hi, Joe," she said gently.

He lifted his head to look at her, his eyes red from crying. "Libby, girl . . ."

He looked so lost and forlorn that she couldn't stop herself from going to him and putting her arm around his shoulders. She kissed him on the cheek. "I wish I could make things better for you, the way you did for me, Joe."

"I wish you could, too," he said slowly. "Things'll never be the same now that my Ann's dead."

"You were a wonderful father. They don't come any better than you," she told him as she slipped into the chair across from him and reached out to take one of his hands in hers. "Ann was very lucky to have you."

"I loved her. It's not going to be the same without her. If only things could have been different. If only Steve hadn't already been married—"

"We can't change the past, Joe," she said with sympathy.

"Lord, what I wouldn't give to be able to turn back the clock. There are so many things I'd do different."

"We all would, but we can't. The only thing we can do is learn from our mistakes and try to do better."

"I'm going to miss you, Libby. Will you write to me?"

She smiled. "You know I will. Where are you going to go? Is there a place you call home?"

"I lived in San Antonio back before Ann's mother died and we joined up with Steve. I'm going back there."

"You be careful and take care of yourself, all right?"

Joe gave her an affectionate look. She was the only one in the world who cared about him. The thought warmed his broken heart. "Thank you, Libby." He paused, gathering his emotional strength. "You make sure you take care of yourself, too."

"I will."

A knock came at the wagon door, and she answered it to find two of the hands there.

"We heard Joe needed help moving out his things, so we brought the carriage over," one of the men told her.

"Thanks, boys," Joe called out.

"You'll be all right getting into town?" Libby asked, knowing that it was time for him to leave.

"I'm a tough old bird. I'll be fine." He managed to give her a weary smile. "Good bye, Liberty Jones."

"You know I really am Weston's lady now. Reed and I eloped last night."

A look of surprise crossed his haggard features. "I knew from that first night in the Diamondback that you two would be good together. I hope you're happy."

"We are, thanks to you."

"Glad I could help."

"Good-bye, Joe. God bless you." She went to hug him.

"You, too." He hugged her back as best he could while sitting down, and then let her go. "Stay in touch."

"I will."

Libby left him then. A short time later, she saw one of the hands driving Joe from the grounds. Joe never looked back.

Libby did not try to hide her tears as she watched him go.

The Stampede's performance started right on time. Reed led the parade on his prancing stallion. He was dressed all in black today, and he had told Libby to wear her white buckskin, so she would look like a bride. As he'd prearranged with everyone but Libby, he reined in before the grandstand.

"Ladies and gentlemen, I have an important announcement that I want to share with you," Reed called out.

The cheering crowd quieted, sensing that something exciting was going to happen.

"I am pleased to introduce to you my wife, Liberty Weston. She did me the honor of marrying me last evening. She is now truly and forever Weston's Lady." He swept his hat off and gave her a bow.

Libby was stunned by his courtly gesture, and the audience went wild.

"Also, since we did elope last night," Reed went on, "there wasn't time to get her a ring, so I'd like to present one to her now. Mrs. Weston?"

Reed sidled his horse over to Libby's, and she held out her left hand. He slipped the gold band on her finger. When he looked up, he saw that her eyes were shining with tears.

The crowd was applauding raucously, thrilled

to be part of such a wonderful moment.

"There is one more thing," he said in a more serious tone.

Again, the people gathered for the show respectfully quieted to listen to his message.

"Today, there was a tragic accident at the Stampede grounds. One of our Stampede family, Miss Ann Shadowens, died. If we could have a moment of silence in her memory . . ."

Reed took off his hat and bowed his head. His thoughts were of Steve as he remained quiet for a moment. As a man of honor, his brother had never cheated on Kathleen or considered divorcing her. He had been a man who could hold up his head with pride, knowing that he had always done his best and had never compromised his principles. By Steve's own hard work and determination, he had put together this show that was bringing joy to thousands of people. He had been a rare man, and Reed sorely regretted that they had been separated for so long. He had loved his brother, and it was too late to tell him and make amends.

A great sadness filled Reed. He had never considered how lonely Steve must have been, but he understood now. He had been surrounded by people, yet he'd had no one close to rely on. Reed knew he hadn't been there for his brother before, but he was going to make it up to him. He would make Weston's Wild Texas Stampede even more successful; he would make it a show that Steve would be proud of. He was also going to make sure he lived life to the fullest from now on. He had learned how important it was to tell those you love that you love them, to help those who need help, and to protect those who need protecting.

Reed cast a sidelong glance at Libby. Her head was bowed and her eyes closed. He knew he was a lucky man to have her. Just the thought of the adversity she'd survived amazed him. Warmth filled him at the realization that she was his. He had been blessed, and he was going to take care of what was his. People were relying on him, and he would not let them down.

The crowd in the grandstand was respectfully silent. When Reed gave the signal and the band struck up a tune, everyone came to life again and began cheering. It was time for the performance to begin.

Hours later, Libby lay in Reed's arms, savoring the glory of the love they'd just shared.

"So, is this going to be our life from now on?" she asked, her eyes twinkling at the wickedness of her thoughts.

"What do you mean?"

She raised herself on one elbow to stare down at him, resting one hand on the broad, hard-muscled width of his chest. "Well, will we do our acts in the show and then hurry back here to perform in private for the rest of the day?"

"I don't know. What do you think?" He grinned up at her. After their riding act, he'd been hard-pressed to get through the grand finale. All he'd wanted to do was ride straight off the field to the wagon with her still in his arms.

"I'm not sure that we've completely perfected

the riding part of it just yet." She was trying not to smile.

"Oh?" he asked, drawing her down to him. "Do you want to practice some more? Do you think we need to rehearse? I'm more than willing to extend the effort, if you are."

"It certainly couldn't hurt to see if we can continually improve," she murmured as his lips explored her throat and then moved lower.

"I thought we had it pretty close to flawless, myself."

"Maybe if I just shift positions a bit," she suggested, moving away from him for an instant and then straddling him as she did in the show.

Reed groaned in pure pleasure at her bold and daring move. "I see what you mean. This was a good idea."

Libby was smiling down at him. "I love you, Reed. Thank you for my ring."

"I wanted to get you something fancier, but that was all I could find in town."

"There's no need. It's perfect," she sighed.

Their gazes met as she began to move, urging him to join her in ecstasy's ride. He needed no further encouragement, but eagerly matched her rhythm. Just having her near left him wanting her again and again. They loved through the night, seeking only to please each other and to show the depth of their devotion.

Dawn found them exhausted, but sated. They were both glad that they didn't have to be ready to perform in the Stampede until that afternoon. Their all-night rehearsal had taken its toll.

Chapter Seventeen

The Stampede had closed out its run in King's Crossing and was packing up and getting ready to travel on to its next scheduled stop, in Coyote Run. It was a four-day trip to the new town, so they had to get on the road as early as possible on Monday.

"Is Mr. Weston here?" a young boy asked Mark as he rode into the campgrounds early Monday morning.

"He's busy right now. Can I help you with anything?" Mark knew Reed was meeting with some of the other workers and thought he could handle whatever the youth wanted.

"I just gotta give him this letter," the boy said, displaying an envelope.

"I'll be glad to take it for him."

The boy looked a little troubled. "Well, I don't know—"

"Is there a problem?"

"I was told to make sure he got this personal-like."

"I see. You're welcome to wait around for him, if you like."

"Thanks." He dismounted and sat on some crates that were stacked off to the side.

"I'll let him know you're here."

Mark went off to find Reed. The last time he'd seen him, he'd been near the stable, so he started his search there. It didn't take long to locate him, and he was just finishing his meeting.

"Something wrong, Mark?"

"No. There's a boy from town who's got a letter for you. I offered to take it, but he said he had to see that you got it."

Reed was puzzled, but assumed that it might be a personal note from either Kathleen or Joe. Something that they'd wanted him to have before they left King's Crossing. "Let's go meet this young man and see what he's got that's so important."

The two men returned to where the boy was waiting.

"I'm Reed Weston. I understand you wanted to see me?" he told the boy.

"Yes, sir. I'm Nat Wilson. A man in town hired me to see that you got this letter." He stood up and handed him the missive.

"Thanks, Nat." Reed tossed him a coin as he started to tear open the envelope.

The boy had just mounted up when Reed opened the letter and caught sight of what was in it.

"Nat!" he thundered.

The youth looked back at him, wide-eyed. "Yes, sir?"

"Who gave this to you?" he asked in a cold, deadly voice.

"Some man came into my mama's store and asked if I could bring it out here. He paid us real good. That's all I know about it." He was frightened by the look on Mr. Weston's face.

"What did the man look like?" Reed demanded.

"I don't know—"

"Did he have a scar on his cheek?"

"No, sir."

"Are you sure?" Reed took a step toward him.

Nat was intimidated. "Yes, sir."

"Did he say anything else to you about the letter?"

"No. Just that it had to be delivered to you personal-like. That's all." He was very nervous, seeing how angry Mr. Weston was. "Can I go now?"

"One more thing—did the man who gave you this letter stay on in town?"

"I don't know. I rode out here with it as soon as he left my ma's store. I don't know where he went."

Reed nodded and said no more. The boy quickly put his heels to his horse's sides and rode off.

Only then did Reed look back down at the letter he held. His jaw tightened as he fought to control the murderous urge that filled him.

"What is it?" Mark asked. He'd watched the whole exchange with the boy and wondered what was in the letter.

332

Since Mark knew about Harris, he handed him the letter without comment. Mark read it over quickly.

Weston,
You may think Libby's yours, but never forget that I want her, and I plan to get her. You can't stop me. When you least expect it, I'm going to be there to take her away from you. Libby belongs to me.

Harris

Mark looked up at Reed. "You were right about him."

Reed gave him a level look. "But where *is* the bastard? The man who gave this letter to Nat must have just been someone delivering it for him. There's no mistaking that scar. If it had been Harris, the boy would have remembered him."

Mark nodded and cast a look around the countryside beyond their campgrounds. "He could be anywhere right now."

"I had a feeling he wouldn't be easy to stop. It looks like I was right."

"I'll tell the men. We'll keep an eye out for him."

"At least I'm reasonably sure we'll be safe until we get to Coyote Run."

"Do you still want to ride into town with Libby ahead of us to do the advance publicity?"

"No, I don't want to take any chances with her safety, but I don't want her to know about this letter, either." He didn't want to worry her unnecessarily.

333

"All right, then I'm going to tell you I'm not ready to run the Stampede by myself and I need you to stay here with me," Mark said, giving him an excuse to remain with the show.

Reed grinned. "I'll tell Libby we're not going to ride ahead this time because you're still new at the job and you need me here to help you."

"Good."

They were both satisfied. As long as they were in camp, they knew Libby would always have someone close to her. She would be safe. That was the important thing.

They moved out that morning and made the trip without incident. Libby was surprised that she and Reed were not going to go into Coyote Run early, but she understood Mark's wanting Reed to stay close at hand in case something did go wrong.

They reached Coyote Run on Thursday morning and settled in a short distance out of town. It was no simple matter getting everything set up. With a show planned for the following evening, the hands went to work right away, setting up the tents and grandstand. Libby and Reed went into town to post the handbills and perform several short demonstrations.

The townspeople were very excited about the Stampede's arrival. Weston's Wild Texas Stampede was the biggest thing to hit Coyote Run in ages, and the Friday night show sold out quickly.

It was near sundown on Friday when the stagecoach carrying Brand and Sheri rumbled into town right on time. They descended, weary but relieved to have reached their destination. They had made it to Coyote Run.

"Look, Brand!" Sheri said excitedly as she stopped to read one of the posted handbills. "Everything's worked out perfectly! The Stampede is here! They're just opening tonight."

"Good. I'd hate to have traveled all this way and missed them."

"Let's check into the hotel and then see if we can still get out to their grounds tonight."

Brand claimed their luggage, and they made their way to the Paradise Hotel, the only hotel in town. It wasn't as fancy as its name indicated, but it looked clean enough.

"We'd like a room please," Brand said as he stopped before the front desk.

"Yes, sir," the clerk answered, turning the registry book for him to sign.

"We saw the signs for the Wild Texas Stampede, and we were wondering where it's set up?" Sheri asked.

"They're camped a few miles out of town. You're too late for tonight's performance, though. It started about half an hour ago. I think it was sold out anyway."

"It's that popular?"

"It sure is. Everybody's real excited about it. Especially with that lady sharpshooter they've got with them—that Weston's Lady. I saw her do some shooting yesterday, and she was really good."

"The Stampede is in town through Sunday, isn't it?"

335

"Yes, ma'am."

Armed with that information, Sheri was ready to begin. They took their bags to the room, then went to the stable to see about renting a carriage. As tired as she was, Sheri still wanted to make the trip out to the campgrounds. They might miss the show, but at least they could make contact with Liberty Jones tonight after her performance and arrange a meeting to start interviewing her tomorrow.

"What are you going to do if she doesn't want to be the heroine of a dime novel?" Brand asked as they started on the drive out to the show grounds.

Sheri looked at him aghast. "Why wouldn't she? The books will make her famous. Everyone will want to meet her and watch her shooting demonstrations. It will be wonderful for her career."

Brand grinned at her. "I don't think I've ever seen you this excited about starting a book before."

"I've never seen a Wild West show. This could be a great adventure." She glanced at him, then qualified her statement. "A much safer adventure than when I was researching you."

"You think so? It might be safer, but what about your readers? If there are no renegades and no rattlesnakes, maybe this story idea won't be exciting enough for them," he teased.

"I'll make it exciting, you just wait and see. *Liberty Jones, Lady Sharp Shooter, or The Adventures of Weston's Lady* is going to be a best-seller."

"Of course, it will be. You're going to write it."

"Thank you." She smiled at him. Brand had

proven to be her biggest fan, and she was glad that he respected her work.

They arrived just as the Stampede's performance was coming to an end. They parked the carriage and got down to walk around and take a look at everything.

Sheri was impressed by the size of the production. It was bigger and much more sophisticated than she'd expected. The grandstand was packed with shouting, happy fans. Banners, posters and advertisements for the Wild Texas Stampede were everywhere. A big tent served as the stable, and there were numerous wagons and smaller tents that she felt certain were the residences of the performers. She had read that there were Indians in the production, and she and Brand located their small village in an area separate from the others. As they were walking back to where they'd left the carriage, the sound of the announcer's message came to them.

"And that concludes our program for today, folks. Thank you all for coming to Weston's Wild Texas Stampede!" There was loud applause in response.

"I guess we'd better talk to someone at the ticket office. They should be able to arrange a meeting for us with Miss Jones," Sheri said, leading the way back.

Brand followed along, fascinated with the workings of the show. He watched as the riders galloped from the parade ground to the sound of the Stampede's band. When they reached the ticket office, they found a man working inside.

"Can I help you?" he asked when they approached.

"Yes, my name is Sheridan St. John, and I'd like to speak with Miss Jones, please."

"I'll be pleased to get her for you, but it may take a minute or two. What's your name again?"

She told him once more, and he left the small office to go find Libby. A short time later, he came back with a lovely young blonde following him.

"Libby, this here is the lady I was telling you about," he told her as he pointed Sheri out.

Libby couldn't imagine who Sheridan St. John was, but she was curious. The stranger was certainly pretty, and the man who was with her was very handsome. He almost looked as if he were part Indian.

"Hello, I'm Liberty. Can I help you?"

"I hope so. I'm Sheridan St. John. This is my husband, Brand," Sheri began. "I'm a novelist. I've traveled here from Arizona Territory because I'd like to interview you in the hope of writing a book about you and your adventures with the Wild Texas Stampede."

Libby stared at her in surprise. "You write books?"

"Yes, dime novels. I've published quite a few. I have some with me, if you'd like to look at them and check my credentials."

"Yes, please."

Sheri took out a copy of *Buck McCade, or Bad Man of the Badlands* and a copy of *Brand, The Half-Breed Scout, or Trail of the Renegade* and handed

338

them to Libby. She watched as the other woman paged through them with interest.

"These are wonderful." Libby smiled broadly at Sheri, impressed. Then, looking at Brand, she asked, "You're the real Brand, aren't you?"

"I am."

"How wonderful that you got to be the hero in a novel."

"My wife is an excellent author, and her publisher, Carroll and Condon, is the best in the business."

Libby looked back at the other woman. "And you want to write a dime novel about me?"

"That's right. If you're interested?"

"Oh, yes. This is wonderful! How did you ever find out about the Stampede?"

"My editor in New York saw an article about you in one of the Texas papers, and he wired me with the idea for the book."

"How would you go about it?"

"I'll need to interview you extensively, and possibly travel with you for a week or so to see what living with a Wild West show is like. Would that be possible?"

"Oh, yes. In fact, we have an extra wagon you can use when we leave Coyote Run on Monday, if you'd like."

"Thank you. We'd love it!" Sheri said enthusiastically. "Will you be available tomorrow morning for an interview?"

"That would be fine. I'll meet you here at nine, if that's good for you?"

"That will be wonderful."

"Can I keep your books? I'd love to read them."

"Of course, and I'm looking forward to the day when you'll have copies of your own."

"So am I."

"We'll see you first thing in the morning."

Libby shook hands with both Sheri and Brand, and she watched as they rode back toward town. She couldn't wait to tell Reed the news. She was going to be a character in a dime novel! She hurried away to find him.

It was much later that night that Libby was sitting up at the table reading *Brand, The Half-Breed Scout, or Trail of the Renegade*.

"Are you ever coming to bed?" Reed asked, coming to the bedroom door.

Libby looked up quickly, smiling a guilty smile. "But this is *so* exciting! I've never read a dime novel before. Sheridan St. John is really good!"

"That's nice," he said, coming to her. "Now, let's go to bed."

"But I'm almost done! Just let me finish this one part." She quickly explained, "Brand has stayed behind to fight the renegades himself, while he's sent the heroine away. Oh—this is so good! Did you know that the hero in this book is modeled after her husband? You'll have to meet him tomorrow morning when they get here."

Reed couldn't help smiling at how enthusiastic she was about the book. Still, he hadn't planned to spend the evening critiquing a novel. He came up behind Libby and bent down to brush aside her hair and press a kiss to the nape of her neck.

"Mmmm," Libby said softly, enjoying his touch.

"I've got an idea of something we could do that might be just a little more exciting than the adventures of Brand."

"Are you jealous?" she asked, hiding a smile as she pretended to continue reading the book.

"Should I be?"

"Never," Libby answered, tossing the book on the table and snuggling into her husband's arms. "Was there something you wanted?"

"Just you, love. Just you."

She kissed him. "I'll have to make sure that Sheridan St. John makes you the hero in my book."

They didn't talk any more as Reed carried his wife off to bed.

Libby didn't get any more reading done that night.

Reed was glad.

Sheri awoke early and lay in the pre-dawn darkness, treasuring the quiet of the moment. Brand was still slumbering beside her, so she had time to think—and to remember.

Gazing lovingly at his ruggedly handsome features, Sheri remembered the first time she'd seen him—it seemed just like yesterday that she had made the trip to Arizona Territory with her cousin Maureen. Tim DeYoung, her editor, had told her that sales of her Buck McCade books were down. She'd been afraid of losing her job and had wanted to prove to him that she could write a best-seller. She'd headed for Fort McDowell to look up a scout named Brand. One of her friends had found an article about him in an Arizona newpaper, and he'd sounded so intriguing that she'd known he had to be her next hero. As the stagecoach they'd been on neared Phoenix, the driver had thought they were being attacked by renegades. It turned out to be some of the scouts from the fort, and that was when she'd seen him for the first time. Brand had been dressed as a warrior, but his blue eyes had disconcerted her.

Sheri had thought him magnificent then, and she still did. Her gaze caressed Brand, taking in the powerful width of his chest. Unable to resist, she reached out to trace the pattern her gaze had just followed. It hadn't been easy winning his love, but now that they were married, she couldn't imagine a life without him. He had become her whole world. She smiled as he stirred and, without opening his eyes, reached for her.

"Good morning," Sheri said, nuzzling his throat as she curled against him.

"Is it?" he asked in a sleep-husky voice, enjoying the feel of her so close to his side.

"I think so. I'm here with you."

"Yes, that is good—very good."

He lost himself in the delight of loving her, thinking there was no better way to wake up in the morning than with Sheri in his arms. It was heavenly letting the rest of the world wait while he sought rapture in her embrace.

Much later, Brand regretfully left their bed to start getting ready for the trip to the Stampede grounds. Sheri, however, lingered there, replete and relaxed, the sheet drawn modestly up over her breasts, her hair spread out around her in a halo of gold.

"I thought you were excited about your meeting this morning," Brand said, trying not to think about how beautiful she was lying there, looking well-loved. He longed to go back to her, but they had to be at the Stampede's campgrounds by nine o'clock.

"I am," she purred, stretching sensuously. "But I'm more excited about being alone with you—with no interruptions."

"It's almost eight o'clock, and we still need to get some breakfast," he said, reaching for his clothes.

"There's only one thing I'm hungry for this morning," Sheri told him. "And that's you."

Brand had been almost ready to put on his pants when her words stopped him. Suddenly, food didn't seem all that important.

They skipped breakfast.

They made it to the Stampede right on time.

"Reed, this is Sheridan St. John and her husband, Brand." Libby made the introduction.

"I'm Reed Weston," Reed said, shaking their hands.

"Please call me Sheri," she said, smiling.

"Well, Sheri, is there a particular way you'd like to handle the interview? Anything special that you want to see?" Libby asked.

"Yes, I want to see everything," Sheri said, her eyes aglow. "But first, we need to find a quiet place to just sit and talk for a while. I want to get to know all about you—about your past and how you came to be with the show."

"Did you know that Reed and I were just recently married?" Libby asked, smiling at her husband.

"No, I hadn't heard that. Congratulations. You really are 'Weston's Lady,' aren't you?"

"Oh, yes, and I couldn't be happier. Reed? Would you like to show Brand around the Stampede and let him see how everything works?"

"It'd be my pleasure. Brand?" Reed glanced at the other man.

"I'm looking forward to it. Thanks," Brand said.

He and Reed walked off, leaving the two women to their conversation.

"Let's sit in the grandstand, shall we?" Libby suggested.

"Whatever you say. I'm here to learn. If I'm going to write about this kind of life believably, I have to know what I'm talking about."

They chose a shady spot, and Sheri took out her notepad and pencil, ready to jot down any ideas that came to her while they were talking.

"How did you come to be 'Weston's Lady'?" Sheri asked.

"It's a long story," Libby began, but she deliberately skipped all the ugliness of what had happened with John. She just wanted to tell Sheri the good things about her life. "I was in Los Santos and needed a job. I saw the handbills advertising the Stampede and went looking for the owner to see if he'd hire me."

"So you approached Reed for the job," Sheri stated.

"Yes, and it was rather awkward, because he was drinking in a saloon and I had to go in there to talk to him."

"Wasn't that a little bit dangerous for a woman alone?"

"It wasn't easy, but I was determined to get a job with him. I knew I could shoot as well as any of the men he had in the show, but he wasn't interested. Reed turned me down." She paused, wondering whether to tell Sheri everything about that night. She knew others in the show would tell her if she didn't, so she finished the story. "I offered to give him a demonstration of how good I was, but he said he wasn't interested. I followed him back into the saloon and shot a card he was holding up, thinking I'd impress him."

"You didn't!" Sheri's eyes widened at this news, and then she found herself laughing out loud at the scene she imagined. "Was he shocked?"

"That's a nice way of putting it." Libby was grinning, too.

"Did you change his mind?"

"No. I only made him angry."

"What did you do?"

"Luckily, one of the older men found me and offered me a job working for him—as long as I disguised myself as a boy so Reed wouldn't know."

"And you did it?"

"Absolutely."

"How long did you manage to carry it off?

345

Somehow, as beautiful as you are, I can't imagine you as a boy."

"I called myself Bert. Joe had gotten me some boy's clothing, so once I hid my hair and got dirty like everyone else working the stock, no one paid any attention to me."

"How did they discover you were a girl?"

"By accident, the night of the first show in Los Santos." She quickly related the story of how Shorty had gotten drunk, and how she'd had to take his place.

"You are very talented," Sheri told her, impressed by her tale. "There aren't many men who could do what you did—let alone women. How did you come to be such a good rider, and how did you learn to handle a gun and knife so well?"

"My parents raised me and my brother, Michael, exactly the same. I'm glad they did. Otherwise, I wouldn't be here right now, or married to Reed."

"Your story is so romantic. How long do you two plan to stay with the Stampede?"

"We've never really discussed it," Libby answered honestly. "The show was Reed's brother's, and he just inherited it a short time ago." She quickly told her what had happened with Ann and Kathleen.

"What a tragic story."

"It was," Libby agreed. "Kathleen left the show in King's Crossing, and so did Joe."

"Are you happy with the show? Is there anything else you'd rather be doing?"

"No," she answered confidently. "I'm here with

my husband, and that's the only place I want to be."

"Well, what do you think of this as the title of the first book—*Liberty Jones, Lady Sharpshooter,* or *The Adventures of Weston's Lady*."

"That's wonderful!" Libby said, trying to picture what the cover might look like. "Do you have any idea what you're going to do for a plot yet?"

"No, not yet. I still don't know enough about the workings of the show to firm that up."

"How long do you have to write the story?"

"I have to have it on my editor's desk in about four months."

"That's not very much time. Will you be able to get it done?"

"Oh, yes. I haven't missed a deadline yet, and you're such an inspiration that I can't go wrong with this story."

"What would you like to see next?"

"I guess I need the grand tour. Is there going to be a practice today? I'd like to watch that with you, so you can tell me everything I need to know before tonight's show."

"Practice is at about eleven o'clock. We've got time to take a walk around and still get back here to see everything."

"Let's go," Sheri said, thrilled to be learning so much about the workings of the Stampede.

Reed showed Brand around the grounds, introducing him to Mark and some of the other hands. Reed made it a point to have him meet with the Indians who were a part of the show, too. Brand was impressed with the way things were run.

"I was just thinking," Reed said, looking at Brand. "You've obviously made quite a name for yourself as Sheri's hero. Would you want a role in the Stampede while you're with us? The crowds would love it—a true dime-novel hero, right here in Weston's Wild Texas Stampede. What do you say?"

"What did you have in mind?"

"You could guide the cavalry during the Indian attack, or, if you've got a better idea, I'm open to suggestions."

Brand wondered what his friends back at McDowell would think about it, but didn't worry. He was enjoying this visit, and he might learn something that could help Sheri. If anyone back home gave him any trouble about his participation, he would just tell them he was helping his wife with research. "That sounds fine to me. I'll do it."

"This will work out great. Come on, I'll introduce you to our 'cavalry.'"

Reed led him off to meet the others, already planning how he was going to introduce Brand at the performance that day.

The stranger approached the bar in the Royal Flush Saloon in King's Crossing.

"Whiskey," he ordered.

The barkeep set up his drink, and he paid for it.

"Get you anything else?"

"No. That's all for now," he answered. "I see that you had a Wild West show in town this past weekend."

"Yes, Weston's Stampede was here. Damned good show. Most everybody enjoyed it."

"Where'd they move on to?"

"They left town last Monday. From what I understand, Coyote Run was their next stop."

The stranger nodded. "That's a goodly ride from here."

The barkeep shrugged. "A man can make it in a day or two, if he's of a mind to do it."

"That would be a hard ride."

"What other kind is here?" The barkeep laughed as he winked at one of the working girls lingering nearby.

"Thanks for your help."

He finished off his whiskey and left the bar. He now knew where Libby was, and he was going to find her—no matter what.

Chapter Eighteen

"Ladies and gentlemen, we have a special guest with us this weekend," Reed announced as he addressed the audience. "I'm proud to introduce to you our new scout, Brand. He's joined us from Arizona Territory. Brand, as some of you may know, has been featured in a series of books by renowned author Sheridan St. John."

A rousing cheer went up from those in the crowd who'd read Sheri's books.

"Miss St. John is here with us, too." He gestured to where Sheri was seated in the stands.

Sheri stood and waved to her fans, and then the performance began.

Sheri was entranced. From the cowboy band in the opening parade to the stagecoach act with Libby, she thought the entire show magnificent. She was especially fond of her husband's cameo role with the cavalry. To her way of thinking, Brand could have had a future with the Stampede. He certainly was handsome enough to be one of the featured stars.

Reed led the closing parade off the parade ground and headed for the stable. Things had worked out well with Brand. Reed had enjoyed seeing the audience's response to the other man's participation. There really was something to this dime novel thing.

Reed was just starting to dismount when he caught sight of someone in dark clothing moving furtively around the back of the grandstand. Libby was still riding from the parade ground, and he realized in that instant that she was completely unprotected. A moment of panic seized Reed.

"Look out!" he shouted at those near him as he unexpectedly whirled his horse around.

Brand had been riding close behind him, and he stopped abruptly. "What's wrong?"

"Get Libby!" Reed shouted as he rode past him. He drew his gun and raced through the milling performers, trying to find the man he thought might be Harris.

Reed reached the back of the stands and reined in. He dismounted and began to search for the darkly clad man he'd seen. After carefully checking behind hay bales and in deserted corners, he finally found him.

"Come on out of there," Reed ordered, his gun still drawn.

"I didn't do nuthin'," the teenaged boy said as he was forced from his hiding place.

"If you didn't do anything, then why are you hiding in there?"

The fourteen-year-old considered a wisecrack, but changed his mind when he realized the man was holding a gun on him.

"I couldn't afford a ticket, so I snuck in," he admitted glumly, fearful of what his parents would say when they found out what he'd done. He was certain he'd get a good tanning from his pa.

"Reed! What is it?" Brand came running up behind him, followed by Mark.

Reed finally relaxed and slid his gun back in the holster. "It's all right. What's your name, son?"

"My name's Sam," the lad answered cautiously, knowing he was in big trouble.

"Sam here just wanted to see the show, but I guess he couldn't afford a ticket. That right, boy?"

"Yes, sir."

Brand noticed the look that passed between Reed and Mark.

"Mark, do you happen to have a few free passes on you?" Reed asked.

"I sure do," he told him, drawing some out of his back pocket and handing them to Reed.

"Here, Sam. Why don't you come back tomorrow and enjoy the show with your parents?"

Sam looked up at Reed, his eyes wide in surprise. "But I thought you'd be mad at me."

"It isn't right to sneak around like this. You can get into all kinds of trouble when you do, understand me?"

"Yes, sir."

"Promise me you won't do it again."

"I promise."

"Good. We'll see you tomorrow night." He clapped the boy on his shoulder as he moved past him.

"Thank you, Mr. Weston." Sam hurried away, thrilled that he'd gotten to meet the real Mr. Weston and had gotten free tickets, too.

Reed nodded as he watched the youth go.

Only when he'd disappeared from sight did Mark speak. "Scared you for a minute?"

"More than a minute," Reed answered tersely, then glanced at Brand. "Where's Libby?"

"I left her with Sheri at the stable."

Reed drew a ragged breath and started back. Mark and Brand fell into step with him.

"What was that all about?" Brand asked. Something had just frightened Reed, and Brand didn't think he was a man who was easily frightened. "Is Libby in some kind of trouble?"

Reed glanced over at him. "No, and I want to keep it that way."

"What is it?"

"She was engaged before she joined up with the Stampede. Her fiancé didn't take kindly to her ending their engagement, and he wants to get back at her. He's dangerous, so we keep watch for him. There's no telling what he might do."

"You think he might show up at the Stampede?"

"He already did once, back in King's Crossing. Luckily, I was close by and was able to help her in time. But I just got a letter from him threatening her again, so Mark and I are keeping a close eye on everything—and everyone."

"What's he look like?"

"His name's John Harris. He's got blond hair. Average height. I guess he was good-looking once, but he's got a scar on his cheek now—from Libby," Reed added, smiling grimly.

"It must have gotten ugly when she ended their engagement," Brand said. "But I guess he was lucky she didn't have her gun."

"Very lucky," Reed agreed.

Brand sensed there was more to the story, but when Reed didn't offer, he didn't ask. It was enough to know that he should keep a lookout for a man with a scarred face. "If I see him, what do you want me to do?"

Reed's smile turned feral at his question. "What I'd like you to do to him, and what we're going to do to him are two different things. If you do see him on the grounds, make sure he can't hurt anybody until we can get the law here to deal with him."

"He's that dangerous?"

"He's deadly."

The three men looked at each other in understanding.

"This sounds like something out of one of Sheri's novels," Brand remarked.

"I wish it was," Reed said. "At least then we'd know that it would have a happy ending."

They returned to take care of their horses.

"Reed? What was that all about?" Libby asked, going to meet him as she saw him come out from behind the grandstand with Brand and Mark.

"Nothing important," he said, wanting to put her at ease. "There was a boy back there, hiding out. He saw me coming and ran because he thought he was going to get into trouble. I wasn't sure what I was up against, so Mark and Brand came after me."

"I'm glad that's all that was wrong. For a minute, there, I thought maybe—"

"It was nothing serious," he said, stopping her. "We took care of it."

"Good. I like it when there are no problems," Libby said, trusting him completely.

Brand and Sheri had moved their things into the wagon that had once been Kathleen's earlier that afternoon, and they returned there now to unpack.

"Why was Reed so worried about Libby right after the performance?" Sheri asked.

"There's a man named Harris who was once engaged to her, who's threatened her. When Reed saw someone hiding behind the grandstand, he was worried that it might be Harris."

"How terrible for Libby! She didn't mention him at all when we talked."

"It's probably one of those things that she'd rather forget about. Besides, she's happy with Reed now."

"Yes, she is, and they are so wonderful together in the show. I especially liked the part of their act where Reed is standing behind her and she shoots the card out of his hand while aiming in a mirror.

Libby said they just added that to the performance recently. It was impressive."

"Are you going to write that into your book?"

"Absolutely. My Liberty Jones is going to be as good as the real Liberty Jones. Just wait and see." She gave him a confident smile. She was getting more and more excited about starting the novel. This was going to be fun.

"I'm looking forward to it."

"And I also like those pants she wears. I think I'll get myself a pair."

"If you do, you're only going to wear them in the house," he ordered.

"We'll see," she said sweetly, kissing him on the cheek.

"Yeah, we'll see," Brand growled, grabbing her to him and kissing her properly. The thought of her in a pair of those pants was very inspiring indeed.

John sat in the back of the saloon, nursing his whiskey. His anticipation was growing. It wouldn't be long now! Weston's Wild Texas Stampede was camped not three miles away from him. He had a plan, and he was certain it would work. He was going to enjoy this so much! Before the night was over, he was going to have Libby to himself again. He downed his drink in celebration and signaled the bargirl to bring him another. He'd deliberately taken a seat where his scarred cheek was hidden from plain view.

"Here you go, big guy," the bargirl said as she put the tumbler of whiskey in front of him.

He shoved some money at her across the table-top. "What's your name, sweetheart?"

"Call me Sugar," she replied.

"You just working the bar, or are you a real working girl?" he asked, a knowing twinkle in his eyes.

"You looking for some fun?"

"I'm looking to do some serious celebrating."

"Then I'm the girl you want," Sugar said. "C'mon! We'll go upstairs right now!"

She reached out and took his hand, pulling him up. Only as they started across the room did she get a look at the side of his face, and it took all her concentration not to react to the hideous scar. Her stomach turned at the sight, and she knew she had to find a way to get out of this. The money she'd make would be nice, but a girl had to draw the line somewhere, and this was it for her. When they reached the foot of the steps, she drew away from him.

"You go on upstairs. My room's the third on the right," she told him. "I'm going to get us some more drinks, so we can really enjoy ourselves."

John was feeling reasonably agreeable, and he went on upstairs alone.

Sugar ran to the back room and grabbed her friend, Della.

"I need your help," she told her quickly, glancing toward the steps to make sure he wasn't coming back their way.

"What is it?"

"You need some money real bad right now, don't you?"

357

"Yeah, so?"

"So I've got a hot one upstairs in my room. He's all yours."

Della tried to read her expression. This unexpected generosity wasn't like Sugar. "What's wrong with him?"

"Truthfully, nothing. He's just got a scar on his face, and it bothered me. You probably won't even notice it."

"He'll pay me good?"

"Absolutely. Here, take this bottle of whiskey with you."

"Thanks," she said, practically bouncing out of the room and up the steps.

Sugar breathed a sigh of relief. Della was much less picky than she was. She was reasonably sure her friend wouldn't object to servicing someone as ugly as that man.

Della had been drinking for most of the night, and she was in a fine mood as she opened Sugar's door and let herself in. The customer was standing, totally naked, staring out the window with his back to her.

"It looks like you're ready for some action, cowboy," Della said invitingly.

At the sound of the strange woman's voice, John turned to face her. He was surprised to see a complete stranger standing before him. "Who are you?" he demanded.

Della gasped at the sight of his face. "Oh, God!"

John saw the horror reflected in her expression

and moved toward her, humiliated and angry. "Where's Sugar?"

"She sent me instead, and now I know why—"

"What do you mean?" he asked.

"Your face—it's so ugly!" she blurted out.

Any desire that had been stirring in him faded before the cruel reality of her words. He had been handsome all his life, and Libby had marred him forever! Cold rage filled him. He wanted his hands around Libby's pretty little neck. He wanted to use a very sharp knife on her. He was going to enjoy carving her up the way she'd carved him.

"Get out of here!" he bellowed, turning away from her, not wanting to see her expression.

Della did not wait around. She fled instantly. He was a strange man, and she didn't want to be anywhere around him.

John had brought his tumbler of whiskey with him, and he downed it in one swallow. Then he reached for the bottle the girl had brought along and sat down on the side of the bed. After uncapping it, he started to drink straight from the bottle.

It was a long time later when he got up and dressed. He went through the chest of drawers in the room, looking until he found what he wanted, and then finally left the saloon by the back door. He did not want to see Sugar or Della again.

There was only one woman he wanted to see— the woman who had ruined his looks and his life! He wanted Libby, and he was going to get her. Emboldened by the liquor, he mounted his horse and rode for the Stampede's campgrounds.

*   *   *

"Fire!" someone screamed.

Reed and Libby heard the cry in the middle of the night.

"Oh, my God!" Reed said in a low voice as he lifted the curtain to look out the window.

In the distance, they could see flames eerily lighting up the night sky in the direction of the stables. They threw on their clothes and bolted from their wagon. Outside, they found the camp erupting in terror. The shrieks of the frightened horses ruptured the night's silence. They ran for the stables, desperate to rescue the trapped animals.

"Grab anything that'll hold water! We've got to try to stop it before it spreads!"

"How could this happen?" Libby cried as she ran beside him.

"I don't know, but I'm going to find out!" Reed snarled.

When Reed reached the stable, he did not even stop, but charged inside to join the others who were already there, leading out the fear-crazed mounts.

Mark raced up and took charge of setting up the lines to bring water. Lines were formed to pass water buckets from the nearby creek, and soon they had a rhythm going.

Sheri and Brand came running up to help, too, as did all the members of the Stampede. This was their home. This was their livelihood. They would do whatever they had to, to save the show.

Huddled by himself in a secluded hiding place

close enough to see the action, yet far enough away to be invisible, John watched all that was going on before him. He smiled broadly as the flames ate at the tent that served as a stable. To hell with Reed Weston! He'd show him a thing or two by the time he was through. He was going to destroy him, his wife and his Stampede. By the time he was done, Weston would have nothing left. He would be sorry he had ever messed with John Harris!

Now, all he had to do was corner Libby alone; then he could snatch her up in all the confusion. He was certain that when she came running out of the wagon, she hadn't even thought about putting on her gun. She would be unarmed and helpless before him. It would be hours before anyone even noticed that she was missing.

John chuckled to himself at the thought of the pleasure he was going to have when he finally got his hands on Libby. The thought of the bargirl's attitude toward him strengthened his need for revenge. He hated Libby. She had disfigured him and ruined his life. He was not going to let her get away with that.

Lifting the bottle he'd brought with him, John drank deeply. Whiskey always helped him see things more clearly, and he was seeing things just fine right now. All he had to do was get Libby alone. He stared out at the scene before him, searching for some sign of her, and finally spotted her helping to lead horses from the burning tent.

She was working with Reed and several others, and that irritated him. He had thought she would stay back where it was safe, somewhere where he could corner her alone. Instead, she was in the thick of the action.

John's frustration began to grow. He wanted her by herself. That had been the whole point of setting the fire! And now, as he was watching, he could tell that the others were succeeding in their efforts to beat back the flames.

Violent curses erupted from John as he moved farther away, fearful of being discovered. He'd chosen the hiding place because it had been close enough to grab Libby and flee. But she had never left Reed's side. She had stayed with him, matching his effort in trying to save all the animals in the stable.

John knew that once they'd overcome the fire, they would start looking for the cause, and he didn't want to be anywhere around when they did. If things had gone according to his plan, the whole place would have been nothing but cinders and ashes, but his luck had failed him again. They had lost only the tent that housed the stable before bringing the fire under control.

Cursing Reed and Libby, John slinked off into the shadows to disappear into the night. Once again she had ruined everything for him. He was shaking with the power of his hatred, and he didn't know what he could do about it. He had to find a way to get to Libby. He had to find a way to pay her back for what she'd done to his face!

Again the memory of the whore's reaction to his looks taunted him, and he roared his disgust into the night, glad that the sounds of the chaos around him drowned out his primitive cry of misery. He mounted his horse and rode off into the enveloping darkness. He would go hide for now, but he would be back—and soon. Libby had gotten away unscathed for too long.

"Mark—look out!" Reed yelled.

Mark was at the head of one of the lines throwing water on the blaze when Reed's shout of warning came. He looked up in time to see part of the tent collapsing, and he managed to dive to safety just as the burning material came crashing down.

Reed ran to him. "Are you all right?"

With a pained grimace, he slowly sat up. Reed offered him a hand up and he took it.

"Yeah, thanks," he said, brushing himself off.

They watched for a moment as the fire fed on itself, and then both grabbed the buckets of water that were being thrust at them and continued the fight.

The members of the Stampede battled on, their determination never fading as they finally got the upper hand. It was nearly an hour later when the last of the flames was doused. The rest of the camp had been saved from destruction.

Reed stood amidst the ruined stable, staring around at the damage that had been done. As horrible as it was, he knew they'd been fortunate. No one had been killed and only a few animals had been slightly injured.

"It's over," Reed said as he looked up at the exhausted workers surrounding him. "We stopped it."

Libby had been passing buckets in one of the lines, and she came to his side and slipped an arm about his waist. "Are you all right?"

"Now that the fire's out, I am," he told her. "That was close—too close. Did anyone see what happened? Who discovered the fire first?"

"I did," Pete told him, coming forward. "I was going over to the stable to check on my horse when I spotted the flames."

"Was there anyone around?" Reed asked.

"I didn't see anybody."

"Did you see what started it? Did a lantern accidentally get knocked over?"

"I didn't see anything but flames," Pete said regretfully as he looked around. "And I guess there's no way to find out now."

They all were quiet for a moment as they stared at the scorched area.

"Let me take a look," Brand offered.

He came forward from where he and Sheri had been working in the line together, helping to pass the buckets. Taking up a lantern, he walked around to where the flames had first been seen. He hunkered down and studied the ground, looking for possible clues. The fire had burned so hot that little was left to reveal the initial cause. Rising, Brand let his gaze sweep over the torched and muddied earth that bordered the stable. He kept the lantern low to the ground as he walked out away from the tent. He searched for some time, checking and double checking the area. There was little to be found, though. What hadn't been trampled by people and animals had been soaked by the efforts of the bucket brigades.

Brand was almost ready to conclude that it had been an accident, when he walked a short distance farther away from the scene to take one last look around. It was then that he saw the single set of footprints circling around the stable. He knelt beside them, trying to determine how long they'd been there.

Reed had been standing with the others watching him as he searched for clues. When he saw him drop down to one knee to check something, he grew curious.

"Have you found something?" he asked, joining him.

Brand looked up, his narrowed gaze studying the direction of the trail of footprints. "I'm not sure."

He rose and followed the tracks to a curtained-off area between the ticket office and the stands. The site offered a good view of the stable, but was secluded enough that someone just walking by would never notice anyone crouching in there.

"Whoever it was, he hid here after he started the fire," Brand told Reed.

Reed swore loudly. "That son-of-a-bitch!"

"You think it was Harris?" Brand remembered his story from the day before.

"I'd bet money on it. Who else would want to sit and watch a place burn down, except someone with a grudge?"

Brand turned his attention back to the ground. He hoped to find the footprints leaving the hiding place and track the arsonist down. It took him a while in the confusion of all the footprints, but he finally was able to locate the man's trail and follow it to where he'd left his horse tied up.

"He rode out from here."

"Can we go after him now?" Reed asked, knowing Harris didn't have much of a head start on them.

"I wish we could, but he went straight into the stream. I'm going to have to wait for daylight before I can try to pick up his trail. There's no telling how far up or down stream he went."

Frustrated, but determined, they returned to where the others were waiting to hear what they'd discovered.

"It looks like the fire was deliberately set," Reed told everyone. "And I've got a good idea who did it. From now on, I want you all to be on the look out for a blond-haired man of medium height."

"There's a hundred men who look like that," one of the hands complained.

"You'll recognize this one," Libby offered. "He's got a big scar down his cheek. You can't miss seeing it. If you spot him, don't confront him, just come and get Reed or me. He's mean, and we know after tonight, he's deadly. So, please, be careful if you do run into him."

"You think he'll be back?" one of the others asked.

"This man is capable of anything."

A murmur of concern went through the group.

"We canceling the show tomorrow?" Pete asked.

"No. Most of the horses are fine. We will have

the matinee as scheduled," Reed answered. "Everybody go ahead and get what sleep you can. Tomorrow is going to be a long day."

Reed and Libby thanked Sheri and Brand for their help, then retired to their own wagon.

"You think John's crazy enough to do something like this?" Libby asked when they were finally back in bed, lying in each other's arms.

"I know he is," he said darkly.

"How?"

He looked down at her, knowing it was time to tell her of the letter. "I received a letter from him as we were leaving King's Crossing. He said that when we least expected it, he was going to show up to get you."

"And you didn't tell me?"

"I'm going to protect you, Libby. He's never going to get anywhere near you as long as I'm alive."

She trembled at his words and clung more tightly to him. "Don't talk like that! John's insane enough to try anything! I don't know what I'd do if anything happened to you!"

Reed kissed her, his mouth plundering hers with deep promise. "John's not going to hurt either one of us, Libby."

She returned his embrace. She loved him with all her heart, her body and her soul that night. She wanted him safe and with her for always.

Though Reed didn't know it, Libby had placed her loaded revolver on the floor between the bed and the small nightstand. John Harris was not going to have the chance to hurt either one of them if she had anything to say about it!

*   *   *

In the darkness of the countryside some five miles away, John Harris sat with his gun and his bottle of whiskey.

"Come on, Weston! You low-life bastard! Come on after me right now! I'm ready for you!"

It had occurred to John after he'd ridden away from the burning Stampede that they might be able to find his trail and come after him. So he was ready, gun in hand, waiting for Reed Weston to show his face. He'd picked a spot on high ground so he could see riders coming, and he was waiting. He was actually anticipating the confrontation. He was going to shoot Weston, too! It was going to be almost as pleasurable as what he had planned for Libby.

Sweet Libby. His lip curled into a sneer as a vision of her danced before him, taunting him. Damn her!

In his mind, he could hear the whore's words about his face, and his knuckles whitened as he tightened his grip on his gun.

How he wished Libby and Reed would both come riding up right now. The joy he was going to feel at seeing them both dead would be overpowering—probably better than anything he'd ever experienced in his life. He was looking forward to it.

If it didn't happen tonight, he was going to make sure it happened tomorrow. There would be no more waiting.

Chapter Nineteen

A fast-moving thunderstorm rolled through the campgrounds in the early-morning hours. It cleared off before dawn, but it had done its damage. All traces of the trail that Reed and Brand had planned to follow that morning had been washed away.

The two men met at sunup and began the search. Brand looked for any telltale sign that the arsonist had traveled in a certain direction, but though he was an expert tracker, he wasn't a miracle worker. There were no clues left to lead them to the man's whereabouts.

"What do you want to do?" Brand asked Reed.

"There's nothing we can do but keep an extra-careful watch today. If Harris was brazen enough to light that fire last night, there's no telling what he might try next. I'll make sure there are more armed guards around."

"If there's anything you need me to do, just let me know. I'll be glad to help."

"I appreciate it. I'm just sorry it rained. We would have found him if it hadn't been for the weather."

"You'll still catch him. It's just a matter of time."

"I don't want anybody hurt in the meantime."

"With your extra guards watching for him, we should be safe today."

"I hope so. Right now, I guess I'll go help the men constructing the new stable. We've got a little time left before the show."

"I'll come with you."

"You sure you want to work that hard?"

Brand smiled at him. "I didn't say I was going to work. I just said I was going with you."

They shared a laugh as they went to help the others.

"Reed!" Pete hurried over to where Reed was working.

"What is it?" Reed asked, not looking up from his labors. It was getting close to noon, and they had to get as much done as they could before the matinee.

"A stranger with blond hair just rode in, and he's asking about Libby!"

Reed instantly tensed. He was glad that he was wearing his sidearm. "Where is he?"

"I told him to wait over by the ticket booth. He didn't have any scar on his face that I could see, but then, he's got a couple of days' growth of beard, so it wasn't easy to tell."

"Thanks, Pete." Reed nodded and hurried off to where the man was waiting.

Reed couldn't imagine that Harris would walk brazenly into the midst of the show and ask for Libby, but as crazy as the man was proving to be, there was really no telling what he might do. Reed knew he had to be prepared for anything.

As Reed neared the booth, he looked around for Harris but saw no sign of him. He wasn't sure whether to be glad or worried. There was one man waiting there, and something about him seemed vaguely familiar to Reed.

"You the one who's looking for Libby?" Reed demanded in a harsh tone.

The stranger quickly turned his way, his expression wary. "I am. Who are you?"

"The name's Reed Weston. I run this show."

"It's nice to meet you, Weston," the man answered, extending his hand toward Reed. "I'm Michael Jones, Libby's brother."

Reed relaxed visibly and suddenly smiled. No wonder the stranger looked familiar. The family resemblance to Libby was definite. "So you're Michael? It's great to meet you. Libby's going to be thrilled that you're here."

"I hope so."

"How did you manage to find us?"

"It wasn't easy," Michael told him.

"I don't doubt it, considering our schedule. Come on," he said, patting his brother-in-law on the back. "Let's go find your sister."

"Wonderful. I've been worrying about her."

"Well, I'd better tell you right now—Libby and I were just married."

"You were?" Michael was truly surprised. "When I left, she was due to get married, but it was to John Harris."

Reed smiled at him wryly. "I guess we've got a lot to tell you."

"I'm listening."

He began with the story of Libby seeking him out at the Diamondback.

"She shot the card you were holding right there in the saloon?"

"She didn't even hesitate. Needless to say, I'm damned glad she's an expert shot."

Michael laughed. "My Libby's something else."

"*Your* Libby?" Libby's voice rang out.

Michael turned, and before he knew it, his sister was in his arms, hugging him and crying for happiness.

"Oh, Michael! I didn't know when I'd ever see you again!"

"Ah, sweetheart," he groaned, holding her close in a cherishing embrace for a moment, then holding her away from him at arm's length to get a good look at her. "You're all right? You're really all right?"

"Now, I'm perfect," she told him with a teary smile. "You're here."

"Thank God I found you," he said, giving her one more intense hug before releasing her. "Is there someplace we can go to talk in private?"

"Our wagon. Come on." Libby took his hand and

led him with her as Reed followed. "I take it you two have already introduced yourselves?"

"We have," Reed affirmed. "Pete told me there was some man asking for you, so I went to see who it was."

"John is around somewhere, Michael," Libby quickly explained. "We have to be careful. He's trying to cause trouble. We think he might have been the one who started the fire at the stable last night." Libby pointed toward where the men were working on the new structure.

"This is so hard to believe." Michael shook his head.

"So much happened after you left—"

"So I found out," he said curtly.

"You did? How? And how did you know where to find me?" She led him into the wagon, and the three of them sat down to talk.

"I managed to get some time off from the railroad to come home for your wedding, but when I got there, you were gone—and so was John."

"Oh, Michael, he was so horrible—"

The look she gave her brother spoke volumes. He had taken the seat next to hers, and he was close enough to slip an arm around her shoulders to comfort her.

"Madeline tried to tell me that you were the one who'd broken your engagement and that you had probably run off with another man. But I knew better. That wasn't like you. Luckily, as I was leaving her house, BethAnne, her maid, called me over and told me exactly what happened—what he'd tried to do to you and why you'd run away."

"Did BethAnne tell you *everything*?" Libby asked nervously.

"Yes, she did," he answered, his tone solemn, his gaze meeting and holding hers. "Libby?"

She gave him a questioning look as he went on.

"I never should have left you alone with them. I had no idea how evil they were. I can't tell you how sorry I am. When I think about what might have happened to you—" He struggled for control. He adored his sister and would never want to see her hurt in any way. He'd thought she was safe in town with John and Madeline.

"It's not your fault, Michael. None of this is. We trusted them. Who would have ever dreamed that they were like this?"

"I confronted Madeline after I'd talked to BethAnne, and she admitted everything. In fact, Madeline was the one who told me where to start looking for you. She's very sorry for what happened to you."

Libby gave a sound of disbelief. "Oh, I'm sure she is."

Michael grinned. "She is. I took her down to the sheriff's office and told him what I knew. He's handling it from here. He's also eagerly awaiting John's return."

"Thank you," Libby said, her eyes filling with tears. She hugged him and kissed his cheek. "I've missed you so."

"I missed you, too. And it seems I missed your wedding. Congratulations, Sis."

"Reed is wonderful," she told him as she looked over at her husband.

Reed smiled at her praise. "Your sister is pretty wonderful herself."

"I'm glad you two are happy together."

"How long can you stay? There's so much I want to tell you!" She grew excited as she thought of all the good things that had been happening in her life.

"The boss told me to get back as soon as I could, but I can stay a few more days."

"Good."

A knock came at the door.

"Reed?" It was Mark. "There's only half an hour until show time."

"Thanks!" Reed opened the door to speak with him. "We'll be ready."

Libby made quick introductions, and then Mark took Michael out to the stands and gave him the seat next to Sheri, after introducing them.

"You're here to do a book about my sister?" Michael repeated, completely surprised and impressed by the news.

"Oh, yes. Libby's fantastic. Wait until you watch her performances today. You're going to be so thrilled when you see how good she is. You should be proud of her."

"I am. I don't know how she's survived all that she's been through."

"It hasn't been easy for her, but she's met every challenge and succeeded. That's why I want her for the heroine of my next book. She's perfect!"

"I can't wait to read it."

"It should be published sometime next year."

"Well, I'll probably end up being your biggest

fan. I'm going to buy at least six copies."

"Only six?" she laughed, delighted with the young man and his open affection for his sister. As the parade was about to begin, she had an idea. "Michael?"

He glanced at her questioningly.

"How would you feel about being a sub-character in the book?"

"Are you serious?"

"Absolutely."

His smile was dazzling. "That would be wonderful!"

They would have talked more, but the band struck up a tune, and they turned their attention to the parade. There would be time for more conversation later.

John was brazen in his approach to the Stampede. He figured if he tried to sneak in, someone would notice him, so he took a different tack. He tied his horse up with the others and walked easily toward the entrance gate with the rest of the crowd. He was glad that he hadn't shaved for a day or two. He hadn't realized until this morning, when he went to wash his face in the creek, that it helped to disguise his disfigurement. Not that the permanent ugly reminder of Libby was hidden, not by any means, but it wasn't as obvious. And since he was pretty certain that Weston probably had people watching for a man with a scar on his face, the more he hid the scar, the better.

John was watchful as he mingled with the others making their way to the grandstand. He saw the extra armed men standing around, trying to look casual, but he knew why they were there—to stop him. That wasn't going to happen, though. This was the day he'd been waiting for. This was the day he would wreak his revenge.

Ahead of him, a small child started crying hysterically. The noise distracted the men who were supposed to be watching for him.

John knew he couldn't have planned the disruption more perfectly. He slipped out of sight between two tents and crept through the maze of wagons until he found the place he wanted. It was an area behind a heavy canvas curtain near the far end of the parade ground. He would wait there and watch until the exact moment when Libby was vulnerable to him. Then he would strike.

He patted the knife he had slipped into his waistband and his gun at his side. He was armed and he was ready. He was going to kill them both, right in front of the audience!

The acts began. While everyone in the stands enjoyed the Stampede, John was purely miserable. He wanted his chance to get Libby, and each minute seemed an eternity.

Mark had had an uneasy feeling before the performance, and he decided to take a quick look around. He could not take any chances with Libby's safety. "Pete, I'm going to do some checking in back to make sure things are all right. I won't be long," he called out.

"All right, Mark. I'll see you by the grandstand in a few minutes."

John stiffened at the sound of their voices so

close by. He recognized one as the same man who'd taken him into town the other night. Reaching inside his coat, he drew out his knife and made his way silently to the split in the canvas where Mark would be coming in if he were going to check this area. John heard footsteps coming nearer, and he readied himself. He couldn't take any chances now. He would strike first and worry about everything else later. He was too close to Libby to run now and let this opportunity slip away.

Mark had seen nothing unusual as he'd walked around the area, but something was nagging at him, so he decided to look in one last place before rejoining Pete. Spreading the canvas divider, he stepped through the curtain.

John struck without warning, savagely stabbing him from behind.

"You—" Mark managed only a pained gasp as he collapsed facedown in the dirt.

John stood over his prone body, smiling. He waited, wanting to make sure his victim didn't try to get up. Satisfied that Mark posed no further threat, John then went back to watching for Libby. It was almost time. The announcer was just proclaiming that Reed Weston and Weston's Lady would be demonstrating their shooting prowess next.

Libby and Reed came out on foot for their next performance. The audience was applauding wildly, thrilled with all the action in the show.

Libby stood before the bales of hay, and John cursed under his breath. The clear shot he thought he'd have at her was partially blocked. He could see Reed, but he couldn't be sure that he'd be able to hit Libby.

John's patience was wearing thin. He had been drinking all night and most of the morning. He wanted to do what he'd come here to do. He didn't want to wait any longer, but one last shred of sanity told him to pick his shot, not to waste this opportunity. Soon Libby would be shooting at Reed, and then, maybe, he'd get his chance.

Reed's shooting was impeccable, and the crowd roared its approval of his flawless marksmanship. Then it was Libby's turn. They switched places, and she showed everyone just how good she was with a gun, too.

John swore some more. He had his gun drawn. He was all set. But he never got the chance to get off a clean round at either of them. And then Libby was done, and they were moving things around in the parade ground.

"And now, ladies and gentlemen," the announcer said. "Weston's Lady is going to demonstrate a new trick shot she has just recently added to the program. Liberty is going to shoot a hole in the ace of hearts while Reed Weston holds the card."

The audience clapped and cheered.

"And she'll do it by taking her aim looking in a mirror."

The audience cheered even louder.

John couldn't wait any longer. It was going to be now or never. They were going to be standing near him and they were both going to have their backs to him! It was perfect! He would fire the moment Libby did, hit Reed and make everyone think that she'd missed. Then in the confusion, he would shoot her, too! It was perfect!

He waited, gun in hand, trigger finger itching for the chance to right the wrongs he believed had been done to him.

Out on the parade grounds, Libby had no idea of John's nearness. She was concentrating on the trick she was about to perform. She knew she had to be steady of hand and eye. She certainly didn't want to risk making any mistakes when she was shooting this close to Reed.

"Ladies and gentlemen," Libby called out. "Could we please have quiet for this part of our demonstration?"

They obediently stopped talking. A hush fell over the grandstand as the audience waited in breathless anticipation for what was to come.

Libby drew her revolver and picked up the hand-held mirror. She lifted it and looked in the reflection, focusing solely on Reed. He was standing some twenty feet away from her, and he was holding out the ace of hearts. She aimed the gun over her shoulder at her husband. She had just started to squeeze the trigger when the face of the man she hated above all others appeared behind Reed.

John!

She froze at the sight of him reflected there. He had a maddened look about him. He was smiling wildly and had his gun trained on Reed's defenseless back.

"Reed! Look out behind you!" Libby cried.

Reed pivoted and drew his gun. In the space of a heartbeat, they fired in unison.

John was caught unawares by Libby spotting him in the mirror. He managed to get off only one shot; then his eyes widened in disbelief as pain exploded in his chest. Searing agony besieged him. He looked down at himself to see blood spreading across his shirt from two distinct bullet wounds. He tried to breathe, but it hurt too badly. Dizziness assailed him.

John looked up in Libby's direction. She was running toward him, her gun still aimed at him, but she was unscathed! His careful planning had backfired. She was going to live—but he was going to die!

The realization terrified John. He wanted to scream at her that he despised her. He wanted to shout out loud that he didn't deserve this fate, but he couldn't form the words. And then suddenly, he was falling backwards into a vortex of blackness from which there would be no return.

Libby stopped and stood over John.

"Libby! Are you all right?" Reed grabbed her up and hugged her close.

"Oh, Reed! I'm fine—and you?"

"I'm fine, too. He missed us both, thank heaven!"

The onlookers didn't know what to think. Some cheered, thinking it was a scheduled part of their sharpshooting performance, but others thought it seemed a little too graphic for their tastes. They were puzzled when the announcer told them that the show was over for that day, and there was some grumbling as they left the grandstand much earlier than they'd expected.

Reed and Libby turned away from the sight of John's body and made their way to the backstage area by a different route, needing some privacy. She held tightly to him, realizing just how close she'd come to losing him. *If John had fired one second sooner—!*

Reed was feeling the same way about Libby. He was certain that John had been ready to gun down Libby while she was performing. He didn't know why they'd been so blessed to see him in enough time to stop him, but he wasn't going to question their good fortune.

"Somebody send for the sheriff!" Reed ordered, as he guided Libby away from the sight of John's body.

Just then, Brand, Sheri and Michael came running.

"Are you two hurt?" Michael demanded, hurrying to his sister's side.

"No, we're fine. I was lucky enough to catch sight of John in the hand mirror before he had the chance to shoot."

"So your Harris did show up, and right in the middle of a show." Brand knew now that Reed had been right to be worried about the man.

"He had to be insane," Sheri put in, going to give Libby a hug. "You are so brave."

Libby's smile was less than bright. "Thanks, but I don't feel very brave right now. I just feel very lucky."

382

"Reed! Hurry! It's Mark!" Pete called out. He'd gone to take care of Harris and had found his friend lying wounded and unconscious.

Reed glanced down at Libby, his expression suddenly fierce. "I'll be back."

He hurried off to where Pete was kneeling beside Mark.

"Is he alive?"

"Yes! But we'd better get the doc here real fast."

Reed and Pete carried Mark to his wagon after sending one of the hands for help. Outside the wagon, Libby came to wait along with Brand, Sherry and Michael.

"What happened?" Libby asked as Pete came back outside.

"Looks like Mark must have found that Harris fella, and Harris stabbed him."

"Is he going to be all right?"

"I sure hope so. Mark's a good man," Pete said.

Time passed slowly as they waited for the doctor to show up, and then it seemed even more tedious once he'd gone inside to tend to Mark's wounds. No word came on his condition until finally, Reed emerged.

"He's going to be all right," Reed announced to those who'd gathered around.

A murmur of thanksgiving went up.

"Libby? Mark wants to see you for a minute."

She was surprised, but left Sheri, Brand and Michael to go to him. Her hands were trembling as she entered the wagon and hurried to Mark's bedside. The doctor had just finished bandaging his wound, and Mark was lying facedown on the bed.

"Mark—" Her heart ached at the sight of this strong, handsome, vibrant man laid low this way, stabbed in the back by a coward. And it was all because of her. "I'm so sorry."

"Libby—" Her name was almost a groan. He couldn't imagine what she was sorry about. "You weren't hurt, were you?"

"I'm fine, and John won't be hurting anyone else ever again."

"Good." Mark managed a slight grin in spite of the pain he was in. "Just as long as he didn't harm you."

For a moment, Libby feared he'd worsened as his eyes drifted shut, but the doctor reassured her.

"He's just weak right now. He'll be fine in a week or two."

"Thank you." She pressed a kiss to Mark's cheek and started from the room.

Reed took one last look at Mark, and then accompanied her.

They emerged from the wagon and told everyone of his condition. All of Mark's friends were relieved, and everyone was thrilled, too, that the one responsible for the fire had been caught.

"I thought coming to a Wild West show would be exciting, but I had no idea it would be *this* exciting," Sheri told Libby as they walked away from Mark's wagon.

"It has been an adventure, but it's over now. John won't be hurting anyone ever again, and Mark's going to be fine." She glanced at Sheri. "I guess we've got a happily-ever-after ending, just like in one of your books."

"It doesn't always turn out like that in real life, but I'm glad it has for you and Reed."

Libby looked over to where her husband was deep in conversation with Brand and Michael. As if sensing her gaze upon him, Reed looked her way and smiled. It was a smile meant only for her, and even at this distance, it had the power to make her heartbeat quicken in anticipation of being in his arms again.

"So am I, Sheri. There is no doubt that I am truly Weston's Lady."

Epilogue

Ten Months Later

Libby heard the sound of the buckboard pulling up in front of the house and went to greet Reed. He'd gone into town earlier that day, and she'd been expecting him back any time now. She was glad he was there. She'd missed him. They'd returned to the Circle W for the off-season, but it was almost time for the Stampede to start up again.

"How was everything in town?" she asked as she went out on the porch.

"Pretty quiet, although we had something at the post office I think you might be interested in," he told her, jumping down and walking around to the back of the buckboard to take out a medium-sized box.

"What's that?" Libby was curious.

"It's from Sheri."

Libby's eyes lit up. "You don't suppose these are the books, do you?"

"Let's take a look."

Reed carried the box inside and set it on the table. He stepped back to watch as Libby quickly tore open the parcel. He would never forget the look on her face as she got her first look at *Liberty Jones, Lady Sharpshooter, or The Adventures of Weston's Lady*.

"Oh, my," she breathed as she carefully lifted out a copy and stared down at it, enraptured. "Sheri did it. She really did it!"

The cover was a picture of the parade grounds; the grandstands were filled with people, and Libby was depicted looking in the mirror and shooting over her shoulder just as she'd been doing when John had tried to attack them.

"The picture is almost perfect! Look at us!" she said in delight.

"How many copies did she send us?"

"Looks like a whole box full."

Libby quickly sat down and started reading.

"I suppose this means I'm not going to get much conversation out of you for the rest of the day," he said, grinning.

Reed knew how much she loved Sheridan St. John novels. After Sheri and Brand had gone back home, Sheri had sent Libby an entire set of her books. He had come to miss his wife during the weeks that had followed, for she'd been caught up reading all about Brand's adventures.

Reed hadn't been tempted to read a dime novel before, but he was now—since this one was about his wife. Unable to help himself, Reed took one of the books out of the box and sat down at the table. He only planned to skim through it.

Liberty Jones, Lady Sharpshooter
or
The Adventures of Weston's Lady
by
Sheridan St. John

Chapter One

Liberty Jones took careful aim at the card Reed Weston was holding slightly away from his body, then squeezed the trigger. She smiled as her shot found its mark, piercing the center of the ace of hearts.

"Well, Mr. Weston, am I good enough to work for your Wild Texas Stampede? Will you hire me now?"

Reed Weston, owner of the Stampede, glared at the beautiful blonde standing before him, smoking six-gun in hand. "I told you before, Miss Jones, I don't hire women for the Stampede—"

Reed smiled and kept on reading.

HALF-BREED'S
Lady
BOBBI SMITH

To artist Glynna Williams, Texas is a land of wild beauty, carved by God's hand, untouched as yet by man's. And the most exciting part of it is the fierce, bare-chested half-breed who saves her from a rampaging bull. As she spends the days sketching his magnificent body, she dreams of spending the nights in his arms.

___4436-6 $5.99 US/$6.99 CAN

Dorchester Publishing Co., Inc.
P.O. Box 6640
Wayne, PA 19087-8640